SINISTER SHADOWS

WICKS HOLLOW

COLLEEN GLEASON

AVID PRESS

AN IMPORTANT NOTE FROM THE AUTHOR

Sinister Shadows was previously published under the title *The Shop of Shades and Secrets*. The book has been significantly revised to make it part of the Wicks Hollow series.

If you've read *The Shop of Shades and Secrets*, I hope you find this updated, revised, and (I think) improved edition even more enjoyable.

Thank you for giving it a read!

— Colleen Gleason
March 2018

ONE

FIONA MURPHY GLARED at the mass of papers on her desk and the files stacked in her overflowing in-box. She had cleaned it out on Thursday. When she left that evening for a three-day weekend, the box had been empty and her desk neat and organized…

She'd only been gone for a *day*. One day, to visit her brother Ethan in Chicago.

One fricking day. And it was like File-Mageddon on her desk.

This was exactly the reason she hated office jobs—other than the eight-to-five, sit-at-a-desk part.

Pushing a corkscrew of auburn hair out of her eyes, she girded her loins and reached for the top file.

The mobile phone on her desk buzzed. Caller ID said *Nath, Nath & Powell.*

She frowned. A CPA firm? An agency? Maybe it was Winona calling from her office—she'd started a new job last week.

Well, whatever. Anything instead of digging through files and bills or assessing purchase orders.

She answered the call. "This is Fiona Murphy." She shoved her reading glasses back onto the bridge of her nose. It was vanity that made her squint most of the time when she looked at menus or the newspaper—whoever heard of a thirty-year-old needing reading glasses at a +2.5 magnification?—but when she was at work, and actually needed to see, she had no choice but to wear them.

"Ms. Murphy, this is Gideon Nath," came a smooth, professional male voice. "Legal counsel for the late Nevio Valente."

Legal counsel. Not an accountant after all. Then the last part of his introduction clicked in her mind.

"The *late Nevio Valente*?" Fiona put down the order for office supplies she'd picked up to peruse and potentially approve, giving the caller her full attention.

"I'm sorry if his death is a shock to you," the voice went on crisply, "but—"

"I probably would be shocked if I knew who Nevio Valente is—er, *was*," Fiona admitted wryly, pushing up her slipping glasses again. "But since I don't—"

"You don't know Nevio Valente?" For the first time, the inflection of the voice changed from unruffled professionalism to show a hint of surprise.

"No, I'm afraid I have no idea who that is."

"*Nevio Valente*," he said, enunciating slowly and clearly this time, as if she were a child trying to learn a foreign phrase. "You're certain you don't know him?"

"I believe I've said that twice already, Mr.—is it Nath?" Fiona frowned. *That* name actually sounded more familiar than Nevio Valente.

"This is Fiona Murphy, of 355 35th Avenue Southwest, Wyoming, Michigan?"

By now she was beginning to giggle. She'd leaned

back in her desk chair and was twirling her reading glasses. "Yes indeed—this is Fiona Murphy and that is my address. I believe you were the one who called me."

Mr. Nath continued in his cool voice, which no longer sounded ruffled but mildly offended. "Yes, well, it's odd that you don't know one of the wealthiest men in Grand Rapids. Especially since he happened to name you in his will."

"*Shut the front door.* Seriously?" The brightly patterned glasses squirted from her fingers and clattered onto the desk. "I'm named in his *will*?"

There was a sigh on the other end of the line that implied this phone call was taking too much of his time. "Ms. Murphy, perhaps you'd better come around to my office so we can discuss this in detail. I—"

Then it hit her. "Wait—this is a joke, isn't it?" She started laughing. "Are you punking me? Is this the radio?"

"Ms. Murphy, much as I wish it were, believe me, it is *not* a joke." The voice became even chillier and more pompous—which had the opposite effect on Fiona as he no doubt intended. She tried to suppress her laughter, but the man sounded like one of those automatons on Westworld whose program had gone awry.

She could picture him: the industrious and oh-so-pompous Mr. Nath, sitting at a massive oaken desk in his tight-collared suit with wispy, thinning hair combed neatly in place. His wire-rimmed glasses would be firmly entrenched on the bridge of his nose just beneath thick, hairy brows with a few wiry grey hairs springing out like little spider legs. *His* glasses wouldn't dare slip, as they'd be wedged into soft, pink skin.

"I think it would be best for you to come to my office

—that's Nath, Nath, and Powell—so that we can discuss this in a more…succinct manner. Tomorrow at eleven?"

She almost said yes, but the imp that always got her into trouble decided to be contrary. "No, I'm so very sorry, but tomorrow won't work for my schedule." She made her voice match his in coolness. As if she were very, very busy.

"Very well. Does Thursday at three-thirty work better for you?" His voice was uber-polite and calm, and she could almost imagine him clenching his teeth.

She bit back on a giggle.

"Yes, I do believe that would work for me. See you then," she said gaily, and disconnected the call—without getting the address.

Damn.

Rather than phoning back and asking the pompous Gideon Nath for the information, Fiona had looked up the address, then casually phoned the receptionist the next day to confirm that was, indeed, the location of her meeting.

Fiona parked her VW bug, which looked like a sassy lemon, on the street about three blocks from Nath, Nath & Powell.

The day was warm, as was to be expected in Grand Rapids in early September, but a cool breeze from the Grand River lifted the leaves that were just turning gold and red.

The receptionist at the law firm, a youngish woman with bleached blond hair cut in a pixie style, looked up with a smile when Fiona walked in. "Good afternoon. May I help you?"

"Yes, I'm Fiona Murphy to see Gideon Nath."

"Yes, one moment." As she picked up the telephone, she asked, "Could I get you anything? Coffee? Tea? Soda?"

"No thanks…unless you have herbal tea?" Fiona took a seat on a large chair in a swirl of her long, flowing skirt. The office was, as she'd expected, sleek and modern, furnished so as to display the wealth—and by extension, the expertise—of its firm.

"Ms. Murphy is here for Mr. Nath," the receptionist was explaining into the phone. When she hung up, she rose. "Herbal tea? Of course. Any sweetener?"

"No thank you."

Another blond woman appeared, this one in her late forties. She had an abundance of hair coiled neatly at the back of her head and a very efficient way about her. "Ms. Murphy, if you'll follow me."

She gestured Fiona into a large corner office, and just as she'd expected, the attorney's desk was large, oaken, and forbidding. Probably weighed two hundred pounds. Near the front edge was a wood and brass nameplate that said *H. Gideon Nath, III.*

The man himself rose from behind the desk as she came into the room, then gestured to a chair placed in front of it. "Have a seat, please, Ms. Murphy."

Fiona had to readjust herself, for her mental picture from their telephone call couldn't have been further from reality. Instead of a fiftyish-year-old man with soft pink skin and wire-rimmed glasses, she was facing a man in his mid-thirties with thick, dark hair—and no glasses in sight. Not even a pair of reading glasses on the desk.

His eyes were piercing grey, cool and reserved, and his shoulders broad and well-proportioned inside his expensive suit. He would probably be attractive if he'd smile—or at least not frown—but at the moment, Fiona couldn't picture it. The man held himself stiffly, as though controlling the barest urge to relax, and his mouth was set in a firm, business-like line.

As she settled in the chair, shoving her bulky leather bag to the side, she once again looked at the nameplate. *H. Gideon Nath, III.*

She immediately needed to know what the H stood for.

Henry? Herbert? Harry?

Yet again, the name Nath stuck in her head...it sounded so familiar. But Fiona knew she would definitely have remembered meeting H. Gideon Nath, the *Third*—if only because of that bothersome H.

On his desk, which seemed to be an extension of his controlled, organized self, there were neat stacks of paper lined up to one side of the huge space, and three fountain pens in three ornate holders off to one corner. A powerful-looking laptop sat on a credenza behind him, along with a stack of files, two flash drives, and a dual charger for cell phone and, she assumed, computer tablet. For someone like her, who left her mobile phone in the depths of her bag half the time, the slew of electronics seemed like major overkill.

The young blond brought Fiona her herbal tea—which smelled of fresh orange and lemon—then left her alone with the attorney.

"What does the H stand for?" she blurted out.

H. Gideon's eyebrows drew together in a dark line. "The H?"

"On your nameplate. What's the H?"

He looked at her coolly. "That's not exactly germane to our meeting today, Ms. Murphy."

Fiona stifled a grin. Struck a wrong chord, had she?

Before she could decide how to proceed, he continued in that formal lawyerly voice. "And speaking of which—before we proceed, may I see some identification?"

"Of course." Fiona gave him a bright smile that seemed to surprise him and flipped out her wallet to show her driver license. "Not the greatest picture, but it's me."

He took it with large, interesting hands and examined the small plastic card before returning it to her. "Thank you. Now," he said, opening a manila folder on his desk, "let's talk about this. You've been named in the will of Nevio Valente, and although there will be a formal reading in short order, I thought that under the circumstances, we should meet prior to that meeting."

"Circumstances?" She couldn't help looking at his hands again. They were beautiful—elegant and tanned, not too big and bulky, but still appeared masculine and powerful.

Now she knew what her mother meant when she said there were some hands that she couldn't resist reading.

He cleared his throat. "Er—yes. You being the only non-family member—other than a few charities—to be named in the will, and secondly, because you claim not to know who Mr. Valente was." His gray gaze probed her face as if to reaffirm her claim.

"I did a little research after you called, but I was hoping you might be able to clear up some more details for me. I still don't know why he would have left me anything in his will. I'm sure I've never even met the man."

H. Gideon cleared his throat again and turned to a different folder—this one green—and sifted through its contents. He pulled a photo from within and placed it on the desk in front of Fiona.

It was a better picture than the blurry images she'd seen online. The lack of good photos was surprising for a man who was supposedly one of the wealthiest men in the city; apparently, he was very nearly a hermit.

"Wait," she said, looking at it as something niggled in the back of her mind. She narrowed her eyes. "Wait a minute. I think I *have* seen him before." But when?

"He owns—owned—quite a few pieces of property in and around greater Grand Rapids. As you are employed by a commercial real estate firm, one might surmise that you interacted with him in a business transaction and perhaps met him that way."

She looked up at him, fighting back a grin at his formal, precise speech. "One might indeed surmise."

He cleared his throat as if aware that he was causing her internal hysterics, then continued, "Perhaps you took some paperwork from him at some point in time when he came into your office. You're the office manager at Thurston & Mills, as I understand it."

"Yes, I think that must have been it. Though, thankfully, I rarely have occasion to interact with our clients," she said, matching her tone and formality to his, "there are times when it is necessary to do so. If I recall correctly, Mr. Valente was a very pleasant man. It seems we had an extended conversation about the weather, and he was quite charming." Fiona still couldn't quite remember meeting him, but if she had, it was safe to say they'd discussed the weather.

H. Gideon's lips twisted into something that may have passed for a wry smile, but looked more like he was swallowing his tongue. "I can't say I've ever heard Mr. Valente described in such complimentary terms.

Even by myself. He was generally considered a…difficult man."

Fiona smiled. "Perhaps his demeanor was merely a reflection of whatever people were around him at the time."

The little dart struck home, and his lips tightened. She couldn't suppress a smile, seeing his smooth, arrogant facade crack. The imp had hold of her now. For some reason, it had become a personal challenge for her to work the stick out from under the behind of H. Gideon Nath, the Third.

At the same moment, Gideon himself was wondering just what he had done to deserve getting saddled with such a flighty, unapologetic female in the midst of this mess Valente had left his firm—and, by extension, Gideon himself.

If his grandfather hadn't decided to embark on a month-long vacation with his current lady love, leaving Gideon as the only Nath available for the clients of Nath, Nath & Powell, *he'd* be the one dealing with this will. Which would likely be contested by the family once the terms came out.

But Gideon Senior could have had no inkling that the wealthiest—and most eccentric, rather sketchy—of his clients would drop dead at an age just shy of a hundred and one during the "Fall Color Tour" the elder attorney had decided to take through Lower Michigan with his girlfriend.

Not that Valente's demise hadn't been long overdue, Gideon thought ruefully, remembering his impression of the stooped, incredibly rude and unpleasant man he'd met only twice.

And not that Gideon actually minded that his grandfather was off with Iva Bergstrom, gallivanting around the state. She'd put a gleam in his eye and had eased the stiff, reserved edges of the elder Nath since they'd met last April. And Gideon absolutely did not begrudge his grandfather the happiness he clearly had found. He deserved it.

He just hoped Iva Bergstrom wasn't a gold-digger. Partly because she made his grandfather—who'd been married thrice before; and for very short stints—so happy, but partly because Gideon himself had come to love her too.

And now here he was with this Fiona Murphy, who'd appeared from nowhere in the old man's will. It had taken him some effort, including combing through social media (which he loathed) and other assistance from his admin Claire to locate the woman named in the will. Because, of course, Valente hadn't made an attempt to identify her other than her name and a basic description. He didn't even indicate how or when he'd met her.

From his phone conversation with Ms. Murphy, Gideon had expected someone younger—in her late teens or early twenties at most. And with a name like Fiona Murphy, she should have been a leprechaun-like creature with springy carrot-colored hair and thousands of freckles.

Instead, according to her driver's license, she was twenty-seven. And she had disconcerted him by being strikingly beautiful, with fair, translucent skin, a faint dust of freckles over high, well-defined cheekbones, and dark, whiskey eyes. And her hair...it was long and lush and curled in large spirals that tumbled *everywhere*.

Somehow her personality—flighty and giddy—didn't fit with the sensual, flower-child figure sitting across from him, but no matter. He had to deal with her in whatever form she appeared, as per the last will and testament of Nevio Valente.

"So," she was asking with a faint smile that implied a joke he had missed, "do I get to find out what he left me, or do I have to wait until the public reading of the will?"

The way she said "public reading of the will" with a hint of condescension in her voice made it sound like she was making fun of him, and Gideon tightened his jaw. He wished there *wasn't* going to be a formal reading, just so he could so inform her, and wipe that sassy smirk off her face. And then he pulled his thoughts back, disconcerted by such a rash, emotional reaction.

"In fact," he replied smoothly, "Mr. Valente did request that you attend the reading of the will. It won't, however, be public, *per se*. Just for the family. He also left this for you." He slid a heavy cream-colored envelope across the table.

She hesitated, then reached for the packet. Her fingers were long and slim, with smooth pink nails and a minimum of one ring on every finger—many had three or four of hammered or twisted metal stacked all the way to the first knuckle. Her fingers were trembling a bit, and when she looked up at him with an awkward smile, his suspicions were confirmed.

She was nervous. The beringed airy-fairy sprite was *nervous*.

"It's odd to get a letter from someone who is dead." Her dark-lashed eyes had lost that giddy spark and were now soft; even reverent.

A curious woman: one moment, carefree and flighty, the next subdued and thoughtful. Gideon didn't know how to respond, so he silently offered her the gold-plated letter opener from his desk.

Ms. Murphy took the opener and slipped it under the

envelope's flap. He watched as she pulled out a single sheet of matching cream paper—he recognized Nevio Valente's personal stationery; God knew he'd seen enough memoranda and letters on it—and looked down at the spidery writing. She stared at it for a moment, peering, squinting, and then finally, with a rueful smile, began to dig in her huge leather bag.

Gideon found himself suppressing his own smile when she pulled a pair of brightly patterned cheaters from the depths of her bag and slipped them apologetically onto her nose. "Much better," she murmured, looking back down at the letter.

There was silence for a moment as she read the letter, and Gideon directed his attention to the rest of the file on Fiona Murphy. He still didn't understand why Valente would make such a significant bequest to a woman he *might* have met once. And there was nothing in the will to indicate the old man's reasoning. Not that it was any of his business anyway.

He could only assume the missive Valente left for Ms. Murphy at least gave her some explanation.

Fiona looked up from the letter at last, and he saw that her eyes glistened. "Thank you. When is the reading scheduled? I'll certainly plan to be there." To his surprise, her tone was modulated and almost businesslike.

"Next Tuesday, at four o'clock. It will be here. I do hope your schedule can accommodate that time slot. Is… there anything I can get for you?" he felt compelled to ask in light of her obvious emotion.

"No thank you. Well, Mr. Nath, if there's nothing else?" She gathered up her bag as if preparing to rise.

"No, no there isn't, Ms. Murphy." Gideon stood and

extended his hand to shake hers. "I'll see you next week. Have a nice evening."

She clasped his hand with a firmness that surprised him, and held it for a moment, looking down as though examining something fascinating.

"Such long fingers," she murmured, then, as though remembering where she was, looked up at him, smiled. "Henry?"

"Pardon me?" She was still holding his hand, and he was very aware of how…interesting it was to have that connection.

"The H. Is it for Henry?"

Gideon withdrew his hand, feeling even more unsettled. "No." He couldn't help that his voice was clipped; he simply didn't know what to make of this woman.

"Howard?"

"No. Ms. Murphy, I—" He stopped himself from commenting that it was none of her business what awful name with which he'd been saddled. "I do hope you have a good evening."

She grinned up at him, and he saw something in her eyes that glinted like a sassy sprite. "Have a nice evening yourself."

He stared after her when she left, flowing skirts and gypsy hair, suddenly feeling like he'd been blindsided by the sun.

TWO

THE READING of the will was as tedious and boring as Fiona had anticipated. She sipped from a goblet of sparkling water studded with a lemon wedge and surveyed the cluster of people around the great mahogany table. There were only four people other than H. Gideon Nath, the *Third*, and his blond assistant, whose name she'd learned was Claire.

The rest were somehow related to Nevio Valente, and Fiona spent her time observing them as H. Gideon droned on, reading the long (*so long!*) document left by Mr. Valente.

Her will—should she ever have occasion to make one—would be one page long, and bullet-pointed.

There was Bradley Forth, the youngest of the bunch, who appeared to be either a grandson or grandnephew of the deceased—she hadn't quite figured out which—and was not much older than Fiona herself. He wore his designer suit with the same confidence and air of professionalism as Nath, and constantly cast his gaze in her direction. His dark brown hair was brushed back from a handsome, sharp-featured face with a cleft chin. He held one end of a marbled fountain pen between each forefinger and thumb, his short fingers spread gracefully on the boardroom table. Square index fingers, Fiona noticed automatically. Must be a lawyer or an accountant. He didn't wear a wedding band, and presumably if he had a spouse, she'd have been there at the reading of the will, so she could safely assume the interested looks he kept casting her were legitimate and not creepy. Plus, *his* name was vaguely familiar.

She slipped out her mobile phone and, holding it in her lap beneath the table, stealthily tapped out the keys to Google him.

Next to Bradley Forth sat an older man, perhaps in his late fifties. Except for the greased back hair, he was a dead-ringer for how Fiona had imagined H. Gideon Nath, III, to look when she'd first talked to him on the phone.

His name was Arnold Sternan, and he wore wire-rimmed glasses that settled into little indentations in his cheeks and had spatulate, manicured fingernails that gleamed while he played with a gold-plated fountain pen. His hair was dark, its exact shade uncertain because it was slicked back with some sort of gel and appeared wet. It was a bit too long so it curled up damply at the nape of his neck. Judging from his age, he was probably a son or nephew of Nevio Valente. She gathered during the general conversation that he was some sort of investment banker or venture capitalist. She thought he looked like an aging mobster.

The two others at the table were obviously a couple, a man and woman of advanced middle age and poor taste —at least in Fiona's opinion.

The woman's clothing, though obviously expensive,

was loudly decorated with beads, lace, and satin-stitch embroidery, and seemed to have no rhyme or reason in its pattern. Aside from its overdone decor, the color of the dress itself was enough to make Fiona feel nauseated: it was the hue of a perfectly ripe navel orange. She'd bet it had been purchased at an exclusive shop in Chicago.

The husband's fashion sense was no more commendable, for, although he wore an unexceptional dark suit and white shirt, his tie looked like a long, narrow quilt. He had a fringe of grey hair that circled his scalp, and the crown of his head shined like a cue ball under the bright lights. The couple was finally identified as Viola Ruthven, Nevio Valente's niece, and her husband Rudy.

Fiona scrolled through her phone, still hiding it under the table, and was able to determine that Brad Forth was an attorney (oh joy) and was running for state senator in this district—but before she could read further, she glanced up at H. Gideon.

He was glaring at her from over the top of the sheaf of paper he held. Feeling like a student caught passing notes in school, Fiona straightened in her seat and locked her phone, endeavoring to look interested in the proceedings. That was easier than she thought—to *look* interested—because her attention was caught by H. Gideon's beautiful hands as they held the sheaf of paper from which he was reading.

They were elegant and strong, and she fairly *itched* to know what truths they held.

But even that couldn't keep her interested for long, and as H. Gideon droned on (how long *was* this will anyway?), Fiona's thoughts wandered once more.

Logically, her mind drifted to the letter Mr. Valente had left for her. It was tucked away in her huge bag, but she could see the words as if the heavy stationery sat on the table in front of her.

My dearest Fiona:

I am certain this will come as a surprise to you—first, that I am dead and second that I've chosen you to name you as a benefactor in my will.

I'm sure you are wondering how and why I should do so. The decision was made for me the moment I saw you at the offices of Thurston & Mills.

You'd just rushed in from a blustering rainstorm—your long, auburn hair was dripping and your bright patterned skirts were billowing—and the picture you made was indelibly printed on this old man's mind because it was an echo of one such vision—a memory—that I have held in the deepest part of my soul for many, many years.

It was as if I were catapulted back in time, sixty—no, perhaps seventy years now; I shan't do the math—to the day I met my Gretchen.

An old, embittered and ravaged heart softened for the first time in decades as I gazed upon you, for you looked so much like my beloved Gretchen that I could barely breathe through the pain of it.

This old man has been through much hatred and ugliness in his life. Your freshness and innocence reminded me of how I once was, and how I could have been happy—how I should have been happy—had things not happened the way they did. Perhaps you will find or create the happiness that I could not.

I charge you, then, in honor of my Gretchen, to take this bequest and make something good from it.

Be assured, however, my dearest Fiona, that should

you shirk your duties, I promise to haunt you for the rest of your life! Ha ha.

Looking forward to seeing what is on the other side…

Fondly,

Nevio Valente

Tears prickled at the corner of her eyes as she remembered the raw hurt and pain in the letter.

And as she'd done for nearly a week now, she mulled over the shock that because she reminded him of someone he'd once known, the elderly man had bequeathed her—what? Some old treasures? Jewelry?

He must have been senile to name a perfect stranger who reminded him of some other woman in his will. At his age, it was possible that anyone he encountered unexpectedly might look familiar.

The attorney continued to pore through the legalese while Fiona's quirky mind was at work, darting down tunnels of possibilities as to the identity and reason for her bequest.

One thought that included forced marriages and other strings-attached bequests was so absurd that she actually had to choke back a giggle. She cast a swift glance at H. Gideon, who flashed an annoyed look her way, and then let her attention sweep over the attentive Brad Forth. Surely Mr. Valente hadn't written a match-making clause into his will. That was for the 19th and early 20th centuries, thank you very much.

Fiona snapped her attention back to the head of the table as she heard her name. H. Gideon (she simply couldn't think of him by any other way) was reading as smoothly as ever, but again, those steel-grey eyes flashed a sharp look at her.

"…Miss Murphy, with whom I recently made an acquaintance, is listed last in this epistle, although she is not, by any stretch, the least of consideration. As one often says, one ought to leave the best for last—and so that is what I've done.

"Nonetheless, it was with great thought that I made the decision to leave to her, upon my demise, the building, contents, and all related business of my Antiques Shoppe, located on Violet Way in Wicks Hollow, Michigan."

Fiona couldn't control a gasp, then quickly stifled it as H. Gideon gave her a *look* over the top of the paper, then continued reading.

"I'm certain that she will make the languishing store into a success, and for that reason, I forbid her to sell the shop or its building for the first five years of her ownership. If in the end she makes the determination to sell before the first five years have passed, all proceeds from the sale will be added to the N. Valente Endowment Fund and she will remain with nothing."

Fiona stared blankly at Nath, whose voice had trailed off with the end of that paragraph.

An antiques shop?

He left me his antiques shop?

I don't know a thing about running an antiques shop.

In Wicks Hollow?

But nonetheless, her insides fluttered. Then, just as quickly, her stomach squeezed alarmingly, and she felt sick.

Holy crap, she was going to be a *business-owner*.

A life without vacations, without sleep, without freedom flashed before her eyes.

"How…generous," she managed to say when she realized everyone was staring at her.

When no one looked away, she gathered her composure and lifted her gaze to H. Gideon. "Is there anything else?" she asked.

"There is nothing more," he replied coolly, adding the paper to a stack that sat off to the left. But, thankfully, he reclaimed the attention of the others by asking, "Does anyone have any questions? I'd be happy to meet with each of you on an individual basis to clarify any of the points in this document."

No one had any questions—at least none they were willing to ask in the presence of the other heirs—but everyone wanted to schedule time with the attorney to finalize the paperwork.

Fiona sat in her chair, cautiously observing the others. She wondered who in the room had expected to inherit the shop—and whether there would be any hard feelings that she had usurped someone else's bequest.

The last thing I need is to be dumped into the middle of some crazy family competition.

"Congratulations, Ms. Murphy."

The deep male voice caused Fiona to look up as she wrestled her bag onto her lap. "Thank you," she smiled, holding out her hand as she stood. "You're Bradley Forth?"

His handshake was brief but his smile lingered. "Yes, of course. Call me Brad, please. I'm sorry I didn't have a chance to introduce myself before the proceedings started."

"I was late, so you wouldn't have had the chance anyway." Fiona remained polite, but she began to ease her way from the table, intending to make her way out of the room. "Now, tell me, how are you related to Mr.

Valente? I'm afraid I didn't quite catch everything that was in the will."

"I'm the old man's grand-nephew—my mother's brother was his grandson." He looked as though he would have said more, but H. Gideon approached them.

"Let me get you both on my schedule for next week," suggested the attorney, "so that we can get some of this paperwork taken care of."

"If you could have your secretary call mine, that would probably be the most efficient way," responded Brad pompously. "I believe you have my card?"

"*My* schedule is perfectly clear, H.—er, Mr. Nath," Fiona said brightly.

Because she just realized *she could quit her job.*

They'd be devastated at Thurston & Mills, but oh well. She was going to be a business owner. Her stomach lurched, and she swallowed hard. *Oh God.*

"How about Tuesday at four, Ms. Murphy?" H. Gideon said, looking at Claire, who had slipped up behind them and was madly tapping on an iPad. "Claire?"

The admin paused to nod, then went back to tapping. "Yes, Mr. Nath, four on Tuesday works, now that your golf league is over."

He nodded again, and Fiona hooked her bag over her shoulder. "Thank you, and I'll see you then. It was nice to meet you, Mr. Forth. Good-bye."

The first thing Fiona did Saturday morning was to make the drive—which was less than an hour along the shore of Lake Michigan—from Grand Rapids to Wicks Hollow.

Since her brother Ethan had bought a log cabin on

Wicks Lake, she'd visited the touristy town several times over the last few years. Though she didn't know all the residents as well as he did, she'd gotten to know Maxine Took, the town's self-appointed matriarch, and her partner-in-crime (for lack of a better term), Juanita Acerita.

The town itself was nested inside a handful of rolling hills less than two miles east of the Lake Michigan shoreline. The ring of hills reminded Fiona of a large hand that protected the collection of houses, shops, and winding streets by holding them in its palm. From what she understood, Wicks Hollow's population was normally about two thousand. Over the summer, however, and in the early autumn, tourists packed the little village and swelled its number to more than twice that.

It was early September now, so the tourists with schoolchildren had gone. This cleared the way for a smaller wave of visitors—what the locals called "the newly-weds and the nearly-deads": honeymooners and senior citizens, who could travel during this off-season and into the Fall Color period, which stretched from late September to mid-October.

From the first time she saw Wicks Hollow, Fiona had been charmed by the treelined streets of mansions built in the late 1890s and early 1900s. Called "painted ladies" for their elegant shapes, ornate trim, and bright colors, the houses lined the streets displaying all the gables, towers, and garrets characteristic of that era. Most were painted in bright colors: cerulean, lime green, purple and violet, and complementary shades of yellow, gold, and pink. Their yards were small, manicured patches of green shaded by mature trees and edged by sweeping landscapes of geranium, hosta, boxwood, and other nursery staples.

To the south and east of the town, there were fewer

houses due to a bank of thickly wooded hills that rose like a natural, protective wall. Shenstone House, a large mansion located on the highest hill just southeast of town, was in the process of being renovated to be turned into a small inn. Through the trees still thick with leaves just beginning to think about turning gold and orange, Fiona could see the peaks of the house's roof and gables.

Before starting her drive, Fiona had used her GPS to locate the address of her unexpected inheritance, and was mildly disappointed to discover it wasn't located in the main downtown area of Wicks Hollow. The intersection of Faith Avenue and Pamela Boulevard—with neither being an avenue nor a boulevard, but barely two-vehicle wide streets—was the heart of the downtown's business and tourist district. From that central location, shops, restaurants, cafes, and other businesses sprang up for two blocks in all four directions. Every building was brick-fronted, although the color, type, and height of their facades varied. Some of the brickwork design was complicated, and some of it merely serviceable.

Fiona came into town via the north-south running Pamela Boulevard, then turned west on Faith Avenue. This took her past Trib's (the trendiest restaurant in town), and on the next block, a second-floor Balanced Chakra Yoga Studio (which she eyed with interest).

Following her GPS (a good sense of direction was not one of Fiona's gifts), she followed Faith two more blocks to Elizabeth Street and turned north. This three block stretch on Elizabeth was known as B&B Row, for it was lined on both sides with painted ladies converted to bed and breakfast inns. Some even had glimpses of Lake Michigan and the Stony Cape Lighthouse from their upper floors.

As she drove by, Fiona noted the names of some of

the B&Bs—Sunflower House, Respite Cottage, Blueberry Courtyard, The Pine Glenn Inn. Each had beautiful hand-painted signs with little flip-cards on them that indicated vacancy or no vacancy. Many showed no vacancy for this weekend in early September, and Fiona was pleased. After all, she was soon to be a business-owner here herself.

At the thought, a little squiggle of nerves made her clench her tummy, but she spewed out a long breath. *One step at a time.*

Elizabeth Street curved slightly west, and Fiona smelled the fresh proximity of Lake Michigan through the open moonroof on her lemondrop VW bug. She took a hard left onto a little street that angled off toward the big lake and found herself on Violet Way.

The road was hardly more than a dirt driveway, stretching less than two blocks between Elizabeth and Frederick Streets. The gravel surface was barely wide enough for two cars to pass each other and definitely room only for one if someone was parked on the street. Though it was several blocks from the main area of town, there were other shops here (probably with lower rent): a small boutique that seemed to carry only black clothing, a tiny pottery store with a cheerful red flag hanging out front, a shop for hiking and camping gear, and, near the Frederick end of the short, gravel road, an old sign that read *Antiques.*

"This must be it." Fiona was just pulling off the road into a dubious parking place when her phone rang. The only reason it wasn't in the depths of her huge bag was because she'd been using its GPS, so she was able to look at it right away. To her pleasure, it was Ethan.

"We're here. Where are you?" he asked as soon as the call connected.

"I'm right—"

"Oh, I see you now. Hard to miss that yellow car. We'll be right there."

She disconnected the phone and stepped out of the car just as he and Diana, his hotshot lawyer girlfriend, walked into view from the opposite direction on Violet Way. She'd insisted they drive up from Chicago for the weekend so they could take a look at her new business as well. After all, what were older brothers—especially ones who dated lawyers—for?

"Hi, Fiona," Diana said, giving her a brief hug. She was a little shorter than Fiona, and had bouncy, dark hair in a flattering cut that left most of her neck bare. As always, she was dressed in neat, tailored clothing—a summer sweater twinset of periwinkle and casual white trousers. Her shoes were expensive Italian flats that Fiona immediately lusted after, and wondered if there was any chance DSW would get them in.

"This must be so exciting for you!" Diana added as she stepped back with a smile. "Congratulations—and what a surprise!"

The first time Fiona met Ethan's hot-and-heavy girlfriend was at Maxine Took's eightieth birthday party last summer, and her first impression of Diana Iverson had been that she was an uptight lawyer who needed to learn to relax. (Didn't they all?)

Fiona's initial opinion hadn't been far from the truth, but after Diana went through some serious upheaval last summer—and hooked up with Ethan during the process —she'd mellowed out quite a bit. Since then, Fiona had visited them in Chicago several times and had come to appreciate and genuinely like the woman whom she suspected would someday be her sister-in-law.

"Thank you," Fiona replied, slipping her arm through

Diana's, her long yellow skirt billowing against their legs. "It is exciting—but I can't decide whether to be thrilled at the opportunity, or scared to death that the place is nothing but a money pit—and something that's going to tie me down forever."

"Yeah, that's my Fifi. Anything even remotely like a commitment makes her hair go frizzy," Ethan said, giving her long, curly hair a tug. "Which is why it always looks like she stuck her finger in a socket."

She rolled her eyes and gave him a sisterly shove as he approached the front of the shop.

There were two large beveled windows that arched out on either side of the door, which created a little covered alcove at the entrance. All of the glass was dingy and looked as if it hadn't been cleaned for years. An ancient sign on the door said "Closed" in large block letters. On one side of the establishment was the clothing boutique, sharing the same interior wall. But the other side of the building ended at an alley no wider than a footpath between it and the next building, which appeared to be a small real estate office.

"Sure doesn't look like much," Ethan said as he peered through one of the door's windows.

Fiona crowded into the little alcove next to him. "Let me look. *I* didn't even get to see yet—I was waiting for you." She gave him a playful bump at the hip and cupped her hands against the glass so she could look.

It was dark and shadowy inside, and she couldn't make out many details. "Looks like a lot of stuff in there," she said uncertainly. "But I can't tell if it's any good or just junk."

"I wonder if the place makes any money," commented Diana as she too squinted through a window, carefully avoiding getting dust on her pale blue sweater. "It's a little off the beaten path, but still close enough to walk—it took us about twenty minutes to get here from the middle of town. Did the estate attorney give you any of the tax returns or balance sheets? Anything like that? Or do you have to wait for probate?"

"I don't have any of that information yet—but I'll find out more when I meet with H. Gideon on Tuesday."

Ethan pulled away from the window. He had a dark smudge on the tip of his nose, and Fiona decided it was her prerogative as his sister *not* to tell him. "H. Gideon?" he said, lifting a brow.

"Yes," Fiona replied, resisting the urge to rub the end of her own nose and risk tipping him off. "*H.* Gideon Nath, *the Third*. He's the estate attorney, and he's got a real big stick up his behind. I think his face would crack if he ever showed any emotion at all. And he won't tell me what the H is for."

She'd been mulling over it all week. Hank? Herbert? Harry?

"He thinks I'm a real ditz—I can tell. And I couldn't help messing with him a little," she added with a grin.

"Why am I not surprised," Ethan muttered. "I don't understand why you get off making people think you're a ditz when you really aren't, Fifi."

"Nath," Diana said, and looked up at him. "Isn't that Iva's significant other's last name?" She sighed, and reached up to brush the smudge from his nose.

"Iva?" Fiona asked, turning away from the shop. There wasn't anything else to see for now. She'd have to wait to have her curiosity appeased. And her anxiety lessened.

What if the shop was nothing more than a big money pit?

Meow.

The guttural cry had her turning as an ink-black cat with a copper splotch over its left eye emerged from the narrow alley next to the shop.

"Well, aren't *you* gorgeous." She knelt in a pool of long flowy skirts and held out her hand for the cat. "All dark and black and mysterious with a pretty pirate eye-patch."

The feline eyed her emotionlessly, her copper-brown eyes cool and remote. Then she gave that low, deep meow again.

"She—or he—doesn't have a tag on his collar," Fiona commented, still holding out her hand in a friendly gesture. "But she's obviously a pet."

"She is a beautiful one," Diana agreed, crouching next to her. "Very striking. Come here, kitty."

The cat was even less interested now that two of them were crooning at her. She lifted her nose as if they were four levels beneath her, then gave one last growly meow before turning away. With her tail in the air, she walked off with clear disdain for the fawning humans—and confirmed that her gender was in fact female.

"Do you want to look around the back, Fi?" Ethan asked. "Maybe there are more windows there, or on the alley side wall."

Of course Fiona wanted to, so they followed the cat down the narrow space between the two buildings. Behind the shop was a slightly wider alley—maybe large enough for a vehicle, if it was careful—and a broken light over the back door. However, there were no windows in the back or along the side, and though Fiona tugged at the door, it was locked tightly.

"I guess I'll have to wait to see more," she said in disappointment. "H. Gideon said he thought probate could settle within four to six weeks, which would put me here in late October. Oh, well. I'm getting hungry."

"Let's go to Orbra's," Ethan suggested with a grin at Diana as he slipped an arm around her waist. "Now that you've come to terms with an occasional cup of tea."

Diana sighed, but her dismay was exaggerated. "Nothing replaces coffee in my book, but at least it's Saturday and I don't need the fuel—so tea is acceptable." She glanced at Fiona, a smile playing about her lips. "The first time I went to Orbra's, I made the mistake of ordering coffee. I thought they were going to kick me out of the place."

Since Fiona had driven, Diana and Ethan climbed in the back of her bug. Her brother showed her a "secret" parking lot in the back of the block near Trib's, and soon they were strolling along Faith Avenue toward Orbra's Tea House.

"Oh, great," Diana said under her breath as they walked in, but just as quickly she smiled with genuine, if exasperated, fondness. "Maxine! And Juanita!"

They'd barely stepped over the threshold when Maxine Took was already giving orders from her customary seat at the biggest round table, right at the front window.

"Ethan and Diana—well, it's been long enough since you been up here, hasn't it? Now that the two o' you are heating up the sheets don't mean you can't drive up here and visit us old ladies! Sit yourself down—and that's your sister, ain't it?" Maxine possessed a head of thick, iron-colored hair in a non-descript style that might or might not be a wig. She had dark skin and large hands with knobby knuckles, and peered through bottle-thick glasses as she gestured violently with her cane. "What's your name again, girl? Look just like a fortune-teller, you do, with that hair and your headband, and those long skirts—you better take care not to trip on them. Break a knee or a wrist, you know. You can read my palm again today—tell me if something's changed. Sit right here."

Fiona, as everyone tended to do when faced with the imperious Maxine Took and her cane, obeyed.

Diana, who'd flushed a little pink when Maxine mentioned heating up the sheets, took a chair next to Juanita Acerita. "Who's winning?" she asked, gesturing to the Scrabble board on the table.

"I am," Juanita replied.

"That's because she's cheating," Maxine grumbled, somehow hearing their conversation even as she was ordering Fiona around. "I saw you swap those letters when you thought I wasn't looking."

"I did nothing of the sort," Juanita replied with such heat that Fiona thought maybe Maxine had a point. "You just can't stand it that I got a Q-word without a U that you didn't know. She had to look it up because she didn't believe me," she added, looking at Diana. "Sheqalim."

"What the hell is a *sheqalim* anyway?" Maxine demanded.

"You looked it up—didn't you read the definition?" Juanita replied archly. "It's obviously the plural of *sheqel*." She was holding a large leather totebag on her lap, and from inside, her seven-pound papillon Bruce Banner was looking around with bright, interested eyes.

"Orbra, *please*, I beg of you, bring us some tea and food," Ethan said as the proprietress approached, putting a temporary end to the Scrabble squabbling.

"Make room—Cherry's on her way over on break from the studio," said Orbra van Hest. At seventy, she was a large-boned powerhouse of a woman, standing six feet tall and sturdy as an oak, with pure white hair Fiona suspected she had washed and set at least twice weekly. "Do you want the whole tea set-up, with sandwiches and scones and all that, or just a sampler, dearie?" She was speaking to Ethan.

"I want it all. Bring us the whole thing—extra egg salad and cucumber sandwiches, though, because Fiona's vegetarian."

Orbra looked at her with a jaundiced expression, but merely asked, "What kind of tea do you like, then, Fiona?" Her tone made it sound as if someone who didn't eat meat would have very strange taste when it came to tea.

"I don't drink caffeine," Fiona replied, prompting a disbelieving look from Diana and a raised brow from Orbra. "So something herbal, or maybe a rooibos?"

"Why don't you give her that canela blend you're trying out for fall, Orbra," said a new voice behind them. "It's herbal—like cinnamon— and it's really good with the cardamom and cacao in it."

"That sounds delicious," Fiona said quickly. "A great combination."

"Hi, Cherry," said Ethan and Diana at the same time.

A slender, toned blond woman in her late sixties slipped into the last remaining chair. She was wearing workout clothing because she was the owner of the yoga studio and had probably just come from a class.

"I'll have my usual after-vinyasa tea," she told Orbra.

"So we've got one full tea set-up, extra no-meat sand-wiches," Orbra said, giving Fiona a side-eye, "an autumn specialty blend, a strong-brewed chai with lots of milk so it doesn't taste like tea" —she gave Diana a quelling look — "and a silver needle tip brewed light, with almond milk on the side. What tea did you want, Ethan?"

"Oh, I'll have whatever you recommend," he replied with a big smile—thus making all the ladies at the table look bad, and himself taking the prize for "best customer."

Fiona rolled her eyes, then re-introduced herself to Cherry as Orbra went off to put their order together. "We've met once or twice before."

"Of course I remember you—you're Ethan's sister. The palm-reader. Good thing Iva's not here—she'd flop her hand down on the table and ask for a reading right off."

"Fiona's going to be in Wicks Hollow a lot more often now," Ethan said, and went on to explain briefly. "In fact, I told her she could stay at my cabin whenever she wants. So you'll see a lot of her."

"Her shop is that old place up on Violet Way? Oh, it'll be wonderful to have someone tending to it again," Cherry said. "I can't remember the last time I saw it even open."

"*I* ain't never seen it open in ten years," Maxine informed them. "And I drive by it all the time."

"You do not," Juanita said, shifting her bag so Bruce Banner's carrier was on the deep windowsill next to her. "And I remember seeing it open a year ago—when there was that sesquicentennial celebration—"

"You don't remember nothing," Maxine told her. "I—"

"My niece just moved here from Philadelphia," Cherry said in a voice designed to forestall anymore arguing. "Her name is Leslie, and she's renovating Shenstone House—getting ready to turn it into a B&B."

"'Bout time someone did something with *that* place," Maxine announced. "Used to be a speakeasy, way back when, according to what my mother used to tell. And there's that story about the missing jewels—"

"And the ghost," Juanita put in, her pudgy fingers reaching for one of Maxine's scones. "There's always a ghost."

Fiona glanced at Diana—the least likely person at the table to believe in ghosts—and was surprised that the other woman wasn't scoffing at their pronouncements. Come to think of it, hadn't Ethan mentioned something about a ghost at her house last summer?

"So," Cherry went on with a smile at Fiona, "you'll both be new business-owners here in Wicks Hollow. And she's about your age too."

"I'll look forward to meeting her—but it'll be at least a few weeks, maybe even a month, before I actually come into possession of the shop," Fiona told them as Orbra wheeled up a tea cart laden with pots and cups and very fragrant tea.

"So what are you going to do about your job, anyway, Fi?" asked Ethan. "Thurston & Mills will be lost when you leave."

Fiona grinned and began to systematically pull off the thirteen rings rings she habitually wore, letting them pile onto the cloth-covered table. "You know I can't wait to quit. I'd give my notice next week if I was sure the shop would support me in the manner in which I'm accustomed."

"I'm shocked at your restraint, Fiona." Her brother grinned, looking up as Orbra placed a small pot with dainty pink flowers painted on it in front of him. "You change careers more often than those Kardashians change clothes, and I figured it was about that time for you to be making a switch anyway. How long have you been there? Eighteen months? Two years is about your max, isn't it?"

"Twenty-five months last week, in fact," Fiona told him haughtily. "I've been at Thurston & Mills for twenty-five months, which, yes, is a record for me—but they treat me well *and* they really do love me."

"Who wouldn't," Ethan said in a teasing voice. "You're so energetic and fun to be around, especially first thing in the morning—"

Fiona rolled her eyes. "Whatever. Anyway, I am looking forward to giving it a real go."

"And there's that hot blacksmith Declan Zyler who just moved to town," Cherry put in. "Though I'm hoping he and my niece will hook up so I can live vicariously through her. You do like men, don't you, Fiona?"

Fiona laughed as Orbra placed a cup in front of her. "I certainly do. Very much."

"All right, well, I just thought I'd ask and not assume," Cherry said. "Like *some* people do."

"Now, don't mind Cherry," Orbra put in as she set a three-tier tray on the table next to Ethan. It was laden with small triangular sandwiches made from paper-thin bread, and spread with cucumber and cream cheese, sundried tomato and spinach, egg salad, ham and Gouda, and chicken salad. "She's still getting over that lady who tried to corner her after one of her hot yoga classes a few weeks back."

"She thought just because I have short hair and am very toned and slender that I was a lesbian," Cherry said, scooping up one of the tomato sandwiches. "And I'm not." She sighed. "Sadly. Because it would probably make life easier."

"Over two years at your current employer?" Ethan commented after he plowed through four little sandwiches. "Maybe you are ready to settle down, then, Fi. Either way, you're going to be tied down for at least that long with this new venture. You won't be able to leave when you get bored. Unless you want to sell it. It's a big commitment—and one you didn't even ask for."

"Yeah. The C word does give me the willies." Fiona laughed. Her brother's honest words spoken like a lecture in public could have bothered her, but they didn't. He was right. "I come by it honestly, I guess, with our mother being the same way."

Despite the fear building inside her—from the fact that she would soon *own* something, that she would be *responsible* for a business—Fiona already had the sense that she wouldn't give up the shop. She hadn't even seen it; didn't even know the details, but there was something about it…

This was an unexpected, once-in-a-lifetime opportunity. There were a lot of unknowns, but something about it felt right…as if she'd been waiting all her life for something to *happen*.

Of course, once she looked at the books and balance sheets and got into the nitty-gritty of the business, she might feel differently…but how could one look at gift horse in the mouth when she hadn't even met the horse?

THREE

FOUR WEEKS to the day after he'd first met with Fiona Murphy, she flowed back into his office, sweeping into the chair he offered her at his work table.

She was once again dressed like an escapee from a Renaissance festival, in a long dress made from some soft, shiny material that looked like layers of gauze. The material glinted with bits of gold, and was edged with some intricate embroidery, and fitted her enough around the bodice and torso to show off some lovely curves.

Her lush red hair was pinned up loosely at the back of her head, and looked as if it might tumble into a spill of corkscrew curls at any given moment. She wore multiple rings on each finger, long, busy earrings, and one wide metal cuff on her wrist. As before, she carried a massive bag that he thought was a purse, but might be a knitting bag or some hobo version of a briefcase.

He hoped for the latter—after all, this was a business meeting.

"So probate went off without anyone contesting my inheritance?" asked Ms. Murphy as she folded her beringed hands on the table in front of her. "I have to admit, I am a little shocked."

Gideon wasn't about to admit that he had been mildly surprised as well. Having gotten to know the extended Valente family over the last two months, he'd expected them to scrabble after every bit of wealth they could squeeze from their deceased relative.

His response to his client, however, was professional and nonplussed. "As you likely recall from the reading of the will, the other family members inherited other, much larger and more lucrative portions of Valente's great wealth. The antiques shop was a relatively small piece of his estate."

"Very well, then. I guess it belongs to me—if I want it. And that brings up a bigger issue. Before we go any further and before I sign anything, I'd like to see just what it is I have to work with."

Ms. Murphy's smile was engaging, but there was shrewdness—and something like apprehension—in her eyes. "I want to know what I'm getting into before I actually get into it. I thought we might have done this even before probate, but here we are."

She caught him by surprise, which, he admitted, didn't happen often. Gideon set down the papers he was holding and reached for another folder. "Of course we can go through all that in as much details as you like, and I apologize if you were expecting to review the documents prior to today. I simply presumed you'd want to wait until everything was final before spending time on it."

Actually, he'd assumed she hadn't a clue in her lovely head about running a business, and that ledgers and accounting would be the last thing she'd worry about. When she spoke again, she surprised him further.

"I'll be the first to admit that I don't know much about running a retail store, but I do know something about business. I'm one hell of an office manager. And I get along very well with people." She gave him a warm smile that inexplicably seemed to have an edge of teasing to it. "However, since I've never had my own business, it's hard to know whether I have a head for the big picture. I'm certain you'll be able to easily answer the biggest question: is the shop financially viable? From what you've said, I get the impression that Valente left me the dog, and everyone else the diamonds. Not that I'm complaining, mind you."

He found himself nodding in agreement while trying not to smile at her bluntness. "Absolutely, Ms. Murphy, I—"

"And," she said, giving him a smile that warmed him like a sip of the twelve-year-old single malt Scotch his grandfather liked, "I think you can stop calling me Ms. Murphy. Fiona is fine. Now," she continued, rummaging in that huge bag of hers, "please, tell me about the whole picture here." She extracted a piece of paper with what appeared to be a list—of questions most likely—followed by the brightly patterned cheaters she'd worn last time.

"Well, Ms. Mur—ah, Fiona," he corrected himself and firmly directed his attention back to the matter at hand, "in a nutshell, you're right—though it isn't a *dog*, to use your term, the shop isn't going to make you a wealthy woman either. But it's not in the red—partly because you now own the building—or will, when and if," he glanced at her meaningfully, "you sign the paperwork. There's a bit of healthy income from rent for the place next door—I believe it's a clothing boutique—and an empty apartment above—from which you could also collect rent should you so desire. Although the shop hasn't been open regularly or staffed for—well, it appears at least five years, possibly longer—the inventory of the shop did bring in some profit, both from walk-in and online sales. You won't find yourself on the street—at least right away."

He pulled the information out of a folder and for the next thirty minutes, went through the property in detail as Fiona fired her questions at him, ticking down her list while looking at him from over the tops of her glasses.

"So I should be able to make a living off the shop and rent," she said at the end. "And potentially live above it if I wanted." Her voice held enthusiasm, but trepidation still hung on her face. "All right then—when do I get the keys?"

Gideon almost laughed, but caught himself in time. It was amazing how she'd gone from appearing so scatter-brained the first time he'd met her, to a serious, business-executive mode, shooting off questions with little pause —and now to guarded enthusiasm. "As soon as you sign these title papers, I'll be happy to relinquish the keys."

It was another thirty minutes before the title work and other papers transferring ownership to Fiona were completed.

"I think we're about finished, and I can give you those keys."

"Excellent." She stood just as he did, and her ankle-length, gauzy dress settled in fluid folds around her. "Oh drat."

She'd knocked over the behemoth of her bag, and as she crouched to pick up the contents that spilled, he noticed how nicely the long, simple shape complimented her, hugging well-proportioned curves and, when she finally stood, swirling about hints of long legs. It was a bronze color, made of a soft, shiny, crinkly material, and with her fair skin and chestnut hair, it made her look soft and golden…and very feminine.

Fiona's fine auburn eyebrows rose as she tucked the last item back into her bag. "Is something the matter, Mr. Nath?"

With a start, Gideon realized he'd been staring and, belatedly, that he hadn't asked her to call him by his first name. "No, I just thought I'd forgotten to do something . . . but, please," he forced a smile, wondering where his head had gotten, "call me Gideon. Now, let me get those keys."

He turned to retrieve the small goldenrod envelope that contained the keys to the shop and all doors of the building that Fiona Murphy now owned. Flipping the metal clasp that held it closed, he poured the keys—twenty-some in all—onto the table.

"You have your work cut out for you," he said wryly. "Most of these keys aren't labeled—although a few are, and, undoubtedly, some of them are duplicates—but as for the rest of them, I have no idea what they're for."

Gideon retrieved one ring with four keys on it and handed it to her. "These are for the shop itself and they're labeled—front and back doors, safe, and storage room."

Fiona took the envelope and slipped it, along with the rest of her paperwork into the cavernous leather bag and extended a hand. "I guess we're all set then," she smiled as he clasped her hand, feeling the ridges of the many rings that adorned her fingers. "Thanks so much for all of your help, H.—er, Gideon. I really appreciate it." Her smile was sunny and warm, and he felt it all the way to his belly.

He walked to the door with her, realizing suddenly that he would probably have no occasion to see her again, and found himself saying, "It's been my pleasure. And if there's anything else I can help you with, please feel free to give me a call."

She stopped in the doorway and gave him another of those dazzling smiles. "I just may take you up on that. Thank you!"

By the time Fiona got in her car after the meeting with H. Gideon, it was just six o'clock. Wicks Hollow was less than an hour away, but since it was almost the middle of October, it would be dark before she could get to the shop. Plus, she'd agreed to meet her friend Winona for a drink to celebrate her change of fortune—so to speak.

That made it an easy excuse to decide not to drive to her property until tomorrow—which was Friday, and would give her the whole weekend to spend in Wicks Hollow.

She realized she was strangely both nervous and relieved that she didn't have to go there tonight and have her dreams either explode—or be realized. Either scenario seemed more than she could bear at the moment.

What if she stepped inside and hated the space? What if she got bad vibes from it?

What if it was full of junk, and H. Gideon Nath, the Third, had only said what he needed to say to get her to sign the paperwork so he could be done with the business?

What if it was *beautiful* inside, and amazing, and it called to her…but it was still filled with worthless junk?

What if it was a treasure trove from which she could create a successful life?

Her palms were damp and her insides churned as she navigated through the traffic to the little pub where she and Winona were meeting.

By the time she breezed in, Fiona had talked herself down from the internal frenzy. *No sense worrying about it now. It'll be what it'll be. One day at a time. Worry about it tomorrow.*

She was very good at putting problems and issues aside, mainly because she rarely was committed to anything long enough that a problem would be so important as to bother her.

This is going to be different, Fi.

I know, I know. Be quiet. Let me have one more night to myself. Consider it my bachelorette party, all right? My last crazy night before I have to be responsible.

"Hey, girl!" Winona rose and gave her a big hug, her dozens of shoulder-length beaded braids making a pleasant clinking sound near Fiona's ear. "Well? Are you a business owner or not?"

"Oh, God, I am. I'm *committed.* I need a drink!" Fiona said with exaggerated desperation.

"Already got your favorite coming—that B-Cubed wheat beer you like."

"The one with the cherry essence? You're the best, Win. Thanks!" Fiona settled in her seat.

While they waited for their drinks to arrive, Fiona filled in her friend about the meeting with H. Gideon. After the long explanation, she gave a sigh. "I have a lot to learn, though—what I know about antiques would fit in my hand."

"Your background should help a little bit there, though," said Winona, sipping from the dark, coffee-scented stout she'd ordered.

"True." Fiona had two undergraduate degrees: one in

art history and one in interior design—an excellent example of her inability to make commitments. "At least I know the time periods and basic styles of furnishings," she agreed, sipping her draft. "And as long as H. Gideon didn't exaggerate the financial viability of the business…" She shrugged.

"Speaking of lawyers, you never got back to me on my text about next Tuesday," Winona said.

"Text?" Fiona reached for her bag. "I didn't get any text from you." She began to rummage in the depths of the satchel. Or did she? If she could actually *find* the phone…

"Did you lose your cell again?" Win shook her head in mock dismay. "I don't know why I bother trying. I should just stick to face-to-face or calling you at work. Not that you'll be at work any more, starting next week anyway…"

"So what's going on Tuesday that you texted me about?" Fiona asked, still feeling around amid the jumble for her phone. When *was* the last time she'd seen it?

"There's a guy I want you to meet," her friend replied, her dark eyes dancing with humor. "He's very sweet and down to earth, and he's never been married."

But Fiona was already shaking her head. "That lawyer you told me about? Vince? No way. You know how I feel about the attorney breed. And I don't trust any blind date you arrange for me anyway, especially after the guy who was supposed to be a veterinarian. The man had hands like the Tin Man—big and knuckly and creaky." She shuddered.

"Girl, you are so weird about hands. And you know that blind date was only to pay you back for sending me flowers from Colin Farrell."

Fiona smirked, remembering how Winona had called

her, babbling uncontrollably about the dozen red roses she'd received the day after meeting Colin Farrell at a charity function Win had managed.

"That was a good one, wasn't it?" she said with a laugh.

"Not as good as the vet I set *you* up with—the one who performs hypnosis on dogs and cats."

Fiona snorted and flapped her hand. "You are nowhere near as good as I am when it comes to great practical jokes. It's because of my inner imp."

"Anyway, this lawyer—"

"Speaking of lawyers," Fiona said, bent on changing the subject. She leaned closer, over her beer. "Why is an accountant better than a lawyer?"

Winona rolled her eyes. "I don't know."

"At least accountants know they're boring."

Winona chuckled in spite of herself, and just as she opened her mouth to speak again, she snapped it shut. Fiona realized why when a deep voice reached her ears. "Ms. Murphy?"

She looked up behind her just as Brad Forth stepped into her line of vision. "Well, hello," she greeted him, surprised that he would approach her.

"I thought that was you," he said, smiling down at her and then over at Winona. "Mind if I join you for a quick minute? I wanted to see how everything was going with the inheritance—the shop and all." His grin was infectious and impossible to ignore.

Fiona shrugged and flickered a glance at her friend, who seemed to be bursting with curiosity. "Have a seat. This is my friend Winona Reed. Win, this is Bradley Forth, the grand-nephew of Mr. Valente."

Winona looked a little confused after the introduction, and it took Fiona a moment to realize she'd probably assumed the man was H. Gideon when he'd mentioned the inheritance.

Forth took a seat, and the waitress was upon them in a second, obviously eager to take the order of the well-groomed, attractive man. Or maybe she recognized him as a political candidate.

After ordering a local IPA, he returned his attention to Fiona. "Did Nath take care of everything with you today? All the paperwork is signed and finished?"

"Yes. We've got everything squared away, and Win and I were just having a little drink to celebrate. You too? I'm guessing your paperwork—which is clearly more complicated than mine—would be all finalized as well."

"Yes—signed, sealed, and delivered. I'm meeting a friend—who's bringing some potential supporters—for a private dinner, and my handler and I got here a little early." He glanced over and Fiona saw the fresh-faced intern, standing near the wall with a clipboard. He was wearing a tie that looked like it was about to strangle him, it was so tight.

"When I saw you, I thought I'd take a moment to say hi. It's always nice to chat with a potential constituent." Brad beamed at Winona, then explained, "I'm running for State Senate in this district. Election's almost four weeks away, so the more people I can meet, the better."

"I'm glad you stopped by, Mr. Forth, because I have a question about your uncle," Fiona said.

"Please, call me Brad. I'm hoping to be your state senator soon, and I like to be on a first name basis with my supporters." He flashed his smile again. "At least, I *hope* I'll have your support."

"Um, well, I suppose I'll have to look at your plat-form," she said, feeling guilty that she didn't already know who was on the ballot for the state elections. "Anyway, I was wondering—do you know who Gretchen was?"

"Gretchen?" He looked at her with genuine confusion. "I'm afraid I don't know what you mean."

"Mr. Valente left a letter for me, sort of explaining his reasoning for putting me in his will, and he mentioned someone named Gretchen. I thought she might have come up at the reading of the will, but she didn't, and I didn't get a chance to ask then. I just wondered if you knew who she was because your great-uncle spoke very fondly of her in the letter."

Brad looked surprised. "Fondly?" He shook his head, glancing up to smile at the waitress who set his beer in front of him. "I'm sorry, I don't know who that could be. Quite frankly, Fiona—that's such a lovely name; I hope you don't mind if I use it—anyway, frankly, I can't imagine my great-uncle feeling fondly toward anyone." He lifted the beer and sipped, then lowered it and shook his head. "No, I don't think I've ever heard mention of a Gretchen. Did he say anything specific about her?"

Fiona took a moment to taste her own brew, wondering how much of the contents of the letter she should divulge. Not that there was anything that important in it, she reminded herself, but she felt odd sharing the nostalgic words from the old man. Not even H. Gideon Nath, the Third, knew what was in the letter.

She finally decided on prevaricating. "He didn't say much, other than that he knew her long ago. Hence my questions."

"I'll ask my mother if she knows," he promised. "My father is dead, and he was Nevio's nephew, but she might recall the name. And I can also ask Uncle Arnie and Aunt Vera."

"That would be great. It's just something that bothers

me a little, in a curious sort of way." She gave him a dazzling smile and noticed when a light of interest and appreciation flared in his eyes.

"I'll give you a call next week," he said, taking the napkin on which she wrote her mobile phone number. Then, with a glance over her shoulder, he stood. "So sorry—my campaign manager just arrived, and it's show time." He shook both of their hands, adding, "I hope I have your support on November 7." He dug into his pocket and pulled out a money clip, flipped through several large bills to find a twenty, and tossed it onto the table. "I'll be in touch, Fiona, if I learn anything about this mysterious Gretchen."

"Good-bye," Fiona said, and returned her attention to Winona as Bradley joined his posse of handlers. Her friend was looking at her through narrowed eyes. "What's wrong?"

"So, what—is he the reason you don't want to meet the lawyer I want to set you up with? He's not bad looking, but seems a little...not your type. Especially with him being a politician."

"What is it with you and setting me up? I go out enough. I don't need to be set up, Win."

"I know you go out quite a bit, but when you do, it's a different guy every time. Don't you get tired of the casualness of it all?"

"I like the casualness. Just because you found Mr. Perfect doesn't mean that I'm interested in that. I'm not. I like things just the way they are. And besides," Fiona added, "now that I have a business to run, I'll have enough responsibility in my life. I don't need to be responsible for a man, too."

Well. This was it.

Fiona gripped the cluster of keys, took a deep breath, and unlocked the door of the shop.

She'd debated about whether to enter through the back, alley-side door or to come in through the front, and decided that her first impression of her new life should be from the same perspective of her potential clients.

So here she was, standing in the little alcove between the two bay windows and unlocking the front door. Her stomach was filled with butterflies and her hands were clammy.

Geeze, Fi. Get a frigging grip.

She pushed open the door, and to her relief, it swung inward easily as delicate chimes tinkled above.

She stepped into the long, narrow shop. The smell of age met her nose: the scent of mothballs and mustiness, old wood and worn damask. The space was dark, and it took a few moments for her eyes to adjust to the faint light. She could see shapes of furnishings and lamps hanging from the ceiling, vases and chests, and other objects unidentifiable in the dim light.

Whatever was here was *hers*.

All hers.

A tingle of trepidation swirled through her middle, curling and squeezing in her stomach. She'd never been responsible for anything this important before. This *big* before.

Heck, she'd hardly been able to keep an orchid alive —and everyone knew they could go weeks without water.

Her palms were sweating…but a grin tugged at the corners of her mouth. Claudia was going to freak when she found out that her daughter owned an entire store.

A business.

Fiona closed the door behind her, locking it, and in the dim light, found a table on which to rest her leather bag. Then, feeling cautiously on the wall just inside the doorway, she groped for the light switch that she hoped was there. Her fingers brushed rough paneling, fumbling over molding and across a myriad of cords that no doubt attached to the collection of lamps that were suspended above.

That front wall of paneling ended, giving way to the chalky brick and mortar of the side, and Fiona had still not located a light switch.

Then, suddenly, with a little laugh, she pulled her hand back to her side. "Fiona, you are an idiot!" She shook her head at her own silliness and reached for a nearby lamp, slipping her hand under its shade to find the switch.

A welcome glow of light filtered into a small area, highlighting the flecks of dust and mites she'd stirred up with her investigation.

In the silence, Fiona heard the floor creak and groan as she moved slowly through a warren of items into the center of the store. Maybe the light switches were in the back. The ceiling hung lower now, giving the back half of the shop a more confined, cozy feeling.

She noticed that there was an unobtrusive staircase on the left side of the space that led to a second floor, which explained why the front part of the store had high ceilings and the rear seemed close and dark like a cave. She began to climb the stairs, hesitating when she looked up into the dark, cavernous stairwell.

Something shivered up her spine. An eerie prickle went cold over her shoulders, and suddenly, she didn't want to go up there.

Abruptly, Fiona stepped back from the stairs, and a

sudden sharp chill enveloped her. The hair at the nape of her neck lifted, and she sucked in her breath with a gasp —smelling, oddly enough, the faint scent of roses overpowering the dust and must.

Her heart began to bump out of rhythm in her chest.

Her hand curling at the collar of her loose peasant blouse, she backed away from the stairs and looked around. There was nothing to see. But it was suddenly *cold*.

Fiona swallowed, tasting dust, and turned to continue her walk toward the back of the shop, berating herself for her skittishness. "I'll get a flashlight," she said aloud...but her voice sounded weak and hollow in the silence.

As she turned, something whispered past her, brushing her fingers. Fiona gave a little shriek, and, pulling her hand away, stumbled backward a few steps, bumping into a table. Something rocked on it and fell to the floor with a loud crash, jacking her heart rate up even higher.

Just then, she noticed a glow of light from the alcove beneath the ascending stairs, and was able to make out three lamps arranged on the top of a massive piece of furniture; some sort of huge wooden secretary desk.

Her breath clogged, for the lamp in the middle of the trio was lit.

It hadn't been lit a moment ago.

And she hadn't touched any other switch.

The hair on the back of her neck turned cold, and her palms dampened. As she stepped toward the light, caution—and let's be honest, *nerves*—making her movements slow, the light winked out.

She froze, smothering a gasp. The smell of roses became stronger and a chill stirred the air.

The light flickered back on.

Fiona shook her head to clear it, to try and find a way to make sense of it.

"There must be a timer on this thing," she said aloud, pushing the heavy chair out of the way so that she could step closer to the large oaken desk. "Or a short in the wire. And that's why it's going on and off."

She reached around and found the cord to the glowing white lamp, following it down to the depths behind the secretary. It wound behind it and disappeared into a corner. Fiona leaned over and because of the light from the lamp, she could see where the cord ended.

Fiona suddenly felt as though she'd been plunged into freezing water, and for a moment, she couldn't move, couldn't breathe, couldn't react.

Then, she was a flurry of frantic movement, whirling away from the alcove, ramming into the corner of the chair, ricocheting against a table, and stumbling toward the front of the shop in a swirl of dust and the scent of roses. Her breath came back, furious and shallow, and her head felt light as she ran to the front door, struggling to flip open the lock.

Without looking back, without even hesitating, she yanked the door wide. The tinkling of the bells above barely registered in her stupefied mind as she burst out onto the sidewalk.

The lamp was unplugged.

FOUR

THE PHONE RANG, its low-key bleep startling Gideon in the silence of his office. Rubbing his dry eyes with a thumb and forefinger, he reached for the receiver as his attention skittered over the clock on his desk.

"Yes?" he said crisply.

"Gideon! I knew I would find you there." His grandfather's voice boomed over the line as if he were in the room with him, despite the fact that static crackled in the background. "What are you doing in the office at ten-thirty on a Friday night? Don't you have anything better to do with your time than to work?"

Tilting his chair back so he could rest his feet on the desk, Gideon smiled faintly. "Someone has to hold this practice together while you and Iva are gallivanting around the state." He loosened the tie he'd been wearing since six-thirty a.m., and snagged open the top button of his starched shirt. *Ahh.*

He wondered vaguely why he hadn't thought to do so before now.

"Good God, man, you've got to get yourself a life,"

H. Gideon Nath, Sr., bellowed over the phone lines. "How the hell do you think you're ever going to find a woman to marry if you're at the office every day till midnight?"

Gideon shook his head at the old man's familiar diatribe. If his grandfather would learn to call him on his cell phone, at least he wouldn't know his grandson was at the office so late. "We've been through this before—you've been married enough times for both of us so I don't need to worry about that. Besides, marriage is not in my five-year plan."

"Fine, fine, whatever you say," barked Gideon Senior. "Tell me whether everything's wrapped up with the Valente estate."

"Yes, it's all finished up. I met with the last of the heirs late yesterday, and everything is settled. I left you a message, Grandfather."

"You left me a message—where the hell—you mean on that damn little phone I can't figure out how to use? All those little pictures on the screen, and—well, blast it all. Next time call Iva if it's something important. She knows how to use hers."

"Well, I'm glad to hear at least one of you has the ability." Gideon looked out his office window at the moonbeam-washed street. It was too late to go somewhere for dinner. He'd have to settle for a frozen pizza—if he had any left from the last time he'd gone to the market.

There was a muffled noise on the other end of the line and the static got worse for a moment, then his grandfather's voice came through clearly. "Sorry about that. Iva wanted me to tell you we're going to be back in Wicks Hollow tomorrow because that big class reunion she's going to is coming up soon. She wants you to join us tomorrow for dinner at that place down there she likes—Trib's. She won't take no for an answer, and since I know you don't have any plans on a Saturday night, I told her you'd be there."

Gideon opened his mouth to refuse, then closed it. There was no good reason for him to do so, and the fact of the matter was, he liked Iva Bergstrom. A lot. Mostly because of how she'd changed his grandfather from an unyielding, business-minded workaholic to a kinder, gentler soul who'd been walking around as if he'd been struck by Cupid since they'd met last April. Gideon had never seen him so *happy*.

He also appreciated Iva because she'd helped his grandfather, who was over seventy, slow down a bit when it came to work. He was even talking about semi-retirement—an idea the younger Gideon fully supported. Not because he was eager to take over the firm and move him out—he had no reason to push on that—but because he was worried about his grandfather's health.

"That sounds fine. I'll be there. What time? Do we need reservations? Shall I call and make them?"

His grandfather laughed over the phone. "No, no, Trib's a friend of Iva's; she's got it all worked out. What, honey? Right, Gideon, it's all set. See us there at five-thirty, all right?"

In Gideon's mind, even six-thirty was far too early for Saturday dinner, but when you were dealing with senior citizens, you went with the flow. He just hoped the place had a decent wine list. Wicks Hollow was supposedly a trendy place that attracted a lot of people from Chicago and Ann Arbor as well as Grand Rapids, but that didn't mean this restaurant would be up to snuff.

"I'll be there. Give Iva a kiss for me, all right, Grandfather?"

"I will. But I think it's time you got yourself home, son. A man doesn't need to work as hard as you do."

You do when your dad is a screw-up.

"All right," Gideon said, shoving away the thought. "I'm closing up the laptop right now."

"Iva sends her love—and promises you a smooshy kiss—her words, not mine—tomorrow night."

Gideon grinned in spite of himself. "Ask her not to wear bright red lipstick then. I'll see you tomorrow." They disconnected the call, and Gideon sighed, then closed his laptop.

He shoved a few files into his briefcase and zipped up his laptop inside. Then he rearranged a stack of papers on the desk so they were aligned neatly, replaced his fountain pen in its gold-plated holder, and turned off the desk lamp.

He started toward the door, his gaze sweeping the office one last time to be certain nothing was awry—for even the cleaning service didn't work on Friday night— and noticed a glint on the floor under the small conference table.

Stooping, he reached beneath it and picked up the flat, circular object. It was a small gold compact with a Celtic design etched on it, and he realized it must belong to Fiona Murphy. No doubt it had fallen out of her huge bag when she knocked it over. He flipped it open and found himself staring at his own steel grey eye in the unsmudged mirror inside.

He snapped it closed, dropping it in his pocket, suddenly remembering the spark in her amber eyes and the thick, wild auburn hair that gave her a tousled, rumpled look. She was a very compelling woman, even if she looked like a wild gypsy.

Gideon closed the door behind him, walking into the

hallway toward the front of the office. He paused at Claire's desk to put a stack of papers in her in-box, and hesitated. His fingers slipped over the smoothness of the gold compact in his pocket.

He could have his admin call Fiona and drop it in the mail to her.

The memory of her mellow lips, puckered in concentration during his explanations yesterday, and the way they quirked in a smile of enthusiasm at the end of their meeting flashed into his mind. Surprising, for he hadn't realized he'd taken such note of her features…other than the objective realization that she was uncommonly striking.

He rubbed a thumb thoughtfully over the compact. He was going to Wicks Hollow tomorrow. Maybe he'd check out the antiques shop and return it himself.

By late afternoon on Saturday, Fiona had run out of excuses to avoid returning to the antiques shop.

Yesterday, after her aborted attempt to explore the little store, she'd gone back to Ethan's house—he'd offered to let her stay at his lake cabin while she was in town—and tried to come up with as many different explanations as possible for what had happened with the lamp.

Then, instead of going back to the shop, she'd spent a few hours on the Internet, doing "research"—which she admitted was just another procrastination.

But when Saturday morning arrived, she knew she had to get up and do something productive. Ethan and Diana were coming in that evening, and she'd be hard-pressed to explain why she couldn't show them the inside of her new property.

It was a very sunny day, and even though it was past the high tourist season, the fall colors were at their peak so there were also weekenders who'd come to town. The result was that with the extra pedestrians, the shop didn't seem as dim and still and lonely as it had yesterday.

But when she got to Violet Way, Fiona still wasn't quite ready to go inside.

Instead, she went to the boutique next door to meet her tenant.

"I heard there was a new owner," said Reba, who introduced herself as the owner and manager of Velvet Express. She was two decades older than Fiona, maybe fifty or so, and skinny as a rail—and modeling clothes that showed off her lack of curves and girth. She was wearing black, of course, and her attire made her look as somber as a funeral director. "Nice to meet you. Our lease expires in twenty months," she added as if to forestall any potential negotiations.

"Yes, I know," Fiona replied as she looked around. "Oh...is that your cat?"

The beautiful black cat with the copper patch around the eye was sitting on an upholstered chair that was probably intended for customers and not felines. Her stunning golden-amber eyes focused on Fiona as if to acknowledge their previous meeting, then she looked away.

"Oh, no. She's actually *your* cat," Reba replied with a smile. "I just sort of inherited her—when the antiques shop was closed, I would take care of her. Since no one's been opening regularly next door for over a year,

Gretchen just sort of became my cat. But she really belongs to you."

"Gretchen?"

At the sound of her name, the cat deigned to look over at the two women with unblinking eyes as if to say, "And what of it?"

"Yes, that's her name. She's a little testy with new people," Reba warned as Fiona started toward the animal. "We have what you might call a tentative relationship. I feed her, let her in and out, give her catnip once in a while, and she doesn't scratch me." She gave a humorless smile and waved a skeletal wrist that jangled with black and silver bracelets. "I'm actually glad you've come down here, because she really doesn't belong in a clothing boutique. She gets hair on everything."

"At least she's black," Fiona replied, looking around at the array of clothing. "Her hair would blend right in."

"As long as my customers aren't allergic to cats," Reba replied in a slightly testy tone.

Right. Good point.

"Well, if I can get Gretchen to leave with me, I'm happy to take her," Fiona said. "I'm going to go up and take a look at the flat above your shop—I just wanted you to know if you heard me moving around up there. In case you thought it was a ghost or something."

Fiona wasn't certain exactly why she said that—certainly she wasn't thinking about ghosts, was she?—but there it was.

Reba merely looked at her as if she were a kook, then said, "A can of tuna will lure Gretchen anywhere. I happen to have one in the back—I keep them for such emergencies. Sometimes she refuses to come inside when the weather is bad, so I've had to resort to bribery."

Any minor irritation she felt toward the caustic

boutique owner dissipated. Reba might be a little abrupt, but if she cared enough about a bad-tempered cat to ensure she was safe from the elements, that made up for any lack in personality in Fiona's book.

Armed with a single-serving can of tuna, and the distinct impression that Reba didn't care to have her new landlady around, Fiona left the boutique through the front door and managed to get Gretchen to follow her.

"Maybe you should go into the shop with me," she said as the cat scarfed down her tuna at the corner of the building by the side alley.

There was something about the idea of having another living thing with her that made Fiona feel braver about going into the place where a lamp appeared to spontaneously light itself, and the scent of roses gathered in the air for no apparent reason.

It had been foolish of her to fly out of there like a bat out of hell yesterday…but maybe it had really been a symptom of her own insecurity—the reality of owning the store and being responsible for it—that had caused her to react so strongly.

At any rate, she was back. "I'm not going to let myself be spooked away this time," she told Gretchen. "There's got to be an explanation for that weird lamp lighting up, and I'm going to find it. Maybe there's a time-operated battery pack attached to it or something."

She looked down at the feline, who wandered over to where she was standing at the front door and meowed. That was a good sign. "You'll probably be happy to get back home to your own place, won't you? Let's go in."

The chimes tinkled elegantly as she pushed the door open, and again that aged smell assailed her senses. Quickly turning on as many lamps as possible in the front area, Fiona finally found a large power strip on the floor, holding with more than twenty plugs. She turned it on, and *whoa.*

The shop came alive with light, and her breath caught.

It's incredible.

That was her only thought as she looked around the shop—a shop filled with lamps and pendants and chandeliers. It was like stepping into Aladdin's cave, for the vintage lights glittered and shone in soft gold and glinted through shades of every color of the rainbow. Hundreds of them dangled from the ceiling like floating candles and low-hanging stars, and still more sat on every surface throughout the shop.

Wow.

She turned in a slow circle, looking up and around, bathed in the soft glow of the golden light.

Unlike when she was here yesterday, there was nothing that seemed amiss or odd. She felt no strange chill, no disruption in the air, no scent of roses or anything else unusual.

Nor did the strange lamp toward the back of the store appear to be illuminated.

Fiona exhaled, and her nerves eased. She looked up and around again. *This place is amazing.*

She left her heavy leather bag on the huge desk that was located partway back into the shop. It was still cluttered with papers, writing utensils, and a large, old-fashioned telephone. Clearing off that surface was one task she promised herself she'd handle today.

Fiona eyed the staircase tucked against the left wall, but decided she wasn't ready to climb up and see what was on the second level. Despite the glow from the myriad of lamps and chandeliers, the upstairs seemed dark and forbidding. And of course she remembered what had happened yesterday.

Instead, she made her way past the staircase and into the low-ceilinged portion of the shop, Fiona fixated on the strange, spontaneously illuminating lamp. It squatted there like an ugly, albino toad.

It was an unexceptional piece. Stocky and white, the base had small nodules texturing its milk glass curves. The shade had faded to a yellowish satin, but the fringe that edged it was still white.

Fiona didn't take her eyes from the lamp and was watching breathlessly to see if it would come on again when a faint jingle from the front of the store startled her.

"Hello? Is anyone there?"

Fiona pivoted in surprise, banging her shin against the corner of a heavy chest. Stifling a gasp of pain, she called back, "I'll be right with you!"

Limping slightly, trying to ignore the throb of pain in her leg, she hurried back to the front. On the way, she noticed the shards of porcelain from the clock she'd broken on her last visit, and knew she'd better find a broom somewhere soon.

When she reached the front, she was surprised to see the broad-shouldered figure of H. Gideon Nath, the Third, looming near the entrance. As usual, he was wearing expensive clothing—but at least it wasn't a suit and tie. A sport coat, yes. A crisp, button-down shirt, yes. But no tie, and the top button (only the top one) was unbuttoned. His dark hair was combed into place, but one tiny little wave curled out of sync over his ear. This must be his "Saturday casual" look, Fiona thought with an inner grin.

He was examining a small end table topped by a Tiffany-style lamp, but looked up when she approached.

He must have noticed that she favored her leg, for he asked, "Are you limping?" in that cut-to-the-chase, professional way of his.

"When you called out, you startled me so much I whirled and slammed my leg into the corner of a chest. So, thank you," she teased lightly. Then she became serious. "Do you have more papers for me to sign?"

H. Gideon shook his head, then turned his gaze from her to scan the shop. "I've never been in here before. It looks like a fascinating place." He reached out almost reverently to touch the stained glass shade of the lamp next to him. "There are some valuable pieces here."

Fiona looked at him in surprise. She wouldn't have expected the stuffy attorney to find an old, musty shop like this fascinating. Surely antiques would be out of place in H. Gideon's life: he'd be all about chrome, and black and white decor with smooth lines. He'd have sleek, uncomfortable leather furniture, with few—if any—color accents.

The illumination in his high-rise condo overlooking the Grand River, she imagined, would consist not of interesting lamps, but of cold recessed lighting, wall sconces, and chilly halogen bulb lamps hanging from narrow black cords.

Abruptly, he returned his attention to her and caught her staring at him. Fiona looked away, controlling a smile, and jammed a hand through her thick hair to push it back from her face.

"Is this yours? I found it in my office after you left." He reached into his pocket.

To Fiona's surprise, she immediately recognized it as her gold compact. She was overcome by relief. "Oh, thank you *so much* for finding this. It was a gift from my grandmother—it must have fallen out of my bag."

She took the compact from his long fingers, noticing how warm it was from being in his pocket, and clutched it to her chest. "I would have been devastated if I'd lost it."

She tucked it into the pocket of her skirt. "You didn't have to come all the way here to return it, though." When Fiona raised her eyes, she found that he was looking at her with something much more than reserve and cordiality.

Gideon shifted his gaze away and straightened his stance—as if he could stand any taller—and said, "How about a tour of your place while I'm here? Are you open for business yet?"

"No. That's why I was so startled when you came into the shop. The sign does say 'Closed Due to Death'."

"Right," he replied, somewhat abashed.

"I think I know the real reason you came by." She gave him a teasing smile.

"And what reason would that be?" he asked warily.

"To tell me what that initial H. stands for."

He choked back a laugh, then shook his head. "I don't think so."

She rolled her eyes. "I don't know what the big deal is."

"Exactly my thought," he replied dryly. "Why does it matter to you?"

"Because it's on your nameplate and your business card. If it wasn't a big deal, then why use the initial?"

He drew in a breath as if to argue, then simply exhaled, refusing to answer.

"Is it Harry? Or Hiram?" she pressed. "Or Hewey?"

There was a flash of humor in his eyes, but still he shook his head in negation. "Will you show me around the shop a little?" he asked in an obvious bid to change the subject.

"All right, then, H. Gideon. I'll show you around, although, honestly, I haven't seen the whole place myself yet. Come on back with me, won't you?" She turned, gesturing for him to follow her toward the rear of the store.

H. Gideon? Fighting an exasperated grin, he shoved his hands into his pockets and walked behind as she led him down the two main aisles, one by one, from the middle to the front and back again. He discovered that he was more interested in watching the shift and sway of her hips in the long, flowing skirt than in examining the shop's wares.

That surprised him, because Fiona Murphy wasn't anything like the type of woman who normally caught his eye. She wasn't polished or professional—for God's sake, her auburn hair looked like it reeked of static electricity. He'd never seen it—or her—resembling anything sleek or styled, and she certainly wasn't a sharp, ambitious businesswoman.

She was as different from the type of women he usually dated—like Rachel Backley—as a White Zinfandel was from an oak-barrel Chardonnay—or, better yet, more like fruit punch compared to a blush Moscato: colorful, sweet, and punchy, but not what one would serve to guests.

Yet, the woman had been drifting into his mind more often than she should...and he felt as though he had no choice but to try and figure out why. Perhaps that was why he'd decided to return the compact himself—so he could try and put his fascination to rest. To move on.

Gideon dragged his attention from his intriguing hostess and focused on his surroundings. The little boutique was surprisingly intriguing and inviting, with the glow of light and the ambience of history and age.

Fiona led him past a large desk, where papers and writing utensils were scattered, and an old fashioned, wired telephone sat buried among them.

"What happened here?" he asked when he noticed a pile of ceramic shards scattered over the floor about three-quarters of the way back into the store.

Fiona stopped to see what he meant, and he fancied she looked a bit uncomfortable.

"I—uh—backed into that table and knocked it off," she explained. "I haven't located a broom yet, so there it sits." She gave a little laugh, then continued to walk along the aisle into the rear of the shop, where the lighting became dimmer and the ceiling lower.

"It's like a cave back here," Gideon commented, watching her turn on lights as they went. The bell-like sleeve of her sweater fell back to the elbow as she reached for a pull-cord. He admired the long, graceful line of her arm and allowed his gaze to continue its logical path over her shoulder, then to wander over the swell of her breasts. In the low light she looked elfin and ethereal with her halo of burnished hair, flowing cloth-ing, and long, slender build.

"It is," she agreed, and for a moment, he forgot what it was she was agreeing to. "It's a little nerve-wracking coming into the back here alone in the dark when you don't know where you're going," she continued after a pause.

"I can imagine." He followed as she turned a corner, and noticed a large desk with three lamps on it, sitting just at the juncture of the bend in the aisle. Something about the walnut secretary caught his attention, and he paused, peering at the wall behind it. Fiona had only switched on one of the lights. He reached to pull the cord of the middle one, the one with the cream-colored shade decorated with fringe.

He thought he heard a sharp intake of breath from Fiona, and when he glanced at her, she was staring at him and the lamp as though waiting for them to spontaneously draw swords.

Her eyes seemed fixed on his hand. "Is something wrong?" he asked, yanking the lamp cord. The cord clicked, and nothing happened.

She puffed out the breath she'd been holding, making him even more confused. "It doesn't seem to work," he said, wondering what was up with her. *Such a strange woman.*

"Why don't you check to see if it's plugged in." Her voice sounded thready.

"All right." Still confused by her sudden change of demeanor, Gideon shifted around the massive desk and followed the cord, which, sure enough, dangled to the ground. He found a plug, shoved it in, and pulled the cord. The light glowed.

"Thank you." Her words were fervent, and the expression on her face still appeared drawn.

"Are you all right?" he asked again. He felt as if he were missing something important.

"I'm fine. Fine now. What were you looking at back here?" Indeed, she sounded more like her easy, informal self.

"I just was looking at this desk a bit more closely." He couldn't explain why he was interested in the ugly piece of furniture. It wasn't his style at all. Heavy-featured walnut with tarnished silver pulls and nicks throughout did not turn him on.

But Fiona did.

Gideon stepped away from her abruptly, wondering if she sensed his suddenly raging testosterone. *Where the hell did that come from?*

"When I came here yesterday, that same desk caught my attention too. Maybe it's because of where it's situated, here in this little corner, kind of under the stairs." She smiled up at him, and for the first time, he noticed the tiniest little dimple near the corner of her full, sensual lips. His mouth went dry and he discovered he couldn't seem to look away.

"I found what looks like a storage room back here," Fiona was saying, pointing to a closet door on the back wall. "The door to it is locked, but I bet the key is in that mess you gave me the other day. I'm hoping to find a broom in there so I can clean up that porcelain. I just have to go back to the front and get the keys."

Gideon allowed her to pass by him in that narrow aisle way, and he caught the same spicy scent that had seemed to filter in and out of his office since she'd been there on Thursday—which was ridiculous. There was no way her perfume still permeated his office. He was imagining things.

He followed her on along the aisle toward the rear of the store. Along the way, the shop morphed from the neatly cluttered arrangement of merchandise into the disorganized array of a back room. There was no door that led to the behind-the-scenes area, nor even any indication that one had left the store and entered a domain available only to the proprietor—but this part of the establishment was clearly not for the eyes of the customer.

The only separation from the front area from the back was the large secretary, situated against the wall by the stairs, and an old wooden and silk divider that had probably been used as a dressing screen.

In the rear of the shop, boxes and crates were stacked against the walls and on top of furniture, most of which were old tables or chests with nicks in them, or broken legs. The lamps were fewer, but he noticed work lights hanging over a long counter that held everything from screwdrivers, nuts, bolts, and hinges to Styrofoam cups, paper towels, papers, and masking tape.

He felt a whisper of movement behind him and turned to find Fiona approaching, a mass of keys jangling in her hand.

"It's a mess back here, isn't it?" she asked ruefully. "It looks as though Valente just brought new inventory in and left the old stuff, and all of its garbage, back here. I'm sure the fire marshal would have a field day if he or she came in."

Shaking her head in exasperation, she gathered her hair back into a ponytail at the nape of her neck, then released the mass of curls. He watched as they sprang back into her face, even more out of control than they'd been a moment before.

"I certainly have my work cut out for me," she said, giving her head a sexy little shake as if to settle her hair back into place.

Gideon's mouth had gone a little dry. "I—uh—hope you're planning on hiring some help."

She walked over to a door on the side wall and was busily trying, key-by-key, to find the right one. He switched on the work lights, and suddenly the area was lit by glaring fluorescent bulbs.

"Thank you," she said without turning. "Yes, I'm definitely planning on hiring someone to help out—preferably someone who knows something about antiques, since I'm woefully ignorant. I have a friend in mind who might be able to help." Her voice became muffled as she bent further over the keyhole. "…because I certainly can't keep the shop closed until I learn enough about my merchandise to be able to sell and buy it, so if you know of anyone who might be interested, send them over."

Finally, she stood upright. "*Aha*. Got it."

He watched as she struggled to turn the key in a tarnished lock, and was just about to step forward to help when it pivoted slowly.

With an unladylike grunt that brought a smile to his face, Fiona forced the key until it clicked audibly. "Whew," she murmured. "Note to self: replace lock." She grasped the doorknob and struggled with it for a moment.

Gideon glanced down at his sportcoat and butter-soft Italian loafers, shrugged, and gently elbowed her out of the way. "Why don't you let me try. It's obviously stuck."

Fiona gave him a look that implied she didn't need his help, but nevertheless stepped out of the way. He turned the stubborn knob and pushed against the door. Nothing happened but a slight creak when it heaved within its jamb. Gideon used his shoulder to shove again, and was rewarded with a louder creak, followed by the groan of wood scraping against wood.

"It looks so much easier when they break in through a door on TV," Fiona said with the light of laughter in her voice.

"One more time," he muttered, and rammed his body sharply against the stubborn door.

It flew open and his momentum was so great that he lost his balance and stumbled through the doorway, landing in an inglorious heap on the floor. Boxes and other unidentifiable items rained down on him, grazing his head and landing in his lap. Dust and dirt swirled everywhere, thrown up by the force of the door opening, and cobwebs swooped into his face and hair.

He heard Fiona gasp, and saw her silhouette as she moved to stand in the open doorway, blocking the light, and looking down at him.

"Are—are you all—right?" she asked hesitantly, and he realized in a blaze of annoyance that she was struggling to contain a giggle.

Something fell on his head—fortunately, it was a small, empty box, and did nothing but dump more dust into his face—and that pushed her over the edge. She lost it and sagged against the doorway, looking down at him as she giggled uncontrollably. Her wild hair shook with violence, and her eyes glowed with humor.

Gideon clenched his teeth and struggled to pull to his feet just as Fiona reached down to offer a hand unsteady with the chuckles wracking her body.

He grabbed her slender fingers to steady himself, and in one brilliantly graceful movement that he would forever be thankful for, she lost her balance, knocking into his unstable crouch, and they tumbled back onto the floor of the storage room.

All of a sudden, his arms were full of a sweet-smelling, soft, feminine body that quaked with laughter and struggled to right itself as all the right curves on her were pressing into all the right places on him. In the light that poured into the room, he was able to see the way humor lit her face, and in an instant his annoyance melted away and then he was joining her chuckles.

When H. Gideon smiled—so close to her, suddenly so handsome—Fiona's heart stopped and her breath caught, silencing her own giggles.

This was the first time she'd seen him relaxed. The air of perpetual annoyance disappeared from his face like a cloud lifting and the sharpness faded away. There was humor in his grey eyes—eyes that no longer looked like angry steel, but like the bluish-grey river—and his full lips became soft and sensual. The smile made all the difference, transforming him into a devastatingly attractive man without the tight collar and stiff professionalism that had been like a wall before.

That smile, that laughter, so casually bestowed, became Fiona's undoing. She suddenly was aware that she was lying on a very attractive, very warm, very masculine specimen of man, and just as quickly, she began to scramble off him.

In her endeavor to escape, she got tangled in her skirts, then elbowed him in the abdomen. He grunted in a gasp for air, then those magnificent hands closed over her arms.

His unexpected embrace stilled her movements without pulling her closer, and, startled, she looked down to find his face mere inches from hers. His powerful thighs stilled under hers, and Fiona felt a shock of heat stab her, then rush up into her face. Her pulse was racing; surely he could see it in the side of her throat.

"What's the hurry, Fiona?" he murmured, something like humor playing about the corners of his lips. "My clothes are already ruined."

She gathered her wits. "But there's still hope for my skirt." Her heart was thudding madly in her chest, and her insides seemed to have melted into hot liquid.

She placed her hands on his chest to lift herself away, and felt the solid slabs of warm, firm muscle flex under the layer of coat and shirt as his hands slid to settle at her hips.

Time suspended for a moment as their gazes locked in the inches that separated them. She was so close she could see the light coat of dust on his nose, and the hint of where dark whiskers would form on his cheeks and jaw. His hands held her lightly, balancing her on top of his long, solid body, and she realized belatedly that one of her legs had slipped between his knees so that she and her skirt were straddling a muscular thigh.

Something changed when his gaze drifted from hers, dropping to her slightly parted lips, and Fiona felt a hot wash of desire flood her. As she caught her breath, he lifted his head and brought her face to his, fitting their lips together in a gentle, tentative kiss.

He tasted of dust—moist, hot dust—and smelled of some subtle male scent that wrapped around her just as his arms did. His lips caressed and coaxed hers, opening them to explore within, and drawing her upper, then her lower, lip into his mouth to taste them. He shifted under her, a rumbling sigh escaping from the depths of his throat, and pulled her closer to his chest as his mouth continued to explore hers.

Fiona was just bringing her hand to touch his thick, dark hair, when, in the very faintest corner of her consciousness, she heard the tinkle of a bell. Someone called out from the front of the store. Jerking back, she rolled clumsily off his body, still tangled in skirts, and banged into the leg of a piece of furniture as she pulled herself to her feet. "Someone's here!"

Stumbling to her feet, she brushed frantically at her sweater and skirt as she stumbled out of the storage room, leaving Gideon behind to struggle to his own feet.

FIVE

GIDEON'S VEINS hummed and his breathing felt like the rasp of iron over wood, rough and unsteady. He pulled himself slowly upright, feeling as if he'd been run over by a Mack truck.

Jesus.

He looked at his hand and saw that his fingers were trembling. His breathing was slowing to normal, but his heart rate and the heaviness between his legs indicated how aroused he was. He took a deep breath and held it, but his body still hummed, and his lips still buzzed from the heat of that amazing kiss.

When he dragged a hand through his hair, more dust and cobwebs floated down to land on his dark pants and leather shoes. *Damn.* He took a few more moments to brush himself off, trying to regain some dignity before joining Fiona and her customer.

Customer? Didn't the sign say the store was closed?

Disregarding the fact that he had ignored the sign himself, Gideon hurried out to the front of the shop, straightening his shirt and finger-combing back his hair as he went.

When he reached the open area of the store, he found Fiona casually chatting with a well-dressed man—who was not the least bit dusty, dirty, or disheveled. And he was standing much too close to her.

Gideon was even less pleased to recognize the man as Bradley Forth.

"Hello, H.—er, Gideon," Fiona greeted him as if he'd just run out for milk. Her cheeks weren't even flushed, and though her lips were a little swollen, she didn't seem at all off-balance by that kiss. "Apparently you're not the only one who decided to ignore the closed sign." She gave them both an exasperated look.

Gideon crossed his arms over his chest to hide as much as he could of his rumpled clothing and offered a polite smile to the other man, who had the grace to look embarrassed by Fiona's comment.

Gideon managed to ungrit his teeth enough to speak. "Good to see you again, Forth. Nice of you to drive down here," he added dryly.

"Yes. I wanted to see how Miss Murphy was doing here at Uncle Nevio's shop. I haven't been here for awhile, but I thought I'd stop by and see how things were going."

Stop by? Forth lived in Grand Rapids. Wicks Hollow was not a "stopping by" sort of place from the big city…

As if reading his mind, Forth continued with the smooth smile of a politician, "There's a large event going on here this weekend—some big class reunion—and with the election being only three weeks out, my team decided it was important for me to be as visible as possible."

And Forth was likely hoping to turn up a nice little

feature in the *Grand Rapids Press* about his deceased uncle and the quaint little shop he'd bequeathed to a mysterious woman…which would of course be accompanied by a spread about the grand-nephew of the old man who'd left it to her, who'd made it a point to visit tiny Wicks Hollow in support of a local event.

Smart and savvy. And annoying as hell.

"Of course, my schedule is extremely tight," Forth continued, shooting a quick look at Fiona as if to make certain she heard his comment.

"Ah, yes, that's right. The other night, you mentioned how busy you are right now."

The other night? What the hell did that mean?

Gideon's irritation grew when Forth modestly smoothed a hand over his thick head of hair—with not a receding hairline or grey strand in sight.

"Yes, but it was very nice to see you. Oh, and I did ask my mother about Gretchen."

Apparently Forth and Fiona had developed quite a friendship, Gideon thought darkly. How the hell had that happened?

"And? Did she know anything about her?" replied Fiona.

"Unfortunately, no," said the politician. "But I will ask Uncle Arnie and Aunt Vera, as promised. I'm sorry I haven't gotten to it yet—so busy with campaign events and fundraisers and press conferences, you know." He smiled winningly. "I'll be sure to let you know once I do."

"Thank you. You do have my phone number," she said matter-of-factly, splitting her glance between the two of them. "You don't have to come all the way over here again if you find out anything—especially since you're so busy."

Gideon smothered a smile as Forth's face showed that her gentle gibe had found its mark, then his niggling aggravation returned.

"Who's Gretchen?" he asked, tired of feeling like he was the odd man out. After all, *he'd* been the one kissing her five minutes ago. Until that slick politician decided to barge in.

"Valente mentioned someone named Gretchen in the letter he left for me, and I was wondering who it is. Do you know?"

Wondering why she had asked Forth for help but not him, and curious about the letter, Gideon took a moment to reply. "I don't recall the name showing up anywhere in the paperwork I've handled. But I'll be happy to double-check it for you." He wanted to know more, but decided not to pursue the matter at this point. Perhaps after Forth left, Fiona would let him read the letter.

Suddenly, a cat appeared seemingly from nowhere, landing lightly on a table near the main pathway through the cluster of tables and other furnishings, drawing the attention of all three of them.

"Meet Gretchen," Fiona said, giving them a rueful smile. "She's the shop cat—and obviously not the Gretchen mentioned in my letter."

Gideon eyed the cat, and the feline eyed him back. He didn't have an issue with cats at all, but this one had an uncanny, eerie expression in her green eyes: they seemed to be measuring him as if to determine whether he was worthy of her attention.

Forth, in the tradition of all the baby-kissing, hand-shaking, pet-greeting politicians, reached over to stroke Gretchen on the head.

She hissed and swiped, then fled the scene, diving

under a nearby chest of drawers as Forth gaped at the thin red lines on his hand.

"Well, I guess I'm not getting *her* vote," he joked, then pulled out a handkerchief to dab at the blood.

"Oh, I'm so sorry," Fiona said with a grimace. "I'd offer you something for those scratches, Brad, but I have no idea if there's a first aid kit or anything like that in the store."

"No worries," he said. "I've got to get on my way anyway. But don't forget—I'll be at the town center with my staff early this evening, just talking to whoever walks by. I hope you'll come and say hi."

But Fiona, who didn't seem overly concerned about the wounds her cat had inflicted, had hunkered onto her elbows in an effort to try and entice Gretchen back out. "Good luck," was all she said, and as far as Gideon was concerned, that was a dismissal for Bradley Forth.

But the other man didn't seem to get it, and instead, he stood there watching Fiona as he continued to wipe off his hand.

Gideon found himself unable to look away from her shapely rear-end, which was lovingly embraced by her silky skirt as she rested her cheek on the floor to look under the chest. Her thick, sweet-smelling auburn hair spilled over her shoulders and onto the dusty floorboards, and she pushed it out of her face with the palm of her hand. "Come on, Gretchen, honey," she wheedled. "Come on out. Mr. Forth won't bother you."

Gideon felt foolish standing there, watching her crouch on the floor, and he flickered his gaze at the silent Brad Forth. He was annoyed that the other man seemed to have just as much interest in the view of her heart-shaped derrière swathed in a flowing blue and white skirt. The fact that Gideon was the one who'd had his hands on it only a short time ago mollified him only slightly.

Yet it was ridiculous to consider the possibility of Fiona and Brad Forth together—they were even less-suited for each other than *he* and Fiona would be. The conservative politician would never make it in the polls with a flighty, ditzy, free spirit like Fiona on his arm.

But what *had* the man meant by "the other night"? Clearly they'd been together…somewhere.

And that bothered Gideon a *lot* more than it should have, which annoyed him greatly.

"Well," Fiona said finally, pulling to her feet without tangling in her skirt this time. "I guess Gretchen's not coming out."

She brushed off her clothing and sighed, then used two hands to scoop up the mass of hair off her face and neck. As before, she let it spill out over her palms, and the thick curls cascaded enticingly around her face and neck before she let the whole cluster drop back over her shoulders.

Gideon swallowed hard and felt a little too warm—and was even more annoyed. What was wrong with him?

Just then, someone knocked on the window.

"Again?" Fiona muttered, looking at the door. Then her face lit up in a smile and she fairly ran to the entrance to fling the door open. "Ethan! I can't believe you're here already. You must have left Chicago before noon!"

She hugged him and smacked a loud kiss on his cheek, then curled the fingers of both hands around his upper bicep and dragged him into the shop. "Well, take a look! What do you think?"

Instead of following her suggestion or answering her

question, the man named Ethan looked at Gideon then Forth, then back at Fiona.

"I thought you weren't open for business yet," he said in a voice that matched his cool, almost warning look. "And yet here you are, already flooded with—er —*customers*."

"Oh, they're not customers," she said with a roll of the eyes.

Fighting a sinking feeling that this Ethan was more of a—well, *concern* would be the word; certainly not *rival*— than Bradley Forth, Gideon introduced himself. "My firm handled the estate, and as I happened to be in Wicks Hollow for the day with my grandfather, I thought I'd see how things were going."

Ethan nodded, still looking at him with a cool expression. When his attention swept down over Gideon's rumpled and dusty clothing, he felt the other man's opinion chill even further. "Looks like you were doing more than just 'seeing how things were going.'"

"Poor H.—I mean Gideon, took a little spill in the back," Fiona replied with a giggle underscoring her words. "He got his nice clothing all messed up."

"Well, I guess I'd best be going," said Forth in a slightly too-loud voice as if tired of being left out of the conversation. He offered his hand to the skeptical Ethan. "Bradley Forth. I'm running for state senator here in this district, and I—"

"Chicago," the other man replied briefly. "Save your pitch. I live in Chicago."

"Right, then. Well, goodbye, Fiona. I hope to see you later tonight."

She made a non-committal reply, and the way she eagerly opened the door for him made Gideon feel *slightly* better. Ethan was still eyeing him suspiciously, and he knew he had no further excuse to stay.

But he really needed to talk to her. About that kiss.

Before he could figure out what to do, the door tinkled open *again.*

What was this, Grand Central Station?

This time, an elegant, expensively-dressed woman in her early thirties stepped inside. She, Gideon noted immediately, was definitely more his type: conservative and stylish in attire and manner, with her lush dark hair coiffed in neat waves. She looked like the sort of professional, career-minded woman he was used to being around.

"Oh, Fiona," she said as she looked around, then clasped her hands over her breast. "It's beautiful in here. Sorry I'm late—I went next door to look inside; their merchandise is a little heavy on the black colors for me. But this place—*your* place is...just wonderful." She seemed to notice Gideon for the first time. "Oh, I didn't realize you had a customer," she said quickly—and her demeanor eased into something more remote and businesslike.

"Oh, he's not a customer," Fiona said brightly, then gushed, "It *is* beautiful, isn't it, Diana?"

"This is the attorney who handled the estate," Ethan said to Diana, still giving Gideon a cool look. But when he slipped his arm around her waist in a proprietary way, he unwittingly answered Gideon's unspoken question.

"And I was just leaving," he said smoothly, feeling slightly mollified. Whoever Ethan was, he was involved with Diana and not Fiona.

"Well, thanks for stopping by, H. Gideon," Fiona said with a warm smile.

Gideon looked for another message in her eyes—something that indicated she wanted to speak with him also, that the kiss had effected her too—but there was nothing but the same warm amber sparkle there. "I really appreciate you returning that compact."

With nothing left to say, Gideon nodded at Ethan and Diana, then made his exit.

Although five-thirty was uncomfortably early for dinner on a Saturday, Gideon was relieved to discover that Trib's was not only trendy, comfortable, and pleasingly appointed, but also had a surprisingly upscale menu as well as an extensive wine list that offered two different sized pours. Their table was situated near the back of the restaurant under what appeared to be an authentic Andy Warhol print, and he noticed several other prints by the artist—most likely copies, as they included the famous Tomato Soup and Marilyn Monroe images—throughout the place.

Gideon was impressed in spite of himself. Maybe Wicks Hollow, which he'd always though of as a kitschy tourist trap, had more to offer than he'd realized.

"Have a seat, Gideon, dear," Iva said, patting the chair next to her. With round, pink cheeks, a hairdo of soft white hair that reminded him of cotton candy, and sparkling blue eyes, the sixty-ish woman had become quite dear to him over the last six months.

"You look lovely tonight, Iva," he said, giving her a hug and kiss before taking his seat. "Grandfather, you look quite rested yourself." He reached over to shake hands with him. "Apparently, vacationing agrees with you."

"I've got a great traveling partner," replied Gideon Senior, smiling down at Iva. "Now if only I could get her to agree to marry me."

"Now, Hollis, let's not rush things. We're having such a wonderful time. There's no reason for you to rush to—as they say—put a ring on it." She giggled and held up her left hand, which was bare of jewelry. "Gideon, thank you for joining us. I know this is abominably early for you for dinner, but you know how we senior citizens are. We turn into pumpkins at nine p.m.!"

"I've missed our bi-monthly dinners," Gideon said, not at all surprised to realize it was true. "And I had some business to attend to here in Wicks Hollow, so it worked out quite well."

"The pizza here is fantastic," his grandfather said, ogling the menu. "Highly recommend it. The Wise Guy is my favorite—it's got sausage, smoked mozzarella, and caramelized onions. In fact, I think that's what I'll have tonight..." He trailed off when he realized Iva was looking at him with raised eyebrows and a pointed expression. "Ahem. Maybe I should have the salmon instead."

"A much healthier choice, darling," she said, looking back at the menu. Without glancing up at Gideon, she said for his benefit, "Your grandfather's doctor is concerned about his cholesterol."

"Well if that's all I've got to worry about at seventy-three, then that's pretty minor," Gideon Senior grumbled. "Don't know why I can't have a pizza once in a while."

Iva looked at him innocently. "Why, of course, Hollis. No one said you couldn't."

But when the server came, he ordered the salmon and a glass of red wine. "Red wine's good for you," he said, drawing his bushy brows together as if to ward off further commentary from Iva.

"I didn't say anything, darling," she replied with an affectionate pat on his hand.

Gideon found himself inexplicably charmed by their interplay, and privately hoped that his grandfather would convince Iva to marry him. He didn't really understand her hesitation; but clearly, Iva Bergstrom was not a gold-digger in any way, shape, or form. She would be the senior Nath's fourth wife—but she was so different from the other three women he'd wed—all of whom had been cut from the same brittle mold—that Gideon knew his grandfather would be perfectly happy.

They chatted about a number of topics as they waited for their food, and the owner of the restaurant stopped by to greet them.

"Gideon, this is Trib—the genius behind this place," Iva said.

The restaurateur was a young fifty and had white-blond hair cut in a very short but fashionable style. He wore a poppy pink bowtie with robin's egg pinstripes, and a crisp button-down shirt in a slightly darker shade of blue. A midnight blue sport coat and charcoal trousers completed his attire—and he managed to look like a Ralph Lauren model instead of an Easter egg. "What a pleasure to meet you," Trib gushed, shaking Gideon's hand. "I've heard so much about you from your grandfather and Iva."

"If the food is as fantastic as it looks on the menu, and as enjoyable as the ambience, I guarantee I'll be back," Gideon replied. "Your wine list is very impressive."

Trib preened a little. "I do my own sommelier work,

and every vintage on it are ones I adore. The Barolo in particular is outstanding."

Gideon smiled. "Either you're very good at assessing your customers' taste, or you cheated and asked what I ordered." He lifted his glass of wine to indicate that he'd already ordered the Barolo.

"I'm just *very* good," Trib replied with a wink, and Gideon realized belatedly that the man was flirting with him. *Yikes.*

He took a too-large sip of wine, nearly choking on the expensive vintage, as Iva eased in to the rescue. "Now, Trib, leave him alone. Poor Gideon is no match for you—and, charming as you are, you're not exactly his type."

"Story of my life," Trib replied with mock dismay, and he and Iva chuckled gaily. Gideon, slightly mortified, looked at his grandfather, who seemed more confused than anything.

"Oh, don't be silly, Tribune," Iva replied, swatting at him affectionately. "You of the trail of manly broken hearts?"

"Well," he said modestly. "I just haven't found the right one yet. Pleasure to meet you, Gideon, truly. I hope the Barolo and your meal meet your expectations."

And with that, Trib was blessedly off to visit and chat with other customers, as the restaurant was beginning to fill.

There was a moment of awkward silence as Gideon tried to assimilate the fact that a *man* had been flirting with him—in front of his *grandfather*. But just then, the server arrived with their meals, and the moment passed.

"So everything's all wrapped up with the Valente estate, then, Gideon?" his grandfather said after the server walked away. "No…er…problems with any of the heirs? Nothing unusual?"

"No," Gideon replied, looking at him carefully. "Did you expect there to be problems?" A sudden suspicion grabbed him. "That's not why you ended your vacation early, is it? To check up on this—on *me?*"

As soon as he said it, Gideon realized he was being foolish. Why would his grandfather do that?

Gideon was *not* his father, and his grandfather trusted him implicitly.

Adjusting his wire-rimmed glasses up and down on the bridge of his nose—a sign that he was uncomfortable—the older man replied, "Not at all, m'boy. It's just—I always felt there was something not right about Valente, and, to be completely honest, I never liked the bastard one bit—even though he was a good—a hefty—client. I always felt like he had something to hide, something that lurked just below the surface…and what better time for it to come out than when he's dead and gone, and his family is quibbling over the estate?"

"But the family didn't quibble over the estate. There was no problem whatsoever with the reading of the will, no one contested anything or even hinted about it—even when they learned about Fi—Ms. Murphy's bequest."

Gideon Senior frowned as he eyed his salmon. "Yes, this Miss Murphy is a mystery. You say she didn't even know who he was? What kind of idiot thing was Valente thinking?" He shook his head, his unruly silver hair gleaming in the low light of the restaurant.

"Not only did she not know who he was, but once I showed her his picture and she thought she remembered him, she commented about how sweet and kind the elderly man was." Gideon took a sip of the very excellent Barolo as his grandfather's jaw dropped.

"My goodness, Hollis," Iva murmured. "What on earth is wrong?"

"Valente was as far from sweet and kind as a piranha is," Gideon Senior informed her, ignoring the fact that he had a mouthful of food.

Clucking, Iva smoothed back a white curl and smiled with mildness. "Now, Hollis, don't tell me that even a piranha doesn't have a soft, warm side—after all, look at *you.*"

Gideon vacillated between merely rolling his eyes and turning away from the sappy sentiment that now flowed between the young-at-heart lovers. Instead, he settled for taking another bite of the branzini he'd ordered.

"Regarding this Miss Murphy's comment about Valente—as I was saying, is it so far-fetched that he might have a soft side? And that, for some reason, she coaxed it out of him? After all, it could just be that he interacted with people who *didn't* bring out the best of him," Iva continued.

Gideon looked at her in surprise. "Fiona said almost exactly the same thing," he said.

"Fiona?" Iva asked delicately. But her blue eyes suddenly became very sharp.

Gideon's face heated. "Fiona Murphy, the woman who inherited the shop."

Just as he said this, he looked away and happened to see a cloud of auburn hair, thick and curly, on a woman whose back was to him at a table across the room. His heart gave an unnatural, off-rhythm thud, then returned to its normal pace as he forced himself back to the meal.

So what if she was eating at the same restaurant?

At a table with another man.

After he'd kissed her—only hours ago.

His fingers tightened around his fork as a wave of memory careened over him. That damn kiss. He'd tried to forget about it, but that hadn't worked. Gideon glanced in her direction again, just in time to see her shift and toss her hair over her shoulder—and he realized it wasn't Fiona after all.

He relaxed, and looked back to find his grandfather and Iva looking at him expectantly.

"I'm sorry, did you say something?" he asked.

They glanced at each other, then at him. "No—you stopped speaking in the middle of a sentence," Iva told him gently.

I did? He was damned if he could remember what he'd been saying.

"About this Fiona Murphy, who inherited the shop," Iva said. She was suddenly watching him very closely. "The shop right here in Wicks Hollow, if I recall correctly. Up on Violet Way?"

Why did he feel like a bug under a microscope all of a sudden? His collar felt unexpectedly tight as he replied, "Yes. That's the address."

Then Iva cocked her head, looking very much like a little bird with her bright eyes...thinking. "Fiona Murphy...I wonder if she's..." Her voice trailed off as she cocked her head to one side like an interested robin.

"What's that, darling?" asked Gideon's grandfather.

"Oh, mmm...nothing," replied Iva in a faraway voice.

But there was a little curl to her smile and a speculative glint in her eyes that, for some inexplicable reason, made Gideon very nervous.

* * *

The following Friday morning, Fiona was humming "Good Day, Sunshine" when she let herself into the shop.

Over the last seven days, she'd enlisted Ethan, who

was on sabbatical from the University of Chicago—along with her friends Winona, Tex, and Carl, who had come from Grand Rapids on their days off or in the evenings—to help her clean and reorganize the shop in preparation for its reopening. Even Gretchen had become marginally friendlier and less prone to swiping out with her claws—especially with Diana, on the one day she'd been able to get away from her law office to help.

Fiona and her friends had accomplished a surprising amount of work in the last week, and she had set the grand reopening for Tuesday: four days from now. The *Grand Rapids Press* had done a nice spread on her and the shop, which would be in this weekend's Lifestyle section, and she was already getting calls and hits on a hastily-constructed website and social media platforms about Tuesday's opening.

She felt as if she could actually *do* this.

Now, for the first time in a week, Fiona was alone when she stepped into her shop and closed the door behind her. She smiled, drawing in a deep, satisfied breath.

This experience was so much different than last Friday, the first time she'd stepped into the place.

No longer were there dust motes every time she moved, and gone was the musty smell of age—to be replaced by fresh lemon polish and a subtle hint of rosemary from the natural cleaning supplies she'd used. An essential oil diffuser had cast a cinnamon-eucalyptus blend into the air overnight to help eradicate the dull, dank scents. She'd replaced the brassy chimes with a more delicate and musical set she found much more pleasing to the ears—and had purchased at one of the shops in downtown Wicks Hollow. The proprietress had been thrilled to hear about the reopening of the store—which would be called Charmed Antiquity.

With the help of Carl, her friend with the antiques background, most of the stock had been priced and organized and she had a basic idea of what was worth dickering over, and what was worth selling at any price. She would be ready by Tuesday. No matter what.

She set her bag down and looked back into the depths of the shadowy shop and, with a little clutch of the heart, she saw: *The lamp was on.*

The lamp's—she knew it had to be *the* lamp; the white one with the nubbly white base—glow was visible from the front of the store. Setting down her heavy leather bag, Fiona walked back slowly toward the little alcove, her heart thumping solidly, wildly, nauseatingly in her chest.

How?

She knew last night when she and Ethan had left, she'd turned off all the lights except for a small collection in the front windows to dissuade burglars.

So, *how?*

But there it was. The lamp was on, sending a small circle of light that followed the angles of the heavy walnut desk—no, Carl had called it a secretary—and the darkly-paneled wall behind it that rose up to the second floor.

The stillness of the shop ate into her bones, but this time, there was no chilly draft to raise the hair on her neck. She saw neither hide nor hair of Gretchen—which wasn't unusual—but she did notice the shade wasn't askew from being batted by a feline paw.

Trying to remain calm, she spoke aloud. "There's *got* to be some kind of remote control or battery on this thing." She pushed the heavy chair out of the way so that she could step closer to the desk. "It's the only explanation."

She dug around behind the desk, thinking perhaps someone had plugged in the cord during the last week of cleaning and reorganizing, and that somehow a short in the wire had maybe caused it to turn on...but as she looked down, following the cord to the side of the secretary, Fiona could see that it wasn't plugged in.

Yet the light was still on.

"A battery pack. Somewhere—maybe it's in the base."

She tugged on the pull cord that turned the light off and on—or *should* have turned it off or on.

But the light didn't change.

She pulled a few more times, a little desperately…

But nothing happened.

The bulb burned, steadily, mockingly.

Her hands grew slick as she picked up the lamp—hesitantly, to be sure—but there was no sign of a battery pack anywhere inside the base, or behind it, or under it.

There was *nothing* that could be construed as a remote control receiver either.

The Lamp was just...*on.*

"What is going on?" she whispered as she realized her hands were prickling and going numb. She was having a difficult time breathing.

Then suddenly, a blast, a full-fledged *gust,* of chill wind blasted over her, rifling the top of her hair.

Fiona felt as though she'd been plunged into freezing water—for a moment, she couldn't move, couldn't breathe, couldn't react.

Then she stumbled back from the alcove, panting as she moved toward the front of the shop. The smell of roses and cold staleness rushed through her, and the chill in the air froze her numb fingers.

Nearly sobbing deep in her throat, without looking back, without even hesitating, she opened the door.

The tinkling of the bells above barely registered as she rushed through the front entrance—and slammed into something solid.

SIX

FIONA PLOWED into Gideon with such force that the breath was knocked out of him.

His hands slid up from her elbows to grasp her upper arms, steadying her as she lost her balance. She looked up, her face pinched and white, her eyes startled and disoriented as she tried to brush past him.

"What's wrong? What is it?" he demanded.

Her frantic expression relaxed a little, and she seemed to focus on him. When she just stared, obvious bewilderment making her speechless, he set her aside and strode into the shop.

It was dim inside, but it smelled so much better than before. The only illumination came from the lights in the front windows—the glass which, he noted, had had a good cleaning. A faint aroma of lemon polish and some other pleasing essence—cinnamon?—filled his nostrils. It was immediately clear that inventory had been moved and displays reorganized. A lot of work had been accomplished in the last week.

He nearly tripped over the heavy leather bag that lay on its side just inside the doorway. The hair on the back of his neck lifted and tension settled over him, his muscles taut and ready as he looked around, waiting. Listening.

When nothing seemed out of place—other than that eerie sensation—he walked toward the back of the shop.

Could she have been attacked? Was there someone lying in wait?

Whatever it was, it had terrified her.

Several feet into the store, he felt a presence behind him and turned to find that Fiona had slipped into his wake.

"Are you hurt?" He paused to look down at her, noting her slim-fitting jeans and curve-hugging t-shirt with the sort of appreciation that made his mouth go dry and heat lick through him.

She looked less shell-shocked now, although her gaze continued to leap around without seeming to land anywhere. "I'm fine. I didn't mean to—to run into you."

"What happened?"

Now, her gaze settled over his shoulder, anchored toward the back of the shop. "There was a light on when I came in today," she replied. "I had turned them all off when I left last evening. But there was one on today. And there isn't a timer on it."

Gideon frowned, looking about again. "Was someone here? Has anything been stolen?"

He admired the slim column of her neck—bare except for a few tendrils of hair that had escaped from the high pony-tail she wore—as she struggled to respond. "No. No, no one was here. Nothing's been taken that I can see. But the lamp…"

"You're certain you switched it off? Maybe the cat turned it on accidentally." He turned to look toward the back of the store, where her gaze seemed to be glued. "Which lamp? Let me take a look at it."

When he swiveled back toward her, wariness had replaced the uncertainty on her face. "That must have been it," she replied, avoiding his eyes. "The cat."

"Which lamp?" he persisted, sensing there was something she was not telling him. "Maybe I can take a look at it—"

"No. That's all right, really. It's…not on anymore."

Fiona turned resolutely to the front of the store, trying to control her churning stomach. The lamp had somehow turned *off* since she went barreling out of the shop, and there was no sense in telling Gideon what she had seen…what she had felt: that sudden, eerie, bone-drenching chill. He'd listen to two sentences from her, then be ready to admit her to the funny farm.

H. Gideon Nath the Third was not the kind of person who believed in the metaphysical. Fiona wasn't sure she herself believed in ghostly lamps, but she *knew* he wouldn't.

Passing a hand over her face, she bit her lip and forced herself to walk away from the eerie alcove and toward the front door.

Gideon must be following behind her…what would she tell him if he persisted in questioning her? After all, he was a lawyer. Wasn't that what lawyers did? Interrogate?

She stifled a giggle at her internal babbling and tried to steady herself. He already thought she was a total flake, and the impish desire to needle him had vanished at about the same moment his lips had touched hers a week earlier.

Oh, yes. That kiss.

She still felt far too hot and bothered every time she thought about it—which was, unfortunately, far too often.

To be honest, she would rather just stay away from him…far away from the danger this rigid, pretentious, self-assured, intelligent, handsome, passionate man portended.

And what the hell was he doing here in Wicks Hollow anyway?

"What are you doing here anyway?" she asked, fixing him with narrowed eyes—her question being a wonderful distraction from The Lamp and its antics.

"Oh, I had to bring some paperwork down to Iva—to my grandfather's friend. She lives here in Wicks Hollow."

"I see. And what brought you back this way? Down here to little, unassuming Violets Way?"

He shoved his hands in his pockets. "Well, I thought I'd see how things were going here."

He was wearing dark mahogany slacks with a perfect crease down each leg, a linen shirt under a jacket, and fine leather shoes. Ever the well-dressed professional. Did the man even own a pair of jeans? Or a ratty t-shirt?

Her mouth quirked. At that moment, he directed his attention toward her, catching her bemused expression.

"Is something amusing?" he asked, walking toward where she stood by the messy desk in the center of the shop.

As he withdrew his hands from the pockets, she noticed again how fine they were—how solid and square and masculine, the long slimness of his fingers, and how smooth and rounded his nails were. They were beautiful hands, and, she remembered in a split second of recall, they had been all over her body only days ago. A shiver jetted up her spine, but she ignored it and chose to respond to his question.

"I was just wondering if that was your way of dressing down," she smiled, looking pointedly up and down his clothing. "Do you even own a pair of jeans? What about shorts?"

He looked down at his garb in surprise. "This is casual," he replied, then, as he looked back up at her, his gaze lingering over her plain white t-shirt and jeans, a sudden, devastating smile flashed over his face. "For me, anyway."

Whoa. Fiona had to steady herself by leaning against the desk, taking care not to knock off a pile of papers. How could anyone who seemed so imposing and rigid become so gorgeous with only a smile? And how could the mere heat in his gaze cause her heart to blip like that?

"You know," she said in an effort to mask her reaction, "you should smile more often. It makes you seem almost human." She turned away before her reaction became obvious and busied herself by straightening a stack of handwritten purchase requisitions that were scattered on the desk.

As she nonchalantly reached for a pen, she felt his presence close in behind her. Fiona jolted and nearly knocked the phone off its stand as he spoke, purring into her ear, his breath wafting warmly over her bare neck. "Aren't you wondering why I *really* came by?"

"To tell me about the H.?" she replied lightly, moving away so that he couldn't hear the thundering of her heart. She couldn't, for the life of her, think of another name that began with an H.

"No."

That simple word hung there—deep, husky, radiating layers and layers of meaning—and caused a shiver to work its way along her arm, raising goose bumps in its path. If nothing else, he was patient, for it was Fiona who finally turned to face him after an impossibly long silence.

"For what then?" But she didn't need to ask the question, for the narrowing of his silvery eyes and the tautness of his fine mouth spoke volumes.

"Surely you don't expect to simply ignore a kiss like that without wondering what more there could be." Despite the arrogance in his voice, the heat in his eyes was very real.

Though her mouth went dry and her knees trembled weakly, Fiona lifted her brows and quirked her lips into an insolent smile. "Kiss? I don't remember any—"

Suddenly she was in his arms and the rest of her words were smothered by his very skillful, very adamant mouth. With a sigh of capitulation—for she had wondered if it had, indeed, been as good as she remembered—Fiona arched against his solid body, sliding her hands up into the thick waves of his hair.

As lips fit to lips—tasting, caressing, slip-sliding—his hands formed to her body, smoothing down the length of her back to cup her rear, pulling her up and to him so that she was in no doubt of his definite interest. A sharp pang of desire low in her groin bloomed into tingling, sparkling heat, and she pressed back into Gideon, sliding her hands to his shoulders, savoring the taste of him.

A soft groan rose in his throat and sighed against her lips as they became insistent, almost rough. Then, drawing in a ragged breath, he pulled away just enough to sweep her onto the desk. The phone crashed to the floor, scattering papers and the cup filled with pens, but Fiona didn't care. She didn't care about anything except touching Gideon—smelling his spicy, male smell, hearing the rasp of his breath, feasting on him— becoming enraptured.

He stood between her knees and she tilted her head, allowing his mouth to trail along her bare neck as she pulled the jacket from his shoulders. He shrugged it to the floor and her hands became free to mold over the hard planes of his chest.

Finally, he broke the kiss. Gently and delicately, he caressed her upper, then her lower, lip with his, gave her one last full-mouthed buss, and pulled away. Her hands were still planted on either side of the placket of buttons on his shirt, and she felt the rapid beat of his heart and steady warmth beneath her fingers while his chest rose and fell with heavy breathing.

"That kiss," he murmured with a sensual smile.

Fiona became more lightheaded. "Ah," was all she could manage.

Dark hair shadowed his forehead and the planes of his cheekbones stood out in relief, as though he'd sucked in his breath. His eyes were dark and fierce, but the words that came out of his full mouth were surprisingly gentle. "All indications are that you see at least some value in finding out what could lie beyond a mere kiss."

She dropped her hands from his shirt. Although she was still trembling with the aftershock of their embrace, she knew she must be honest.

"I don't go in for casual sex, Gideon." She gave a short laugh, almost in derision. "I don't go in for sex much at all, in fact." Which was why, she thought in shock, it was so shocking that a simple kiss had turned her into a shuddering mass of skin and bones. She gave an easy shrug.

The surprise that washed over his face was quickly masked behind that stony, lawyer-like countenance. "The evidence speaks otherwise."

Fiona struggled for a moment, but her innate honesty won out. "What I mean is, I don't very often find someone I choose to have sex with. It… complicates…things."

"It doesn't have to. Complicate things." He slipped a finger under one of her loose, wild curls and flipped it behind her ear, allowing the tip of his thumb to trace along her jaw line, leaving her skin jumping in its wake.

"Hmm." She cocked her head and looked up at him, aware that the sound of her thundering heart was deafening only to her, and considered.

Her mother never let sex complicate things in her life. She'd been a free spirit and had no qualms about sleeping with anyone, anytime, anywhere: male or female. A child of the 'Sixties, Claudia lived a carefree life, even to this day—currently in Costa Rica. She had instilled in her children a love for fun and mysticism and all things natural, but not a moving sense of responsibility nor a taste for authority.

Fiona was, ironically, the precise opposite of Claudia when it came to sex. While she lived for the moment in most areas of her life, intimacy and relationships were the one area she didn't.

Because it scared the shit out of her.

Fiona's hands curled tightly in her lap, pressing six rings into her fingers, and her throat was dry and tight. The ridge of the desk on which she sat bit into her upper calves as her fingers curled around the same sharp edge, clenching the wood to keep them from touching him again. She did want him...there was no doubt about that...but—

The glow of a light flickered at the back of the shop, freezing her mind.

With a muffled shriek, she launched herself off the desk into Gideon's arms. "The lamp! It's the lamp!"

"What?" His arms slid around her, but then she pulled just as quickly away. Bewildered, he peered down at her as Fiona tried to steady her breathing.

"The lamp is back on." She pointed behind him with a finger that trembled even as she clutched the sleeve of his shirt with a death grip. "See it?"

Gideon took a hesitant step toward the back of the shop, then, when she started to follow, he lengthened his strides.

"It's not plugged in," she babbled, feeling light-headed and confused. "And it keeps coming on. That one lamp."

When they came around a tall escritoire and full-faced into the alcove, Fiona stopped short. The tension flooded from her, leaving her limbs weightless and numb, and immediately, embarrassment replaced her fear.

On the mammoth walnut desk, where the three lamps stood like a row of gateposts, Gretchen sat calmly cleaning her paw. She was, no doubt, cleaning the paw that had just batted at the dangling chain-switch for the Tiffany-like glass lamp of red and blue...the light which now glowed there in the alcove.

Gideon shot her a confused look, but, thankfully, he didn't say anything. Fiona wanted to sink into the floor. How much more of a madwoman was she going to be around him?

Gamely, he reached around behind the lamp, pulling its cord and following it down into the dark recesses of the corner as Fiona had done with the other lamp shortly before.

"It's plugged in," he said, straightening, looking at her closely.

Fiona darted a glance at the other lamp—*The* Lamp— which sat innocently in the far corner of the desk and didn't even hint at being alit. She forced herself to give a short laugh and turned away—wanting to get out of there as quickly as possible.

"Must've been the cat," she said lamely, curling her fingers into the palms of her hands. It was a good thing she had no nails to speak of, or she would have drawn blood.

"Yes, it must have been the cat." Gideon's voice was carefully level and neutral. He gave her a long, steady look, then turned away, starting back toward the front of the shop.

After glancing over her shoulder at the lamps again, Fiona followed, feeling like a complete idiot...but at the same time, frightened and disconcerted.

She was *not* crazy.

When she rejoined Gideon, he was pulling on his jacket. Flipping the collar down and smoothing the sleeves, he looked up at her. "So, when are you planning to open for business?"

"Tuesday." *As long as the place doesn't keep freaking me out.* She gritted her teeth. "Baxter James—he's the owner of B-Cubed Brewery here in town, if you don't know, and he also does freelance writing—did a feature on the shop for the *Press* this weekend. Hopefully that will spur lots of folks to come and check it out."

He still looked bewildered—like he was ready to bolt

—so she decided to make it easy on him. "I'm glad you stopped by, Gideon, but I have a lot of work to do before Tuesday. I'd enlist your help," she said with a teasing smile, "but you're not really dressed for the occasion."

She started to walk toward the front door, hoping he would take the hint. She couldn't stand to have him continuing to look at her as if afraid she'd turn into a screaming idiot at any given moment.

"Ah, yes. Well, let me know if there's—err—anything I can do. If you have any other problems with the—the lights."

Fiona's cheeks warmed. "Certainly. Thanks again, Gideon." She nearly pushed him out the door, and watched covertly as he started down the street. As soon as he rounded the corner out of sight, she grabbed her leather bag, shot out of the store, and slammed the door behind her.

He was beginning to get worried.

In more than six weeks, he'd found no sign of old Valente's journal or the bank statements he knew existed.

Fiddling with his gold-plated fountain pen, he pursed his lips and tried to quell the nervousness that roiled deep within. If he didn't know for certain the journal existed, he wouldn't be so damned concerned—but Valente had mentioned it more than once, so he knew all of the old man's dirty secrets were written somewhere. His nostrils flared as if he smelled something rank.

Why the hell had the bastard insisted on writing everything down anyway?

He slammed his hand onto the desk, and the fancy

pen flew from his hand and clattered onto the floor. What kind of fool would leave a paper trail of sins behind him?

He'd torn apart every file, bookshelf, box, and drawer in Valente's home since his death—very carefully, of course, for the others knew nothing about the old man's secrets or his egotistical need to write them down. He had only learned about it by chance...but once Valente realized out he knew, the old man seemed to feel the need to divulge every aspect of his sordid life—as if he was unburdening himself.

That was the best thing Valente had ever done for him, besides leaving him pots of money—for if he didn't know enough to be concerned about that damn journal showing up, he wouldn't be looking for it. And then, when it did appear someday, as it was bound to, he would be broadsided and lose everything.

That could not happen. He'd worked too hard to get where he was to allow the old man to bring it tumbling down around him—especially after the bastard was dead.

There was only one more place left to look.

His hand sidled over to the well-creased *Grand Rapids Press* and picked up the weekend section, where there was quite an admirable spread about a little antiques shop and its grand reopening.

The perfect opportunity to do some snooping.

The food was excellent, the wine beyond compare, the music perfect...and the woman at his side lovely enough to garner envious looks from men in every direction.

Given all of these assets, Gideon should have been having a wonderful time. However, he detested political fundraisers as a rule, and attended them only under duress. This one was a big one, however—for the governor—and his duress tonight was in the form of the very lovely Rachel Backley, principle at The Marage Group.

While she did not hang on his arm, for Rachel Backley was in no way a clinger, she did hover near him. That made it quite evident to the other men that the slender, elegant beauty was with Gideon and quite happy to be so.

He sidled his glance over the black dress with the plunging neckline, down past the table to admire her shapely legs, and back up to the chestnut hair pulled into a neat chignon at the nape of her neck. There it would stay—those shiny strands of honey-brown a sleek cap until late tonight when she—or he, if he were in the mood—would loosen it into the straight, heavy curtain that fell to her shoulders.

Rachel laughed at a joke made by an elderly man—one of the biggest political contributors to the party—who was drooling down her décolletage. She brushed her arm against Gideon's shoulder in a casual manner, sending a waft of the expensive, woodsy scent she wore. No florals or sweets for Rachel. Only fragrances that hinted of the Orient, or the subtleties of sophistication. She glanced up at him, her red lips glistening and blue eyes dancing as she shot him a look that suggested she was not interested in going home alone tonight.

Warmth slid over him at the blatant heat in her eyes and he responded with a subtle curl of his lips. It had been awhile, and he had been feeling rather on-edge lately. Ever since he'd fallen into Fiona Murphy's dank, dusty closet.

Before he could push it away, the stubborn thought of Fiona Murphy—the one that had been hovering in the back of his mind since yesterday, when she'd practically chased him out of her shop in Wicks Hollow—descended upon him and planted itself in the forefront of his mind. Along with the image of her wild eyes and strange babbling about lights and unplugged lamps came the searing memory of the kisses they'd shared in that musty old shop.

Sex only complicates things. He frowned at the memory of her words, her lame excuse for not pursuing what they obviously both wanted. He didn't want complications any more than the next guy, but, hell, he was attracted to her—that sexy, sensual, fruitcake of a woman who was always giddy and shamelessly honest. He hadn't been able to keep from thinking about her all week; which was why he'd made an excuse to visit Wicks Hollow again.

For Christ's sake, she'd even intruded in one of his memos. He'd written the name Fiona instead of Finley.

Claire had returned the memo for his review with a quirked eyebrow and a knowing look that annoyed him so much that he made the required edits himself and filed it away without letting her see it again.

He was irritated by the amount of energy he'd spent trying *not* to think about her over the last week—and the fact that she had turned him down flat yesterday, when he'd finally given in and sought her out.

Truth be told, his pride was more than a bit wounded, and, if he were to be honest himself, showing up at this fundraiser with a beautiful, powerful, sophisticated woman on his arm was a balm to that bruised ego.

To placate himself further, he tried to picture Fiona here, at a black-tie event such as this, surrounded by some of the richest, most powerful conservatives in the state. She, with her unruly cinnamon hair, fey manner, and unabashed openness would be nothing if an anomaly in this urbane environment. She'd be a fish out of water—fruit punch mixed in with champagne—at a function as conservative as this.

She would smile and chatter and ask interesting, naïve questions, and look up at a man like he was the only person in the room as he expounded on everything she wanted to know…

With a grunt of disgust, Gideon brought the glass of wine to his lips and tasted it. She would make a fool out of herself, he thought, and turned his attention to Rachel.

But as he shifted to look at his date, his gaze wandered past her, glancing randomly over a cluster of people across the room…and then jerked back in disbelief.

Impossible, he told himself, staring without trying to be too obvious at a figure with a mass of crazy, curling auburn hair. He almost rose from his chair before catching himself. Settling back into it, he slid a hand over to cup Rachel's cool fingers.

She turned a smile on him, which he answered absently, still scrutinizing the clique of people that seemed to be surrounding the auburn-haired woman. He had made a similar mistake before, he reminded himself. What was wrong with him, seeing Fiona wherever he happened to be?

"What is it, Gideon?" Rachel asked in her well-modulated, even tones—a voice that, while pleasing to the ear, had little inflection or emotion, and seemed always to carry the stiffness of a cold-blooded businesswoman.

"I believe..." Gideon began, then paused when the woman shifted and he could clearly see her face. *Hell.* "I just noticed that a client of my grandfather is here."

"Shall we go speak with him?"

He nodded, rising to his feet before he could think twice about it. It wouldn't be a bad thing for Miss Fiona Murphy to see that he hadn't slunk off like a dog just because she wasn't interested in pursuing matters with him. "Her. Yes, I think I will—would you like to join me?"

Rachel rose gracefully to her feet, retrieving her small, beaded black bag from the table, and smoothing her very short dress. "Please excuse us," she said with a smile. "Duty calls."

As they drew nearer, Gideon noticed that the cluster of people seemed to be formed around Fiona, who appeared to be examining the hand of a senior partner of Laslow, Yonke and Greiber—one of the oldest and largest accounting firms in Grand Rapids. She said something that caused the small group to explode with laughter while she merely looked up at the distinguished, white-haired man and grinned a meaningful grin.

The man withdrew his hand, still chuckling, just as Gideon and Rachel approached the crowd. "So there *is* more than one meaning to having your left hand knowing what your right hand is doing, eh, my dear?"

"Absolutely." She nodded once, emphatically, and just then, noticed Gideon and Rachel. A flare of surprise lit her face, then receded immediately as she gave them a friendly smile. "Why, Gideon, I didn't expect to see you here."

Words stuck in his throat when she turned to face him. *Jesus.* Someone—probably an engineer—had taken on the task of piling that glorious mass of coppery curls at the crown of her head, leaving thick, corkscrew wisps trailing down the nape of her neck, and a few locks framing her face. Her features were flawless, colored faintly by all shades of cinnamon and nutmeg, peaches and cream, with thick, dark lashes and gracefully-winged brows. The silky halter dress she wore—a simple black affair so different from Rachel's elegant, sexy, short-skirted one—revealed alabaster shoulders and arms dusted generously with tiny, pale freckles. The bodice sleeked over her curves, then fell in graceful folds from hips to floor.

Then, to top it off, he noticed for the first time that Bradley Forth stood behind her, watching her with a possessive demeanor.

Forth's presence was enough for Gideon to find his voice, but the words came out stilted and flat. "It is a surprise to see you as well." He shifted his glance to the other man and offered his hand. "Forth. I suppose I shouldn't be surprised to see you here—with the election less than three weeks away."

Rachel interrupted the odd moment with the tact of someone used to all aspects of social situations. "Mr. Forth, I'm Rachel Backley, one of the partners at The Marage Group. It's a pleasure to meet you—I've been quite interested in your candidacy." She extended her hand, following it with a warm smile, then transferred it to Fiona. "I didn't catch your name," she said easily, "and I suppose I could wait for Gideon to introduce us… but that doesn't seem to be imminent."

"Fiona Murphy." She shook Rachel's hand and while trying to suppress the shock and—well, *fury* was the word—that Gideon should have shown up here with this ice-cold babe (who was just his type, actually) on his arm after propositioning her, Fiona, just yesterday afternoon.

Of course, she *had* turned him down. But still. She gave him a very dark look.

"Fiona is a client of my grandfather—as is Brad Forth," Gideon finally said, dragging away his silvery gaze. "They're both heirs of Nevio Valente's estate."

"Valente?" One of the other men in the crowd—Fiona remembered his name was Norm van Delt—spoke up, drawing attention away from her and allowing Fiona an opportunity to compose herself.

It was a sin, she mused as the conversation picked up around her, that anyone should look so good in a tux—especially a man that she knew had a tighter rump than Al Gore. A little giggle threatened to burst free, and damn if Gideon didn't happen to look at her at that moment.

He fixed that same haughty, arrogant glare on her that he had the first time they'd met—the one that was so very much like her third grade teacher's pointed stare. The one that failed, as it had twenty years ago, to have any sobering affect on her whatsoever.

But as she transferred her attention to the sleek Ms. Rachel Backley, Fiona's amusement once again trans-formed into ire.

How dare that man kiss her like he had and try to get her to sleep with him, then appear with this trophy-woman the very next night?

This time, when Gideon looked at her, she caught his eyes with a cold glare of her own, firming her lips and jutting her chin in an unmistakable show of her feelings.

Surprise flitted in his eyes, then, to her shock and chagrin, he turned to his escort and said, "Excuse me, Rachel, for just a moment. I believe Ms. Murphy needs to speak with me on a confidential matter."

"Of course," she replied casually, returning to the

conversation and, to Fiona's surprise, batting nary an eyelash that her date was going off with another woman.

As her escort, Brad showed mild annoyance, but he didn't say anything other than, "I hope you won't be long, as there are a few other people I think you should meet, Fiona."

She was given no chance to protest as Gideon gestured firmly for her to step away from the group of people. As soon as they were out of sight, he closed those elegant fingers over her wrist and led her out of the Grand Ballroom to the vestibule of the hotel before she shook herself free.

"Let's step outside," he suggested, glancing toward the smattering of people milling about. "It's a beautiful night."

In fact, it was a *chilly*, mid-October night, and that only fueled Fiona's aggravation. She was sleeveless and backless in her halter dress, while he was wearing a coat and tie.

Men.

She walked brusquely ahead of him down the semi-circle steps that led to a flagstone path that meandered along the Grand River. Across the stretch of water was the Gerald Ford Presidential Library, its lights winking on the ripples of water.

Fiona chose to sit, and did so with a small flourish that caused the full, gauzy skirt of her dress to settle over the majority of the bench—leaving no place for Gideon to place his stiff rump without mussing her skirt. She crossed her arms over her chest and eyed, eyebrow raised with the same slant she imagined Queen Elizabeth would use.

"You wanted to speak with me?"

"What are you doing here—with Forth?"

That was the last question she'd expected him to utter, and she rolled her eyes at his audacity. "The same thing you are, I presume—placing myself in an environment where I'll be induced to contribute money to a political cause. Not that I have any to contribute. Brad thought it would be good publicity for my shop's reopening." Then, she realized she was angry with him and the small talk would do nothing to alleviate that. "I can't believe you have the nerve to make a pass at me —*twice*—and then show up here with someone you're obviously involved with."

"Twice?" he exploded. "Don't be ridiculous, Fiona. I made a—a *pass*," he spat the last word as if it were vulgar, "as you call it, at you, after *you* kissed the *hell* out of me—then acted as if nothing happened."

She stared up at him, unable to keep a slow smile from creeping over her face. He was *so* hot when he unwound a little. "So you do have some emotion in that stiff-necked body after all, H.—um, Gideon. Other than related to passion, I mean. I was beginning to wonder."

He gaped at her, clearly flummoxed. Despite the brainless expression on his face, she had to admit he looked delicious there in the moonlight. Tall, dark, his figure vibrating with emotion she hadn't thought he'd possessed, he stood with his hands slung onto his hips. His stance pulled the tux jacket open to reveal a cummerbund and white shirt stretched taut over the defined muscles of chest and abdomen—slabs like iron that Fiona remembered feeling all too well. His thick, wavy hair had obviously been trimmed, as it was close-cropped by his neck, and only one small curl flipped out of line, over his forehead. By now, he was gritting his teeth—she could tell by the way the muscle along his jaw moved—and his brows had drawn together in a frown.

Before he could speak, she seized the opportunity to keep the upper hand. "*You* came on to me, H. Gideon. And just what would the *lovely, elegant* Ms. Backley say if she knew about that?"

To her surprise, he relaxed slightly. "Actually, that's just what I wanted to talk to you about." He glanced longingly at the bench, still covered by the fabric of her skirt, but she made no move to accommodate him.

"What is she—your fiancée? Your girlfriend? Don't tell me she's your *wife!*"

He was shaking his head. "No, none of those. Fiona, she's a friend—that's all. If neither of us have a date, we often attend business or professional functions with the other. That's it."

"That's it? You don't sleep with her?" Fiona didn't believe that for a minute—and her suspicion was rewarded when his eyes flitted away, then back to her. He began to make some sort of mumbly noise that she took to be an excuse, and she stopped him. "I don't sleep with men who sleep with other women—when I *do* choose to sleep with a man. So, forget it, H—Gideon. You're wasting your time."

With that, she stood up and stalked past him, brushing close enough to feel the warmth of his arm and the sexy, musky scent that clung to him.

"Not only did I tell him where to stick his stiff rump after he admitted they weren't exactly platonic," Fiona told her friend Carl Pelham, "but I also had to shut down Mr.

Kiss-as-Many-Babies-As-Possible-For-a-Vote when we got back to my place."

Carl's deep laugh rumbled through the telephone. "I'm sure you had no problem whatsoever doing that. Fiona, you are the Master—er, I mean Mistress—of Shut-Down. The poor bastard probably didn't have a chance."

"Well, you know power doesn't do a thing for me, and the guy's good looking—in a politician-y sort of way…but *so* not my type."

"Did you let him in for a nightcap?"

Fiona snorted. "No. I figured once he stepped foot in my house, I'd be fighting off Mr. Octopus, based on the way he'd been gawking all night. You should have seen his face when H. Gideon dragged me off to read me the riot act."

"Ahh, H. Gideon. Have you found out yet what the H is for? And is he really that much of a jerk?"

"I don't know about the H yet. I keep asking and he won't budge. But I can't deny he's a good kisser. I mean… a really good, knock-your-socks-off, seeing-shooting-stars kisser. And he seems to be loosening up a little. I think he actually smiled at me once the other day." He sure had… and it had sent her veins tingling all the way to her fingers.

"But, Carl, darling, you know me…I'm not into any kind of relationship or responsibility." As she spoke the words she'd uttered so many times before, Fiona suddenly realized she didn't feel any power behind them any more. Her stomach felt heavy at the thought. When had that happened?

"Yep. I know. You just like to hang around with the guys. No responsibility, no ties, no commitment—hell, you sound just like one of us. Wanna come over and watch some football?" Carl chuckled dryly into the phone. "I promise not to make you cook for us this time."

Fiona tried to laugh back, but it stuck somewhere between her lungs and throat. Was she really that transparent? That shallow? *No responsibility, no ties, no commitment…*

"Hey, Fi, you still there?" Carl, one of her oldest and dearest friends—which was why he could be so blunt with her and she'd still love him—sounded concerned. "Hey, you know I'm just giving you shit, you know. Fi?"

"Just like I do to you, I know. It's just that…well, with this shop thing…I feel like I might want to turn over a new leaf. Make something worthwhile out of my life—something long-term." She hadn't known she felt that way until the words came jumbling out. "I think I never wanted permanency because I hadn't found a place or thing that called me to *be* permanent. But there's something about this little shop that calls to me…that really makes me want to be there."

Well, despite the weird and creepy light.

"There's one thing about you, Fi. Once you set your mind to something—once you actually *commit*—I know, you hate that word—to putting your all into it, you do it. If you've got your mind made up that you want to make the shop work, then I've no doubt you will."

She smiled, her cheek moving against the phone receiver. He was right. She might be flighty and noncommittal at times, but once she jumped, she was in all the way.

"By the way, did you tell your lawyer guy about your not-interested-in-sex deal?"

"Yep. Went over like a lead balloon, to quote Robert Plant."

"Keith Moon, you mean."

"Whatever." Fiona tapped her fingernails on the table. "Anyway, he didn't understand, of course, but then, he's a guy."

"Yep. Guys don't understand not wanting to have sex if the kissing's as good as you said it was. Probably shocked the hell out of him."

"Oh yeah." Fiona smiled again at the thought, then sobered as a rash of heat flashed through her. The chemistry between them *had* been amazing.

And, if she had to be honest, she hadn't seen any chemistry between Gideon and Rachel Backley…which was the only reason she semi-believed him that there was nothing between them but some friends-with-benefits benefits.

Regardless, she had no intention of being tied down, responsible for, or committed to a man at this point in her life—and, she realized, she might never feel that urge. Claudia certainly never had.

"I've got a hard enough time managing my own life. You know I'm as low-maintenance as they come." She ignored Carl's scoff from the other end of the phone line.

"Yeah, well, you know, some day you're going to be eating those words, Fioney-pony. You're going to fall flat on your face for some guy who's the exact opposite of every one you've ever dated. So, anyway, thanks for the reminder to pick up some extra plates and napkins. I'll see you in about an hour for the party. I'll have my best suit on, plus my charm, and be ready to woo all those lady customers of yours."

She was glad to hear a lighter inflection in his voice. "Thanks so much for agreeing to help out, Carl, and for listening today. See you in a bit."

It was Tuesday morning, three days after the political fundraiser where she'd seen Gideon and his date, and she stood in the middle of her shop. As she hung up the phone, Fiona looked around with eagle eyes and a churning stomach. She would open the doors for business as Charmed Antiquity in less than two hours, hopefully welcoming in a new, refurbished clientele.

Over the weekend, Fiona had spent pretty much all of her waking moments in the shop—doing last minute cleaning and rearranging, sorting files, and other preparations—but never alone.

No, she'd refused to be in there alone. And she hadn't told anyone—even Ethan—why.

Perhaps after the reopening, after people began to rediscover the store, whatever it was that made those odd things happen would stop, and she wouldn't feel such eeriness when alone in the shop.

Thank goodness for Carl. He was one of her old friends from school and had remained a perpetual student. Now in grad school at the University of Michigan, he was working on an improbable dissertation concerning early 20th-century households.

He'd worked for an estate sales company all through high school and college, and knew far more than she did about antique furnishings. She'd had pounced on the opportunity to snag him for a part-time job Thursdays through Sundays—especially since his charm and good looks matched his knowledge of antiques.

For the next hour and a half, she fussed and fretted, rearranging the displays, trying not to think about how much money she'd spent on the catering (even though she'd used Winona's company and got a discount), welcoming Carl when he arrived in his suit as promised (and with extra plates), and just generally driving herself crazy.

Now, she flicked a dust rag over the top of a grandfather clock for the umpteenth time and glanced nervously at its face.

It was already eleven-thirty.

Just then, Carl wandered from the back of the shop, which had been put into order in the last week. "Win's caterers are here. Do you want them to put the food in the back, or out in front?"

"Out here is fine—I thought we could put the wine on that table over there and the cheese and fruit on that —er—what did you call it?"

Carl had a pained look on his handsome, tanned face as he replied, "A Hepplewhite lowboy, circa 1793, in near-mint condition, and…is it possible you'd reconsider? I don't think…you really wouldn't want to…uh…take a chance on having an accident on it."

"Fine with me," she replied, gesturing widely through the shop. "Knock yourself out and find somewhere safe to put the food. I'm going to turn on some music." She'd wanted to have a live harpist for the day, but it hadn't fit in her budget, so the customers would have to settle for excellent hors d'oeuvres, decent wine, and canned music.

By the time the new-age instrumentals of Enya were filtering through the shop, and Fiona had checked her image in the spotty bathroom mirror in the back then breezed to the front of the store, the chimes had tickled three times and guests—*customers*—were strolling about.

Her nervousness faded as she became busy welcoming people, offering them sparkling water, wine, coffee, or tea, and half-listening to Carl as he chatted about various pieces of furnishings throughout the store. He always seemed to have at least two women, if not more, clustered around him, daintily holding their wineglasses and looking up at him from under their lashes.

Fiona suspected it wouldn't matter what the conversation was about—as long as he was standing there—for Carl Pelham had been blessed with incredible good looks, an unassuming personality, and the ability to listen.

In fact, she thought idly, he looked like a living, breathing Ken doll, with his perfect blond hair, startling blue eyes, golden tan and swimmer's body, and a gentle, calm nature that caused him to appear as if he had no idea the effect he had on women. Most women anyway.

Fiona knew that, objectively, he was very attractive, but he didn't do a thing—never had—for her hormones. She preferred dark-haired men with a sense of humor. Who weren't lawyers.

The afternoon passed quickly, as there was a steady stream of clientele coming in, out, and through the shop—and most of them leaving with small bags, larger bundles, and other receipts. Fiona greeted and chatted with customers, skillfully turning them over to Carl whenever they began to sound as though they might be interested in making a purchase or wished to haggle over a price.

It was early in the evening, just an hour or so before closing. Fiona turned, a glass of wine in her hand for one of the patrons, and she came face to face with Bradley Forth.

"Looking for someone?" he asked, smiling down at her. "Me, perhaps?"

Apparently her brush-off last weekend hadn't cooled his jets enough, if the expression in his eyes as they slipped down her figure was any indication. But, now he was a customer—not a date—so Fiona decided to cut him some slack.

"How did you know?" she smiled back, looking at

him from under her eyelashes and thinking of Carl's court of flirtatious ladies as she did so. "I wanted to give you this."

She handed him her untouched wine, gave him another very warm smile that made his eyelids flicker, and patted his arm as she turned away. "I'll catch up with you in a minute, but I need to say hello to that couple over there."

Before Brad could respond, Fiona slipped off to greet a silver-haired pair who'd just entered the shop. The man was tall and distinguished-looking, and his companion neat as a pin and charmingly enthusiastic.

"Welcome," she smiled at them. "I'm Fiona, the new owner. Thank you for stopping by. Please feel free to help yourself to refreshments over there, and if you have any questions, or would like to know more about the shop, let me know."

The woman rewarded her with a warm smile that curved her apple cheeks, and the man with her— possibly her husband—gave Fiona a nod and an appraising glance.

"Now, Hollis, why don't you dash over there and get a glass of wine for me—white would be perfect. And, I'm sure I won't be able to wait until our reservations at Trib's, so a nip of cheese and fruit—and those mini crab-cakes look fantastic—would just tide me over." The lady gave her directives in a well-modulated tone, with just the slightest air of helplessness to it, even though Fiona could see the sparkle of determination in her bright blue eyes. "I'll just chat with this young lady here for a moment."

The man—Hollis—seemed to hesitate, but one look from the woman prodded him on and he sifted into the small crowd of people around the food.

"Well, now, this is very nice," the woman said. She looked as though she was a young-at-heart mid-sixty, with silvery-white hair in a short, fashionable cut and round, rosy cheeks. Glancing toward Brad, she leaned closer as though to share a confidence. "Is that your young man over there, that I saw you speaking with as we walked in? I wouldn't want to take you away from him…"

"No, no," Fiona shook her head vehemently. How kind of the old lady to be so considerate. "He is just an acquaintance, but it's very nice of you to be so concerned."

"Ah. I see." Fiona thought she saw a crafty look slip into the woman's eyes as she slid her frail hand—one that had surprising strength—into the crook of Fiona's arm and led her over to examine a table.

No *way*.

Gideon couldn't believe it.

He'd taken such great pains to not mention to his grandfather and Iva where he intended to go this evening—in fact, he'd made sure not to discuss the Valente case in any detail at all in the last week, and he'd certainly not mentioned the spread in the *Press*.

But it was all for naught, for whom did he see the minute he walked into Charmed Antiquity?

And with whom was Iva having, by the looks of it, one hell of an interesting conversation?

"Damn," he muttered under his breath, pausing in the doorway of the shop.

For a moment, he was actually torn as to whether he should slip out before he was noticed, or brave the tidal wave of questions that was sure to follow. But then he saw another unwanted figure, and his mind was quickly made up. He was staying.

Gideon sauntered casually over to Brad Forth. "Well, now, Forth, fancy seeing you here. I thought you'd be out fund-raising or at least stumping for votes. It's getting pretty close to the election."

The other man was holding a glass of red wine, and he frowned, moving it in the barest of greetings toward him. "Nath." His gaze flickered toward Fiona, who was still chatting with Iva, then back around the room. "She's done a nice job with the place," he commented. "I told her food would be a nice touch—it adds a bit of elegance to the affair. Too bad she couldn't afford a live harpist."

So she'd been taking advice from the smarmy politician, had she? Gideon managed to control a sneer, but barely.

Instead of responding, he took a moment to actually look around the shop and see what she'd done to it.

The place had become inviting and warm. It was charmingly cluttered in an eclectic fashion that somehow made sense. Fresh flowers, trailing plants, or succulents graced nearly every gleaming, polished surface. There were countless sources of light illuminating the place with a soft, golden glow: glittering chandeliers, colorful Tiffanys, twinkling string lights, elegant sconces, Japanese lanterns of all shapes and sizes, and dangling Art Deco pendants. Some tinkling, New Age music provided a suitable, subtle background—although Gideon thought a string trio would have been even nicer than a harpist.

More importantly, the place was filled with people milling about as they sipped beverages and nibbled on tapas. As he finished his perusal, he noticed a large, brightly-colored object descended from the stairway near the back of the shop.

"Isn't that Mrs. Ruthven?" he asked Forth. "Your cousin, Viola?"

The politician turned just as the object materialized into the carrot-red hair of a woman sheathed in what appeared to be a multi-colored quilt, followed by a slender but just as colorfully dressed figure of a man. "It is. I hadn't noticed they were here," he said dismissively.

"It's hard to miss that," Gideon muttered, eying the couple.

At the reading of the will and during their subsequent meetings with him, the two had been dressed in similar clothing of screaming colors and unusual design. He'd learned through their conversations that they owned a small boutique in Traverse City that carried items such as the ones they wore today. Viola's dress appeared to be little more than a shiny bedspread with beads and fluorescent embroidery embellishing its hem, and Rudy wore a man's vest of ornate damask pieces patchworked together.

But apparently, somehow, their boutique was highly successful—and had been profiled in *Midwest Living* as well as several other national magazines. A number of celebrities had even been photographed wearing what amounted to eyesore quilts and blankets.

For the life of him, Gideon couldn't understand how anyone found the style attractive, but, he acknowledged, it took all kinds.

"Why hello, Mr. Nath!" Viola trilled as she steamrolled her way over to them. "And Bradley, darling. Why I didn't even see you here." She seemed a bit out of breath and fluttered a plump, lily-white hand at her throat. "We just had to see what was hiding upstairs," she gushed.

Her husband came up behind her and gave Gideon a brief handshake. "Nothing up there but a bunch of dust and an old table or two," he said. "Don't know why we had to waste our time up there in all the dust, but you know how women are." His chuckle sounded too hearty. "What are you doing here, Brad?"

"And there's Uncle Arnold," Forth pointed out, neatly avoiding answering the question.

Gideon turned, and sure enough, there was the well-dressed investment banker with the gelled-back hair, emerging from the dim rear of the shop.

They were all here. All of Nevio Valente's heirs.

For some reason, that bothered Gideon.

He glanced over at his grandfather and saw Fiona leaning toward Iva, looking down at something she was probably holding while Gideon Senior looked on.

He wondered if his grandfather's instincts about Valente's estate—and the man himself—were correct. Now that the man was dead, it would be just the time for ugly secrets to come out.

Then, just as quickly, his uneasiness left and he berated himself for allowing his grandfather to put wild ideas into his head. The remaining family of Nevio Valente was most likely simply interested in seeing what had become of their relative's shop—and were probably simply curious about the stranger who'd inherited it.

"Well, we'll be going now," Rudy said, extending a hand to Arnold.

"What? No purchases?" Arnold lifted a thick black brow as he deigned to accept the handshake. "You didn't find anything worthwhile up there in the attic?"

"No, no–just some junk up there. You know how

Nevio was." Rudy appeared a little flushed, but he gamely smiled all around the little cluster.

"Oh, but I wish we'd found something to buy," Viola chimed in as though to ease some building tension. "I'd give anything to get the *personal* attention of that shop clerk for just a few moments."

Gideon followed her gaze to the man in question and felt himself go cold.

That guy was a shop clerk? *Fiona's* shop clerk?

The man looked more like Adonis than a minimum-wage smurf. Christ. And the ladies were hanging all over him, cooing, and listening to his every word.

"He's the best piece in *this* shop, at any rate," muttered Viola unabashedly. Her husband must have elbowed her, for she shifted away. "Well, he is!"

"Come on Viola, let's get out of here." Rudy took his wife's arm and directed her through the crowd.

As they brushed past Fiona, she looked up to say good-bye, and Iva happened to look toward Gideon.

And the jig was up.

"Gideon!" Iva cried in ingenuous surprise. "Why, I didn't know you were here. Come on over and say hello to Fiona."

"Hello, Fiona." Even to his ears, there was a rich layer of warmth to his voice, and he saw her eyes widen slightly as she returned his greeting.

"What a nice surprise to see you, uh, Gideon." She actually sounded like she meant it. "Thanks for coming." She looked at Iva, her eyes narrowing in comprehension. "Wait a minute...you know each other?"

"As it happens, we do. Gideon here is Hollis's grandson."

"I *knew* your name sounded familiar to me!" Fiona

said with a laugh. "Iva. Iva Bergstrom. Ethan talks about you and the Tuesday Ladies all the time."

"And I believe I just missed meeting you at Maxine Took's eightieth birthday party last summer. You'd had to leave early, and Hollis and I had arrived late."

"That's right. Well, it's a pleasure to meet you at last."

"It is indeed. It seems we have much in common besides an affection for Ethan and a place in Wicks Hollow," Iva replied.

While the two women smiled at each other as if they'd just found their soulmates, Gideon found himself looking at Fiona without trying to be too obvious about it. She'd pulled back just the front of her hair, away from her porcelain face, and the rest of the cinnamon tangle fell in crazy curls around her shoulders. Soft curls. He remembered how soft they were, and he curled his fingers into their palms so he didn't reach out to touch.

Tonight, Fiona wore a sophisticated ivory pantsuit, sleeveless, with wide-legged pants—a departure from her usual fortune-teller-like garments—and it made her sexy, sleek, and elegant. Huge, jangling, gold earrings and a matching necklace depicting a Celtic design set off the outfit…along with some incredible, musky scent that seemed to head straight for his nose.

Gideon shifted his stance in order to get a stronger nuance of her perfume, and realized Iva was prattling on excitedly about something. "Did you know that?" she was asking him.

"Know what?"

"Fiona reads palms, Gideon—and she was right on when she looked at mine just now." Iva's eyes danced and she slipped her hands around Gideon's upper arm.

His heart sank. He knew Fiona was odd, but this took the cake. "You what?" He couldn't quite keep the disdain from his voice. There was no way he could even *think* about getting involved with her—even though that was pretty much all he'd been doing for the last week.

He'd be a laughing stock. And besides…no one knew better than he how unreliable and irresponsible artsy people could be.

A smirk pulled at the corners of Fiona's mouth, as if she knew what he was thinking. "My mother does a better job than I do, but I can make my way around a hand if need be." For some reason, although the words blared innocence, they caused a strange frisson to run across his shoulder. Maybe it was the way the timbre of her voice dipped into duskiness just a little at the end.

"Hollis, let her look at yours," Iva was insisting.

"Now, Iva—" his grandfather began.

"Hollis?" Fiona asked lightly—then speared Gideon with her eyes. Her face shifted into a feline grin that made his knees go weak. "So that's it," she murmured for his ears only, still looking at him with that knowing smile. "Hollis."

Gideon spoke quickly and a trifle loudly in an effort to save himself. "Iva, I'm sure Fiona needs to attend to her guests." But then, too late, he saw the trap into which he'd been so expertly led.

"Oh, dear, of *course* she does. I'm so sorry, Fiona, I realize your guests come first. But the shop closes in just a few minutes, doesn't it? Then, why don't you join Hollis and me for dinner as our guest—we have an eight o'clock reservation—at Trib's, of course. I would just *love* your company. We have so much in common!"

Whatever happened to turning into a pumpkin at nine o'clock? Gideon thought, eyeing Iva suspiciously.

Then he swore to himself, cursing meddling potential

step-grandmothers, when Fiona agreed to join them for an unusually late dinner.

Now why would she do that?

* * *

Fiona didn't know herself why she agreed to join the senior Naths for dinner. Perhaps it was because she really had been enjoying her conversation with Iva—after all, the older woman was a good friend of her brother's. There was a reason Ethan enjoyed her company and that of the other Tuesday Ladies.

Or maybe it was because she knew Carl had to leave right at eight o'clock, and she didn't want to be in the shop alone, especially at night...

Or perhaps it was because the moment she'd seen Gideon, standing there so dark and handsome—and for some reason, glowering—she'd become very much aware of him. And then there was the fact that now he was standing just in front of the desk where she'd been sprawled beneath him only a few days ago.

Regardless of the reason for her capitulation, Fiona was even more unsettled when Hollis Gideon the Third also agreed to join them for dinner.

"Just so I can keep an eye on you," he murmured to Fiona.

It was a few moments later that she realized another, unexpected benefit of accepting Iva's invitation as she escorted her last guest—Brad Forth, of course—to the door.

"How about dashing off with me to grab a bite?" he asked, his gaze flickering toward the Naths and Iva, who stood near the desk, chatting in low voices. Actually, it looked as if Gideon the Third was doing all of the speaking. He had a lecture-ish expression on his face.

"Thank you so much, Brad, but I have a previous engagement. Maybe another time?" she asked, fervently hoping that he would win the election in a few weeks and be too busy to keep contacting her.

Carl saved her as he called from the back of the shop, "Fiona, I have to run—but could I see you before I go?"

Giving Brad a last, distracted farewell, she swept past Gideon and the older couple to meet Carl at the back of the store.

"Tonight went really well, don't you think?" she asked.

"It went very well. You cleared a nice chunk of change, Fi."

"That means you'll be getting a nice cut yourself," she replied happily.

"For sure." His smile faded as he stepped back. "I want to show you something I just noticed." He propelled her to a far corner of the back room, near the little closet where Gideon had taken his tumble and kissed her for the first time. "Looks like someone was a little too nosy."

Fiona peered closer, ducking her head under a low shelf, and saw what he meant: several boxes that had been stacked neatly were misaligned, and one flap was open. Beyond them, an old rusty file cabinet's bottom drawer was ajar. These were items they hadn't had time to sift through yet, but had moved back into the corner behind a screen to get them out of the way. She certainly had not left the bottom drawer ajar.

"Hmm. Must have been a customer." Fiona dismissed the uneasy prickle that zipped down her spine. She pulled back out of the corner and her head bumped into the bottom of the shelf, knocking the combs that held her hair away from her face askew.

"A very nosy one," Carl pointed out to her. "Well," he said, casting a look at his watch, "I really have to get going—I'm supposed to play basketball in thirty minutes, and I'm twenty minutes away."

A vision of the muscular Carl dribbling a ball up a court, dripping sweat, and garbed in loose shorts that would show off his rear still had little effect on Fiona's hormones, and she sighed mentally. By all rights, she should be drooling over the man.

"Hope you win. See you tomorrow," she smiled, fumbling to readjust her loosened hair combs as he turned to leave. She walked back out to the main area of the shop, still stabbing the comb into a twist of hair.

"Shall we?" Iva asked. "Hollis and I will drive you both to Trib's—you'll never get a parking place otherwise."

Gideon looked as if he were about to argue, but clamped his lips shut and acquiesced. At this point, he had the uneasy feeling he was just along for the ride— whatever ride his grandfather's girlfriend had picked.

Five minutes later, they were seated inside Trib's at a table near the front window.

Fiona paused to greet Baxter James, a handsome black man with a close-trimmed afro, mustache, and goatee. He was sitting at the bar making notes on a laptop while sampling a beer. She thanked him again for the writeup in the *Grand Rapids Press*, then joined the others at the table.

"I didn't realize you knew Baxter," Iva said as Fiona took a seat.

"He and Ethan are friends, so he connected us. Bax is the one who did the great spread on the re-opening for the store," she said as she slid into her seat. "He came by the shop earlier today, right after we opened, and is going to do a follow-up article as well. Very nice guy."

Iva looked at Gideon. "Baxter James is our local brewmaster. Baxter's Beatnik Brews—B-Cubed. You might have heard of them. He moonlights as a freelance journalist."

"Makes a damned good IPA," Hollis Nath said, looking up from his menu.

Any further conversation was pre-empted when their server came over to give the specials.

"Do take a look at Hollis's hand for me, will you," Iva said, leaning toward Fiona just after their round of drinks was delivered. Her eyes sparkled. "He doesn't put any credence into any of this, and I want you to tell him something that will change his mind."

"Now, Iva, really, I—"

"Please, dear, just indulge me, won't you?" Iva patted his hand and gazed up at him with such an endearing expression that Fiona could see the elderly man melt into a puddle of wax right before her eyes.

They must have been married a long time. An uncomfortable feeling jetted through her mind. What would it be like to be attached to—*responsible* to—another person for decades?

She risked a glance at Gideon, and found that instead of paying attention to the byplay between his grandfather and Iva, he was watching Fiona with an inscrutable expression. Their eyes clashed for a mere second, then he quirked a grin and raised his wine glass as though to say, "You asked for it."

"It's been around for centuries, you know," Iva was saying earnestly to Gideon Senior. "Palm reading. And there is some scientific proof to its validity. The Hindus are credited with its inception—and it's believed that the people we know of as the Rom originally came from India." When she caught Fiona looking at her in surprise, Iva shrugged. "I'm a librarian," she explained with a modest smile.

"And a killer player at any trivia game," the elder Nath said with an affectionate smile.

"If you don't mind, Mr. Nath, I would like to take a look at your hands. I've been admiring them all evening," Fiona said truthfully.

They were the kind of hands she loved, with long, well-shaped fingers, well-defined lines, and a solid, square palm—easy to read and interpret.

"And never fear, Mr. Nath—I don't tell fortunes. One's hands are merely an insight into the personality of a person, and, sometimes, their potentials—or lost potentials. Now, if you're right-handed, I'll need to see that hand."

The blustery man was really a soft old teddy bear, as Fiona was beginning to learn, and, with an awkward glance at his grandson, he set his glass down then extended his hand toward her. His palm rested in the center of the round table, and Iva hastily moved a vase of orange and yellow mums out of the way.

"You have a generous nature, but an ambitious strain as well," Fiona told the elder Nath, smoothing her thumb along his palm. She was surprised when she saw the marriage lines on the side of his little finger and looked up at him suddenly. "How long have you two been married?"

He stiffened, then glanced at Iva. "We aren't married. *Yet.*" He moved his free hand to pat Iva's. "She's the love of my life—but I didn't find her until I was seventy."

Fiona relaxed a little. "And this would be your—uh—I mean, how many marriages?"

"I thought you were supposed to be able to tell that from looking at his hand," Gideon snarked.

"I'd be his fourth wife," Iva replied, giving him an arch look. "*If* we get married."

Fiona smiled with relief—there were only four marriage lines. "And you'd be his last," she said, then looked at the older man. "And only one child? A son?"

He nodded, although some of the light went out of his face. "Yes, that's right." Then he smiled at Iva. "I doubt we'll be having any of our own, hmm, dear?"

"No, but some grandchildren would be nice," she said brightly.

Fiona looked at his thumb—how it angled away from the rest of the hand, its length, and the way the top curved back from the nail. Many palmists felt that the thumb was the best indicator of personality overall, and she liked what she saw. "You're ambitious and organized, not willing to take too many risks. You're not easily influenced."

She was murmuring to herself more than anything now. She moved her attention to his long middle finger, the Saturn finger, and continued. "This indicates that you're serious and down to earth—but not overly inclined to pessimism. It's slightly inclined toward your forefinger, the Jupiter, indicating your assertive personality toward business...but," she looked up at him, "you're much more tentative about your emotional life."

She could tell by his expression—and Iva's—that she was accurate in her suppositions. But, feeling the heavy, sarcastic weight of Gideon's gaze on hers, Fiona decided not to continue her thoughts aloud. She released Gideon Senior's hand.

"Well," she said lightly, "that was just a quick look. Hope I didn't spook anyone." She gave a pointed look toward Gideon, who was all but glaring at her. Yet, heat simmered beneath his look and caused her stomach to flip slowly over and around like a lava lamp.

"Why don't you take a look at Gideon's hand?" Iva suggested.

Gideon snorted, but Fiona, feeling the devilish imp prodding her once again, turned to look at him. "I'd be happy to see what secrets he's hiding."

SEVEN

"ABSOLUTELY NOT." Gideon tightened his fingers around his drink as though she was trying to pry them open. How on earth had he gotten into this mess?

"But why not?" Fiona looked at him, training her big, Madeira-colored eyes on him. "I'd love to look at your hands."

Her voice was a purr: intimate without being too suggestive, the depth of it meant for his ears only. He felt himself drowning in her gaze—right there in front of his grandfather and Iva in the middle of Trib's.

Never mind that she was nearly begging to read his palm, for Christ's sake, like some charlatan fortune-teller.

Never mind that she'd come from the back of the shop with Carl, the blond god, with her hair all mussed, sticking her combs back into place.

Never mind that she'd probably had fewer serious thoughts in her lifetime than his screwed-up father.

He just couldn't resist her.

Avoiding his grandfather's eyes, he set down the drink and extended his hand.

"You're left-handed, yes?" she asked as her fingers closed over that hand. When he nodded, she continued, "Good."

She held his hand, brushing her thumbs over the inside of his palm, right there in the restaurant...and he felt as though she were undressing him. There was something about the intimacy of fingers slowly, carefully touching fingers... Even though they'd kissed—their bodies smashed up against each other, every curve and hard plane outlined against the other...this was different. It was as though they'd never touched before.

She wasn't unaffected either, if the faint trembling of her fingers was any indication. He felt the ridges of her fingertips, the finger pad whorls that made her Fiona—unique, odd, exciting Fiona—as they brushed over his own.

"It looks as though you'll be marrying soon," she said suddenly, breaking what had become—to him—a charged silence, but was in reality only moments of quiet. "And at least one child."

He almost pulled his hand away as anger spurted through him. What the hell kind of game was she playing?

Iva nearly burst from her seat, barely able to contain herself, and he shot her a dark glare. "Don't get all excited, Iva—she's just telling you what you want to hear. Grandchildren, remember?"

Fiona remained cool, and her gaze continued steadily on him. "I'm just telling you what I see, Gideon." Did he detect a hint of sadness in her gaze? Regret, perhaps? "Unless you've already been married?"

"No." He snapped the word out and this time did

start to pull his hand away. Her fingers held on and he relented, for, despite his anger, he liked the feel of her small, warm hand around his. And he didn't want to make a fool out of himself by making a scene.

She bent to look at his palm again, her pale, slim fingers caressing the darker skin of his own flesh, straightening his digits with her thumbs, smoothing the underside of his hand where the skin was softer and more sensitive. Then she looked up at him, and he could see the surprise in her face. "Let me see your right hand," she said, frowning slightly.

"What is it?" Iva asked, leaning forward.

"Nothing major…just one of those secrets I mentioned." She was waiting for him to show her his other hand. "Since you're left-handed, your left hand shows what you are or have been, while your right hand indicates potentials that may or may not have been realized."

Gideon was just about to comply when he was saved, rescued from something that would certainly be uncomfortable, by the waiter serving their salads. By the time all of them received their plates, Gideon had firmly picked up a fork and knife—to keep his hands busy—and managed to swing the conversation to the success of the open house for the antiques shop.

The rest of the meal passed slowly but at least without further discomfort on his part. Fiona and Iva had hit it off famously, discussing things he knew nothing about—*ta'i chi*, aromatherapy, *feng shui* and yoga.

Gideon Senior managed to bring up the Valente estate only once—when he casually asked, "How did you say you knew Nevio Valente, Fiona?"

She flickered a glance at Gideon as if to measure how

she should respond, but replied, "Do you mean Gideon didn't tell you? I believe I only met him once, when he came into the office where I worked."

The older man shook his head, then dabbed at his mouth with a napkin. "Odd man, Valente was. Even odder for a crotchety old bastard—pardon me, ladies—to do something nice for anyone, let alone someone he didn't know. Everything else going okay with the shop?" His eyes focused sharply on Fiona, and Gideon held his breath.

Don't mention the light.

He couldn't bear for the older couple to think she was a flake—talking about lit lamps that weren't plugged in. Obviously, it was something that had rattled her—and, odd as she was, probably for good reason…but he wasn't sure his grandfather would understand.

In order to forestall that from happening, he reached over and, resting his hand on top of hers, said, "Speaking of the shop, I'm sure you need to get back and get closed up for the night, hmm, Fiona?"

He ignored the frown directed at him by his grandfather and kept his attention on Fiona. He was ready to get out of there—away from the suggestive looks from Iva, but more importantly, away to where he could have Fiona to himself.

Heat shot through him, straight down through his belly, as he realized exactly how much he wanted to run off with her…and just what he would do when they did.

When his grandfather insisted on settling the bill—a legitimate business expense, since Fiona had been there —Gideon was able to get his wish. Less than ten minutes later, they were strolling up Pamela Avenue toward Violet Way.

As it was a Tuesday evening in October and after

nine o'clock, the quaint streets were nearly empty and most of the windows had gone dark, except for eating establishments. Victorian-style streetlamps cast warm circles of orange-gold every block. On each corner was a small barrel planter spilling with rust, gold, and white mums. A banner strung over the main intersection of the town announced a large multi-class reunion. The air was smooth and almost warm, but there was still the bite of autumn in it.

Gideon hadn't spoken a word to Fiona since they'd parted from his grandfather and Iva—for suddenly, now that they were alone, he didn't know what to say. He knew what he wanted to *do*...but not what he wanted to say.

Fiona broke the silence at last. "Your grandfather and Iva are lovely people—and it was so kind of them to invite me to dinner."

"Yes, well, you should know that Iva had an ulterior motive." He glanced down at her as they passed under a streetlight, and saw the delicate planes of her face outlined by the stark light when she looked up at him.

"Well, of course she did, Gideon—it was pretty obvious. She—and probably your grandfather even more—is dying for you to settle down and find happiness just as they have, so they'll take advantage of any possible candidate for you." The smug smile she sent him should have tweaked his annoyance, but instead, he grinned at her candor. "Even an oddball like me."

His gaze flickered away. "You're no more odd than Iva, believing in all that New Age stuff," he heard himself say. "Do you actually think that by rearranging your furniture, you can become wealthy or happy?"

Fiona laughed out loud, delightedly. "Do I detect a bit of sarcasm, there, Gideon? You'd best be careful—

sarcasm could be mistaken for a sense of humor, and I'm sure you wouldn't want that." She laughed again, her bare arm brushing up against him as they ambled along. Then, to his surprise, she slipped one hand around his bicep, hugging it to her without breaking her stride.

They walked easily, their steps matching, thighs brushing, her thick, wild hair tickling the underside of his chin, and it felt like the most natural thing in the world.

When she smiled up at him again, the sparkle in her eyes showing even in the half moonlight, Gideon felt an unfamiliar twinge deep inside and he almost stopped right there on the sidewalk. He must have hesitated anyway, for she looked back up, shifting against him as they walked.

"Almost there," he said, just to make sure his voice still worked.

"Yes."

They turned onto Violet Way, which was dark except for a single streetlight at each end, and a soft glow from an upper floor window in the realtor's office building.

"Do you need to go in?" he asked as she paused in the little exterior alcove of her shop. She peered in one of the windows, cupping her hand around her eyes as if to see better.

"No. Carl locked the back door when he left, and everything looks fine from here."

At the mention of her shop clerk, Gideon's veins froze and his earlier irritation returned. "Yes. Your assistant. How could I have forgotten?"

Fiona looked up at him, puzzlement etched over her shadowed features, and nodded. "You met him?"

"No, I didn't meet him—but all the ladies were gushing on about him."

Fiona grinned. "Yes, he does tend to have that effect on the ladies. Well, I'm not complaining—it can't be a bad thing for business, can it?"

She stepped away from the door and turned to walk past him. "My car is parked in the alley. I'm really glad you're here to walk me back there since Carl's gone." She tossed him a warm smile and slipped past, back onto the sidewalk.

Gideon felt outrage bubbling in his veins, but he mutely turned to follow her. So he was an acceptable escort when her boy toy wasn't around, was he? A mere stand-in?

He wondered furiously whether their backroom embraces meant anything in light of the fact that she'd been kissing her assistant so passionately earlier that she'd had to replace her hair combs. His mouth settled into a hard line as he stalked just behind Fiona when she turned into a narrow but well-lit alley between two storefronts. The thought of her passionate, pliant, willing responsiveness under another man's mouth infuriated him, driving coherent thoughts from his mind.

The only thing that stayed there—the pinpoint of lucidity in his haze of anger—was the desire to remind her of those moments with *him*. He wanted to mutilate any last trace of Carl's kiss on her lips, and replace it with his own...and to make her understand that he wanted more from her.

Fiona rounded the sharp corner to the alley that led to the back entrance of her shop, walking as quickly as she could. She felt Gideon on her trail as if he were already touching her, and her skin prickled with antici-pation. She thought about how it was going to feel— pressed up against the side of her little VW, sandwiched between it and the hard, muscular frame of Gideon, his mouth on hers and his hands everywhere else.

He was going to kiss her—and if he didn't, she would kiss him—and after that…well, she couldn't make that decision right at this very moment. She was too nervous, too on-edge to think about where this could lead…and whether she wanted to take that step.

"Fiona!" He caught up with her in the middle of the alley, a narrow, brick-walled passage just wide enough for a car to pass through. A glimmer of streetlight cast shadows and shards of light down upon them. At the end of the narrow throughway, in the small loading area behind Charmed Antiquity, Fiona could see her VW Beetle gleaming like a sleek lemon drop right next to a large Dumpster.

She didn't need to turn, for Gideon's hand closed over her arm and tugged her, firmly, around to face him. She was close enough to feel the heat of his body, and prickles erupted on her bare arms. The intensity in his eyes shocked her, sending a thrill of sensation—and a bit of nervousness—through her belly.

"Are you going to kiss me now?" she asked, looking up at him. "I was hoping you would."

Gideon stilled as his fingers closed around her arms and he looked down at her, obviously astonished. Then his mouth settled into a dark, slashing line, shadowed by the uneven light. "Is that what you say to all your boy toys?"

"Boy to—?" Fiona choked on her surprise as he reeled her in to him, smothering her abrupt confusion with those hard, persuasive lips. Desire won out over shock, and she allowed her mouth to mold to his for a few moments before she yanked herself away.

"What do you mean, boy toy?" she demanded, stepping back as far as his arms would allow. The further away from temptation, the clearer her mind would be.

"Your muscle-bound minion Carl. And Bradley Forth. And whoever else you may have stringing along. I don't count myself in that line-up, by the way." His eyes glittered dangerously.

That kiss had not been one of uncontrolled passion, Fiona realized, but one borne out of fury and frustration. Even so, it left her all hot and fluttery—wanting more. *Damn.*

"Don't be ridiculous," she retorted, gathering up her indignation—which was difficult, considering what she wanted mostly to do was step back into his arms. "And if you really believe that I'm somehow juggling Carl and Brad, *while* kissing you, then you're only degrading yourself by kissing me back."

She stepped out of his loosening grip and planted her hands on her hips. "And you're one to talk, *Hollis* Gideon Nath—considering the fact that you were with your friends-with-benefits ice queen on Saturday."

"I didn't sleep with Rachel," he said, his eyes dark in the shadowy light. "I wouldn't do that then—then kiss you."

But Fiona wasn't finished with him, even though her lips were still full and ready for his kiss. "And, by the way, *Hollis*—when and *if* I choose to be involved with a man, that's it—it's him and no one else."

He'd taken a step closer during her tirade. She felt the presence of the brick wall behind her, brushing it with her fingers, but she did not feel trapped.

Not trapped. Excited.

"Don't call me Hollis," he muttered just before his mouth descended on hers once again.

She should have continued to berate him, she should

have insisted that he apologize for such a rude comment…she should have stayed in control, walked away…but she didn't. She let go.

Dropping her one-ton leather bag, Fiona slipped her arms up around him, smoothing her fingers down the sides of his warm neck and over the breadth of his wide shoulders, thinking vaguely that it was odd—scary, almost—that she should be so affected by his kisses, and the closeness of his body.

And then, she had no further coherent thoughts. She concentrated on *him*, on the skillful way his mouth moved over hers, the taste and heat of him…every plane and angle of his body and that of the wall behind her… the ridges of brick pressing into her spine.

He must have realized she wasn't going to push away, so Gideon released her arms, planting his hands on either side of her shoulders, pinning her back against the rough wall with his mouth and thighs. Fiona shifted, kissing him back, pushing her breasts up into him so that he exhaled long and raggedly as he trailed his lips along her jaw-line.

"Fiona…."

"Ever done it in the back of a VW bug?" she murmured with a husky chuckle that ended in a gasp as he circled his tongue around her ear. "Gideon . . ." she began, but then forgot what she was going to say as he returned to taste her mouth again. His hands had long since left their anchor on either side of her, and were deftly unbuttoning the back buttons of her pantsuit top.

He slipped those long, elegant fingers up under the silky fabric, smoothing them over the satin of her strapless bra, then into it to cup her nipple-hard breasts in his hands.

The cooling night air breezed over her hot skin

through the open back of her shirt, and the sandpaper roughness of the bricks grazed her bare back, but Fiona was conscious of little other than what his fingers were doing to her body. She was just about to yank his shirt open—damn the buttons—when there was a crash, followed by a shrill alarm.

Gideon staggered back, pivoting to look toward the back entrance of the shop—but the view was hidden by a large Dumpster. "What the he—"

"That's my alarm!" Fiona pushed him away and started toward the Dumpster and her shop's back door.

Just then, a figure burst into view from behind the Dumpster, started toward them, then spun to run in the opposite direction. Gideon was after him in a flash, with Fiona stumbling behind in her high heels.

"Hey! Stop!" she shrieked as Gideon tore along, gaining on the intruder and leaving her far behind.

She hurried after them, damning herself for the little bit of fashion sense she'd chosen to follow this evening, but unwilling to kick off her shoes and run barefooted through a back alley. She saw Gideon disappear around the corner of the opposite end of the alley and sped up her pace. Her foot landed awkwardly on a stone or some odd object, wrenching her ankle enough to bring her to a wincing halt.

She forced herself to hobble along at a much slower pace, realizing belatedly that the cool breeze on her back was due to the fact that the top of her pantsuit was unbuttoned. She angled her hands up behind her, fumbling to connect at least one button before the whole thing fell off as she rushed to catch up to her date.

When she finally rounded the corner around which he'd disappeared, she nearly ran into him. "What happened?" she exclaimed, breathing heavily, looking around past him. "Did he get away?"

Her hands landed on the center of his chest, and she felt it rising and falling rapidly. Only then, when he didn't reply, did she look up to see a dark stream running down the side of his face, and the hand he had pressed to his head. He was leaning against the wall.

"Gideon! What happened?" she cried, pulling his hand away.

"Don't fuss," he muttered, placing his hand back onto some type of wound. "Let's get back to the shop and see what damage he did." His voice, though weaker than usual, still held the stilted command of a man used to no-nonsense—and dripped with self-disgust.

"He crowned me as I came around the corner—caught me right in the gut, then knocked me against the brick edge there." He had begun the walk back to the shop, and Fiona could do little but walk along with him.

"Are you all right? Are you hurt anywhere else?" She wrapped her arm around his waist as though to support him, already feeling guilty that he should have been hurt.

"I said don't fuss," he repeated, but he did not move away from her embrace. In fact, he may have shifted a bit closer to her. "I didn't get a look at the guy at all—did you? Just that he was fairly tall, and average build. Fat lot of good that'll do us."

They had reached the back of the store now, and Fiona saw that the bathroom window next to the back door was shattered where someone had obviously tried to break in.

"He must not have seen us—we were blocked by the Dumpster and that edge of the building. But when he broke the window and the alarm went off." She drew in a breath. "Good thing Carl set the alarm."

She checked to see whether the door had been jimmied, but the lock was intact. The opening of jagged glass was much too small for any person to pass through. Since the alarm had gone off just after the window was broken, the intruder obviously never made it inside the store.

That was also the conclusion of Wicks Hollow Police Chief Joe Longbow, who arrived moments later, having been notified by the alarm system.

"Store's still locked up," he said in his drawling voice. "You say nothing was taken, Miz Murphy?"

"I haven't been inside, but it doesn't appear that he made it in."

"That's all right, then. You can confirm when you file the report tomorrow up to the office," Longbow said. He was a rangy man approaching fifty with the high cheekbones and sienna-toned skin of his Native American heritage. His demeanor was calm and professional, and instilled a sense of trust and confidence in Fiona. "If nothing's taken, we'll file it as vandalism and suspected attempt of breaking and entering."

"All right," she replied. "I'll be in first thing tomorrow to file the report."

"Sorry about this being your welcome to Wicks Hollow," Longbow said with a grim smile. "But I did hear your re-opening was a success. My wife and daughter came in and brought home a small porcelain lamp." He scratched his head. "Has a turtle for a base," he added as if uncertain about it.

Fiona smiled. "Oh, I know the one. That turtle was a cheeky little critter. I'm glad he found a home."

Through their conversation, Gideon had leaned

propped against the side of Fiona's yellow Beetle, holding a rumpled handkerchief to his head and refusing to allow her to minister to him. "Finish up with this first," he growled when she tried to pry it away to look at it.

Apparently he was not the type that liked to be mothered, yet he looked wan and drawn even in the dim light.

Longbow jerked a look toward him. "Might want to have him looked at by an EMT or at the ER. Nasty cut there." Then he shook her hand, took a few more photos with an actual camera instead of a mobile phone, and bid them good evening.

"I'm not going to the ER," Gideon said from between clenched teeth, heedless of the blood that had dried all over his temple and the side of his face.

"All right, then. But at least let me drive you home, Gideon."

He seemed about to argue, then apparently thought better of it. "Fine," he said shortly. "It's about thirty minutes away," he added as if in warning.

She shrugged. "I figured you lived in Grand Rapids. I'm glad you're on this side of town and not the other."

With that, she opened the passenger door of her car. It would be interesting to see how he managed to get all six-foot-plus of himself in the little bucket seat.

She nearly had to shove him into the vehicle, but when he acquiesced with little reluctance, she realized how badly he must feel. He gave her basic directions and they fell silent as she maneuvered the Beetle out of Wicks Hollow to the highway that would take them to his house.

The seriousness of tonight's events struck her as she was waiting for a light to turn green. Up until now, it had been a foggy realization, overshadowed by the passionate kisses shared with Gideon, concern for him, and her factual conversation with the police.

Now, her focus sharpened as she recognized the hard facts: someone had broken into her shop. A random thief, or maybe even one of her guests from the open house today. Maybe someone had noticed one of the few pieces that caused Carl to positively drool, and decided he didn't want to pay for it? Regardless, it wasn't likely the police would ever find him—particularly since neither she nor Gideon had gotten a good look at him. She shivered. She was just so lucky that she hadn't come back to the shop on her own.

Fiona turned to look at Gideon, whose face was still raised to the ceiling. "Are you sure I can't take you to the ER?" she asked, noticing the lines of pain etched on his face.

"No. Stupidity does not deserve to be catered to." His voice was flat, but he lifted his head as they exited the highway and gave her further directions.

Moments later, Fiona pulled into the drive outside the garage to his condo, which overlooked Lake Michigan. "Lake view," she said, impressed. "Nice."

He let them into his condo, which was of newer construction, and Fiona had to readjust her previous assumptions about his living space.

It was not the cold, sleek, black-leather-and-chrome decor she'd imagined. Although definitely a bachelor pad, it did, nevertheless, have a warmer feel than she'd anticipated, with plump—not sleek—leather sofas, Scandinavian-style wooden furnishings, and interesting texture everywhere: in a tile display on one wall, on the subway-style backsplash in the kitchen, in an interesting metal piece on a two-storey wall, in a modern fabric tapestry stretched in a mahogany frame.

A small gas fireplace opened on two sides into the living room and kitchen, and a worn armchair was positioned next to a closed, but very large, wall-to-ceiling, entertainment center. The ugliest afghan she'd ever seen —olive green, chartreuse, and off-white—was folded across the back of the rich navy sofa.

"Nice blanket," she commented sincerely, smoothing her hand over its worn comfort. Ugly though it might be, it had been well-used and obviously provided some great measure of solace to its user.

"My mother made it."

The level of emotion in his voice told Fiona that it wasn't just pain from his injury that made it short and flat. She filed the information away for future contemplation and turned her attention from the residence to the man himself.

"Sit down and let me take a look at that. No, better yet, let's go into the bathroom where I can clean you up right there." She didn't wait for him to reply, but started down a hallway that passed a staircase, a den, and ended in a spacious powder room, certain he would follow.

He set his keys and phone next to the sink. Fiona made him take the handkerchief away from his face, and she couldn't help a small gasp when she saw the gash and nasty scrapes from the brick wall all along the side of his face. "Wow, he got you really good, hmm?"

Gideon's jaw tightened—she could feel it shift under her fingers as she gently wiped away the blood, grit, and dust from the wound—and he replied, "Yes, he certainly did." She could tell by the tone of his voice that he was angrier with himself than the would-be intruder for doing it to him, and she chose to remain silent.

Instead, she concentrated on ministering to him, and feeling the warmth of his tanned skin, the heavy weight of dark waves, and the slight prickles of end-of-the-day stubble. It didn't take long to clean it up, but by the time she was finished, all Fiona could think about was picking up where they'd left off in the alley.

Obviously, Gideon was feeling the same way, for when she turned to leave the room, he caught her wrist and pulled her back. "Not so fast," he murmured.

She stood, looking down at him where he sat next to the sink, then shifted to look at their images in the mirror. Gently, almost reverently, holding her gaze with his own in the mirror, he half rose from his seat and brought his lips to hers.

As their mouths touched, lightly, tentatively, she sighed and closed her eyes, allowing the rush of desire to flood her in powerful contrast to the carefulness of their kiss. She felt him lower back to his seat, allowing her to stand over him, hands on his shoulders, bending her face to his as they kissed slowly, thoroughly…as if they had all the time in the world.

And they did, until his cell phone chirped.

Fiona began to pull away, but Gideon grabbed her wrists, and held her in place. "No," was all he said.

It chirped a second and third time, and at that point, Fiona pulled away. "Someone's trying to get in touch with you."

"It's just a text," he murmured. But they both looked down and there it was, lit up on the phone's screen. Fiona didn't mean to pry, but she took in the message at a glance.

Tried to call you. Wanted to confirm the party next week. Had a great time Sat. Lmk.

It was from Rachel. And it was signed with a heart-eyed emoji.

Fiona extricated herself with deliberate care, and the fact that Gideon allowed her to do so was a measure that he understood how serious the situation was.

She stepped back, passed a hand over her face, then let it drop to her side. She saw herself in the mirror—saw the rueful smile pasted on her face, saw the flush of her cheeks and the fullness of her lips—and tried very hard to keep from losing her temper.

"I knew better," she said, turning to walk out of the powder room. "I knew about her, I knew you were involved…and somehow I let myself forget it. Stupid." She was speaking more to herself than to him, but she didn't care that he heard.

"Fiona…."

She heard him start behind her, but kept walking. "Gideon, I'm not angry. I swear it. I knew exactly what the situation was, but I let myself forget about it. You are a supernova kisser, you know," she said, turning to look at him as they reached the living room. Her smile turned wry. "You made me forget about my rules and every other precaution that I'm used to taking."

"Fiona, really, this is ridiculous," he began.

"I'm not sure I follow that line of logic," she said sharply, taking back the control she'd lost to him twice this evening, "but let me just say one thing to you—again. I don't sleep around, and I certainly don't sleep around with men who are also sleeping around. It would have been fun, it would have been nice…but as long as you have Rachel Backley—or whatever her name is—on the short list, then I'm removing myself from it."

"I told you, Fiona, Rachel is just a friend," he said, his

words taut and flat. He reached to slide an open hand down her bare arm.

She stepped away before he could touch her. Her insides, which had been bubbling with fullness all evening, suddenly felt starved. "But you don't deny sleeping with her. You have. And you're still connected. And that's all I need to know."

She picked up her heavy leather bag, and miraculously found the mass of keys immediately in its depths. "Thank you for a wonderful evening, and for getting yourself beat up for me. I really do appreciate it...and, truly, you are one incredible kisser." And just to make sure she had the last word, the last moment in her corner, she pulled his face to hers for a short, thorough kiss. "Good-bye, Gideon. It's been real."

EIGHT

DAMMIT.

How could he have known that the old bastard had installed an alarm at the worthless shop?

He leaned against a nearby building, resting his forehead against the harsh brick. That had been close—too close. If she or Nath had seen him…it'd be all over.

He looked around to be certain no one had followed—but no one had. He'd slammed Nath into the wall hard enough to stop him in his tracks, and that had given him the chance to get away.

He *had* to find that journal and those bank statements. Desperation crawled up his spine, and he ruthlessly shoved it back.

Not for the first time, he raised his face to the heavens and cursed the old man…then gave a harsh laugh when he realized if there *was* a place to go after this life, he had gone down instead of up.

Bastard. Nevio must have known what he was doing, leaving that diary to chance. He must have known how it would make him crazy, wanting to get his hands on that money and fearing those secrets would be made known. The old bastard had hated him anyway—and leaving him a nice chunk of something in his will was just a slap in the face when he knew that the important things—the journal, the statements—were nowhere to be found. He'd know how crazy it would make him.

But, dammit…if they were anywhere, the papers had to be hidden in that antiques store.

Then he finally understood.

That was why the old bastard hadn't left the shop to a family member.

It was crazy, but he couldn't get Fiona out of his mind. Maybe it was the way she'd said, "You're an incredible kisser," and then laid one of her own mind-boggling kisses on him…and then breezed out the door without a glance.

Gideon pulled his gaze from the window back to his laptop. Somehow, work didn't seem so necessary any longer. He had other things on his mind…at least, one other thing.

He gave himself a sharp, mental shake. Thoughts like that—distractions and obsessions—and diversion from good, hard work were what had ruined his father. Chasing pipe dreams and setting aside practical pursuits had screwed him up—diverted him into drugs and deals and a lifetime in jail.

It had ruined his mother's life as well.

God, he missed her.

Gideon firmed his lips and sternly returned to his work, poising his fingers on the smooth, concave keys of the laptop.

Men like his father were poison for any woman, and he knew he had the same tendencies his old man had. Good thing he'd basically been raised by his grandfather —the old slave-driver. The old man, who'd actually begun to soften since meeting Iva, had never had time for unimportant things—like self-expression or daydreams. That was just as well. Gideon's father had allowed self-expression to rule his life and daydreams to ruin it.

Gideon was a good attorney—an excellent one—he reminded himself again, and he was not about to allow himself to be swayed from what was really important.

Stability. Predictability. Nose-to-grindstone. Professionalism. Integrity.

Besides, allowing a woman to dictate to him who he could or couldn't see was not going to happen in this lifetime. He didn't need that from Fiona Murphy, or anyone. It was her loss, after all.

A week after the open house, Fiona and Carl were just closing up the shop. It was late Monday evening, and it had been a slow day—but an appreciated reprieve from a surprisingly brisk weekend.

"I'm glad we had a bit of a break today," Fiona commented, leaning against the heavy walnut secretary that held the three lamps. Since Carl had come on board, she'd become ambivalent about that piece of furniture, and the weird lamp as well. Once he told her that the desk was pretty worthless—except for the fact that it was made of walnut—she lost her sense of awe toward it. They'd moved it out from the small alcove where it had been nestled under the staircase, and now it sat off to one side in the main part of the shop.

There had been no more unexplained lights, no more cool breezes. Everything seemed completely normal.

Carl nodded in response to her comment. "Yes, it was nice to spend time pricing some of that inventory in the back and upstairs. Listen, Fiona, do you mind if I take off now? My headache is raging, and all I want to do is lie down and take some aspirin. I don't mean to leave you in the lurch or anything, but do you mind if I go?"

"No, not at all," Fiona said breezily, although a wave of panic washed over her. She quashed it firmly. What was wrong with her?

She couldn't avoid being alone in her own shop forever, for pity's sake.

"Go on home and take care of yourself," she said breezily, in case anyone—or anything—was around to hear.

He looked at her strangely. "Are you all right? Is something wrong?"

"No, no." Her cheeks heated. "Please, go on home. I'll see you tomorrow."

As Carl left, Fiona realized that she *had*, in fact, been alone in her shop since he'd started working for her. Not for long, and not at night as she was now, but she had been alone. That made her feel better, and after Carl left, she turned on Janis Joplin and sang about Bobby McGee as she cleaned up for the night.

Fiona was sweeping along the back of the hall when she looked down in the place where that large walnut secretary had been sitting and noticed something yellow on the floor. When the broom didn't pick it up, she crouched to see what it was.

Suddenly, a breeze—icy cold, sudden and cutting—

zinged across her cheek and over the nape of her neck. The air moved so sharply it buffeted her hair.

Fiona swallowed hard, freezing in an awkward crouch. Her heart thudded nauseatingly as her stomach twisted, turning into a big, tight knot.

Then she smelled something, and a cold sweat broke out over her torso. *Roses.* Strong and sweet—it was definitely roses.

She breathed slowly, waiting.

Nothing happened. The scent of roses faded slightly, but the air was still cool, still stirred up.

Silence.

After a long moment when nothing more happened, she started to pull to her feet and noticed the yellow object again. Now she was close enough to see that it was a feather—dusty, old and mangled, but a feather nevertheless. It looked as though it was stuck under the wall. Fiona tried to pull it free, but it wouldn't come.

"What's the deal?" she asked, inexplicably frustrated. "It's just a feath—"

A sudden moaning breeze whistled through the shop, and one of the crystal chandeliers began to vibrate. The tinkling, rocking of the ice-like obelisks was at first gentle...then became more insistent, almost as though someone was violently shaking its suspension chain.

Fiona looked up, her stomach wringing inside her. The fringe on one of the lamps ruffled with the gasp of air, and she closed her eyes, cold seeping through her numb body as the chandelier jumped and clinked with more urgency.

What is it?

Maybe it's not just a feather...

Her hands icy and her skin clammy, Fiona looked at the feather again and saw there was a narrow space between the wall and the floor. Somehow, through the panic that trundled through her, it registered in her frozen mind that the wall was more uneven than the rest of the shop, and it looked different. She stared at the wall, wondering....

"Is there something behind there?" She spoke aloud to be certain she was heard. "Are you trying to tell me there's something behind here?"

The wind roared louder, like a small cyclone circling above her and she stifled a small moan, covering her head as glass clinked and shades rattled. The entire room seemed to vibrate with rage and fear, and she was just about to try and make a run for it—to escape—when the wind stopped.

The chandelier quieted.

All was still.

"So," she said softly, hugging her knees close to her chest and trying to keep her voice steady. "Just to be clear...no need to get loud again, all right? Just...if you're trying to tell me there's something behind the wall, could you just—"

The Lamp blinked on.

Her words caught in her throat, and Fiona swallowed hard, tensing. But the Lamp went off again, and the room —the entire shop—was silent and still.

Except for the remnant of roses on the air.

Even the temperature had changed, warming slightly.

"All right, then. Message received." Fiona looked around, and when all remained silent, she rapped firmly on the wall.

It *sounded* hollow. She thought.

She sat back on her haunches and looked up—not yet brave enough to try and stand. Her heart rate had slowed, but her stomach still felt as though it was on a roller coaster. Her gaze followed the line of the wall, and she realized for the first time that the partition could have been added to enclose the area under the stair-case…that same staircase that felt so cold and forbidding on her first day in the shop. It couldn't be some sort of closet, for there was no door—nor was there any other way to access the area in the shop.

"What was he trying to hide?" She tried that idea aloud to see if there would be any response from what-ever it was that made the cool breeze come.

Out of the corner of her eye, Fiona caught a move-ment behind her, and, stifling a shriek, she twisted around.

Gretchen landed softly on the floor next to her and looked at her with golden-brown eyes that were very knowing. She meowed, then rubbed her head along Fiona's arm.

Swallowing the heart that had leapt into her throat at the cat's sudden appearance, Fiona stared down at the introverted feline.

This was the first time the creature had made an over-ture toward her—usually, Gretchen stayed far out of everyone's way. Her favorite perch was on the top of the stair railing that led to the small, dusty loft above. There she sat most days, her ink-black tail dangling, its end flicking as though disgruntled with the world.

"You like that idea, do you?" Fiona asked, reaching slowly to scratch Gretchen's soft head. She felt more relaxed now—the cat was not reacting as though there was any sort of supernatural presence.

But she couldn't deny that there was *something* going on in this shop.

She gingerly pulled to her feet, ready to duck if something rushed toward her again, and walked, half-stooped, down the hall to the back room of the shop. Perhaps there was some tool she could use to get through the wall.

But in the back, Fiona only found a broom and a toolbox with hammers, screwdrivers, and wrenches much too small to be of any use.

She spoke to the room at large, just to let whatever it was know she would follow through on this odd situation.

"Tomorrow I'll bring a crowbar or something and get Carl to help me pry that plywood away," she said, hastily reaching for her keys and purse as she sidled toward the back door, just in case the entity was of an impatient nature. "And I'll see what it is old Valente had to hide."

Fiona had no help from Carl the next day—for he'd called, explaining that he had the unexpected chance to meet with an historian from Williamsburg who was visiting the Henry Ford Museum across the state about a topic in his dissertation. Her head began to swim when he went on to describe the details—something to do with the way the floorboards in Colonial homes were laid compared to those in England—and Fiona cut him off and told him not to worry about it.

But much as she wanted to, she wouldn't wait for his return. Despite her nervousness, she was dying to know what was behind that wall…and aside from that, she felt as if she'd made a promise to whoever or whatever was in the shop.

Fiona locked the front door of the store so that any

arriving customer wouldn't surprise her, then she hurried back to the little alcove under the stairs.

Hefting the crowbar, she glanced around to see Gretchen watching her avidly from a step halfway down the stairs. Her amber eyes seemed to glow with anticipation, rather than appearing sleepy or miffed as they usually did.

"Well, I hope I'm not about to make a fool out of myself over nothing," Fiona murmured, shoving one end of the crowbar under the bottom of the wall.

She heaved and immediately felt the flimsy wood give. She heaved again and it cracked, splintering along near the floor. She found the seam between two thin pieces of plywood and shoved the crowbar between them. They came apart easily, splitting along under the thick paint job that hid the woodwork.

By the time she pulled a good chunk of plywood away, a dark hole yawned behind it and Fiona felt vindicated. There was some kind of room or storage area behind there, under the stairs, and obviously it contained something with a yellow feather.

Perhaps it was some old clothing—hats or costumes —and she might be able to sell it to a vintage clothing store. Or—she wrinkled her nose against the dust as much as from the thought—the feather could be attached to some victim of a taxidermist.

A rattling at the front door drew her attention from her task, and Fiona whirled to look toward the front. Sighing, she pushed a spiral of hair out of her face, tucking it back into the loose twist at the back of her head, and let the crowbar fall onto the floor. Dusting her hands over the jeans she'd chosen to wear today, she hurried to greet the customer at the locked door.

By the time she got to the front, though, no one was

there, and she tsked in annoyance at the unnecessary interruption—and the potential loss of a customer.

She started back toward her project, pausing at the desk to grab a flashlight, and felt her stomach tingling. She couldn't help but remember those Nancy Drew books she'd read growing up.

The titian-haired sleuth peered into the cavernous darkness, her flashlight beam glancing off the walls. The secret had to be there—the last clue to the Mystery of the Antique Light! Nancy's pulse quickened when the flashlight illuminated a metal chest in the far corner....

Fiona smirked to herself as she thrust first the flashlight into the hole, followed by her head.

Then she screamed.

NINE

"MR. VAN DER BLOEST, the contract can be revised," Gideon repeated for the fourth time in fifteen minutes. He was able to keep his voice smooth, but the back of his jaw ached. "It's not an unusual circumstance at all. It—"

A light tap on his door interrupted him, and, with an apologetic glance at the fussy, skinny man with him, he called, "Yes?"

Claire cracked the door and poked her silvery blond head in. "I'm sorry to interrupt, but Ms. Murphy is here. She says she needs to see you as soon as possible."

Gideon felt his heart lighten, and he almost smiled. But, then, remembering himself, he kept his face placid. He wasn't surprised that she'd come crawling back... only that it had taken her a week to do so.

"We don't have an appointment, do we, Claire? If not, then I'm afraid she'll have to wait until I'm finished with Mr. van der Bloest—or come back at another time." It wouldn't do to give her the impression that she had the ability to get him to drop everything to see her—even though that was precisely what he most wanted to do.

Did he imagine it, or did Claire—his ultra-professional, poker-faced assistant—give him a nasty look? "Mr. Nath, she appears rather distressed...."

"She always looks that way." Gideon waved it off with a casual gesture, but he felt a prickle of concern. He expected Claire to take that as a dismissal and to handle Fiona—as she did all of his other situations, but she did not.

"Mr. Nath, I apologize for belaboring this," she cast a smile at the fidgeting Mr. van der Bloest, "but Ms. Murphy expressed her need to see you immediately... and if you weren't available, she requested that I see her in to Mr. Nath, Senior." The woman looked as though she'd actually tossed a trump card onto the table, a slight smugness playing about her face.

Gideon caught himself before he uttered the outraged exclamation that came to his lips. "I see."

Apparently she wasn't there to see him on a personal note—unless she was using his grandfather as a way to get to him. No, Gideon dismissed that thought immediately, Fiona was completely guileless. She wouldn't do that.

Now concern washed over him, and he stood behind his desk. "Er—well, Claire, I—"

"I can certainly see to Mr. van der Bloest's last minute items," she stepped in smoothly. "I believe your meeting was almost over anyway." She turned the full force of her attractive smile at the man, and Gideon saw the fussiness drain from his countenance to be replaced by a dazed, hungry look.

He nearly snorted. God help him if he ever got that look on his face in the presence of a woman.

"Yes. Please, if that's all right with you, Mr. van der Bloest?"

"What? Oh, yes, of course," he stammered.

Claire disappeared out the door, and moments later returned with Fiona. Both men rose from their seats—van der Bloest, whose jaw nearly dropped to the floor at the sight of both women in close proximity, and Gideon, who felt his whole body tighten when he saw how damn good she looked in jeans and a vintage Nirvana t-shirt.

It was skin-tight.

Then he saw her face and knew something was terribly wrong. When he turned to release his client from their meeting, and saw the man's eyes fastened on the very well-defined breasts under the blue-gray shirt, Gideon could do nothing but pity the man.

"Thank you, Claire," he said to his assistant, and reminded himself to give her another raise.

As soon as he shut the door behind them, he crossed over to Fiona, who'd begun to pace around the room. "What is it? What's wrong?"

Her face was white, and lines of worry etched around eyes that seemed dazed and lost.

"There's a body in the shop." Her voice came out rough and uneven, and her hand shook as she pushed a thick curl out of her face.

"What?" He caught her on one of her paces, taking her gently by the arms. "A body? Someone is dead? Someone broke in—"

"She's definitely dead," she said, shuddering. "All that's left of her is a skeleton." She took a deep breath and pressed her hand over her mouth.

"Why don't you sit down." He propelled her into a chair, then turned to his desk and jammed a finger into the intercom. "Helene, please, I need some—uh—sparkling water?" he glanced at Fiona to be sure, and she nodded absently. "Sparkling water, and…why don't you bring a small brandy too."

"I found a skeleton under the stairs—where that big desk used to sit," she explained rapidly, as though it was a relief to get the words out. "It was boarded up under there—and when I pulled the wood away and looked in there, I saw a skeleton on the floor."

"How—this is stupid that I'm asking this, but how do you know it's a woman?"

"Her clothes are still on her." Fiona shuddered once, hard. Then she seemed to lose the rest of her control and suddenly she was out of the chair and into his arms all at once. "I didn't know what to do or who to call…so I came here."

"You…drove all the way here from Wicks Hollow?" he said. Something inside him gave a little pittypat.

She came to me.

He smelled her hair and held her close, his mind working rapidly even as his body leapt and sizzled at the feeling of her against him. *Feels so right.* "Did you call Captain Longbow? What about Carl? Does he know?"

She shook her head against his shoulder, her curls tickling his chin. "No," her voice was muffled. "I—I just got in the car and drove here."

"All right, then. Let me wrap up a few things here and I'll drive you back down. Then I can be there when you call the police."

White bones glowed in the dim light, easily visible in the small closetlike room.

Gideon didn't consider himself a squeamish person, but the sight of the skeleton, still clothed, collapsed against the wall, sent an uncomfortable ripple through his middle.

Her skull tilted back, empty sockets and gapping mouth yawning at the ceiling. One of her knees was somehow still propped upright and the other had fallen to the side, stretching her skirt like a canopy between them. Judging from the style of her dress, she appeared to have been there since the mid-fifties. A hat lay fallen to one side and its decoration of pale yellow feathers matched the trim on some other type of garment sitting in a crumpled heap next to it.

Gideon jumped slightly when something touched him from behind, but it was Fiona, coming to stand next to him at the gaping hole in the wall.

"Did you talk to the police?"

"Yes. Captain Longbow is on his way. I asked them not to use their sirens—it's going to be bad enough having a cop parked in front of my shop so soon after my reopening."

Fiona was calmer than she'd been when she first came to his office. Still, there was grief and shock in her eyes.

He started to reach for her, but she stepped away, putting distance between them. "Gideon." Her voice was a soft warning, and she shook her head slightly.

A pang shot through his belly. He didn't want her pulling away from him, keeping her distance, banning him from her life. The realization came quickly—its force a shock that actually made his eyes widen.

He wanted her, physically, sexually, of course…but her energy and casual personality intrigued him against his will, bringing an air of the unexpected into his staid world.

He realized that, in spite of himself, he enjoyed that about her.

And he wanted to *know* her.

That conclusion both lightened the regret that had clouded his life for the last week, and scared the hell out of him. He'd been playing the game of hard to get, carrying the need to be in control like a shield in front of him...but in that moment of clarity, he realized he couldn't do that with Fiona.

She was too open, too honest...and crazy though it was, she had begun to insinuate herself into his mind. He couldn't shake her loose.

That simple warning—the sound of her speaking his name—made something click inside him. He realized how foolish it would be to hold onto a non-relationship with Rachel just so that it didn't appear he was capitulating to Fiona's demands...and in the process, lose the opportunity to be with her.

To get to know her.

Just then, a knock at the front door—which still displayed the Closed sign—drew his attention.

He followed Fiona to the door, unable to help admiring the back view of her jeans.

"Captain Longbow. Thank you for coming."

"This is Officer Helga van Hest," the police chief said, introducing his companion. "She worked a few homicide cases in Detroit before moving back home to Wicks Hollow."

A young woman in her late twenties, Helga was tall and toned, and wore a uniform that was pressed and creased and starched to within an inch of its life. Her honey-streaked blond hair was pinned back in a no-nonsense bun at the nape of her neck, and the smattering of freckles over her cheeks and nose did nothing to detract from the professionalism that exuded from her.

"Van Hest?" Fiona asked, shaking the woman's hand. "Any relation to Orbra?"

"My grandmother," replied Helga with a smile, then gestured to the yawning opening of the hidden room. "Because it's a homicide, the sheriff will be here too, and we've got a forensics team on its way. We're going to be here a while."

"I understand," Fiona said. "Though there's not much left to her but bones."

She showed them the hidden alcove, and Longbow and Gideon pried the rest of the boards away from the space under the stairs. Helga took photographs of the bones, and she and the captain searched the small area to be certain there weren't any other items in there.

"Pretty obvious cause of death," Longbow said, kneeling next to the skeleton.

"Massive head wound," Helga said, crouching next to him. "Blow to the back of the head."

Gideon felt Fiona give a little shudder, but she, too, looked down when Longbow gently tipped the skull forward—which clearly showed the injury at the back.

"The question will be accidental or murder," Helga said, pulling to her feet. "And that will be up to forensics to determine." She smoothed back her hair, which hadn't moved that Gideon could see, and said, "You don't have to stay here any longer than you want to, Ms. Murphy. We have everything we need from you, and to be honest, you look wiped."

"Fiona," she said. "Thank you. I'll stay a little longer, then I'll leave you to your work."

Helga nodded. "Whenever you like, you're free to

leave. We'll have you make a formal report tomorrow, once we have everything finished here."

But Fiona stayed until nearly seven o'clock in the evening—until all of the police and detective personnel had filed out.

She was surprised to find that Gideon was still there. He'd been beside her all along, of course, fielding questions, helping Longbow and Helga, and keeping the peace in his own direct, structured way, and it felt natural for him to be there…but when the activity finally settled down hours later, Fiona realized that she should be surprised that he'd stayed.

"You're so busy," she said, suddenly feeling awkward now that they were alone in the store. "I can't believe you're still here."

"I wouldn't have left you to handle such a thing on your own." He looked at her, and she felt the weight of desire in his gaze, warming her, but she also saw something softer there. Concern, and tenderness…not merely attraction or desire.

"Thank you, Gideon. I can't imagine what sort of havoc being here today wreaked on your schedule."

The truth was, when she found the skeleton, she'd had one coherent thought: get to Gideon.

In that instant, she'd forgotten her need to stay away from him, ignoring her resolve that, as attracted to him as she was, she couldn't give in and share him with another woman. When she looked up at him now, and her attention rested on the planes of his face, gliding over the firm, manly chin and to his mouth, she felt that resolve falter.

"Let's grab a bite to eat," he suggested in a voice unsteady with some emotion. "Unless all this ruined your appetite."

"Yes. That would be great." Fiona seized on an opportunity to move past the heavy moment.

His car, so different from her tiny yellow Beetle, had butter soft leather seats that embraced her in comfort. It was a sleek black Mercedes, and it had been parked quite imperfectly in a slot in the back of the shop. She hadn't noticed before, but now she couldn't resist the opportunity to comment—after all, the mood had to lighten up soon or she was going to go mad at the thought: *a skeleton in her closet!?*—so she teased, "Nice parking job, Hollis Gideon."

He paused in buckling his seatbelt and looked up at her from under a thick shock of hair. "I thought I told you not to call me Hollis," he said dryly. "But why am I not surprised you still do?"

She grinned at him. "You shouldn't be. I'm sassy that way."

He looked at her and for a moment their eyes locked, and time seemed to freeze. "You certainly are," he murmured.

Then, abruptly he turned away and finished buckling his seatbelt. "So…since your car is still near my office, we should probably head back in the general direction of Grand Rapids."

"Right." She'd forgotten that salient point; he'd insisted on driving her back to Wicks Hollow. "What do you have in mind?"

"I could cook," he replied casually. "Or we could go out somewhere."

"What? This sounds suspiciously like a date," she replied with an arched brow. And then she added, "You cook?"

"Yes, well, I usually wait at least a week after finding

a skeleton in her closet before I ask a woman out, but I decided to make an exception in your case."

Fiona stared at him. "Did you—just make a joke? You?"

Gideon frowned, tilting his head as though contemplating a deep thought. "Yes, I guess I did. Sorry about that. Now," he turned to fit the key into the ignition, "what's your preference? Eating in or eating out?"

"Depends what you're cooking," she replied, still staring at him.

The decision was made. "My house." He started the car with a low purr and the Mercedes slid onto the street.

Suddenly, Fiona panicked, picturing them at his house, enjoying an intimate meal, picking up where they'd left off…. "Gideon, I don't think—"

He glanced at her, his face inscrutable as the streetlights flickered over his features. "You don't have anything to worry about, Fiona. I'm not planning to jump your bones or any—ouch!" He directed a definite glare on her and rubbed the arm where she'd smacked him.

"That was two too many jokes in as many minutes," she said, giggling. "I don't even know who you are anymore, Hollis Gideon."

"All right, all right, I'll stop. I probably used up my quota of jokes for the week anyway." And then his frown turned into that devastating smile of his. He grinned at her and Fiona nearly swooned right there. She was saved from making a fool out of herself when he floored the car, zooming along the entrance ramp and onto the highway.

She was still slightly unsettled from the effect of his sensual mouth curving in such an unfamiliar manner when they pulled into his garage and he stepped around to help her out of the car. She slipped past him, afraid to let him touch her even in the most innocent of ways.

This was going to be a tortuous meal.

Gideon waited until she was sitting on a bar stool at the counter in his kitchen before telling her.

"Wine?" he asked, pulling two balloon glasses down from a cupboard and setting them on the counter between them.

"Sure."

He could tell she was nervous—like a cat ready to spring—and he was pretty certain it was only partially due to the heap of bones in her shop. He forced himself to be nonchalant as he poured the smoky garnet wine into the glasses. He handed her one rounded goblet and raised his own in a slight toast.

"To skeletons…and to us. We're going to be magnificent." He caught and held her eyes firmly as he sipped the rich Cabernet, looking at her from over the rim of his glass so that she would be in no doubt of what he meant.

Fiona took a drink and set her glass down quickly. "Gideon," she began, her voice surprisingly firm for the consternation she must have felt. "You can't seduce me. I won't let you."

"No, Fiona…I'm going to let you seduce *me*. But first…."

He paused, reaching to cover her sexy, parted, angry mouth with two fingers. Her lips were plump and warm, and he felt their faint moisture as he pressed lightly against them.

"Let me tell you one thing: there is nothing between Rachel and me. What there was, was convenient, occasional sex when we both wanted it, and an agreement to act as each other's escort at certain functions. That's it, that's all it ever has been, that's all I ever wanted, and now it's *over*. It's *been* over, except for the escorting part."

"Oh." Fiona settled back onto the counter stool from where she'd half risen in irritation and just looked at him. She took another sip of wine, narrowing her eyes as she glowered over the rim. "And what makes you think I'm going to believe *that* convenient story?"

He settled on his elbows across the counter from her, and, leaning toward her, stared into her eyes. "Because you want to. And…because I don't lie." The words came from deep inside him, laced with some emotion he wasn't entirely comfortable with. But he knew it was vital that she believe him.

She looked back at him, her eyes clear and steady, and he felt prickles of awareness travel up his spine. The situation couldn't be more innocent, for a whole expanse of counter yawned between them, but tension zinged through the air as they gazed at each other.

Finally, she spoke. "Let me see your hand." Resting her own palm on the counter, she opened her fingers to take his.

He obligingly offered his hand, and the prickles turned into a surge of heat when she began to examine the lines on his palm with her delicate, beringed fingers: tracing, smoothing over them with the pads of her fingers as she'd done in the restaurant. What did she think she'd see there? Whether he was telling the truth?

At last, she released his hand and returned hers to clasp the wineglass. She caught his gaze with her own, and he saw that her lids had dropped slightly, giving her a sensual, come hither look that set his blood racing to a particular, throbbing location. She smiled very slowly. "All right."

He started to come around from his side of the counter, wanting only to yank her into his arms and dispose of that horrible t-shirt...among other various items of clothing.

"When are you going to show me your art?"

Her words, low and warm, stopped him cold three feet away. "What?" He stared at her, visions of having her sprawled on the stone counter scattering with the rest of his thoughts.

"You're an artist, Gideon. I'd like to see your work. While you make us something to eat." Her face was the picture of innocent interest, but he saw the way the corners of her mouth curled up in a smug smile.

"How...never mind." He stared at her, fighting within himself the fear of exposing that part of him to someone he didn't know well, but, who, it seemed, knew him even better than he could have imagined. He had no choice. "They're in the den—my most recent ones. In the big drawer in the desk."

She slid off the stool, brushing past him, sauntering out of the room as though she hadn't just escaped being laid on his countertop. He watched her go, knowing he'd just lost the upper hand in this tête-à-tête...and wondering what she would do next to catch him off guard.

Then his stomach squeezed as he realized she would be looking at his work. He knew the drawings weren't bad...but would she think they were good? Gideon took a healthy drink of wine and forced himself to open the refrigerator. Better to keep his mind occupied with tasks other than Fiona Murphy's reaction to his most personal items.

He'd rubbed two filets with garlic and cracked peppercorns when she wandered back into the kitchen. "Something smells good," she said casually, and he heard her slide onto the stool behind him.

Gideon forced himself to remain focused on preparing the steaks, refusing to turn to face her for fear he'd see disinterest, or even antipathy, for his work. A rejection of his creativity would also be a rejection of himself. "How do you like your steak?" he asked as he turned.

"Steak? Oh."

He looked over to see that she was biting her lower lip. "Oh?" he repeated, standing there with two beautiful filets mignon on a plate—one-inch-thick, perfect dark pink steaks that would just round out that Cab he'd opened.

"I'm vegetarian," she confessed, her eyes wide and apprehensive. "But I—"

Gideon, who considered himself the most patient of men, would have thrown up his hands in defeat if he hadn't been holding the steaks. Perhaps he should just give up on this—on trying to connect with a palm reading, esoteric, disorganized New-Ager who didn't know how to enjoy a good steak. How the hell did he think they could ever get over their differences enough to find their way to bed?

"How about some pasta, then?" he replied, eyeing the rich, aromatic steaks with regret. This was definitely not going as planned.

"Pasta is fine, but I...oh, Gideon, I'm sorry," she wailed in frustration, "the truth is, I have a real weakness for filet...I can't resist it...even though I haven't had red meat regularly for years...or, well, at least since last New Year's...."

He stared at her, more baffled than ever. She was a vegetarian with a weakness for filet mignon? Did that mean she would eat the steak...or not? He was almost afraid to ask.

Fiona rested her head in her folded arms, wondering why she couldn't stop babbling such nonsense. She was making a complete idiot out of herself. "I'd love to eat the steak," she managed to say, her voice muffled. "Medium."

She was afraid to look up and see the incredulous expression that must be plastered on his face. She'd been as nervous as a cat since arriving at his home...and that tension had just about set her heart to choking her when he made his blithe announcement that there was nothing between him and Rachel. It had been all she could do to seize the opportunity to get away from him—from the chemistry that sizzled between them, from those hungry eyes that did not rest from taking her measure—and escape into the den.

And then when she saw his drawings, Fiona had been moved...and more unnerved than ever. The monochrome sketches were bold and expressive, almost alive.

And she'd recognized herself in two of them. Yes, she'd recognized herself—but as he saw her, and that made her stomach flutter even more. How could she possibly be—live up to—*match?*—that siren-like, sensual woman he'd drawn, with hooded, bedroom eyes and wild, erotic hair?

When she raised her head at last, her cheeks heavy and warm from being huddled in her arms, she first saw the heavy chopping board in front of her on the counter. As she watched silently, unwilling to speak, Gideon sharpened a serious looking knife and began to chop tomatoes and cucumbers into bite sized cubes.

"I love your drawings."

The rhythm of his knife slowed, then sped up. He didn't speak, and didn't look at her—and it confirmed her suspicion that the artwork meant much more to him than he'd readily admit.

"They're full of emotion—simple emotion. Raw. I love that with only a few strokes, you can make a picture say something."

"Thanks." His response, brief, short, tried to be nonchalant, but it failed. She heard the underlying notes of relief and delight and smiled inside herself. Sensitivity was a good thing in a man. Especially one who informed her that she was going to seduce him.

She became quiet again, watching him. As always, she was fascinated by his hands, and admired the long, tanned fingers sprinkled with fine black hairs. She watched the tendons shift on the back of them, giving texture and life to his hands, and admired the solidness of his angular wrists.

"Have you ever thought about exhibiting?" Fiona sensed that she'd inched her way out onto a limb, but if she was going to make love to the man...well, she felt she had the right to get to know him.

At that, Gideon snapped up his head to look at her. "Exhibit? My work?" The stark horror in his eyes threw her for a loop. "I would never even consider that."

"Why in the world not? They're definitely good enough. With some nice matting and frames, you could easily sell them."

"Absolutely not. I'm an attorney, not an artist."

Fiona arched her brows. Keeping her voice gentle, for she realized that this was some kind of red-hot button for him, she reminded him, "They're not mutually-exclusive."

"To me they are." His mouth drew up firmly, and Fiona decided it would be wise to stop there. She could pursue the issue later.

She wanted to end with one last comment though. "I think they're beautiful, and if you ever wanted to gift me with one of them, I would be very flattered."

"How did you know about my work?"

She smiled, resisting the urge to reach across the counter and touch his hands. "The lines on your palms told me you had artistic abilities—but since they were fainter on your left, dominant, hand, I suspected that you'd pushed the urge to create aside, in favor of more structured pursuits."

Her guess had paid off not only by being accurate, but also by catching him off guard and giving Fiona a chance to catch her breath—away from him, in the den.

She'd come back into the kitchen, knowing she was going to have to play this cool, or she'd be lost in no time —succumbing to the strong attraction she knew sizzled between them, and very likely losing her own self control.

Being out of control was not something she was willing to risk.

TEN

"DO YOU THINK SHE WAS MURDERED?"

Gideon looked up at her words and shrugged easily, his shoulders moving under the starched shirt he still wore. At least he'd removed the tie and unbuttoned the top button. "It could have been an accident—but it's possible she was murdered." He set his fork aside and raised his wineglass to take a sip.

Fiona swallowed and looked down at her plate, her stomach curling inside. She knew it wouldn't be much longer…and the anticipation was making her crazy. Here they were, settled at a smooth, mahogany table in a cozy dining nook, eating calmly and discussing the remains of a body that had been found in her store…when all she wanted to do was touch him. Everywhere.

And if the glint in his eyes, and the tic in his jaw were any indication, he was just as distracted. So why did she continue to delay, to play the game?

He can make me lose it—lose control. I have to keep the upper hand.

"I wonder if Valente put the body there, or if someone else did."

Gideon's movements were smooth as he settled back in the chair and pushed his empty plate aside. He unbuttoned his shirt cuff and rolled it back, exposing a muscular forearm. "That's the million-dollar question. Perhaps they'll find something in her clothing that will at least help identify her." He rolled up his other sleeve and watched her with hot, steady eyes.

Fiona had finished everything she was going to eat—which was to say, a very, *very* small portion of her steak and *lots* of vegetables—and she stood to begin clearing the dishes away. "I'm going to make sure I look through everything Valente left behind to see if there's any clue as to who she was."

A little shiver danced up her spine—not, for once, caused by Gideon. This was a real-life Nancy Drew mystery, and she wasn't about to sit aside and let the detectives have all the fun. When would she get another chance like this again?

The shiver turned into steaming lava when her gaze was caught by Gideon's. She hesitated, leaning over a corner of the table toward him to take his plate, then began to draw back. He reached out with deliberate slowness and grasped her wrist, tugging just enough to bring her to eye-level with him. "What's the hurry?"

She boldly leaned forward to press a light kiss to his lips, pausing longer than she'd meant to when it felt so good. Just as her eyes were sinking closed and she started to forget who she was, Fiona gathered her senses and pulled away. "Remember, you promised you weren't going to seduce me." Her voice, meant to be light and playful, came out much too breathy to be taken seriously.

"I didn't make that move," he replied casually, but she could see the rise and fall of his chest under that starched shirt and she knew he was fighting just as hard as she to remain in control of himself.

Then, abruptly, something inside her snapped. Why was she waiting? It was time.

"Come on—let's get settled in the living room," she suggested, taking his wrist. Her fingers barely fit around it, but when she tugged, he obliged and pulled to his feet.

"I thought you'd never ask," he murmured, allowing her to pull him into the living room. He would have propelled her over to the couch immediately, but she released him and paused.

"How about some music?" she asked.

Gideon forced himself to sit—because if he didn't, he'd make himself a liar and do the seducing himself—watching from the plump leather sectional.

"There's music through the TV cable," he told her, doing his best to keep from sounding impatient. "Or you can plug in to my speaker system—I've got two streaming services. Anything in particular you're wanting to hear?"

She tossed him a slow, meaningful smile. "Mood music."

Mood music. Well, that was a good sign. He raised his feet, resting them, ankles crossed, on the big square ottoman that fit in the middle of the sectional.

She scrolled through the options on his music for what seemed like forever, then finally seemed to settle on something. Then she fiddled with several buttons and knobs—and it was to his credit that he didn't say anything about her adjusting his wildly complicated speaker system. The music seeped into the room, softly at first, then just loud enough after she found the volume control.

Nirvana? The hard, rough beat of the grunge rock band pulsed into the room, Kurt Cobain's scratchy but pleasing voice driving from a speaker near Gideon.

If he hoped Fiona would have joined him on the sofa after choosing her mood music, he was bound to be disappointed and frustrated. Instead, as the music forced its way into his being—the bass-line and solid electric guitar permeating his veins in a way not unlike Fiona's presence—he watched as she moved around the room. She dimmed the lights, leaving only one corner lamp on low, and the rest turned down to a bare burn.

He began to burn, and shifted on the couch. If she was trying to drive him crazy, she was doing an excellent job of it. "Fiona," he said firmly, resting his arm along the back of the sofa.

"I'm setting the mood for your seduction," she told him—from safely across the room. "Where can I find some matches?"

Gideon almost groaned aloud, but he managed to respond, "Third drawer in the desk. What do you need matches for?"

"The candles." She glided out of the room, leaving him a moment to gather his patience.

Only Fiona would take over someone else's house to set a seduction scene, he thought wryly. It would be worth it, though, his seduction, he thought, resting his head back against the couch and closing his eyes.

The snick of a match striking sandpaper brought his eyes open, and he saw the flare of a wick being lit—she must have taken the candles off the bookcases in the den. Fiona lit three fat white pillars that smelled like vanilla (a gift from Iva) and moved them onto the low square table.

Warm, glowing light spilled onto the ottoman next to the couch, setting off the thick curls of her hair in a glowing aura.

She came to stand in front of him, and he remained lounging back against the couch, his arm still resting across the top. Closing his fingers around the leather to keep from reaching for her, Gideon looked up and felt his heart move. She looked so beautiful...earthy yet ethereal at the same time in her scuffed jeans and nimbus of coppery hair.

"Fiona...." This time, it was his voice that shifted roughly, bespeaking his need for her.

"I'm a little nervous," she confessed, reaching out with two slim white hands. "I don't think I've ever planned a seduction like this before."

"You're doing just fine," he replied, his throat dry. "But I think you should kiss me now."

She moved forward suddenly, straddling him where he sat on the couch—taking him totally by surprise as her jean-clad thighs embraced him, knees against the back of the sofa...her mouth suddenly pressing into his as her hands slid to cup the corners of his jaw.

"Christ," he groaned as he went abruptly from famine to feast—just as he had that day she fell into his arms in the closet.

Her mouth demanded from his, fitting boldly to his lips and tearing his breath away. Her weight sank into him—her hands on his shoulders, fingers sliding over the sensitive skin of his neck, and her breasts leaning into his chest. He smoothed his hands down over her back around her rear, pulling her closer, on top of him, imprinting her body onto his.

Fiona pulled away, sitting back on his thighs, her legs

bent on the sofa on either side of him, and pushed a hand through her wild hair. He was about to protest between the deep dragging breaths she'd caused when she started to slip the buttons loose from his shirt. He fought the urge to shrug out of the crisp, rough cotton on his own and enjoyed the feel of her hands on his bare skin.

The way she sucked in her breath when she touched the firm planes of his pecs told him she was as appreciative of his curves as he was of hers.

Her fingers smoothed over him, light, then heavy, then gently brushing through the hair that covered his chest. His nerves were singing, and his skin wanted to shift to meet her touch as she explored its texture.

Fiona slid the shirt off his shoulders and he leaned forward to shrug out of it, catching a faceful of thick, musky, coppery hair and the opportunity to taste her neck. She paused as his lips touched the sensitive, silky skin next to her throbbing pulse, tilting her head to one side and catching her breath in an audible sigh of pleasure.

That did it—that small little moan from her ended his restraint, and the next thing either of them knew, they were tumbling off the sofa onto the carpeted floor, lips locked together as somehow their shirts were torn off and her bra unclasped.

Gideon felt the vibration of the steady, driving rock music beneath his knees as he kissed Fiona against the big ottoman, tasting the pair of lips he couldn't seem to get enough of, kneeling next to her on the floor.

It was an anomaly—the deep, thumping bass chords, the wailing twang of electric guitar, and the scratchy, husky vocals—hard, and fast, and rough...featured in a place where the lights were low and soft and the smell of vanilla gently permeated the room, mingling with the spicy, musky scent of silky Fiona.

The juxtaposition of these two opposites inflamed him, two worlds colliding in his consciousness…and then it all became nothing but a faint awareness as he focused everything on the woman before him.

Grasping her wrists, one in each hand, he drew them up over her head, pulling her to her knees, pushing her so that she splayed on the top of the ottoman. He transferred one wrist to his left hand—holding her loosely, so she could tug free if she wanted—freeing him to slide an open palm down her arm, to her torso, and around to hold a perfect breast. He bent to kiss the tight, tempting nipple, reveling in the shudder that coursed through her under his mouth.

Gideon pulled back to look down at her—at the scene before him. His mouth felt cottony, and the beating of his heart leapt out of sync then back into rhythm, faster now, faster than he could remember feeling it before.

She looked like a magnificent goddess—sprawled back on the ottoman—torso bared and golden in the flickering candle light, long fluid arms raised over her head, held there by his taut, dark fingers. Her hair fanned over the beige suede leather furniture, cinnamon-colored spirals cast over his arm, her hands, her face, her shoulders. Her skin glistened like a honey-colored pearl under the burning lights, the faintest smattering of freckles over her shoulders and arms. She looked up at him, lips parted, moist from his own mouth, eyes dazed and half-closed.

He worshipped her—touching, kissing, licking, sucking—feeling her writhe and sigh beneath him. It would only get better, he thought, his head pounding. With a flick of his wrist, he freed her belt from its buckle and yanked her jeans open, still one-handed, still keeping her gently imprisoned there before him.

She was wet and hot and very vocal when he slipped his fingers into her. Gideon had to close his eyes at the wave of need that sliced through him, struggling to keep from losing his weakening control.

She jerked once at the sudden onslaught, then her eyes slid closed and an erotic smile curved her lips as she drew in a long, deep, solid breath, her white neck tensing with pleasure. Then, when he brought her over the edge —easily—she opened her mouth in one soft, puffy sigh, sinking her teeth into her bottom lip as she shuddered, shifting and arching against him.

Fiona was lost in a haze of sensation—trapped in a place she had no desire to escape. She opened her eyes when her wrists were released, and she looked up into Gideon's burning gaze. He stared down at her, his face immobile, jaw tight, eyes narrowed, as he worked the rest of his clothes off, slicked on a condom…then, before she even had the chance—or desire—to move, he recaptured her wrists, one in each hand, splaying them outstretched over the ottoman, and slipped inside her.

The pleasure was so intense, Fiona cried aloud, and he stopped suddenly to look down at her, his eyes focusing on her with instant clarity.

"Don't stop," she whispered, her voice thick, lifting her head to kiss him. He met her lips, quickly and savagely, then began to move firmly and steadily, then hard enough that the smack of their bodies could be heard over Cobain's raspy voice. He released her arms in order to slam her hips into him one last time, then held her there just in time, just as he found what he was looking for. What he needed.

Intense pleasure rolled through him as she gave the

soft cry of her own erotic peak, shuddering against his trembling body.

Before Fiona had begun to return to herself, Gideon slipped his arms around her, hugging her against his solid, lightly furred chest, and shifted to one side, rolling onto his back on the floor.

The vibrations of the music were more pronounced now, thumping up through him and into her body, which was, itself, still singing from pleasure. She let her weight collapse onto him, felt his arms hold her close, then the adjustment as he reached up and pulled something off the couch to cover her naked back.

His hands, fingers widespread, smoothed up to her shoulders, then down, down her spine, over her rear, and back up. She noticed his breathing slowing and his heart, against her ear, calming. The thick hair on his chest tickled her nose, but she didn't move. She couldn't. She was boneless.

"Fiona," he said in her ear a long while later. It must have been a *long* while, for Nirvana had long since ended and silence reigned but for their easy breaths. "Why did we wait so long to do that?"

"Because sex complicates things," she murmured, for the moment not caring that it was true. "Even mind-boggling stuff like that."

"Mind-boggling?" She could hear the smile in his voice. "I'm glad you thought so too."

"Are you saying that wasn't bad for a first-time seduction?"

"That's what I'm saying." He kissed the top of her head and gently moved her aside, helping her to sit up and lean against the side of the sofa. "Can I get you something?" He reached to touch her, sliding a hand along her jaw, his mouth firming as he looked at her.

"You are incredibly sexy and beautiful, Fiona. I don't want this to be a one-time thing."

She felt a tear sting in her eye. He was sincere, so heartbreakingly handsome, at that moment, and her lungs swelled to fill her chest. "It won't be." And, petrified though she was, she meant it.

ELEVEN

GIDEON PUSHED OPEN the door to Nath, Nath & Powell, feeling unusually empty-handed without his laptop and briefcase—which he'd left at the office in his haste the day before. He stepped into the reception area just as Claire appeared from the back, and Helene Montgomery, the receptionist, looked up from her desk.

"Is everything all right?" asked Helene, her eyes concerned.

Gideon frowned, pausing in his route toward the hall leading to his office, just as Gideon Senior came barreling from the back, moving much faster than his grandson had seen him move in years. "Gideon! What happened? Is everything all right? I just saw you pull into your parking place."

"Yes, everything is fine. Why do you ask?" He looked at the others—Helene, who still looked concerned, Claire, who looked extremely wide-eyed and innocent, and his grandfather, who seemed to be fighting a grin.

"It's nine-thirty—we were worried about you."

"I know what time it is," Gideon replied, suddenly feeling the weight of their stares.

"But you're over two hours late," his grandfather continued, rubbing his hands together as if pleased about something.

"Two hours late? The office opens at nine. I didn't have anything going on—what's the problem?" He began to edge toward the hall, suddenly desperate to escape to his office.

"You're always the first one here," Helene said earnestly. "Seven o'clock, sure as the sun rises, you're here. We were afraid something had happened to you!"

Gideon began to feel even more uncomfortable. "I decide to come in late one day and you automatically assume something's wrong?"

"I even tried to call you on your cell phone to see if you were all right, but all I got was voice mail," his grandfather added, watching him closely.

Gideon's neck heated. "I—uh—forgot to charge it overnight." He shook his head, stepping away from the group. That was so unlike him—he was always prepared, always thinking ahead.

"—was just getting ready to come over and check on you," Gideon Senior was saying.

Gideon jerked to look at him, suddenly immensely grateful that Fiona had hustled them both out the door so she could get to her car and drive back to Wicks Hollow before he coaxed her back to bed again.

Having his grandfather show up and finding Fiona there would only open a huge can of worms.

No, a basket of rattlesnakes would be more like it.

And was that a damn twinkle in the old man's eyes?

"Why didn't you just call me on the land line?" he

asked, his voice short and annoyed. He managed a few more steps before his grandfather replied.

"I tried, but no one answered."

The flush rose up Gideon's neck and over the back of his skull. He must have called while they were in the shower. The heat intensified as he remembered the short exchange afterward with Fiona, and he had to fight to keep from grinning like a schoolboy.

She'd stepped out of the shower, her hair a mass of sexy, wet zigzags plastered to her head and neck. A smile quirked her face when she caught his reflection in the mirror. "Somehow I pictured you as a Norelco man."

Gideon allowed a grin to curve his lips, taking care not to crinkle the skin he was shaving. "No, I've always been a blade man." He smoothed his fingers and thumb over his chin. "Much closer shave."

Fiona wrapped her towel closer around her, and stepped over to touch his chin. "Mmm. Yes, I see what you mean." Her hand slid from his chin down to the damp mat of hair on his chest, sending a renewed wave of lust through him.

He pulled her closer and her other hand came up to wrap around his neck. The thick towel slipped away, crumpling to the floor, and suddenly, they were skin to skin.

Something his grandfather was saying forced Gideon's attention back to the matter at hand.

"—skeleton in the closet."

"What? How did you know about that?"

The older man crossed his arms and leaned against the wall. "Not too difficult when it was on the six o'clock, ten o'clock, eleven o'clock, and early morning news. Not to mention all over Yahoo! and CNN.com. Weren't you watching?"

That did it. Gideon tossed a last annoyed, faintly embarrassed glare at his grandfather and stalked off to his office. He thought for sure he heard a snort of laughter just before he slammed his door.

He sat at his desk, turning to the credenza behind him to the laptop that had gone to sleep sometime yesterday. The computer sizzled and hummed as it woke up, and Gideon moved back to the stack of files on his desk that had to be attended to.

He opened the first beige file folder and began to peruse the contract, looking for anything that might be a problem for his client.

What a night.

The thought popped into his head, right in the middle of a clause about indemnification, and he smiled. Actually, it was more of a goofy grin than a smile.

The words on the page in front of him faded away as he sat there, smirking like a fool, remembering...

It was only the chime on his computer indicating he had email that pulled him back into the present.

Gideon shook his head and closed the file folder. He could look at that later. He spun in his chair to face the laptop and began to work his away through the programs to open his email.

He got through the first three messages, memories and sensations from sharing his bed with Fiona hovering in another layer of his consciousness. Then he remembered what she'd said about his drawings.

The warmth curling in his middle expanded, seeping up into his throat and heating his face—like he was a high school kid who'd just made the honor roll *and* was receiving kudos from the sexiest teacher at school.

She liked them.

She loved them.

She wanted him to sell them.

His thoughts plummeted. There was no way he was going down that path. It was certain to lead to trouble. He'd lose focus at the office, he'd spend all his time drawing, sleeping, drinking—trying to find that combination that would give him his Big Break, his Breakout—wealth and fame….

Foolish man. He let his forehead sink into his palm.

He wasn't his father…but he could be. Very easily.

There was no chance of that. He wouldn't do that to himself, or to his grandfather. He had to stay on the straight and narrow—work hard, be successful, find a woman to marry—maybe—in five years or so….

But his art.

"It has nothing to do with…Us."

He'd spoken aloud, and without meaning to, he'd capitalized them, making it official. That, at least, he had no qualms about—no qualms whatsoever.

Damn. He wanted to see her again—tonight—five-year plan or no.

What if he wanted to see her again? Soon?

Fiona dragged a hand through her hair, yanking mercilessly through the thick curls. She sat at her desk in the middle of Charmed Antiquity, examining—or, rather, trying to keep her mind on examining—some bills of sale from the open house.

She pushed away the warm, mellow feeling that crept over her when she thought about lying in bed next to Gideon, touching his smooth, damp, warm skin after making love with him. This was so very unlike her—to dwell on the memory, to think of nothing but a man.

A dull pounding on the glass of the shop's front door had Fiona's thoughts jolting back to the present—thank goodness.

She removed her reading glasses and rose from the desk to make her way toward the front of the store, mildly curious as to who would be knocking when the sign said "Closed."

Maybe it's Gideon.

She'd kept Charmed Antiquity closed today because it had taken until well after lunch for her and Carl to clear out the mess that was left behind from yesterday's investigation by the police, and also because of the news and public interest generated by the finding of the skeleton.

But now Carl had gone home, and she was finishing up some listings on eBay…when she wasn't distracted and daydreaming about Gideon.

The door rattled in its hinges; whoever was knocking was growing impatient. Then Fiona saw who was there, and she gave a short laugh.

Well, that explained the impatience and determination.

Her step hitched, but by then, Maxine Took, Juanita Acerita, and Iva Bergstrom had all seen her through the glass.

It was too late for retreat.

She sighed in acquiescence, and opened the door. "Hello ladies," she said.

"We heard about the skeleton," Maxine said, barging past Fiona, her cane gripped tightly in her fist.

"Who is it?" asked Juanita, squeezing into the shop more carefully so as not to squish the bag carrying Bruce Banner, who peeked out with his bright black eyes. "Who's the dead person?"

"Hello, Fiona," Iva said gaily, pausing to embrace her in a cloud of White Shoulders. "I could hardly believe when I heard about it!"

Fiona could only blink as the tornado of Tuesday Ladies filled the small space near the front of her crowded shop. She peeked out to make sure that was all of them—apparently Orbra and Cherry, like normal people, had other things to do.

"How about a seat?" she asked quickly, envisioning a fiercely-wielded cane or large leather bag smacking into a table and upending a vase or porcelain lamp. She started to pull up a chair, but Maxine was already charging into the depths of the shop, with Juanita and Iva in tow.

"Back here, I suppose," Maxine cried, as if going into battle. "I can see where the wall's been torn down."

Fiona followed, watching for stray cane swings and gasping quietly each time Juanita passed a fragile item with her dangling tote bag.

Miraculously, the three elderly ladies made their way to the newly revealed storage room with only one minor mishap—when Maxine's cane caught under the leg from a chest of drawers and nearly sent her flying.

But the old lady caught herself on the solid top of the dresser, and no harm was done. *Thank God*, Fiona thought, envisioning the elderly woman crashing to the floor amid shattered lamps, bulbs, and vases...

"This is where you found it?" Iva asked, taking Fiona's arm as soon as she got close enough and urging her forward. "How startling that must have been!" she exclaimed enthusiastically. "To find a skeleton hidden away for *decades*."

Fiona had the feeling Iva had been a Nancy Drew fan as well.

"Yes," she replied, and, having no choice, went on to describe in detail how she'd come to discover the gruesome find.

"And they have no idea who she is? Was, I mean?" Juanita asked. She'd set Bruce Banner's bag on the floor, easing some of Fiona's concerns about antique casualties.

"Not so far. From her clothing, she looked as if she'd lived during the fifties."

"Must have smelled *awful* in here when she was decomposing," Maxine growled. "Don't know how no one could stand it. Would have been weeks, if not longer. Depends on the humidity and the temperature, and all that, you know." Her voice was accusing, as if there was no excuse for Fiona *not* to know.

"The stench would certainly drive away customers," Iva said, slowly lowering herself to a crouch so she could examine the floor—presumably for clues. Fiona didn't have the heart to tell her that the forensics team had swept up anything that might have been important, and she and Carl had then cleaned up in their wake.

"Don't even know what the building was at the time," Maxine snapped. "Mighta been something else back then. Not an antiques shop." She spun a look at Fiona, startling her by the sharp, discerning expression in her dark eyes. "When did Valente buy the building?"

"Uh…I'm not certain. I believe someone mentioned he'd owned it since he moved from Chicago to Grand Rapids in the Fifties," she said, trying to remember who had made the comment. "That means he might or might not have owned the building when she was—uh—locked up."

Maxine's eyes glinted with interest and sass. "Needs looking into, missy. If you ain't got the time, I'll take Juanita to the library and we'll look at them old newspapers. Damned microfishers are hard to read, but at least we can blow 'em up big enough on them screens. Poor Neety can't see hardly nothing, you know, without her glasses."

"I can see enough to beat your patootie in Scrabble," Juanita, who was *not* wearing eyeglasses, retorted. "That reminds me, dear," she said, looking at Fiona. "I'm so sorry I missed your grand re-opening last week, but Maxine and I were at a Scrabble tournament in Kalamazoo. I kept my 1500 rating," she added with a sly smile at her partner in crime.

"But you lost two games," Maxine snarled. "And I only lost one."

"The rating's what matters," Juanita replied archly. "As you well know."

"Well, I—"

There was another rattling at the front window, and Fiona was relieved that, apparently, someone else had paid no attention to the sign. "Excuse me," she said, slipping away from the two bickering ladies—and at the same time, wondering how Iva could tune them out, as she appeared to have done while creeping along the edge of the wall where the skeleton had been found.

When Fiona saw a tall, half-shadowed figure at the front of the shop, her heart leapt before she could stop it. She had to plant her feet firmly on a faded wool rug to keep from rushing to the door.

Gideon.

Quelling her anticipation and pleasure that he had, indeed, wanted to see her again, even though it went against her very grain to wish for that, she walked casually to the front of the shop.

She had every intention of throwing open the door and saying, "Can't you read the sign? The shop's closed," and giving a coy smile. Then he would sweep her into his arms for the kiss he'd been waiting for all day....

It wasn't Gideon.

"Mr. Sternan?" Fiona opened the door to the investment banker and nephew of Nevio Valente, ignoring the way her heart now sank to her knees.

Of course it wasn't Gideon. And she was a fool to have her hopes riding on it being him.

"Ms. Murphy. I'm sorry to bother you—could I come in?"

As her brain processed that it wasn't Gideon but Arnold Sternan standing there outside her front door, Fiona blinked, then stepped aside for him to enter.

"Yes," she replied. "I'm guessing you heard about my little surprise, then."

"I couldn't believe it when I saw it on the news." He glanced at her, then swept his attention over the shop. "You've certainly done some nice work here, Ms. Murphy."

"Thank you." A little uncertain as to what he wanted, she merely stood and waited.

"I'm rather surprised you didn't contact me or Brad —or any of us—when you made the—er—unpleasant discovery," Sternan commented.

She nodded. "It didn't occur to me, quite frankly— but I can see why you'd be interested. The detectives took it—her, I mean—yesterday, and they're going to try and identify the body. If you haven't heard the details," she looked up at him, raising her eyebrows in question— since he'd obviously heard something, "it's a woman and she's been here about fifty or sixty years."

"I wondered about that." Sternan leaned against a table, crossing his arms. "Incidentally, how are *you* doing, Ms. Murphy? I'm sure it was quite the shock for you to find a skeleton hidden away."

"Please, call me Fiona. And I'm fine. I was a little freaked out at first, as you can imagine—but, well, she's been dead a long time."

"Yes. So, the authorities are saying she's been dead for more than fifty years? I certainly hope that they don't try and attach Uncle Nevio to this mess."

"I hardly think that a fifty-year-old skeleton in your deceased relative's shop is going to ruin your reputation." She smiled to take any sting out of the comment.

Sternan chuckled, and he appeared more pleasant than she'd ever seen him. "I suppose you're right. But it's difficult to know what will affect one's reputation and what won't—and I work with a lot of very important, very rich, and very powerful people in my line of work." His smile faded suddenly.

Fiona felt a little chill skitter over the back of her neck. Had that been some sort of warning? Or had all of this activity made her exceptionally sensitive?

"Well, nothing was found with the body; at least, nothing to identify who she was," Fiona told him.

"Er…well, then, I expect they won't be making any assumptions about how the skeleton got there. I'm just concerned my uncle's name will be dragged through the trash."

"Do you actually think your great-uncle smashed her on the head and stuffed her in a secret room for fifty years?" Fiona said, a giggle bubbling up inside her.

"Certainly not. Uncle Nevio might have been odd, but he wouldn't have hurt a fly," Sternan replied in a tone that sounded far too hearty to be real.

She looked at him with narrowed eyes as she became aware of a sudden chill brushing her cheek.

And was that the scent of roses?

The hair on the back of her neck and arms prickled. The temperature had definitely dropped.

"It was so long ago, I'm sure he didn't even own the property at the time," Fiona said, a trifle louder than necessary. "Surely he didn't."

A loud crash startled them, and she whirled. "Oh dear." An antique china shepherdess lay in smithereens on the floor, several yards away—and nowhere in the vicinity of the Tuesday Ladies, who remained huddled in the rear of the shop.

She spared a worry as to what they were discussing or planning, but then she was distracted when she realized the shattered figurine had been close to that old walnut desk with The Lamp on it. Fiona swallowed.

"How on earth did that happen?" Sternan asked in astonishment, staring at the mess.

Fiona forced a nervous laugh. "It must have been the cat—Gretchen. I wonder where she went." She made a show of stooping as if to look under the nearby tables, but she knew the cat hadn't knocked over the figurine.

But the fringe on the white milk-glass lamp was swaying slightly, as if a breeze—or something else—had passed by. Yet the door and windows were closed, and there weren't any fans to stir up the fringe.

And still, the air had cooled. Suddenly and noticeably. The tip of her nose felt icy.

"I'd best get a broom and get that cleaned up," Fiona said, hoping to take advantage of the diversion to bid her unwelcome guest goodbye. "Thank you for coming by, Mr. Sternan. I'm sure you understand, but I have to get back to work. The forensics team left quite a mess. Thanks again for stopping by." She moved toward the door and opened it, letting the cooling evening breeze sift into the store.

Left with little choice, Sternan nodded and began to walk out, but, like Colombo, paused for one last entreaty. "If you don't mind keeping me in the loop on what's going on with the body, I would appreciate it. He was my uncle, you know."

"Yes, of course I will," Fiona promised. He was a relative, after all. "Have a good night."

As soon as she closed the door behind him, Fiona returned to the scarred, oaken desk in the middle of the shop and began to yank open the heavy drawers.

It hadn't even occurred to her that Valente—that harmless old man—could have been responsible for the woman's death, if it was indeed murder, until Arnold Sternan had appeared so concerned about it. But now that the thought had struck her, she agreed with Maxine: she needed to know when Valente had bought the shop.

"If it was less than forty years ago, he's innocent," she murmured, bending almost double to look in the back of the bottom-most drawer.

"Who was that?" demanded Maxine Took.

Fiona nearly shrieked as she bolted upright. How had the old woman sneaked up on her like that? Usually, you could hear her shuffling feet and thumping cane from miles away. Not to mention her peremptory voice.

"That was Nevio Valente's nephew," Fiona replied. She looked at the elderly woman, who was frowning and staring around the shop. Iva and Juanita joined them. "You—uh—did any of you notice how chilly it got in here a few minutes ago? Was the back door open by any chance?"

"Chilly?" Maxine replied. "It was downright *cold* back there. Like being in a freezer."

"That wasn't the back door, dearie," Iva said, patting her arm with a soft hand. "That was a Ghostly Presence." The final two words were, very obviously, capitalized.

"The sudden cool breeze, the scent of roses...of course that's what it was," Juanita put in. Her eyes were wide and earnest.

Fiona stared at them. They all seemed perfectly lucid. "So you noticed the roses too," she said after a moment of resetting her brain.

"Of course, dearie. Obviously, some spirit has been disturbed," said Iva. "Probably the skeleton."

Maxine's voice was more of a screech than a comfort. "What did you—"

"Did these sorts of things happen before you stumbled upon the skeleton?" Iva spoke over her in a gentle but firm tone.

"Um...yes. A little." Fiona couldn't help but look up and around as if expecting to see some evidence of the Ghostly Presence. "There's a lamp—"

"Well, we gotta find out who it is. Who's haunting the place."

Fiona nodded. She couldn't argue with that.

"A Ghostly Presence means there's something unresolved," Iva told Fiona, patting her hand as if she was consoling her over the loss of the figurine, which, now that Fiona thought about it, was probably due to said Ghostly Presence.

"I suspect it means whoever killed that woman killed her here, and locked her up in that room to disintegrate," Maxine said, looking around. Her eyes were sharp and clear, and her voice matched them.

Fiona knew that back in the late Sixties, Maxine had earned her PhD in chemistry and worked as a chemical engineer in an industry nearly exclusively populated by white men—not unlike the women of *Hidden Figures*. In this moment, the sharp, brainy, determined woman she'd obviously been was evident as she looked at Fiona and said, "And once you figure out who'd do such a thing, you'll damned well know why there's a ghost."

"Then," Iva said, "you'll have to find a way to set things right."

"That's right," Juanita said earnestly. She'd once again taken up her bag with the beady-eyed Bruce Banner peeking out of the top.

Fiona knew better than to reach out and pet the darling pooch. Despite his sweet face, soft fur, and butterfly-like ears that were too big for his face yet fit him perfectly, she knew from experience that he was aptly named. Bruce Banner was no fun when he was angry—and an unexpected pat on the head was a sure way to turn him into a small canine version of The Hulk.

"How does one set things right?" Fiona asked.

"It depends," replied Iva, "on what's out of order. I'm sure it will all come clear."

I just hope I don't go mad before it does.

"I want to look at one more thing before we go," Iva said, gesturing to the back of the shop. "And then we're out of here."

"Knock yourself out," Fiona said, finally returning her attention to the paperwork she'd been doing before all of the interruptions. As she slid her reading glasses into place, she said, "Lock the door behind you, please."

Sometime later, she pulled off the glasses and put the last sheaf of papers aside. Bending over at the desk to stretch her back, she went on to do a few minor yoga twists in her chair, then and stood to stretch tall on her toes.

She stepped back to the desk. Fiona was just reaching

across its wide expanse for a new pen when a firm touch at the base of her exposed back sent her snapping up and around.

She shrieked in surprise, and banged her elbow on the heavy side rail of the desk as she looked up, flinging her hair away from where it'd stuck to her mouth, to see a silently-amused Gideon, arms tucked behind his back.

"What the hell are you doing here?" she sputtered, trying to swallow her heart back to where it belonged.

"My…I would have thought after last night…and this morning," he said, giving her a very slow, sensual smile, "I'd have a warmer welcome than that."

"Stop doing that!" She glowered at him, angry at herself now because the erratic, merry tripping of her heart had nothing to do with being startled.

"What? Walking up behind you?"

"Stop showing that you have a sense of humor. *And* sneaking up behind me." Fiona tried to hold it back, but the nervous giggle escaped and she succumbed to the smile while her heart did a little flip.

He moved, and suddenly a mass of pale purple tulips —at least thirty of them!—appeared just under her nose, sending their sweet scent to her senses.

Fiona couldn't help the sigh that gushed from her throat. "These are *gorgeous*." Smoothing a fingertip over one delicate flower lip, she looked up at him. "What a gorgeous color! Almost lavender. And tulips—well, it's not spring, so they're extra special. They're beautiful. Thank you."

"I thought roses—especially red ones—would be far too cliché for you." Gideon sat on the edge of the desk and reached to pull her chin toward his mouth. Holding the flowers carefully so they wouldn't get crushed, Fiona lifted her lips to his. After several moments of reacquainting themselves with each other's kiss, they broke away and pulled back to look at each other.

Fiona was unnerved as she recognized not only the intense emotion in his eyes, but also the depth of feelings that swelled in her chest when she gazed up at him.

"How did you get in here, anyway?" she asked, frowning. She would have heard him if he'd come in through the front door.

He shrugged and half-grinned, and she couldn't help but notice how his shoulders moved. And now that she knew exactly what those shoulders looked like, and how smooth and hard and broad they were, it had an even stronger effect on her than before. "Iva let me in. She and Maxine and Juanita were just leaving."

"Of course she did," she said dryly. "I meant to check that they'd locked up after them, but I got so distracted after Arnold Sternan dropped in—"

"Sternan dropped in?"

The tone in his voice had her stopping cold. "Yes." Why did he sound so…annoyed? She lifted a brow as if in challenge. "Is that a problem?"

"No. Just…curious."

Her lift of irritation eased. "He was curious about the skeleton. As one might imagine."

"Yes. But I find it interesting that he should drive all the way down here to ask about it."

She gave him a flirtatious smile. "*You* drove all the way down here."

His eyes narrowed on her. "I came down to see you. Not to nose around about a skeleton. As you very well know." Before she could stop him, he tugged her to him by the shoulders, nearly crushing the tulips between them as he covered her lips with his.

If the earlier kiss made her melt like hot wax and

want to collapse into a pile of nothing, this kiss made her nerve endings sing and singe with heat.

When she pulled away this time, she was breathing heavily, and he looked as though he'd willingly toss the cost of three dozen out-of-season tulips aside, just to get to her again. In fact, he reached for her, staring at her with some dark intensity in his eyes, but she slipped away.

Keeping the flowers between them like an aromatic, yet delicate, shield, Fiona forced her scattered thoughts into order. "Gideon, when did Valente take over this shop? When did he buy it?"

He blinked as though trying to refocus, looking at her for a moment without comprehension before frowning slightly. "I have no idea." He reached for her again, but she thrust the flowers at him.

"All right, then. There's a big vase in the back, by the sink—would you stick these in water for me? I've got to find something that shows when Valente took over here."

Aware that Gideon hadn't moved, she fought with a desk drawer containing old files she hadn't yet gone through. The ancient drawer groaned like wind through the trees as she forced it open.

"Why does it matter so much to you?" he asked, perching his very fine ass on the edge of the desk. "Even if Valente was involved, you didn't even know the man."

Barely glancing up at him, she rifled through an old, yellowed file and replied, "Because I'm a curious sort of gal. It's a mystery—and it's fascinating. I feel like Nancy Drew—you probably don't even know who she was, do you?"

"Girl detective," he retorted immediately. "Very goody two-shoes."

Fiona snickered as she thumbed through old, yellowing files. "That would be true. She never even kissed her boyfriend that I remember. And she was a red-head!"

"Foolish, foolish girl," he murmured, lifting a coil of her hair to spin it around his finger. He had, she noticed, conveniently forgotten her suggestion that he get a vase for the flowers.

"True that." She scanned an official-looking document that turned out to be nothing more than an old insurance policy. "Valente was a freaking pack-rat," she muttered, noticing the expiration date was February 19, 1963. "Sternan was all worried that the skeleton in the closet here would be damaging to his career. I'm surprised Brad hasn't shown up, worried about the same thing, to be honest."

"He probably will," Gideon said in a perturbed voice. "If nothing more, it would be an excuse to hang around you and invite you to another fundraiser, or to dinner, or—"

"Either way, I thought I'd better check and see if Valente did own the shop when the woman was murdered."

"Fiona, we don't even have a date yet for her death, let alone know whether it was foul play or not. Why don't you let the cops worry about it—"

"What a great idea! Gideon, they'd tell *you*. You could ask for some official reason, couldn't you—as my attorney or something—so they'd have to tell you what they've found out. Will you?" She looked up at him with pleading eyes—coming as close to batting her lashes as she'd ever done before—and she could almost hear her mother's disgusted groan.

"Will I what?" The calm, cool, and collected Gideon

actually seemed distracted by her fluttering eyelashes. Maybe Marilyn Monroe'd had the right idea.

"Call the police and find out what they know." She allowed her lips to part just enough that he would notice, and she was gratified when she saw his throat convulse in a hard swallow.

He looked away, down at the cluster of flowers he still held. "Fiona, it's not that easy—I'm not sure what grounds we—you'd have to have for asking. But," he held up a hand as she began to protest, "I'll try it. Okay, I'll try it—but can we just drop it for tonight?"

Beaming, she nodded, pushing her hair back behind her shoulder. "Thank you Gideon. I really appreciate it."

He smiled at her then—a slow, taunting one that sent a rush of heat through her. All at once, the distraction of playing amateur detective was not enough to ward off that heavy emotion—the emotion that was easing into need….

It was Fiona's turn to swallow and she turned away, crossing her arms in front of her. She would not melt into his embrace again. She needed some space…before he got too close and she got lost.

"Let's grab something to eat," Gideon suggested, his hands settling on her shoulders from behind.

She was fumbling for an excuse when a soft buzz vibrated near his waist. His hands left her shoulders and he pulled the sleek phone from his trousers.

"Hi." His familiar greeting told her it was someone he knew casually. There was a pause, then he flickered a look at her, then away. "Uh…well, all right. No, that's all right…I'm sure you did. Where are you?" He was quiet again for a moment, then replied, "Okay. Give me at least forty-five minutes and I'll be there. I'm…not in town."

He disconnected the call and slipped the cell back

into his pocket. "Fiona, I'm sorry—that was a friend of mine who's stranded with a broken down car and asked if I could help out. I need to take off. Can we hook up later for something to eat?"

"No thanks, Gideon," she replied, sensing that he was uncomfortable about the situation and wondered if the "friend" was a woman.

Rachel.

She felt her stomach tighten, then ease slightly. It shouldn't bother her—he'd told her they were friends and that anything beyond friendship was over. She could handle this.

After all, all she and Gideon had done was sleep together. Once. Hell, if her mother had tried to put the ball and chain on every man—or woman—she'd slept with, Claudia would be living with more lovers than Fiona could fathom.

But still…the uneasiness moved in her stomach and settled there like a bowling ball. A big, murky green one.

She'd be brave and elegant. She twisted her fingers into her skirt, hiding them in the flimsy rayon folds. "I'm kind of tired after yesterday's excitement, and I'm just going to head home—I'm staying at Ethan's here in Wicks Hollow—and try to get to bed early."

"Well, all right." He still looked like something was bothering him. She could have made a comment to relieve his concern—that she understood, that it was no problem—but, perversely, she didn't. "You're going to close up now, aren't you? I don't want to leave you here alone."

"What, do you think a skeleton might leap out and grab me?" she countered, smiling slightly. "I'll lock up if you'll just give me a minute. I don't want you to keep your friend waiting, but I appreciate you staying around."

Moments later, he bid goodnight to her at her yellow VW, leaving her with a kiss that left her breathless...and with trembling knees.

TWELVE

IT WAS PAST DARK, but lights illuminated the Wicks Hollow streets, so Fiona wasn't nervous about walking along by herself. After Gideon left, she'd pulled her car out of the secluded back alley and drove down to The Roost, a dive only a few blocks from Trib's, to grab a quick dinner.

As she sat at the bar's counter—sticky from years of spilled beer and cocktails—and ate what the place called a veggie burger (something frozen with the consistency of cardboard), she refused to let herself dwell on the image of Gideon picking up Rachel at seven o'clock at night.

Just in time for dinner.

"Oh, Gideon, I'm just starving. Maybe we should stop at a fancy-schmancy restaurant and share a bottle of very expensive wine now that we're together." She could just hear Rachel's cultured voice and low, throaty laugh.

Stop that, Fi.

The problem was, she'd met the elegant, self-assured, polished woman...so it was no hardship for Fiona's mind to conjure up all types of images and scenes—detailed and very disturbing.

Why should she trust Gideon anyway? Why should she even care?

Because I don't lie.

And his hand—that elegant, sexy, powerful one—had told her the same. He didn't lie. He was honest and filled with integrity.

Despite the meal she was picking at, her stomach felt hollow—like she hadn't eaten for days.

A short time later, as she walked the block to her car after the unsatisfying meal, Fiona realized she'd left Ethan's house key back at the shop. She'd been so determined to leave when Gideon did—blithe and uncaring that the man she'd had *ahhh*-mazing sex with was rushing off to help his friends-with-benefits-friend, that she'd neglected to grab the ring with her brother's key.

For crying out loud, Fi—you spend one night with a man and you're miserable the next time he's got to run off and do something that doesn't include you.

Well, she retorted smartly to herself, *I think it's justified since the so-called problem is* another woman.

At least he'd brought tulips for her.

She shivered—partly because of the chill night air coming in from nearby Lake Michigan, and partly at the thought of her mother's reprimand—a reprimand that had reverberated in her head since she was ten.

"Don't get attached to them, don't rely on them, don't feel for them," Claudia Murphy had told her over and over again. "They're good for a good time, but we don't need them for anything else. They'll only take advantage of you."

Not that Claudia spoke from experience. No, she'd never been the one to tell the men in her life when to come and when to go. It wasn't that her mother was promiscuous—she didn't sleep with men indiscriminately. She just didn't have much use for them other than sex, and to move heavy things around the house. In fact, Claudia was an equal-opportunity lover, as Ethan called it—sleeping with whoever caught her fancy, male or female.

Regardless, Claudia had instilled in Fiona the need to be in control in any situation with a man, and to always call the shots. But nothing her mother had ever told her prepared Fiona for the confusing feelings Gideon Nath created in her.

The problem was, as irritating as he could be, as arrogant and stuffy as he was, she liked him, liked being around him...and, horror of horrors, had begun to actually care about what happened to him.

And that was exactly why, Fiona told herself firmly as she navigated her Beetle onto Violet Way, it was good that Rachel—for who else could it have been?—had called to ask for his help. It served as a reality check for Fiona, and she was going to force herself to remember that getting involved with a man was the last thing she wanted or needed to do.

Fiona spewed a huge puff of air from her mouth and rolled her eyes heavenward. What she really should do was back off from the man for a couple days to catch her breath. There'd been too much, too soon.

Of course, it had only been one night...one glorious, crazy, incredible night. Maybe it was a fluke. Maybe—

Fiona stopped short in front of her shop door, keys dangling in her hand. There was only a faint light in the back of the store. She peered in the window, cupping her hand around it to peer closer.

Sure enough, the store was dark except for the

faintest flicker of light shining from the rear of the shop. Hadn't she turned the front lights on? After the break-in a few weeks ago, she'd always left at least three or four of them on. She really had been distracted when she walked out the back door with Gideon.

A little nervous in spite of herself, Fiona fitted the key into the lock of the door. A prickle skittered up her spine as she opened the door. Now that she had found the skeleton—*especially* now that she had found the skeleton—she slightly nervous about being in there alone, at night.

"I'll just step in and turn on a few lights," she said aloud to calm her nervousness. "Right at the front. The tall one right by the door, and the table lamp on the other side."

The chimes above tinkled faintly in the silence, seeming to echo in her ears long after they stopped. She reached for the lamp next to the door and yanked the chain. Light, welcome light, spilled into the store, casting a golden glow around her at the front door.

Fiona was just reaching for the table lamp on the other side of the entrance when she noticed a metallic glint on the floor by the desk. Frowning, forgetting her apprehension, she stepped into the body of the store and the door tinkled shut behind her.

The glint formed the shape of a circle as she drew closer, and when she stooped to pick it up, Fiona saw that it was a flashlight—its glass face reflecting the light at the front of the store. Her stomach plummeted as she realized that it had not been on the floor by the desk when she and Gideon left that evening.

Just then, something stirred behind her and she shrieked, whirling, just as pain—and then darkness crashed—down upon her.

"Thanks so much for rescuing me, Gideon," Rachel said as she slid into the leather seat. She smiled her brilliant smile, displaying perfect teeth and great self-confidence, as she clicked the seat belt buckle into place.

"No problem," he replied, steering the car out of the parking lot where Rachel's silver Lexus sat waiting for service. "I wanted to talk to you anyway."

"Good. Want to grab a bite? I'm starving." She settled back in the seat, resting her head against the headrest. "I'm so tired." Her eyes fluttered closed.

"You've been running yourself ragged lately since the awards were announced," he said automatically, then kicked himself for bringing it up. He was supposed to be her escort to the party celebrating the fact that her firm had won the prestigious, sought-after *Hottest Midwest Company of the Year* from *Fortune* magazine. She wasn't going to be too happy when he backed out of it.

"I know. I thought that I'd be so energized by the award that I'd get through these weeks like a breeze… but maybe I'm just getting old. It's starting to wear on me." She turned, opening her eyes to glance at him. "What did you need to talk with me about?"

He swallowed. This really shouldn't be that difficult. "Rachel, about the…about us. I—"

She sat upright and turned her full attention on him. "Yes?" Was there a bit of concern in her eyes? It was hard to tell when the only illumination was the rhythmic flash as they sped under streetlight after streetlight on I-96.

"I—uh…our arrangement has suited me—both of us, I hope," he glanced at her. "But I think it's time we—er—reevaluated things."

She stared at him for a moment, and he didn't have to

look at her to feel the assessment in her gaze. Then, to his shock, she smiled and gave a little laugh. "So you've found someone, have you, Gid?" Her short chuckle was laced with a bit of hardness, and he tensed, closing his fingers tighter around the soft leather steering wheel.

"Well, yes. At least, someone I'd like to…pursue… without feeling like I have other obli—uh, string—interests." Even as he said the words, corrected himself, he knew he'd blown it.

A woman didn't want to think of herself as an obligation, or a string, to any man. He clenched his teeth, waiting for the explosion. It wouldn't be tears with Rachel—no, she wasn't that type. It would be anger or— he shivered at the thought—calm, cool, female manipulation that he had absolutely no idea how to combat.

"I'm guessing that redhead at the fundraiser, right? Fiona Murphy. She just opened a little antiques shop in Wicks Hollow. Wasn't there something about a skeleton?"

Gideon swallowed back bile in his throat. This was going to be worse than he expected. "What makes you think that?" he asked casually.

She laughed again, and this time it sounded more natural. "It was pretty obvious, darling Gideon. You were practically drooling all over her right in front of everyone." —He thought he detected a little bite at the end of her words.

"Drooling?" He tamped back his irritation, knowing that he needed to keep his cool if he were to make it out of this scene with his dignity. Still, he didn't like to think he'd made a spectacle of himself in front of his colleagues.

Her laugh was beginning to grate on his tightly-strung nerves. "I think it's wonderful, Gideon. She—

even though she did look at me with a bit of a catty eye
—seemed very…engaging. But I suppose I would have
done the same thing in her shoes. Give me the catty eye,
I mean."

There was a long silence as Gideon tried to figure out
what that meant. Was she not angry? Did she not get that
he was trying to end things? Or was she refusing to
acknowledge what he thought he was making
very clear?

Or was this the manipulation he'd expected, and had
no way to identify?

"So…are you trying to tell me that our arrangement
is…defunct?" she asked lightly.

"Yes." Tension seeped from his shoulders to his neck
and the back of his head.

"All right." She sighed, frowning slightly. "I knew we
couldn't go on this way forever, but I guess I thought it
would end…differently."

"Oh." Running a hand through his hair, Gideon knew
he couldn't just leave it as it was. They'd been together—
well, sort of together—for three years, and he did care
for her. "Rachel, I hope you…I hope you're all right with
this." They'd exited from the highway and stopped at a
light at the end of the ramp, so he turned to look at her.

She nodded. "I am—I'm happy for you. I hope this is
something…good for you." She wiped her eye with a
forefinger, and Gideon felt his heart sink.

The blare of a horn behind them jerked his attention
to the front, and he saw the green light. He jabbed the
accelerator and they leapt forward. "Dammit, Rachel, I'm
sorry. I—"

"No, Gideon, it's not you. Honest. I'm sorry—I'm
just…emotional."

"What's going on?"

She rested her head back against the headrest and spoke through a definitely weepy voice. "I'm just under a lot of stress from the press related to the award and all the new business coming from it—don't get me wrong, it's great, but it's just, well…to tell the truth…I always thought it was going to be me who found someone and wanted to end it." And with that, she burst into tears.

Fiona forced her eyes open to darkness broken only by irregular shafts of light. Her head screamed with throbbing pain, just above her left temple, and the rest of her body was one big ache. And she couldn't move.

She was tied, trussed like a turkey, arms behind her back, ankles lashed together, and on her side…somewhere.

Something disgusting filled her mouth—a cloth—sopping up every bit of lubrication she might have had or mustered, and she couldn't spit it out even if her tongue could have worked, for something like tape was stuck from jawbone to jawbone.

She closed her eyes, nausea flooding her, and prayed desperately that she wouldn't have to vomit. Deep breaths, she told herself, repeating the mantra over and over, and tried to pull in soothing gulps of air, sprinkled with dust, through her nose. She didn't allow herself to think of anything else until the danger of puking was past.

When her stomach finally settled, it was some time later. In fact, she may have weaved in and out of consciousness a few more times. The ache in her head had lessened, but the pain was now centered in her shoulders and wrists from her arms being pulled back.

Fiona blinked several times while her eyes focused in the darkness. The same slashes of light fell awkwardly across the floor and over the wall, and that was when she recognized where she was.

Chills crept up her spine when she realized she was in the very spot where the skeleton had been found, and only the fact that there was a faint light reflecting into the small alcove under the stairs told her that she hadn't been boarded up in the darkness herself.

Gulping back terror, her throat scratchy and dry, Fiona cleared a path through her addled mind and tried to calm down. She was alive, basically unhurt, and in her shop. Since there was filtering light, she knew she wasn't enclosed in the closet. Whoever had done this must be gone, for there wasn't enough illumination, or any sound, to indicate that someone might be there.

Using her elbows, she shifted and squirmed, rolling over to her other side. Now she could see out into the shop from under the stairs, and could see that all was still. She had no idea what time it was, but if the deep darkness that hung around the edges of the shop was any indication, it was the dead of night. The lamps she had come in to turn on were off, and only one light cast a pool of warmth into the shop...and it was, of course, The Lamp.

Fiona closed her eyes as terror welled inside her—cold chills sending wracking tremors through her body. She knew without a doubt that whoever had left her here had done so in the dark.

She knew that with the same certainty that she knew the lamp was not plugged into the wall, even though it was illuminated.

Yet, nothing happened—nothing was going on. There

were no breezes, no clinking of chandeliers, no flickering lights, no scent of roses…all was still. Almost peaceful.

And, she told herself, grasping at one logical aspect: it was no ghost who'd bashed her on the head and tied her up. That had been the work of something very human. Her shivering eased and she forced herself to breathe more slowly.

At the worst case, she would lie here on this cold, musty floor—at least it wasn't dirty, thanks to the meticulousness of the forensic detectives and her cleaning up after them—until tomorrow morning, when Carl showed up for work…or, perhaps, that was the best case. After all, she had no idea whether her attacker would come back…or whether the ghost would have something to say about the situation.

Fiona shook her head hard, scraping it against the hardwood floor. She would not think that way. She would not. She would think about other things…nice things.

Clenching her hands, wriggling her fingers to keep the numbness at bay, she focused her thoughts on Gideon, and for a long moment, as she basked in the memories, warmth seeped through her. And then she remembered his phone call tonight, and, with a lurching stomach, realized that right now—at this very moment, whatever time it was—he could be with Rachel.

That path was not an attractive one for her mind to take, and she firmly steered it away.

She was just about to try and roll herself out of the closet in hopes of making her way to the phone when she heard a rattling at the front door. Tensing, fear shooting through her, Fiona followed her first instinct: to roll as quickly as she could back into the depths of the closet.

The door rattled again, then there was the telltale tinkling sound of the bells as it swung open. Her heart in her throat, Fiona inched her way into the farthest corner she could, out of the wavering light.

"Fiona?"

The sound of her name in a voice she recognized was enough to allow the tears to burst forth.

"Fiona, are you in here?"

She rolled again, this time toward the shop, out from under the stairs, as Ethan walked back into the shop, turning on lamps as he went. "Fiona!" He came to a screeching halt when he nearly stepped on her. "My God, what happened to you?"

In a flash, he was kneeling beside her, tearing the tape none-too-gently from her face and helping her to sit up. She couldn't help the tears that gushed from her eyes, and her running nose, and she buried her face in his coat.

My brother. My big brother.

"Oh, my God, Fi—Let me get something to cut you loose with, Fifi—I'll be right back." Ethan hurried away, his dark coat fluttering behind him. He was back almost immediately with a packing knife, and made short work of the ropes.

Fiona could not stifle a groan as her arms were freed and fell forward back to her sides. Her wrists and shoulders screamed with pain, and her skin was chafed from the rough bonds. Her head still pounded, pain resonating through her forehead, and she reached up gingerly to touch the tender spot at her temple. When she tried to talk, to thank Ethan, nothing would come from her desert-dry mouth except a little mew.

He dashed away and was back with a cup of water, which she drank thirstily. "I'm going to call Longbow," he said, fishing out his cell phone as she gulped the water.

Fiona nodded, and, setting the cup aside, began to rub her ankles with numb fingers. "What are you doing here?" she croaked as he hung up the phone. "You're supposed to be in Chicago."

"You found a skeleton in your shop," he said as if that explained everything. "And you didn't call me. I had to hear about it on the news—anyway, I tried to call you on my way back from Chicago, and you never answered your cell phone—so I drove by here on the way to the cabin to see if you were still working. I saw your car out front, but realized that none of the lights were on in here, and I thought that was funny because I knew you always left something on since that break-in—so I thought I should check. When I opened the door —*which was unlocked*—I nearly tripped over that big-ass bag of yours, and I nearly had a heart attack. By then, I knew something was definitely wrong."

She nodded wearily. "Thank God you came by, or I'd have been stuck here all night." Her voice was a little better now. "What time is it?"

"Almost midnight."

Officer van Hest had arrived, and her smooth competence and neat professionalism were a balm to Fiona's nerves. She described her experience, acknowledging the fact that she was lucky to be relatively unhurt.

"But I'll take her over to the urgent care center to have her looked at," Ethan said, giving her a quelling look. "And she's not coming to work tomorrow."

Fiona didn't protest, for she was no martyr—and her head still made the room spin when she tried to stand. In fact, she was more than glad to rest herself against her brother's solid, comforting body, his arm around her waist, as he helped her to his car.

"Ms. Murphy." Helga hurried out after them, just as Ethan was ready to slam the door shut. "Have you seen this before?"

She handed Fiona a white sheet of paper—it was the back of one of her invoices—and on it, someone had scrawled three ugly words: *You'll be next.*

THIRTEEN

NANCY DREW NEVER FAINTED, Fiona rebuked herself. No matter what she went through—whether it was being tied up and left in the path of a black widow spider or a scorpion, or thrown in an abandoned ski lodge—she never lost her consciousness…or her cookies.

Fiona rolled her eyes, crimping her mouth, disgusted with her own weakness. Having done both last night after seeing the threatening note Helga van Hest found, she knew she was no Nancy Drew—nor did she want to be.

"Oh, good, you're awake. How do you feel, Fifi?"

She turned her head—which still ached like crazy—to see Ethan. To her surprise and delight, behind him was Diana. The latter walked into the bedroom, and was carrying a steaming pot of tea on a tray with some food.

"Diana! When did you get here?" Fiona asked, struggling to sit upright in the bed. Crashing waves of pain in her temples slowed her movements, and she stifled a groan. "And, actually, bro, I feel like shit. Thanks." She forced a wan smile.

"I drove up as soon as Ethan called to tell me what happened." Diana leaned closer and added in an undertone, "He was nearly hysterical and I figured he wouldn't be much help if he got you all riled up too."

Fiona managed a smile as her brother looked at them with a wary expression. "Thank you."

She'd considered—only considered, and only for the space of thirty seconds or so—calling Gideon last night, to tell him what had happened…but no.

It wouldn't do to begin to rely on him at all. Besides, he might not even be at home. Or alone.

She simply hadn't wanted to find out that he wasn't alone at four in the morning.

"You look like hell." In the no-nonsense way of many of his gender, Ethan blurted out the raw truth.

Though she couldn't see herself, Fiona was well aware the skin at her wrists, ankles, and jaw was raw and chapped. And from when she was at the urgent care center last night, she knew that the welt on her head gave her forehead an off-balance tilt. No doubt her hair was its usual scraggly mess, and God only knew what the rest of her face looked like.

"Thanks for the breaking news, dear brother," she retorted as Diana set the tray on the bed next to her. Along with the tea—which smelled like mint and lemon —there were two pieces of toast, a boiled egg, and a small pot of jam. "Thank you," she added to the other woman in a dry, raspy voice. "I just realized I'm really hungry."

"And the tea will help your throat," Diana said, lifting the pot to pour for her. "Orbra told me to put a lot of honey in it."

"Uh, Fifi, there are a few missed calls on your cell," Ethan said as he edged closer to the bed and set her smartphone next to the tray. "I dug it out of your bag last night to charge it—how the hell do you ever find anything in there any way? It's like the depths of hell in that bag. And why do you keep your phone on silent all the time? Do you know how many calls and texts you probably miss?"

Fiona flapped a hand, batting him away as if he were an annoying gnat. Which he was, often enough. "Well, I check it a few times a day. When I remember. Plus I don't like the sound of the ring. It's too loud and jarring."

"You know you can change the ringtone," Diana said mildly.

"You *can?*" Fiona's battered voice cracked. "To what?"

Ethan and Diana exchanged glances. "To pretty much anything you want, Fifi," he said, fighting a grin. "Any sound, or a song, or a chime—whatever. I can do that for you."

"Thanks, Ethan." Then she looked at Diana. "Make sure he doesn't change it to something like 'The Bitch is Back'."

"I was thinking more of something like 'Ding-Dong the Witch is Dead'," her brother replied with a grin. Then he sobered, as if remembering the warning note from last night's break-in. "Look, Fi, this might seem like fun and games—getting pampered in bed and everything—but someone *attacked* you last night. I think you're going to really need to amp up your security, and I don't want you to be there by yourself anymore."

"Well, duh," she replied airily—even as the insides of her stomach twisted. "And I didn't plan to be there by myself last night, anyway."

"To state the obvious, clearly someone wants something they believe is in the shop," Diana said, sitting on the edge of the bed near Fiona's toes. "And I'm certain it's no mere antique."

"It's got to have something to do with the skeleton," Fiona said, looking down at the cell phone Ethan had returned to her.

Three missed calls…from Gideon.

And two texts.

She felt a swell of something warm bubble in her stomach. Gideon hadn't spent the night with Rachel. And he'd called her.

Fiona couldn't help a smile as she sipped from the tea—definitely mint—as relief coursed through her.

"So, uh, who's this HG3 person who was trying to reach you last night?" Ethan asked, obviously noticing her reaction to the phone. "And this morning?"

Diana's eyes shot to Fiona's, and she gave her a knowing smile and furtive nod. *She* knew.

"Oh, it's just—"

Ethan's black lab Cady suddenly exploded into wild barking from somewhere out in the house, and he gave Fiona an exasperated look. "That's her 'someone's here' bark," he said, rising from where he'd been sitting on the other side of the bed. "Probably the UPS man. I'm expecting a contract from my agent. We just sold the Spanish rights. Cheers to me!" Ethan was an anthropology professor at University of Chicago who'd written a very successful, mainstream book about death and dying.

"So…" Diana said as Ethan left to check on Cady. She had a wicked gleam in her eyes. "HG3, hm? This wouldn't be that tall, cool glass of water I met at the shop the other day, would it? The very handsome lawyer?"

"Maybe." Fiona couldn't completely stifle a smile.

"The stiff and stuffy Gideon Nath the Third?" Diana teased. "Maybe he's not so stiff and stuffy after all?"

Despite her headache, Fiona gave a soft laugh. "Let's just say…he's only stiff in the right ways, and at the right time…if you get my drift. And otherwise…he's very, very…*warm*."

Diana—who was a little stiff and stuffy herself at times—gave her a shocked, wide-eyed look, then burst into gales of laughter. "Well, well, well," she said, wiping the tears from her eyes. "Nothing like saying it like it is."

"Yes. But…there's no need to mention it to Ethan at this point. It's not serious, and he'll just get all weird and brotherly and—"

She trailed off at the sound of voices from the hall, and purposeful, heavy footsteps.

"Fi," called her brother from outside the door. "You've got a visitor."

Diana looked toward the voice and frowned a little. "He doesn't sound happy."

"It's probably the police. Officer van Hest said she'd come by this morning to take my report since we weren't sure whether I'd feel up to coming into the station."

"I don't think that's—" But Diana's voice trailed off when the bedroom door opened to reveal Ethan—wearing a scowl—followed by Gideon and a very excited Cady, who immediately charged over to the bed and nosed under Fiona's hand.

"*Fiona*." Instead of appearing horrified at her battered state, Gideon sounded furious.

"Well look who the cat dragged in." Fiona tried for a nonchalant drawl, but with her raspy voice and surprise at seeing him, it sounded more like a husky invitation to join her in her bed. "Hello, Gideon." She saw Diana wink and slip out of the room—dragging Ethan with her.

"For Christ's sake, I leave you alone for two minutes and look what happens," Gideon said, looming over her like a furious specter. "I thought you were going *home*. You *should* have gone home. What the hell were you thinking, going back in that shop alone?"

He stood at the edge of her bed, fists planted at the hips of his neat, designer suit. Dark silvery eyes flashed as he glowered down at her, as though expecting that she would actually respond to such outrageous accusations. His hair wasn't as neatly combed as it usually was, and his conservative navy tie, half twisted so that its Versace tag showed, was another sign that he was agitated.

Fiona couldn't resist. She reached out to flip the tie back into place, and responded, "Better fix that before you get back to the office. And, by the way, I feel fine, thanks for asking, Gideon."

"You look terrible," he commented, but his voice was soft and bumpy. "Are you all right?" He looked around, then with a shrug settled on the very edge of her bed.

Absently petting Cady, Fiona nodded, warmth swimming through her at the concern in his eyes. "My head hurts, but otherwise I'm doing fine."

"You didn't respond to my calls or texts last night," he said. "I was a little worried."

"Oh," she said, her cheeks warming. "I hardly ever look at my phone because I can't read it without my cheaters. Ethan was just lecturing me about that." She forced a smile. "I just now saw that you called."

"Ethan's your brother." It sounded more like an accusation than a question.

Fiona nodded. "For twenty-seven years, in fact. How did you end up finding me here, anyway?"

"Iva, of course. Helga van Hest—she must have been

there last night, after you were attacked..." His voice trailed off and the corners of his mouth tightened. "Helga told Orbra, and of course Orbra told Iva, and Iva and my grandfather called me. I don't even want to know what they were doing together at six in the morning," he added, rubbing his temples with a thumb and index finger.

Fiona giggled and took another sip of tea. "I have an idea, but you don't look like you—"

"Fiona, this isn't the time to make jokes." An angry line creased between his heavy brows as he sank onto the edge of the bed. The mattress buckled a little, and she tipped slightly toward his muscular thigh. "Fiona, this whole situation—it's not good. It's not just a simple break-in. We've got a homicide to deal with."

"Do you think you need to tell me that?"

"Longbow told me about the note they found," he added flatly. "That was one piece of information Iva didn't seem to have. Fiona, that's a direct threat. Toward you."

The memory of that black, scrawling threat still made her stomach churn, but she said, "You talked to Captain Longbow?"

"Yes. I called him on my way over here and he told me about it."

"Well, that wasn't very circumspect of him," Fiona replied. "You can't just call up the police and expect them to tell you everything like they do on television. It doesn't work that way—does it?"

"Well, I think he thought I already knew about the note," Gideon confessed. "And probably since he knows Iva and the Tuesday Ladies, he figured I'd find out through them anyway."

"Small town," Fiona said with a sigh. "What else can

I expect?" She picked up her toast to slather strawberry jam on it.

"I did talk to Detective Hinkle—the homicide investigator from the State Police—like you'd asked me to, for an update about the skeleton. The only news he had was that they found traces of lime in the fabric of the woman's clothes. He wanted me to ask you if you'd had any, or seen any lime anywhere else in the shop."

"Lime?" Fiona would have frowned, but her head hurt too much.

"Yes—you know, limestone."

The fog cleared. "Oh, limestone. As in, to help bodies decompose faster—or slow them down decomposing. I can't remember which." She sighed and gave a rueful chuckle as she replaced her toast on the tray. "Anyway, I guess my mind is more addled than I thought. No, I haven't seen anything like that around."

Gideon took her hand and fumbled with her fingers between his own, touching each of the three rings she wore, and smoothing over the freckled skin on the back of her hand. His breath hissed out when he saw the red roughness around her wrists, and he touched that too.

"I should have made sure you went home last night," he said finally. "I'm afraid I just didn't see any reason that a fifty-year-old skeleton would be the cause of anyone's concern. But apparently it is."

Fiona swallowed and reached for the tea to moisten her throat. His stiffness and arrogance seemed to have faded, and the warmth emanating from him was so unlike the cool, business-like attorney she'd first met that it threatened to work its way past her barriers.

"Do you think...could it be Brad Forth?" she said. "Or Arnold Sternan?"

Still holding her hand, he shrugged, and she felt the

gentle jolt. "Forth's been sniffing around ever since you opened the place…but, frankly, I think he's more interested in you than a skeleton or scandal. And I don't think he'd do anything to jeopardize the election, with it being so close. And as for Arnold Sternan…well, I suppose it's possible. He did come to your opening. And he was in the back of the shop. I saw him come out from back there."

"You did?" She gave him a sidewise look. "You never mentioned anything about it."

He shrugged. "I didn't think anything of it—between Iva and my grandfather meddling in the whole—well, I didn't think it was worth mentioning. But now that we're talking about it, I should also state that I saw Rudy and Viola Ruthven coming down from the upstairs of the shop. They were definitely poking around up there."

Fiona felt sick. "If someone's broken in twice, they're looking for something," she said. "It's not just a thief. But the first break-in—the night of the grand opening—was before I found the skeleton. Is it possible they're not related?"

Gideon reached up to tuck a coiling curl behind her ear, fighting internally with himself. He didn't want to say anything that would put an even greater edge of fear in her eyes, but at the same time, he wasn't about to downplay her safety. If she was concerned about the situation, she would take more care than to be in the store alone at night.

He ground his teeth at the thought of her lying bound and gagged on the floor of the shop for *hours*, then forced himself to unclench his fists. "It's possible the first break-in was a random thief. Last night, though…well, you must have surprised the intruder and we don't know whether he got what he came for."

He stroked the back of her hand. If he hadn't leapt to answer Rachel's call and dropped everything to help her…

He thrust the thought away. There was no way he could have known Fiona would return to the shop, and absolutely no indication that she would interrupt another burglar. Still…if he'd listened to the message his heart had been telling him, he'd never have gone to Rachel.

Gideon's stomach churned at the memory last night of the terrible, heart-rending scene that had ensued after he told Rachel how he felt. It had ended with her in a storm of tears, and him unable to comfort her…and all the while, he'd been thinking about Fiona.

"I suppose the reason he tied me up and left me was to scare the hell out of me," Fiona said in a small voice, breaking into his thoughts and jerking him back to their conversation. "Well, it worked."

Her eyes, framed by thick, winged lashes, carried the shine of fear, and she fluttered her lids down as though to hide it. "But why scare me? I haven't done anything."

"That you know of, anyway," Gideon agreed. "Fiona, we don't know what's going on here—so I want you to promise me that *no matter what,* you won't be in the shop by yourself in the evening, or at night—or even early in the morning. Not until we figure out what's going on, and why you seem to be a target." The very thought was enough to make his throat close up. "That note was definitely a warning, and it was definitely personal."

She pulled to adjust herself upright in the bed, exasperation showing in her drawn features. "Don't be ridiculous, Gideon. I'm not going to be stupid about things—especially now, after this—but I can't schedule

Carl to be there with me every waking hour. He lives in Ann Arbor and only comes out for the weekends."

He began to talk, but stopped when she pressed two firm fingers to his mouth—which had the added benefit of distracting him as she touched his lips.

"I promise I won't be in the shop after hours by myself. And I've already scheduled to have the security system updated, so I'll turn the alarms on when I'm there alone. Customers will just have to knock to be let in when I'm alone. Plus, I'm going to get some Mace and have it with me all the time. Unlike my cell phone— which, I promise I'll try to keep handy. Or, at least, handi*er*. Okay?"

What else could he say? She made sense, even though it left him with a nervousness that would not abate. However, her fingers were still pressed to his lips…and it was rather distracting…

He smiled under her touch, then, with a quick movement, he opened his mouth and let a finger slip in. He nipped it lightly, quickly, and pulled away, grinning at the shocked look on her face. Gideon leaned to press her back into her pillows, covering her lips with his in a gentle, sensual kiss.

She tasted *wonderful*…hot and lush and exotic. Like Fiona.

A wave of desire washed over him, surging to his groin, and he slid a hand along the length of her neck, tracing over her shoulder to the curve of her breast. Oh…yes….

The rumble of a throat clearing sharply behind him froze Gideon.

Half sprawled on Fiona, he swallowed deeply and with a wry smile, pulled away and sat on the edge of the bed as Fiona's bloody, interfering brother entered the room.

"I'm sorry to interrupt," Ethan said—sounding not the least bit sorry at all, "but Diana thought I should check to see if you need any more tea, Fiona." He gave Gideon a very cool look.

"Diana did?" Fiona replied with an arch expression.

"Diana did *not*," said the woman herself, coming into the bedroom from behind Ethan.

Despite being caught out, Fiona's brother didn't waver from his stance in the doorway, nor from the dark look directed at Gideon. Deciding it was time to take the bull by the horns, so to speak, Gideon rose from the bed and turned, extending his hand to the brother.

"Thank you for taking care of her last night," he said as Ethan reluctantly shook his hand. His grip was probably a trifle stronger than it needed to be, but Gideon gave it back as well. "I'd hate to think of Fiona lying there all by herself all night—and maybe longer."

That, at least, he and Ethan seemed to agree on, and the brother nodded briskly. "It was only luck that I happened to drive by," he said. "But you can bet she won't be doing *anything* in that shop by herself anymore. At least until this stops."

Gideon agreed. "She wasn't supposed to be there by herself anyway," he said, giving her a chilly look. "She'd promised."

Ethan lifted a brow at his sister. "She did?"

"All right, you two. I need to get dressed, so why don't you run on out of here and go do manly things for a while."

She lifted the bedcovers as if to throw them off her, and Gideon and Ethan both reacted immediately—though likely for different reasons.

"Okay, okay," Ethan said, holding up a hand as if to block the view of his sister in her scanty sleepwear. "Nath, let's go do manly things—like throw the ball for Cady or something." At the sound of her name, and, presumably a word she recognized, the black lab clambered to her feet and began to whine with excitement.

Gideon wasn't so easily distracted, however. "Why do you need to get dressed?" he asked suspiciously as Diana shoved Ethan out the door behind the dog.

"Well, I've got to get to work—"

"To *work*?"

"Yes. To work. To my shop. To my *livelihood*. To my—"

"Are you mad?" he exploded, even as she tossed back the covers to expose her lovely body covered by a short —*very* short—little night shirt.

He was momentarily distracted by the flash of creamy white thigh and the curve of her hip as she climbed out, then he continued. "You need to stay in bed and—"

"Yeah, no." Fiona padded over to the largest suitcase he'd ever seen, bulging with clothing, and opened it, book-like. A heavy shoe fell out from one of the pockets, landing with a clunk, and a hot pink and lime green scarf fluttered to the floor in its wake.

Gideon tried to keep his irritation in place, but seeing her floating around the room in a tiny scrap of blue silk was enough to get his heart racing again. The tone of her voice indicated that she wasn't about to capitulate to his demands that she get back into bed, unless.... He shifted gears and decided to try a different, more rewarding tactic.

He slipped up behind her, resting his hands lightly on her shoulders as she dug through the colorful, gauzy mass of dresses and flowing skirts that tumbled out of the suitcase she clearly hadn't taken the time to unpack.

"What's the hurry?" he murmured in her ear, trying not to wince when he saw her hand pause over a flame-red dress with bead-studded fringe that looked like something a cowgirl/gypsy would wear.

"No hurry," she said crisply, and chose a long blue sweater, pulling it from the tangle of fabric. She turned right into him, and that was a very fortuitous event.

He slid his arms around her waist, his hands slipping sensuously over her skin with the shift of silk. The dark circles under her eyes solidified his decision that keeping her in bed would be the best thing for her, and that was all he needed to justify the way his mouth covered hers —telling her what would happen next.

When she murmured a protest, he shook his head, smothering her words with his lips.

At the moment, he didn't give a rat's ass about Ethan Murphy.

He sat outside, trying to enjoy the musky, musty taste of a Puerto Rican cigar and a tumbler of golden brandy. Sucking hard on the smoke, he held the taste in his mouth for a count of ten, then expelled it in a straight shot toward the twilight sky.

God *damn* Nevio Valente.

He clenched his teeth, then forced himself to relax. He would find the papers if it killed him...or someone else.

His lips tightened as he thought of that idiot woman who'd interrupted him last night—again. She always seemed to find a way to interfere. The hardness relented into a nasty smile and he set the cigar on the edge of a marble ashtray.

He doubted she'd be around to bother him for much longer. He hoped he'd succeeded in scaring her so much she sold the shop—or at least closed it for a while. All he needed was some time to do a good, uninterrupted search, and he'd be able to find what Valente tried to hide from the world.

Then when he found it, he'd keep it hidden too, of course, except for the money it would lead him to. The money would be his. After all, it was his due.

He tapped his neat, clipped fingernails on the table and imagined how much those bank accounts would be worth now…and his heart began to race. Valente owed him…for all he'd put up with over the years, Valente owed him.

FOURTEEN

THE FOLLOWING FRIDAY—TEN days after Fiona had discovered a skeleton in her shop's closet and that a stuffy lawyer could take her to the moon—she found a bracelet belonging to the skeleton.

It had to belong to the skeleton, she reasoned, staring at the delicate gold links that clasped a heavy oval plate, because it had somehow got caught up on the inside of the wall she'd broken through.

She'd forgotten about the debris that she'd removed before finding the skeleton, and only now had she enlisted Carl's help in moving it from the back room out to the Dumpster. The detectives had missed it too—although they'd gone over every other inch of the small closet under the stairs with a fine-toothed comb. Now she understood how some of the celebrated errors in police investigations happened.

Fiona turned the bracelet over in her hand and saw the faint engraving on what looked like an old-fashioned identification bracelet. Stepping toward one of the fluorescent lights that spilled into the back room in a decidedly un-designer-like fashion, but even then, she couldn't read the small engraving without her reading glasses.

Once she had her cheaters in place, she finally could discern the plain, neat letters that read: "GJF liebe NV 17/6/40."

Fiona felt a swell of sadness rise within, and, without truly being conscious of why she did so, she looked out toward the main shop—toward The Lamp—and spoke very softly. "Is this yours? GJF?"

The sudden rush of wind past her face made her nape-hair stand on end and brought sourness to her mouth, but Fiona stood there, unmoving. The scent of roses filled the air as tears dampened her eyes. Chills shivered over her skin, and her hands trembled while her stomach surged sickeningly. A chandelier hanging high overhead tinkled alarmingly.

"It *is* yours." Sadness washed over her, slowly, almost lovingly, as she held the bracelet. "Who are you?"

The tinkle of the chandelier above the heavy walnut desk was the only answer. She sifted the cool links through her fingers, smoothing the pad of her thumb over the engraved gold plate.

"Fiona?" Carl's voice rang from the front of the shop, where he'd been waiting on a customer. He came around the corner, a questioning look on his face. "Did you say something?"

Before she could answer, he frowned and rubbed his arms. "Feels like a bad draft in here somewhere."

"Look what I found," she said, with a quick glance up at the now-still chandelier. Gretchen the cat sat up on her regular perch—on the rail at the top of the stairs, her tail twitching like a thick whip. "It must belong to the skeleton, because I found it caught up in that garbage we were going to take outside."

Carl took it and read the engraving aloud. "GJF—something—NV?" He looked at her. "What's the middle word?"

"*Liebe*. You know, love. And—NV…that must be Nevio Valente." She looked up just as the nubbly white Lamp, behind Carl, flickered twice. "Oh!" She swallowed the startled exclamation as her companion looked at her with raised eyebrows, then whirled to look behind him.

"What is it?"

"N-nothing." Fiona's heart thumped rapidly, but she smiled at him. "I'm sure the NV must stand for Nevio Valente." Then, her pleasure at the discovery faded as she realized what that could mean. "If he knew her…if it was him…then he probably knew she was here." Her stomach dropped.

"What?" Confusion dotted Carl's expression, then he returned to the bracelet. "This must be a date after it—written in European format. Makes sense because of the German. June seventeenth, nineteen-forty."

"Yes." Fiona tried to push away the heaviness that had settled over her shoulders, and she held out her hand for him to return the bracelet. "I guess I'll need to let Detective Hinkle and Captain Longbow know about this. It might help them identify the body." She shivered suddenly. Could Valente have known about the woman all this time? Could he have put her there?

Had he killed her?

She stopped the thought and refocused her attention on Carl. "What did you say?"

He glanced at his watch. "Gideon should be here pretty soon, hmm?"

Fiona started to reply in the affirmative, but stopped to glare at him. "Why would you think that?" she asked, starting to feel uneasy. She knew exactly why he thought that.

"Because ever since you spent the night with him, he's come by here every evening—all the way from Grand Rapids—just like clockwork, to take you home." His face crinkled into a warm smile. "I'm glad you two are getting along so well. Although he is a little tight-assed at times, he seems like a good guy."

Then Fiona's lips firmed. Carl was right—she and Gideon had spent just about every evening together for the last week, either at Ethan's cabin (if her brother was back in Chicago) or Gideon's condo; sometimes spending the night together, other times not.

She smiled at the memory of last evening, when he'd shown up with an outrageous bouquet of Birds of Paradise for her. In the last week, she'd hardly thought of him as stuffy or anal-retentive at all. She'd thought of him as the most romantic, tender of lovers.

She didn't understand why irritation—and something like alarm—flitted through her, then, at the soft look on Carl's face. "Yes, well, he's been kind enough to make sure I don't have to leave by myself. He's just making sure I get home all right."

And making sure I get a very good night's sleep.

A smug grin tickled the corners of her mouth at the thought. Yes, Gideon definitely knew how to put her in the most relaxed, lazy, satisfied moods.

The bells above the front door tinkled, and Carl craned his neck to look around the corner. "Speak of the devil. Why don't you run along—I'll close up here."

"Thanks, Carl—you're a darling." She stood on

tiptoes to kiss his cheek, then turned to greet Gideon, who had a stormy expression on his face.

Grinning up at him, Fiona linked her arm through Gideon's, drawing him to her for a full-body embrace. She knew he'd seen her kiss Carl, and it gave her the smallest, admittedly immature, thrill to know that it irritated him. To make up for it, she tipped her face up to meet his mouth in a slow, sensual, it's-you-I'm-involved-with kiss.

"Hello baby," she said, smiling against his mouth. He felt *good*.

His expression softened as he looked down at her. "How was your day?" He smoothed a hand over her mass of thick hair, down her back, rubbing and caressing as he kept her close to his side.

She told him, and showed him the bracelet, which he examined with interest.

"Yes, it's a good assumption that NV is Valente. It's not as if those are common initials." He glanced toward the front of the shop where Carl was doing a poor job of using a feather duster, then back down at Fiona. "Did I hear him tell you to take off? Let's get out of here...I'm hungry and I missed you today."

Warmth bubbled through her and she smiled up at him. "I just need to grab my bag." She slipped out of his embrace and hurried back to get the leather abomination she called a purse.

The night breeze was still warm, and it caressed her face with light coils of hair. She slipped her arm through his, hugging close to his side, as they walked through the alley to where he'd parked his car.

"Why don't you get a smaller pocketbook," he suggested as the bag bumped between them. "That thing could be dangerous."

"I need a big bag to hold all my stuff," she replied, adjusting the heavy tote on her shoulder. "What do you want to do about dinner? I can make something at Ethan's cabin, or we can grab a bite somewhere else."

"Is your brother in town?"

She looked up at him, fluttering her eyelashes. "No. He went back to Chicago this morning."

"Sold." His eyes smoldered.

A shiver raced up Fiona's spine, curling around into a pang in her belly. "Sounds good." Her voice came out husky. "We don't have anything exciting to eat at the cabin—we can order pizza, or stop and pick up something to cook."

To her surprise and pleasure, he said, "Let's cook. Together."

By the time they stopped at the little grocery store on the south end of Wicks Lake and got to Ethan's cabin, it was after nine o'clock.

Gideon helped carry the groceries in, then settled to meet her in the kitchen. He had to hand it to Ethan Murphy—the place was very comfortable, and tastefully furnished.

The cabin—though that was really a misnomer; it was more of a full-fledged house—was enclosed by a thick forest in a clearing on a small hill. He suspected there was access to Wicks Lake down a pathway into the forest, and though it was dark, he could see a few lights twinkling from lakefront homes in the distance.

The great room was furnished with a taupe sectional made of luxurious suede, and a large stone fireplace bisected one tall wall. Evidence of Ethan Murphy's travels to places like Macchu Picchu, Angkor Wat, and Bangkok hung on the walls in the form of drawings, photographs, and in one case, a woven tapestry.

From the living room, he could see Fiona unpacking groceries and grouping them on the counter in the places they would be used. Then she disappeared into her bedroom to change.

Gideon took off his coat and loosened his tie, laying them neatly over an armchair in the living room. He thought about the casual shirt and jeans, along with the tee and cut-off sweatpants he'd left in the car. And the toothbrush.

He'd put a small bag in his trunk last week, planning to change into them some night when they were together...but somehow, even though they'd been almost inseparable after working hours, he was a little apprehensive about letting her know he'd planned to stay overnight.

Perhaps his uneasiness wasn't unfounded. After all, on the three occasions he'd spent the night at Ethan Murphy's cabin (that alone bothered him), when he went into the bathroom in the morning, there was a new, wrapped toothbrush on the counter by the sink—three different times. Fiona didn't even recycle the ones he'd used previously. Was she just trying to be a good hostess —or was she trying to keep him at arm's length?

Gideon smiled wryly as he worked the cork out of the bottle of Chenin Blanc. For the first time in his life, he was worried that he might be moving too fast for a woman...rather than the other way around. He knew Fiona was skittish about getting involved on a regular basis with a man...and in the last week, he'd realized the last thing he wanted to do was to scare her off.

At that moment, it struck him. He was falling—hard. And fast.

Oh, man.

She could be...she might just be...the one.

The One.

Still reeling with this unexpected development, he poured two glasses of wine and tried not to panic.

Then Fiona breezed into the kitchen, and every bit of panic evaporated. His nerves settled and his thoughts calmed.

She's the One.

She just was.

"Mmm. That looks good." Fiona said as she fussed with a small gadget that looked like something Iva had in her bathroom.

She snicked a match and it flared into light, leaving an acrid scent trailing in the air after she lit a small candle and extinguished the match.

That was something else he liked about her that Gideon never realized he would: she was always fussing with something, setting up some kind of mood or environment, turning on music, talking about gobbledy-gook like numerology or reflexology, or palmistry.

He stilled.

Palmistry…that reminded him of her prediction when she'd read his palm those weeks ago. That he'd get married soon, and have at least one child.

Suddenly, his palms became damp and he needed a good-sized sip of the wine. He took it too fast and began to cough and sputter.

"Are you all right? Not a good one after all?" Her fine brows were raised in question.

Gideon took another drink of wine to smooth his throat, and managed to respond, "Went down the wrong way.

"Mm. Let me try?" Could she know how much that huskiness in her voice turned him on?

Gideon handed her a glass, feeling suddenly, overwhelmingly happy. And what was wrong with the woman he was involved with being so sexy, so interesting, so warm and caring, even if she was a little quirky?

Her eyes covered him from over the rim of her glass. Amber tiger's eyes with a glint of humor and the depth of passion: a combination he'd never expected to find—or to want—in a woman. In that moment, he almost took the plunge...he almost mentioned the clothes he had waiting in the car. But that would open up too much, lay too much out on the table...and if she wasn't ready for it, then he'd be facing a setback that he had no patience for. No, better to just enjoy the evening.

Steering his thoughts firmly away from clothes—either getting into them, or getting out of them—he sniffed delicately at the faintly citrusy air. "What's that?" he asked, looking at the little gadget under which she'd lit the tea candle.

"An aromatherapy diffuser," she replied, brushing past him to pull a large chunk of gingerroot out of a bag.

Gideon looked more closely at the object, which appeared to be a large crystal rock, cut in half so that the insides showed the pale lavender crystals in a small, cup-like shape. The outside of the stone was rough and grey, but the inside had a small hollow in which the smallest bit of liquid glistened. It sat on a small metal stand, and the tea light burned merrily under it. The room had begun to smell like...citrus and cinnamon.

"What is that smell?"

Fiona had begun to peel the ginger, and its pungency tinged the air now too. "It's a mixture of essential oils used for relaxation and calming—bergamot and cinnamon." She looked up at him from under her lashes with a decidedly meaningful expression and added, "Well, actually, the cinnamon is for something else."

A pang twisted deep in his middle and he became breathless with the intensity of emotion that swamped him.

Jesus, but she always manages to get me off-guard.

"And what might that be for?" he asked, knowing full well what that coy, sensual look on her face meant.

"Well, cinnamon is also a wonderful massage oil. It has warming elements, and it has antiseptic purposes as well."

Cinnamon—like her hair, her lips, her eyes, the faint freckles on her creamy skin… Cinnamon wasn't just warming to him. It burned him.

"Oh?" he asked, deftly unwrapping the thick tuna steaks they'd purchased and trying to hide the fact that he was working through a maze of desire and some other deep-seated emotion that he would not name.

Not yet, anyway.

Fiona scooped the ginger into a haphazard pile and went to work on peeling and chopping garlic cloves. Ginger, cinnamon, citrus, and Fiona all combined—along with the wine—to make his senses sharp and hazy at the same time. His mouth watered, thinking about the meal they were preparing together, and about tumbling her onto the old-fashioned, white, wrought-iron bed piled with pillows…and about waking up next to her in the morning.

"It's also good for other things." She still had that look on her face—that slight smirk that tipped her mouth to one side. She turned to pour a bit of oil into a pan, then pivoted back toward him and the tuna steaks. "Brush these with the oil," she directed, handing him the bottle.

"What other thing?"

"Oh…dry heaves…." She shot him a look that told

him she was enjoying their banter, even though they both knew where it was leading.

When she reached up past him to pull a jar of sesame seeds from the cupboard, he slipped his free hand around her waist and pulled her up against him.

"And what else?" he murmured, tasting her lips, savoring the hint of wine on them.

A ginger-and-garlic-scented hand reached up to stroke his cheek as she kissed him back. "Foot fungus," she gasped a laugh against his mouth and he smiled too.

"How appropriate, since I ran out of foot powder yesterday. Aren't you sweet—always thinking of me."

She chuckled against his mouth, then dropped her voice low and dusky. "Sexual stimulation."

She started to pull away, but he held her tightly with the one hand. "What? Should I be offended that you think we're in need of help in that area?" He tasted her mouth again—delicious with wine and warmth and Fiona. "And I know *you* certainly don't need any help in that area. Unless..." some of the teasing note crept from his voice as a bit of insecurity wafted in, "you do need it."

"Oh, *Gideon*." Laughter lit her eyes, and he felt better —and foolish for his moment of nerves. "You know better than that."

"Just kidding," he said, smiling. He released her and she slipped away to continue making their dinner.

But all the rest of the evening, all during the wonderful meal of broiled tuna steaks with spicy Asian noodles, sesame seeds, and green beans sautéed in garlic and ginger, and even that night as he tenderly undressed her and made her cry and keen with passion, he wondered.

And then he wondered why he'd worried so. Everything was fine.

FIFTEEN

"SO, what about that new Thai restaurant in Grand Rapids for dinner tonight?" Gideon spoke into the phone as he scrolled through his latest batch of email. "That new one over by the river? One of the guys at the gym said it was great." Another email from Gordon Borowy? Did that man ever let up?

"Oh, no thanks," Fiona replied.

"All right. Well, we could just stay in, make something at my place. I saw some great-looking crab legs at the market yesterday. How about surf and turf? I'll do the turf, you do the surf? You can pick up some wine—if you don't mind driving up my way." He opened another email, scanned it, and deleted it. Then, he froze as her words sunk in.

"I have plans tonight," she was saying casually…very casually.

"Oh." He paused then asked, "Well, are you going to be late? I could come by afterward. I don't mind driving down there. Unless you're going to be up this way."

There was a short silence, then she replied steadily.

"I'm not sure how late I'll be—but, anyway, Gideon, I think I'm just going to head home afterward."

He let out a long breath—silently so that she wouldn't hear—and told himself to ignore the unease rising in him.

It was, after all, Friday night.

Maybe her brother was in town. He fought the urge to ask, to reassure himself...and he won. "All right, then, darling," he said with forced casualness. "Have a good time tonight, whatever you're up to, and I'll talk with you tomorrow."

There was obvious relief in her voice when she replied. "You too, Gideon. Good-bye."

He placed the phone deliberately back on its cradle and swiped a hand over his hair.

Dammit. He shouldn't be surprised. He *wasn't* surprised. But that didn't ease his apprehension. Was this her way of putting space between them? Was this how she was going to blow him off? Or was he just making a big deal about nothing?

Why should it bother him that she'd made other plans? It didn't...except that she'd waited until he called to tell him. Almost as though she'd wanted to catch him off-guard. Gideon felt his mouth tighten and his shoulders tense.

Then, practicality swept over him and he forced the tension away. Fiona was the most guileless person he knew. She probably didn't know the meaning of the word manipulation. And, besides, it was only one night. The first night they hadn't seen each other since the attack on Fiona two weeks ago.

It wasn't that he didn't trust her. He did. It was just that he'd been looking forward to—*expecting*—to see her all day...and now he was just disappointed.

With a frown, he gamely returned his attention to the latest barrage of emails from Gordon Borowy.

Fiona set the shop's phone on its cradle with a flourish of satisfaction. That had been easier than she'd expected. Perhaps it had been too easy. Perhaps she was making a mountain out of a molehill. Perhaps—

"Fiona," she exclaimed aloud, forcing her mind to stop its runaway path. "Don't be an idiot!"

She knew bloody damned well that Gideon had expected her to be available tonight…as he had for the last two weeks. Declining his assumed invitation gave her a sense of control—control which she'd felt slipping in the last two weeks, especially since she'd been attacked in her own shop.

"Did you say something?" Carl poked his head around the corner from the back room.

"I was just talking to myself," she told him without a hint of shame.

"So what time is the man coming by?" he asked, sauntering about with his lambswool duster. She wondered if he just carried it around to make him look useful—for he truly hadn't a clue how to use it—or if it was a ploy to make unsuspecting female clients think he'd be a good partner. She'd seen a calendar once featuring pictures of hot men doing housework—not a bad idea, in fact. Maybe he'd gotten the idea from there.

"He's not coming by." Her reply reverberated with satisfaction.

Carl's bushy brows rose as he looked at her. "Wasn't that him on the phone?"

Fiona glowered at him, wondering how he'd known. "Yes. But I told him I had plans tonight."

Carl looked at her with pity in his eyes. "Getting cold feet, huh? Better be careful—I don't think he's the type that plays hard to get."

"What are you talking about?" she flared, her heart bumping nervously. "I don't have cold feet about anything—and I'm not playing hard to get. I just needed a break."

He leaned against the desk and looked down at her. "So you lied to him. You don't have any plans, do you?"

Misery flowed through her. "No. I just needed to—well, to make sure I could still do it." That she wasn't relying on Gideon to make herself feel safe, and whole, and happy.

"Still do what?"

Fiona shifted uncomfortably. "Still spend time without him. Not count on him or need to see him…" She pushed her hair out of her eyes, tamping down the anxiety that welled inside her when she thought about being dependent upon someone, especially someone as strong and overwhelming as Gideon.

It would be so easy to relinquish control, to let such a capable man take care of everything. Of her.

Carl reached across the desk and squeezed her hand. "Well, I think you're playing a little dangerously…but let's not make a liar out of you. I'll take you out to dinner and to a movie so at least you can have a clear conscience about that."

She smiled, a bit shakily, and said, "That would be great. And let's make it a comedy, all right?"

"What are you still doing here on a Friday night?"

Gideon lurched in his seat, dropping his feet from the credenza on which they'd been resting as he stared out the window over the river. Spinning in his chair, he turned to face his grandfather.

"I should ask what *you're* doing here so late. Are things cooling off with you and Iva?"

Gideon Senior strode into the room, pulling a cigar from his pocket. "Ah, Iva had some psychic party she was going to tonight—said she wouldn't be home until later. Thought I'd catch up on some work I've been putting off."

"Psychic party? You mean you actually let her go to those things?" Gideon rolled his eyes and opened the drawer of his desk to retrieve a cigar.

His grandfather chuckled as he handed the younger man his cigar guillotine. "Don't be an ass, Gideon. There's no 'letting her go' about it. Iva does what she wants to do—and what do I care?"

"Doesn't she come back spouting all kinds of nonsense about what the future holds, and tall, dark strangers and lots of money, et cetera, et cetera?" Gideon snipped the end of his cigar with vehemence and leaned forward to light it from his grandfather's proffered lighter.

"Nothing more unusual than hearing that you're to get married and have a baby." Gideon Senior spewed a stream of smoke toward the ceiling. "Hope the damn smoke detector doesn't go off in here."

Gideon didn't have the energy to deny the path his grandfather's thoughts were obviously taking. The truth was, the thought of getting married—someday in the future—had occurred to him once or twice in the last week. And the possibility didn't unsettle him the way it would have only a few months ago.

But he wondered whether Fiona's palm-reading that portended this future had actually put the possibility in his mind.

"I take it you're not going to see your young lady tonight," his grandfather asked casually.

"No." Gideon couldn't help his voice sounding clipped.

"She's a lovely young woman."

"Yes. Yes, she is." For a moment, warmth surged through him...then ebbed back to be replaced by the faint chill that had descended upon him since their phone conversation.

"Well, why don't we go grab something to eat—your place is closer. Let's go over there and order a pizza. Or ribs. Or Chinese." His eyes danced in their crinkled pockets.

Gideon raised his eyebrow. Pizza did sound good. "I'll meet you there—why don't you stop and get a couple of six packs?"

"Deal."

Several hours later, Gideon Senior's cell phone buzzed. Iva's name came up on it and he reached across the coffee table littered with empty pizza boxes to grab the sleek black instrument.

His grandson watched in amusement, noticing that apparently Gideon Senior knew how to work his phone when his woman was calling.

From his casual position on the leather sofa, Gideon watched his grandfather's face relax. "Hello, darling.... No, I'm at Gideon's." There was silence, then his attention flickered to Gideon and away. "No, no—they didn't have any plans. I'm not imposing . . .What did I do for dinner? Uh…oh, nothing much—just some pasta and a big salad. Light dressing."

Gideon raised his eyebrows and gave a short laugh, which he smothered into his beer. He was feeling pleasantly warm and buzzed, even relaxed—though his mind continued to wander to Fiona.

"On your way home? You're taking a cab, I hope." Gideon Senior was saying into his sleek black phone. "Well, I'm sure Gideon won't mind." He raised his eyebrows and his grandson nodded in affirmation. "How long…about ten minutes? That close? Well, all right—see you then." He pushed the button to end the call, dropped the phone on the table, and leaped to his feet. "We've got ten minutes—really only five, considering how she'll be egging on the cab driver. Come on!"

He scrabbled about, shuffling the pizza boxes together as his grandson watched in amusement. "Get those bottles out of here, will you?" he snapped at the younger man.

"It's no use, Grandfather. She'll smell the beer and cigars, and, besides, she knows you better than that." He remained lounging on the sofa, tilting the beer bottle gently to his lips.

"You're a whole lot of help," Gideon Senior growled as he carried a tilted stack of pizza and garlic-bread boxes from the room.

He returned nary a moment too soon, for the doorbell pealed and the door swung open. "Hello in there!" came Iva's cheery voice as she flowed into the room, carrying two large shopping bags.

'Flowed' was the right word, too, for she wore a brilliant blue caftan-like garment embroidered with silver and sapphire designs. A matching blue scarf that was tied around her face and over her ears embraced her silvery hair. Bracelets, earrings, and necklaces clanked and clinked as she bent to embrace her guilty-looking lover.

Gideon looked at her in askance. "I thought you were *going* to a psychic party—not *being* the psychic, Iva. You look like a fortune-teller yourself." Much as he loved her —truly he did—he sometimes couldn't understand how his staid, conservative grandfather had become so besotted with her. She was just so…odd.

Iva came over to him, brushing her sweet, powdered cheek against his as they hugged, then kissing him just next to his lips. "Thank you my dear," she said merrily.

He could smell the faintness of alcohol on her breath, and by the look in her starry eyes, surmised that she'd been having as good a time as he and Gideon Senior had. "I'll take that as a compliment! Although there is no way I could even think to match Salton's talents. She is absolutely wonderful."

"What's all that stuff?" the elder Nath asked, eyeing the two large bags she'd dropped on the floor next to him. "And where did you get that outfit? Christ, Iva, you look like a gypsy!"

Instead of being offended by his comments, she giggled at him and twirled around so that the gown spun in a whirlpool of rayon. "What, you don't like it? Gideon, dear, do you have any more of that lovely Michigan Riesling you always have on hand? I'd like a glass while I show you two the wonderful things I got tonight."

"I always keep some just for you, Iva, my love." Grinning broadly, he pulled himself from the sofa and sauntered into the kitchen to do her bidding.

His grandfather's words followed him out of the

room: "I thought you were going to a party—not to the mall, Iva."

When he returned, he found his apple-cheeked guest cozied up to his grandfather on the loveseat, and they both looked up guiltily as he came in the room.

"Did I interrupt something?" Gideon asked innocently. "I can go find something to do in the kitchen if you two would like to be alone."

"Nonsense," his grandfather blustered. "Iva, let's get this over with."

"Now, dear, don't be so impatient. You know, Salton said that impatience is one of your greatest weaknesses…but then again, she said it was also one of your greatest strengths." She gave him a huge smile and he settled back in his seat, abashed.

Gideon couldn't help but roll his eyes. "So do you really believe all the stuff this Salton tells you?"

Iva turned to look at him, and the humor eased from her face, replaced by earnestness. "Ah, Gideon, darling." She pursed her lips and reached over to touch his hand, patting it where it rested on the sofa next to him. "Salton says you're trapped in the past, and afraid to—"

"What?" Gideon interrupted, sitting upright. She'd been talking to a fortune-teller about him? "That's nonsense, Iva. I'm sorry, I don't—"

"She says," Iva continued, as though he'd never interrupted, "that you've been smothering your talents and that they'll waste away if you don't allow them to come forth."

"Iva—" Gideon swallowed, feeling his stomach twist. How could a strange woman know these things about him? "She just made broad statements that could be interpreted in many different ways."

Iva patted his hand again, still looking at him with

something akin to sympathy in her eyes. "She mentioned Fiona." Her eyebrows rose delicately as Gideon froze and looked at her.

"What?"

"She said that a breath of fresh air had come into your life. That she had reddish hair and that she likes hands, and that she was good for you. I didn't tell her anything about Fiona."

Gideon stared at her. "And you don't know this woman? This psychic?" he asked, reaching blindly for the beer bottle at his side.

"Gideon...." Iva took his hand, clasping his long fingers in her small, soft, wrinkled ones, "she said that you would have a very difficult decision to make...that it would turn your life around...and she said that, although it would be very painful, you would do the right thing in the end."

He eased his hand away. "I can't believe I am actually half-believing this," Gideon said faintly, shaking his head. "Well, Iva, what can I say?"

She gave him a tender, motherly smile. "Nothing. Just file it away in the back of your mind for when you need it. Now, tell us...is there any news from the police about the break-in at Fiona's shop?"

Gideon shook his head, his mouth grim. "None really. If it weren't for the note he left that said *you'll be next*, I think they'd be writing it off as a random robbery." His grandfather and Iva had learned about the threatening note a few days after the break-in, of course, because of Orbra's connection to Helga van Hest.

"But there've been *two* incidents," his grandfather reminded him.

"Yes, and the police will say that there are valuable items in that shop, and it backs up to a dark alley, so it's a target. There's a lamp in there worth more than five thousand dollars." At least, according to Carl the shop-smurf.

Gideon thrust that thought away and added, "Fiona's being smart about it. Taking care not to be alone at night, and always having the alarm system on if she's at the shop by herself during the day. What other choice does she have?"

"Do they think it's all related to the skeleton?" Iva asked, her eyes bright with interest—not unlike Fiona's were, when she talked about the mystery of the skeleton.

"How can it be?" Gideon Senior asked. "The first incident was long before she found the bones."

"True. But maybe someone knew or suspected the skeleton was there. Or...that *something* was there," Iva said thoughtfully. "But, still, I can't imagine what urgency an old skeleton would have for someone. Unless it's a member of the family? Maybe there's a family secret hidden in the shop. Or maybe the *skeleton* is a family secret." She drew back into her seat on the sofa, bringing her wineglass to her lips, eyes sparkling.

Gideon Senior nudged the shopping bags on the floor. "What in blazes is all in here?" he asked, exchanging glances with his grandson.

Allowing herself to be distracted, Iva leaned forward to pull one of the bags onto her lap, then tilted it so that its contents tumbled onto the ottoman. Tissue paper flew as she unwrapped her treasures. "This is an aromatherapy diffuser, and here are the essential oils that I bought to go with it," she explained, holding up a device that looked similar to the one Fiona had used at her house, but it was made from metal instead of stone.

"And here are some aromatherapy candles, too—a stress-reliever for you, dearest," she smiled at Gideon

Senior. Then she looked at the younger Gideon and her eyebrows knit. "Hm. I should have gotten one for you too."

She opened up a small box and showed them a stack of cards with designs and alchemical symbols on them. "When I learn how, I'll do a Tarot reading for you, my dear," she told her host, with such sincerity in her voice that he had to look away to keep from grinning.

"What on God's earth is this?" Gideon Senior bellowed, lifting a rather large, heavy box from the second shopping bag.

"Oh, yes, that's my favorite of the bunch," Iva chirped enthusiastically, relieving him of the box. "It's a mini waterfall. You can put it on your desk…or I could put it in my bedroom." She slanted a look at him that made the younger Gideon raise his eyebrows and grin. "Or yours."

"A waterfall? On my desk? Iva, what—"

"Now, dear, remember your blood pressure." She patted his hand, then returned to the task of pulling the waterfall from its packaging. It was a bowl-like object stacked with rocks of varying sizes and shapes, and a long black electrical cord snaked from the back of it. "Isn't it cute?"

Gideon himself could hardly believe what he was seeing, but just as he was about to ask what one actually used a small waterfall for, the doorbell rang.

Iva looked up. "Oh, and, Gideon, I forgot—there was one more thing Salton mentioned. She said that you'll have a surprise tonight."

Riiiiight.

Gideon glanced at his grandfather and asked, "You didn't order any more pizza did you?"

"No!" he sputtered as Iva turned an accusatory glare on him.

"Pizza? Any *more* pizza?" she asked, shaking a finger. "What have you been eating, Hollis Gideon Nath?"

Gideon didn't hear his grandfather's reply as he stepped into the foyer to look out the peephole.

Fiona.

His heart stopped. She stood there on the doorstep, her mass of hair illuminated by the porch light, her beautiful face upturned toward the door.

He opened it, trying to keep his delight to a minimum in case he misunderstood the situation. And as he looked out, he was glad he had—for a shadow moved behind her, stepping onto the porch, and metamorphosing into her shop-smurf Carl.

"Hello Gideon," she said, smiling, but tentative in her look. "Are you...busy? It looks like you might have company, and I don't want to intrude."

"It's just my grandfather and Iva," he explained, looking at Carl, wondering what this meant.

"Oh. Good." Obvious relief broke out over her face. "I knew I was taking a chance in coming here, but...I...." she trailed off, and shot a glance at Carl, who stood leaning against the porch column, arms crossed over his abdomen.

"I guess you don't need me any more, hmm?" he asked, glancing at Gideon, and pushing away from his relaxed stance. "Is it all right if I take off now? Mission accomplished."

She looked back at Gideon, and warmth flooded him at the blatant uncertainty in her eyes. "Of course. Fiona, you're always welcome here," he said, trying to keep the emotion from gushing in his voice.

No sooner had the door closed behind Carl and the

chilly October air than Gideon pulled Fiona into his arms and, jamming his hands into her hair, pushed her up against the door to kiss the life out of her.

"You're here," he murmured.

"Mmm," she sighed against his mouth, and he felt her lips curl in a soft smile.

"Gideon, who is—*oh.*"

They broke apart and Fiona shifted to see Iva standing there with a pleased smile on her face. "So you did come, after all."

"Yes." She looked up at Gideon. "Yes, I did."

Then, noticing for the first time how the older lady was dressed, Fiona clapped her hands together. "Oh, Iva, I love your outfit! You look so bright and happy."

Iva slipped her hand through Fiona's arm and tugged her toward the living room. "I just have to show you this deck of Tarot cards I bought tonight. At least *you* will appreciate them. They're all angels!"

"Tarot cards? Do you read them?" Fiona asked curiously as she sat on the floor next to the ottoman. "Didn't your friend Jean read them too? The woman who died last summer?"

"She was murdered," Iva replied calmly. "And she used her cards to help Diana and Ethan to find the killer."

Gideon looked at her. "What did you just say?" He blinked, then looked at his grandfather.

Gideon Senior harrumphed a little. "Yes, well, she's right," he said. "Jean's—well, you tell it, Iva. I can see that my grandson won't believe me."

"Jean came back as a ghost at her lake house—the one Diana Iverson, Ethan's girlfriend—inherited, and she used her Tarot cards and some other *activity,*" Iva said with a smile, "to give them messages that helped them find the killer."

Gideon sank onto the sofa. He felt as if he were in some sort of alternate reality. "Really."

"It's true," Fiona said, giving him a bright grin. "Ethan told me all about it." She seemed to revel in the fact that he was stunned and confused and completely upended.

"All right." What else could he say? The rest of them —even his very staid, grounded grandfather—seemed completely okay with the direction this conversation was going.

Fiona grinned at Gideon's obvious confusion and skepticism, and turned her attention to his grandfather. "Hello Mr. Nath. It's so good to see you again."

"Nice of you to stop by here," he smiled down at her, where she'd settled on the floor among Iva's bags and purchases. "Poor Gideon didn't know what to do with himself tonight before you came around."

"Grandfather—" Gideon started, but Iva interrupted smoothly, "Have you ever seen such beautiful cards? They're all angels—did I mention that? Archangels, and..."

Fiona turned her attention to the items scattered all over the ottoman just as Gideon Senior pulled a large, folded piece of paper from the pile.

"What's this? A map of your foot?" He glared at Iva, but, to Fiona's delight, she merely smiled at him. "What the hell do you need a map of a foot for?"

"It's a reflexology map," Iva told him calmly, taking the paper from him. As she began to gather up the rest of her items, dropping them back into two large shopping bags, she said, "Now, dearest, it's time we got on our way and let these two have some time together."

Gideon Senior looked at her for a moment and then a slow smile eased across his face. "Yes, m'dear, I believe you're right. Let's pack up your stuff. I'll—er—drive you home."

As they strolled to the door, followed by Fiona and Gideon, Iva turned to speak to her. "Would you like to have lunch sometime soon? I'd love to talk with you about your palmistry—maybe learn a little bit from you. Salton did some palm-reading tonight, and it was just as fascinating as the ones you did. And I'd like to show you these runes I picked up as well."

"I'd love to have lunch," Fiona said, meaning it. "How about on Monday? I don't open until three on Mondays."

The two Gideons exchanged glances as though they weren't sure whether to approve or disapprove of this alliance—but, Fiona noticed with a private snicker, neither of them had the nerve to say anything.

She hugged Iva goodnight, and pressed a kiss to the smooth cheek of Gideon's grandfather—a little sorry to see them go, but very glad to have their grandson to herself.

The last thing she heard before the door closed was Gideon Senior's demand, "What the hell is a rune, anyway?"

SIXTEEN

LATER THAT NIGHT, much later, Fiona smoothed a thick lock of hair off Gideon's forehead, looked deeply into his eyes, and said, "I acted like a fool earlier today."

She faced him, lying on her side, propped up on one elbow.

He kissed her mouth, swollen and pink from passion, and replied, "I wouldn't say *fool*…but whatever you want to call it, I confess I expected the utopia to take a turn for the worse. But I didn't expect you to come back so soon." He sighed, pulling back slightly, running his hand down her arm. "I thought I'd be waiting a week or two…and the thought was unbearable."

She smiled at him, but there was more than a hint of shame around the corners of her mouth. "I was afraid. I still am, I suppose…but I couldn't stay away—and I realized I was just playing a game with you. I don't want to play games with you, Gideon. I can't promise you I won't be afraid again—because I probably will, regardless of where this goes—but I can promise you that I won't play games like that ever again." Her voice was low, rumbling, husky, and heavy with emotion.

He looked away for a moment, gathering his thoughts, curling his fingers around her long, slim hand. "Tonight made me realize how much I care about you… and how much a part of my life you've become." It was probably more than that, but Gideon wasn't ready to verbalize it just yet. Not to her, and not to himself.

Her eyes flickered down, then back up to look at him, and the intensity in them was gone, replaced by laughter and perhaps, in the deepest part of them, a bit of fear. "Your grandfather is such a dear. And Iva is *so* lovely. She is the neatest lady—I'm so glad to know her, too. They are ridiculously cute together."

Taking his cue from her—the subject was over for now—Gideon smiled and yanked lightly on a long copper coil, then rolled onto his back. "You and she are two peas in a pod with all your new-age stuff, and that scares the hell out of me and my grandfather. I'm not sure Wicks Hollow will survive you two reading runes and picking out Tarot cards."

It occurred to him at that moment—surprising that it never had before—how alike Fiona and Iva *were*…and how alike he and his grandfather were. Was there a parallel here?

A shiver sneaked up his spine and he shoved that thought away. He was feeling amazing things about Fiona, but he certainly wasn't ready to admit she was the love of his life.

Not quite.

"It's *picking* runes and *reading* Tarot cards," Fiona corrected him with a giggle. She rolled backward, threw her arms enthusiastically wide and looked up at the ceiling with a joyous smile. "I think we'll have a lot of fun terrorizing you two Naths, mark my words."

"That's just what I'm afraid of." His words sounded glum, but in fact, her joy made him feel warm and expansive and so very content. It glowed onto him—from her blushing skin and over the sheets, covering him with a blanket of happiness.

But her next words whisked that blanket away.

"Gideon, tell me about your mother. And father. You never talk about them…and when I was reading your grandfather's palm and mentioned his one child, he seemed a little—well, uncomfortable about it."

He went cold.

He didn't really want to talk about his parents. They didn't matter. They weren't part of his life any more—thanks to his father—and they certainly weren't going to be part of his legacy.

"My mother is I guess what you'd call a hippie," Fiona continued, her voice steady and quiet as she laid there, her face directed toward the ceiling. "She lives in Costa Rica with her partner—currently a man, though she's been known to hook up with a woman. She weaves baskets and reads palms and makes quite a comfortable living off the tourists. He's an electrician, and works for one of the resorts."

She turned toward him and started to stroke his arm, lightly running her nails up and down, from wrist to elbow. His hair lifted in the wake of the sensation, and the rhythm soothed him.

"My mother—Claudia—raised me with the notion that men are disposable and dispensable. Good for sex once in awhile, and moving heavy things, and whistling for the dog when he wouldn't come. That's about it."

He couldn't help but chuckle at the last part of her

comment. "Very practical. Not something I'd expect from you, my dear."

"I can be very practical, Gideon, and you know it. In fact, I'm learning to be more practical every day now that I'm a small-business owner. Look at how quickly I called you when I found that skeleton. Pretty practical if you ask me...to call my attorney when I find a dead body." He could hear the lilt of laughter in her voice. "And please don't change the subject on me. I really want to know about your parents. Tell me."

"My mother's dead. Suicide." Even after twenty years, he could barely say the words.

"*Gideon.*" Her voice was just right—not gushingly sympathetic, not shocked. Just...right. It gave him the courage to speak further.

"My father's in jail. Life in prison. Drug dealing, once killed a guy during a deal." He laughed, a grating, ironic chuckle. Fiona's hand brushed over his chest to rest across it and onto his shoulder, half-hugging him. "He was a musician. Music was his life. He lived it, breathed for it, was addicted to it—to the detriment of everything else in his life.

"He attracted women as most musicians do, and my mother was no exception. She loved him, but eventually couldn't handle the gigs, the drugs, the focus on only living for the moment...which was all he ever did. She took a bottle of pills along with an alcohol cocktail when I was sixteen. They couldn't save her."

Fiona didn't speak. Her breathing had increased, but its waves still moved, soft and smooth, next to him. He was aware of the length of her body lined up along his, her breasts pressing into the side of his ribs, her arm a vee over his chest.

"My grandfather—my father's father, of course—

took me in, thank God. I wouldn't admit it at first, but it was the best thing for me, to have a solid, stable home. He made sure I had the best education, and even though he wasn't around much—and when he was, he was always focused on work—I felt like I had a place. I was so grateful to him for taking me in that I was determined to be a better son than his own son had been. Make him proud of me."

"You've obviously succeeded." He felt her lips move against his shoulder when she spoke and a bit of husk tinged her words.

"I'm not so sure about that. He came rushing home from his vacation the minute he found out about Valente's death, as if I couldn't handle a simple probate."

"Gideon, your grandfather is very proud of you. I can see it in his eyes, and the way he acts around you. There's no doubt about that. He adores you. What does he think about your art? Your drawings?"

He had to resist to keep from pulling away, but he knew she felt him tense because her face snapped up to look at him. "He doesn't know about them. He…he believes art is a waste of time, and in truth, so do I. It's a silly hobby left over from high school."

Gideon felt her draw her breath to speak, so he headed her off. "I don't want to talk about it anymore, Fiona. Tell me what it was like growing up in a commune."

You are a fool, man.

Gideon frowned at himself in the rearview mirror as he pulled into the parking structure of Rachel Backley's building. What ever had possessed him to make good on his promise to escort Rachel to her company's big award-ceremony shindig?

He wouldn't worry about it so much except that he was wasting an evening he could be spending with Fiona...lovely, fiery, the-only-woman-for-him-Fiona...to play trophy-man at an event he had no interest in whatsoever.

At least Fiona had been understanding...and she really had been. Although there had been just the slightest flare of irritation in her cinnamon eyes, it had disappeared with his earnest explanation—stolen from Rachel's own imploring speech not to leave her high and dry on such an important night—and she sent him off with kisses, and promises of her own.

"I'll be home as soon as I can," he'd vowed, kissing her at the door of his condo, where he'd suggested she spend the evening.

"I won't wait up if it's too late," she teased, her cinnamon eyes hot and inviting.

Damn. He should have blown off Rachel and stayed home. But at least he knew Fiona would be waiting for him, warm and soft and curvy and sweet-smelling in his bed.

Straightening the bow tie of his tux, he took a quick, last glance in the rearview mirror before leaving the car to rush up and collect Rachel. She would be ready, and pacing her condo's living room, as always.

A flash of familiarity washed over him as he rode up in the elevator. This would be the last time he would do so, he mused, unless, somehow, he and Rachel maintained their friendship. Which...he didn't really see happening.

Rachel was, as expected, waiting for him. She was fairly pacing, like a caged tiger. Although she was put together perfectly as usual, he noticed tightness and stress in her face, and unusual weariness around her eyes. Her sleek hair was pulled back into a simple black velvet bow studded with sequins that matched the sparkles on her floor-length gown.

"You look stressed, Rache," he commented as they rode down in the elevator.

She jerked and looked at him, as if pulled from some deep thoughts. "I am. But soon this night will be over." Then she busied herself by digging through her impossibly tiny handbag—tiny, as compared to Fiona's monstrosity.

"I can't even imagine what you've been going through."

She shook her head as the elevator doors opened. "No, you can't," she murmured enigmatically.

The Amway Grand was the locale for The Marage Group's huge celebration. Gideon pulled smoothly into the valet parking lane and escorted Rachel into the crisply elegant hotel, already counting the minutes until he could leave.

Once inside, he made a trip to the bar for a Scotch, and wine for Rachel, and then remained at her side as she turned on her corporate persona and schmoozed her way through the cluster of people—clients, potential clients, press, and representatives from *Fortune*.

She worked the crowd, and Gideon watched her, realizing suddenly that this was a lot more boring without Fiona at his side. He used to enjoy these types of functions —still did, sometimes...but he had been spoiled by a fiery, funny, feckless redhead who always made him laugh.

Even when he was trying to be proper.

Especially when he was trying to be proper.

Rachel approached to guide him to the head table, where they'd sit during dinner. After the meal, she and her partner would do their overview of the company's milestones and successes over the last year, and accept the award. Looking covertly at his watch, Gideon guessed that he could perhaps make it home by midnight, crawl into his warm bed, and gather that soft, supple body into his arms.

A tiny tremor raced through him. It was wonderful to be in love.

It was nine-thirty, and Gideon couldn't stop thinking about Fiona. He'd been a good companion this evening, making conversation, complimenting Rachel and her team—which was well-deserved—but now he was getting a bit antsy. He firmed his lips, jutting his chin out, just as Rachel turned to look up at him. He immediately rearranged his features into a more relaxed expression, but he saw the question in her eyes.

"I think I'd like to get some air," she told him, squeezing his arm.

"All right." He nodded to their companions while feeling mild surprise.

It was very unlike Rachel to want to leave the spotlight, but she seemed strangely unlike herself tonight, and he thought, in a moment of guilt, that perhaps she was annoyed with his lack of attention this evening.

Indeed, once they had stepped outside into the crisp autumn night, she looked up at him, scrutinizing him with sharp eyes.

"Are you all right tonight, Gideon?" she asked, slipping her hand from his arm and stepping back to look directly at him. "You're so quiet."

An easy smile crossed his face. "Just a bit distracted," he responded. "I'm sorry if it was noticeable. I hope I didn't make you feel awkward."

"No, no. I know you'd rather be elsewhere. Thank you again for coming with me, even though things have changed. I know all of this talk about finances and awards and milestones can become tedious, but it's going to be well worth it."

A smile curved her red lips, reminding him how attractive he found her…when he wasn't thinking about a redheaded woman with wildly curling hair. "I'm nearly ready to leave myself—I've already made my excuses. All I have to do is say goodnight to Blake, and we can go."

"Great." Though it seemed odd she was willing to cut the evening short, Gideon wasn't about to question her desire to leave early.

Moments later, they were in his Mercedes, gliding silently through the streets of Grand Rapids.

"I hope you'll come up for a drink," Rachel commented idly as they pulled up to the valet parking at her high-rise condo not far from the river.

Gideon would have refused, but he felt more than a bit guilty about his distraction this evening—it was such an important night for her, and he'd been barely there. And it was early yet. Hardly past ten. "A quick one would be nice."

Rachel was unusually silent in the elevator, and Gideon stood with his hands plunged into his pockets, staring at his gleaming black shoes as the car rose to the sixth floor, again, feeling the familiarity of the situation. Once inside her spacious condo, Gideon stripped off his tux jacket and loosened the hand-tied bow tie around his neck, stuffing it into one of his pockets.

Rachel was more deliberate: she slipped off her shoes and, tucking them under her arm, took off the one-carat diamond earrings she wore, gathering them into the palm of her hand.

"Help yourself," she said unnecessarily—for Gideon had already made his way to the gleaming glass-topped bar to pour a short whiskey. He made her a drink as well —her usual dirty martini with a double-olive garnish.

As he turned back, absorbing the scene in which he was in the midst, realization zipped through him. They moved about with the ease and familiarity of an old married couple—he flinging his clothing on the sofa, she divesting herself of earrings and shoes without a thought for him as a guest. He helped himself to her bar, even going to far as to pour her regular drink.

It was a routine. It felt natural…yet it did not.

If he hadn't met Fiona, would he have gone on along with this arrangement until his five-year-plan indicated it was time to get married?

And then would he have asked Rachel? Someone like her, for certain.

If he hadn't met Fiona.

Gideon took a large sip of whiskey, suddenly uncomfortable. Wordlessly, he handed Rachel her drink, then sank onto a thick leather chair, hanging his hands over his knees.

She took the glass, stirred it with her finger, then took a quick sip and set it on a nearby table. "I'm glad you came up," she said, looking at him with a sudden intensity in her expression. "We need to talk."

Oh Jesus.

Gideon's head begin to pound and he took another

drink. "Oh?" he replied belatedly, trying to keep an even expression on his face.

She raised her glass to her lips, sipped, and then, frowning, pulled it away. "Are you still seeing that redhead—Fiona? How's it going?"

Gideon swallowed. What was she up to? "Things are fine. We're seeing each other. Occasionally."

Why he chose to downplay his relationship with Fiona wasn't clear to him in that hazy moment, but perhaps it was merely an attempt to keep Rachel from feeling bad. The last thing he wanted was her crying on his shoulder again.

"How about you?" The moment the words left his mouth, he regretted them. Of course she wasn't seeing anyone—or else why would she need him for an escort tonight?

"I need to talk to you about something."

The look on her face was weary, resigned, and a bit fearful. Rachel Backley, woman executive, fearful? It made him distinctly uncomfortable. In fact, it made him suddenly, inexplicably *ill*.

"Go ahead," he said cautiously.

"I know this is something you're not going to want to hear," she began, looking down at her perfectly mani-cured fingernails, "but I felt it only right to be perfectly honest. We had an arrangement for years, and…well, there's something I need to tell you."

"Yes?"

"I'm pregnant."

SEVENTEEN

GIDEON SILENTLY OPENED the door to his bedroom, stepping in with care so as not to disturb Fiona.

The last thing he wanted was for her to wake up and want to talk.

Like a wraith, he moved about the room without a sound, slipping his shoes off, unbuttoning his shirt, folding it and his tux trousers over a chair. He didn't want to think, didn't want to talk…he just wanted Fiona.

A very heavy sleeper, she lay unmoving in an embryo-like lump under the thick duvet in the middle of his bed. The faint scent of some pleasing fragrance hung in the air, and he noticed two candles that had burned low next to her side.

Gideon slid under the covers, reaching for her, *needing* her. She sensed him, turning in her sleep, and rolled into his arms. Her soft hair amassed under his chin, and he tilted his head to bury his lips and his nose in its warm comfort.

His body, his mind, his emotions—all were numb, stuck, frozen back in that moment at Rachel's house.

He shouldn't be here, with Fiona—that one thing was certain; he should sleep on the couch—but when he'd left Rachel's, after downing a second whiskey, he found himself unable to keep away from the one thing he was clear about.

He needed her. And she was here, waiting for him.

Damn. Oh, God…

He squeezed his eyes closed tightly, trying to banish the knowledge, the reality…the truth.

Fiona sighed in her sleep, adjusting her warm body, brushing against the hair on his chest. He held her closer, breathing in her scent, staring into the darkness over her head. Trying not to think.

When he moved to drop a kiss onto her cheek, Fiona sighed and wriggled slightly in his arms. "Gideon?" she murmured, half asleep. "Mmmm."

She stretched, shifting against him, brushing her breasts over his chest, and sliding her knee up between his legs.

Gideon pulled back, still holding her, but away so that he wouldn't be tempted into the glorious web she spun. He swallowed a hard lump, throat convulsing against her head, and closed his eyes.

It was hell.

She rolled toward him, and her hand moved into the hair on his chest, then she smoothed slim fingers over his shoulder as she nuzzled against his throat. His body, numb though it was, began to respond to her touch and he couldn't still his fingers from brushing over the mounds of hair and across her soft cheek. Fiona arched against him, sighing, still half-asleep, but with a small moan that sent a pang of arousal straight into his belly.

Even as he knew he shouldn't, he did: he slid his hands to cover her breasts, one thumb brushing over a nipple that tautened beneath it like a flower awakening. He covered her mouth with his, he pulled her hips tightly against him. The moan from the back of her throat was louder this time, and he could see her eyes flutter in the dim light as she tipped her head back to leave her neck bare to him.

With a fierceness that still surprised him, Gideon bent to her, covering her body with his, sliding his fingers into and around the deepest, warmest part of her. He closed his eyes and coaxed from Fiona the deepest, most shattering response he'd ever done with any woman.

And when it was over, he felt, rather than heard, her lips move against him.

I love you, Gideon.

He closed his eyes and cursed his life.

Fiona hummed as she dumped a cup of fresh blueberries into the bowl, carefully folding the batter over them with a spatula.

"Good morning," came Gideon's scratchy voice.

She looked up at him, tossing a coil of hair out of her face, and smiled. "Hello, cutie. Sleep well?"

"What are you making?"

"Whole wheat blueberry muffins. My specialty…one of them, anyway." She flashed him a coy smile, but he didn't seem to notice. "Coffee?"

He grunted an assent as he sank onto a chair at the small breakfast-nook-like table.

She poured him coffee, then returned to her muffin batter—dropping healthy spoonfuls into the battered muffin pan her mother had given her. "How was the party?"

"Boring."

Fiona flashed him a glance. It wasn't like him to be so reticent. Maybe he was just tired. She slid the muffin pan into the oven and came over to the table, sliding onto Gideon's lap and wrapping her arms around his sleep-scented body, burying her face in his neck. His hands moved to caress her back for only a moment before dropping away.

"You know, Gideon," she murmured into his shoulder, her heart thumping madly at the suggestion she was about to make, "I've been thinking."

"Oh?"

She pressed a light kiss onto his warm, smooth shoulder and allowed her lips to curve into a smile there. "We've been seeing a lot of each other, lately…and…"

He shifted so that she was forced to sit up, away from him. "Fiona, could you get me some sugar?"

"Sugar?" she looked at him in surprise.

"For my coffee?" He stared intently at the cup of sable liquid, not meeting her eyes.

"Sure." She got up, mentally shaking her head.

Gideon always took his coffee black.

Ah well, maybe it would be easier to say it when she wasn't cuddled in his arms. "Anyway, I was thinking… you've been staying over so much lately that I thought you might want to…leave a toothbrush at my place—I mean, at Ethan's place. And maybe some other things."

"A toothbrush?"

Fiona banged into the corner of the big oaken desk, and winced and swore, tears springing to her eyes. Her thigh screamed with pain where the edge—though dull and rounded, but lethal nevertheless—met her tender skin.

She dropped the bundle of dust rags that she'd been carrying and stood there, soundly rubbing the sore spot while moaning in frustration. "For crying out loud!" she groaned, glaring at the monstrosity of the desk on which The Lamp sat. "I should have moved your big butt much earlier instead of letting you block my aisle way."

The pain ebbed and she stooped to pick up the rags. Just as she stood, she saw a flicker from The Lamp on top of the desk…and saw the fringe on its shade shift and sway as though someone had run a single finger through it.

As always, a prickle of coolness shimmered up her neck, but Fiona felt too annoyed and ornery to even care. Of course, it didn't help that Gideon had been acting remote and distracted for the last few days, either. He'd been really busy with work, and they hadn't seen each other since the morning she made blueberry muffins for him the morning after his "date" with Rachel.

She tried not to worry about it, so for now she focused her irritation on the lamp.

Thus far the ghost—or whatever it was—hadn't caused her any harm other than a few startles, and she wasn't about to let it start bothering her now—especially when she was going to have the mother lode of bruises on her thigh.

"What do you want?" she snapped at The Lamp. "I sure wish you'd do something other than flicker at me. If you're trying to tell me something, why don't you find some other way to communicate?"

Abruptly, everything went still.

The fringe stopped *in mid-sway*, every light in the

shop went black—even the constant hum of the air conditioning ceased as though strangled into silence.

Fiona swallowed and looked above her, half-expecting to see some specter-like apparition hovering overhead—but there was nothing to see except the railing of the balcony above…and Gretchen—sitting in her spot, tail twitching, amber eyes gazing coldly down at Fiona.

The room became cooler, and then the stillness began to soften as a faint whisper of rose-scented breeze brushed her cheek.

"What?" she whispered. "What is it? What can I do?"

She looked around, but there was nothing to direct her. Then, as though the spirit gave one last sigh and succumbed to the effort its activity had caused, the breeze disappeared and everything stilled once again.

Fiona remained frozen for a moment, but nothing else happened to stir the air. The lights remained dark and the shop silent. The heavy stillness was punctuated only by the sounds of slamming car doors and voices from out on the street.

She turned toward the back of the shop where the circuit breaker was and took two steps before she tripped went flying, landing in a heap on the hardwood floor.

Even as she swore in an extremely specific manner, she reached out to touch what had tripped her, and felt something solid protruding from the bottom of the mammoth desk.

It was too dark in that small bend of the aisle to see what it was—but one thing was certain: *it hadn't been there when she walked by moments earlier.*

A prickle danced up her spine. Ghosts couldn't actually *move* things, could they?

Suddenly freezing, she looked around warily.

Maybe they could.

Taking better care now, in the dark, Fiona pulled herself to her feet and limped toward the back of the shop. Fortunately, sunlight streamed through one of the back windows—the one, in fact, that had been smashed and since replaced when the burglar had broken in—enabling her to find and flip the correct switches in the circuit box.

Since she had by no means been certain that action would work and re-illuminate the shop, she breathed a small sigh of relief when the lights came back on and the air conditioner hummed to life.

Hurrying back toward the center of the store, under the balcony in that small cubbyhole where the desk sat brooding like Jabba the Hut, Fiona crouched at the spot where she'd tripped and saw that a small drawer had popped from the bottom of the desk.

"A secret drawer!" she squealed, looking up at Gretchen. The feline had deigned to descend several steps and now sat next to the desk, watching her with condescension. The single patch of copper fur in a swath of black made the eye it surrounded look even larger and more intense than its partner.

Gretchen, at least, seemed very interested in what Fiona was up to.

When she pried the drawer completely out of its slot, Fiona was elated to find a manila envelope stuffed inside with what felt like a small book. Just as she was tearing the paper to open it, the bells jingled as the front door opened.

Fiona shot to her feet, narrowly missing the lethal desk corner, and hurried out to greet her customer.

"Fiona!" greeted Iva as she started toward her, arms outstretched for an embrace. "I hope you don't mind I'm a little early. I wanted to browse a bit before we left for lunch."

"No problem. You look marvelous!" Fiona hugged the soft, sweet-smelling woman as a wash of grief for her own grandmother came over her. But she was too keyed up by her discovery to dwell on that thought.

"I just found a secret drawer in that big old desk," she told her excitedly. "The Ghostly Presence led me to it!"

"At last! We're making progress." Iva clapped her hands together, a little drawstring bag dangling from her wrist, and demanded to see the drawer at once. "What's in it?"

Fiona produced the manila envelope, tearing it open as she spoke. "I banged myself on the desk and yelled at the ghost—and then the lights went out and this drawer popped open." The envelope tore and its contents spilled onto the floor. She and Iva stooped, nearly bumping heads, to gather up the sheaf of papers—which appeared to be letters, newspaper clippings, and some old photos.

"I think we should go to lunch *right away*," Iva said as they gathered them up.

"I agree!" Fiona said gaily. "Orbra's?"

"Definitely!"

***

The manila envelope contained clues that would make Nancy Drew green with envy.

The two of them had the contents of the mysterious envelope spread out on the table before Orbra even noticed they were there.

Fortunately, for once, the nosy and argumentative Maxine and Juanita weren't at the tea shop. In fact, it was nearly empty, so Fiona and Iva had taken a table near the back of the charming cafe.

"That way if Maxine comes by, she might not see us," Iva said. Then both of them began to laugh, because of *course* Maxine would see them, and of *course* she would horn in if she did.

That was what Maxine Took *did*.

"What's going on here with you two?" Orbra demanded as she approached. She was watching Iva scrounge through the sheaf of papers covered with spindly writing that had faded so much it was mostly illegible. "What's all this?"

Iva explained far more succinctly than Fiona had expected her to do—with hardly any mentions of a Ghostly Presence—then went on to order a pot of Earl Grey for herself and a full afternoon-tea menu.

Fiona, too engrossed with some yellowed newspaper clippings to pay much attention to the menu, merely waved her hand and said, "I'll have the same, and something herbal for tea. You pick, Orbra. No meat." And then, as an after-thought, she added, "Some kind of scone too, please, Orbra."

"Right," said the efficient woman as she glanced back toward the kitchen as if to recall what she had in stock. "I have a violet rooibos that just came in—how about that?"

"Sounds great," Fiona replied, looking up with interest as the words penetrated her consciousness. "Violet, did you say? That sounds very nice."

"Of course it'll be nice," Orbra grumbled. "I don't serve anything that isn't nice."

"Thank you."

"Oh, there goes Cherry—and that's her niece with her," Orbra said, looking out the front window. "They're heading to Grand Rapids for a shopping trip for the bed and breakfast she's opening. Too bad they can't stop in and chat. Did you meet Leslie yet, Fiona? She's turning Shenstone House up on the hill outside town into a bed and breakfast. Leslie's the one who's hooking up with that hot blacksmith Declan Zyler, you know."

"Blacksmith?" Fiona asked. "There are still people who do that? Does he work at Greenfield Village?"

Orbra laughed. "No, no, he's been doing lots of restoration work. He's doing the staircase at Shenstone House."

"Shenstone House is haunted too, you know," Iva said.

"It is?" Fiona asked, looking at the two older ladies. "There are two haunted buildings in one town?"

Iva and Orbra looked at each other and began to hoot with laughter. Jowls shook, eyes filled with mirthful tears, and cloudlike, wispy hair floated and danced like nimbuses as they laughed and laughed.

Finally, Orbra contained herself enough to gasp, "Only two?" And then she and Iva were off in another round of chuckles—though not quite as uncontrolled that time.

Shaking her head at the two of them, Fiona couldn't help a smile at their antics. Whatever it was that was so funny, the two Tuesday Ladies were certainly enjoying life.

She returned her attention to the curling corners of a newspaper article that had been shoved into an envelope with some kind of letter.

Fiona began to read, with difficulty, the faded printing—then stopped cold. Prickles erupted all over her skin.

"Iva! Listen to this headline: 'Woman's Disappearance Still Unsolved.' And here's the article—it looks like it's from the *Chicago Tribune*: 'Police still have no leads in the disappearance of Miss Gretchen Freudenhofer, 22, a recent immigrant from Berlin, Germany. Friends with whom she was staying reported her missing after she did not return from a shopping trip on August 25. The woman was last seen disembarking from a bus near Lake Shore Drive. If anyone has any further information on this woman's whereabouts, they should report to the 153rd Precinct Office.'"

She raised her eyes to look across the table. "It's dated August 31, 1948."

"What were the initials on that bracelet?" Iva asked, her sharp blue eyes gleaming with interest across the table.

"G...J...F." Fiona smacked her hand on the table next to the teacup that had appeared without her notice. Hot tea sloshed onto her hand, splattering onto the blue chintz tablecloth. "Gretchen. Our skeleton must be Gretchen!"

As Orbra emerged from the kitchen wheeling a large tea cart, Fiona waved the small clipping. "We figured it out!"

Then she sobered. "If the skeleton is Gretchen, then..."

Iva was nodding from behind her tea cup. "Yes, it would seem that your Mr. Valente knew about her...or possibly—quite probably—had something to do with her appearing in that store room."

Unease flooded through Fiona. Had the old man been a murderer after all?

"Maybe something happened and she died in his shop—an accident—and he was too afraid to call the authorities, so he hid her body. Or someone else could have killed her and forced him to hide the body—or they could have even hidden it there without him knowing…" Fiona's voice trailed off as she realized she was defending a man she didn't know—and who could very well have been a murderer.

"Is there a picture of Gretchen in the article?" Iva reached across the table, her silver and sapphire charm bracelet jingling merrily.

Fiona handed her the curling paper then realized a tray of tea sandwiches had materialized. The super slim cucumber and cream cheese one, sprinkled with dill, caught her attention and she popped one in her mouth.

Iva was looking at her with a strange expression. "Fiona, did you look at this picture?"

"Yes. Of course," she replied, swiping up another elegant cucumber sandwich. She hadn't realized how hungry she was.

Iva looked at her as if expecting her to say more. When Fiona didn't, she went on, "Well, didn't you notice, my dear? You are the spitting image of Gretchen."

"What?" Fiona took the paper Iva offered back and looked at the grainy photo.

"*Wow*." The resemblance was uncanny, now that she actually realized it.

Almost unnatural.

How had she missed that?

"That's what Valente said in his letter," she said slowly. "That I reminded him of Gretchen. And so that's why he left me the shop. Guilt, maybe?"

"Stranger things have happened," Iva told her, her face grave. "Being intimately involved with a male senior citizen," she said with a delicate blush, "I'm constantly surprised at the way his mind works." She took another sip of the bergamot-scented Earl Grey.

"What else is in that envelope?" She pulled out a piece of paper folded in thirds.

When Iva unfolded it, Fiona could see the impressions of a typewriter's keys through the thin paper—the small dots where the sentences ended, an A and an F and other black marks as well.

As Iva read aloud, Fiona's heart pumped faster.

"'Hadn't you better report to the 153rd Precinct, Mr. Valente? If not, you will leave $50,000 in unmarked bills in a plain paper-wrapped package under the stairwell on the third floor of 350 Arch Street. Tomorrow, by 3:00. Come alone, or I'll be contacting the precinct *for* you.'"

There was no need for either woman to speak when Iva was done reading. They just gaped at each other, unmoving, as Orbra came with a small plate of scones.

"What is it?" asked the Dutchwoman, sliding into a chair next to them.

Iva explained—she really was quite good at the brief rundown—as Fiona discovered the delights of Orbra's blueberry scones.

"What's the date on the letter?" asked Orbra.

"Why, it's only fifteen years ago." Puzzlement washed over Iva's face. "Why drag up something like this so many years later?"

Fiona spread a good hunk of clotted cream on her scone as she replied, "Why indeed? Maybe whoever it is had just found out about it."

"They could still be blackmailing him—or, I mean, they could have been before he died." Orbra looked sharply at Fiona. "Do you know—was there anything odd about the way he died—like Jean, last summer?" Now she was looking at Iva.

"I thought Valente just died from old age," Fiona said slowly. "I'm sure Gideon would know, but I don't think it was anything sudden. I got the impression that he—Valente, I mean—had been declining and it was expected."

"A blackmailer isn't going to murder his golden goose," said Iva.

"Right. That doesn't make any sense," agreed Orbra. "But Poirot always asks the questions, you know. And so does Helga!" She smiled proudly at the mention of her granddaughter.

"Here's another envelope—very similar." Iva didn't seem to be interested in eating any longer. She pulled out a second letter with a very small scrap of newspaper just large enough to depict a very old, yellow photo of a man with his name imprinted under it.

"Josef Kremer." Iva said his name aloud, pursing her lips as she frowned. "That name's familiar to me, though I don't know why. Josef Kremer."

"What does the letter say?" Fiona asked, reaching to take the paper clipping.

Josef Kremer was a young man, not bad looking, with a thin, Hitler-like moustache and heavy brows. The photo was of terrible quality, and that in combination with its age, left much to be desired in the way of details.

"There's a letter with it. Another blackmail note!"

"Read it," Orbra ordered, snatching up a slender egg salad sandwich that had gone unnoticed on the tray and slipping it into her mouth.

"'Another missing person, Mr. Valente? Tsk, tsk. I'll look for another package of $50,000 as always. Tomorrow. By 3 pm.'" Iva looked up. "Dated almost a year later than the other one."

"He was definitely being blackmailed," Fiona said. "But by whom?"

"And what exactly for? The letters don't actually say," Orbra commented.

"Murder. Maybe Gretchen's murder?"

The three of them stared at one another for a moment, eyes sparkling at each other with interest and enthusiasm.

Then Fiona's heart surged into her throat, choking her. "Someone's been breaking into the shop—looking for something," she said. "Could it be this—the proof? Could they be looking for these letters?"

"It must be someone who knew Valente who's breaking in. It's the only thing that makes any sense—someone who knew him well enough to blackmail him fifteen years ago. And maybe still was blackmailing him until he died."

"And he—or she—is trying to find the evidence of whatever Valente's crime was before someone else does?" Fiona drew her brows together. "Or maybe it's the blackmailer…trying to destroy the evidence of the blackmail so *he* isn't implicated."

The three of them looked at each other and nodded soberly.

"It could be either one of those scenarios," Iva said.

"I'll call Helga. She should know about this, considering all that's been going on," Orbra said, and Fiona nodded in agreement.

"And you should tell Gideon too," Iva said. "I'm sure he'll have some ideas."

Fiona's giddiness faded abruptly.

Gideon had been acting so strange lately. Remote and…disconnected.

She bit her lip and studied the paper scraps in an effort to hide her thoughts.

But Iva wasn't fooled, and she said quietly, "I think

something's been bothering him, Fiona. Lately, he seems so preoccupied. I meant to mention it earlier, but we got distracted. Hollis and I had dinner with him on Sunday night, and he was definitely not himself."

"I've noticed it too. Just this week. He's been withdrawn and quiet...and almost short-tempered. Gideon might be a stick in the mud sometimes, but he's not usually impatient and snappish." Fiona sipped her tea—which was a lovely, floral brew with a slight purplish hue because of the violets.

"We were going to see a movie on Sunday night, but he called and said he was going to have dinner with the two of you," she went on. "Just the three of you. It didn't bother me at all, truly. I just thought it was odd the way he did it at the last minute."

Iva reached across the table and patted Fiona's hand. "You're right not to let it bother you, my dear. He cares about you very much. Truly. I have a...well, I have a sixth sense about these things. This is so cliché, but I can't think of any other way to say it except this: I've not seen Gideon this happy since I've known him.

"You've brought him to life. Whatever is bothering him will work itself out. I *know* it."

EIGHTEEN

FIONA DECIDED to wait to tell Gideon about what she and Iva had found, thinking it would be better to show him the letters in person.

But when he called to invite her to dinner that night, she knew it was a bad sign.

It was the way he did it—the way he called and, in a very business-like manner, invited her to dine with him that evening. It reminded her too much of the scene in *When Harry Met Sally...* when Harry and Sally meet for an uncomfortable "it was a mistake" dinner after they slept together the first time.

Not a good sign.

At least he hadn't had his assistant call, Fiona thought morosely.

Her hands felt clammy for the rest of the day whenever she thought about it. When evening came, she took off the scarf she'd taken to wearing as a headband and pinned up her hair on the sides so that it kept her face free and fell down her back. Of course, now she wouldn't have the benefit of the nervous habit of pushing her bangs out of her face—or hiding behind them if she needed to cloak her expression—but Fiona was too miserable to care.

She knew this was not going to be fun. Her antennae had been singing ever since the morning she'd asked Gideon if he wanted to leave his toothbrush at her house.

Something was wrong.

Terribly wrong.

Navigating her Beetle through Grand Rapids, Fiona smiled a wry one. She finally got comfortable enough with a guy to want to build something permanent out of hot sex, great meals, and wonderful conversations—not to mention a literal skeleton in her closet—and she'd somehow scared him away.

She might have scared him, but she'd scared herself more.

Hell, she might as well be honest with herself—she always was, Fiona thought as she jerked her steering wheel to grab an on-the-street parking place.

She was in love with the most amazing, sensitive, talented man she'd ever met—and he had scheduled a Dear Jane Dinner.

***

Gideon had never been more miserable in his life. He'd spent the entire weekend after the evening with Rachel carrying what felt like a mason block in his stomach.

Now, as he sat across the table from Fiona—who looked as disheveled and New Agey and lovely as always—he found himself taking a larger drink of his martini than he should have. It was very dry, with Grey Goose, smooth and clean…but the way he swallowed it

—hard, fast, and large—ruined it, and left him with a rasping throat.

He'd have been better off just shooting the vodka, or something just as strong, without the fancy dressing of a martini glass and olive.

Fiona sat across the table from him, watching as tears sprang to his eyes while he battled the urge to cough and choke.

Her hands rested on the table, folded neatly, her fifteen rings (he'd counted them more than once—and the number was always the same) glinting silver and platinum in the low light. She looked at him with large cinnamon eyes, and there was an eerie calmness about her that made him feel even worse.

When the server approached and asked if they were ready to order their dinner, Fiona folded her menu and laid it precisely next to her plate.

"Not yet," she told the waiter. "We'll need at least fifteen minutes. Come back then, please."

Gideon closed his mouth and stared at the menu. After the server walked away, he looked up at Fiona, who was watching him steadily.

"I don't see any reason to order dinner," she told him calmly. "But I didn't want to mention that in front of the waiter. Why don't you tell me what's on your mind?"

"Fiona." He took another drink of his martini—this one went down much better, though his stomach was in square knots. "I hardly know where to begin."

"Let me help you. It has to do with Rachel, I'm sure. And it has to do with us." She linked her fingers in front of her and looked at him.

Gideon heaved a deep sigh. He might as well put it all on the table—Fiona was already halfway there. "I found out on Saturday night that Rachel's pregnant."

He waited while she digested the words. She blanched, then her expression settled.

Then, most horribly of all, it became bleak.

Cold, dead, empty and bleak.

"I see. Well, that makes it easy for me, then," she said in a voice so calm his heart stopped.

"What do you mean?"

"I realized after I made that stupid comment the other day about you leaving your toothbrush that I probably scared you off. I know that it scared me; and pretty much as soon as I said the words, I wanted to take them back.

"I was going to tell you I wanted to slow things down… but I guess that would be a moot point, now, wouldn't it? I have to assume you're telling me about Rachel's pregnancy because you're the father. This just makes things *so* much easier. For both of us." She gave him a very bright smile.

Gideon felt like he was standing on the edge of a sand pit, and the sand was falling away under his feet as he stumbled backward.

He delved into her with his gaze, searching her expression to see if he could read anything behind her words. She appeared calm, sincere, and collected. He looked closely into her eyes, and they matched his without guile as she held her smile.

Maybe for a trifle too long.

"We're too different," she said. "But it's been a lot of fun and wonderful hot sex—and a few laughs, too…but, you see, I've been feeling a little cramped lately." She chuckled, the sound clear and unstrained, and Gideon suddenly knew—with a sharp blow to the heart—that she was telling the truth.

That it didn't matter what he'd planned to say. That

his carefully-thought-out decision and position on the future no longer had meaning.

"I don't know for sure that the baby's mine," he managed to say, trying to salvage some ounce of control. "I don't want to stop seeing you, Fiona—"

"Well, that was obvious since you slid into bed with me the night you found out—the night you must have found out about the baby," Fiona said with the faintest harsh edge to her voice. "I know it was Friday night, because you were...different after. But...I suppose you didn't have much choice coming to bed with me, seeing as I was already there."

The smile on her face had become brittle and Gideon felt that sand rushing away from his feet faster now, and he could almost see the funnel through which it was spiraling down.

"Fiona—"

"Look, Gideon, you've said it before—and I do agree. We're just too different. You live and move in a totally different world than I do. Rachel's pregnancy is a perfect excuse—a valid *reason*—for you to take a step back, and I understand that. I *truly* do." She reached across the table and patted his hand—like he was back in second grade and had lost his favorite Matchbox car. "You'll make a wonderful father, Gideon. You really will. I have no doubt of that."

His heart plummeted, then surged back up. "I don't even know if the baby's mine, Fiona," he repeated, hearing the desperation in his voice. The vodka in his stomach sloshed.

He wasn't ready to be a father. He wasn't certain he'd be strong enough to put his weaknesses aside, unlike his father had.

And he wasn't ready to let Fiona out of his life. Even though she…she was already ready to let him go.

"Gideon." Her simple word—similar to her response when he'd told her about his mother: quiet, full of feeling without being smothering—made him focus on her sad face. "Remember what I saw in the line on your hand? A wife and a baby."

With both of hers, she gathered up his left hand, gently turning it so that the palm faced up. Her index finger traced a crease on the side of his pinkie, then carefully swept over his open hand, whispering over his skin and raising every nerve ending in his body.

No. God, no…

He was losing her—he'd *lost* her, faster than that sand funneling away underfoot.

It was in her face, and in his head. *No. No!*

Suddenly, he recalled what Iva told him, the message from Salton: *You'd have a very difficult decision to make… that it would turn your life around…and she said that, although it would be very painful, you would do the right thing in the end.*

It seemed like everyone knew his future but him.

Fiona rushed out of the restaurant, blinking back what she refused to consider might be tears.

No way. It was allergies that made her eyes sting.

It was for the best. No doubt in her mind.

She'd done the right thing.

Gideon was wishy-washy-ing around about telling her the whole story—but she knew what his palm had said, and she knew what had to be done.

He had to be cut loose so that he could become a

father with a little less guilt than he would already have, having had a father of his own who was such a screw-up.

The baby might not be his.

So? she told herself, jamming the key into her car door lock. She knew Gideon. She'd come to learn his soul during their time together.

He was the *responsible* type—the ultra-vigilant uber-responsible type; the exact opposite of his father—and even if the baby wasn't his, he would do right by Rachel because it could just as easily *have* been his.

And because he couldn't stand to see the child of someone he cared about—perhaps even loved, she thought miserably, cranking up a Katy Perry song on her car stereo about being hot and then cold—grow up in a broken home.

He would fix it as his grandfather had fixed his.

Oh God, oh God…why did she have to fall in love with such a conservative, stick-in-the-mud, responsible, do-the-right-thing guy?

The truth was, she told herself firmly, if he wouldn't have been looking for a way out of their "relationship," he would never have brought it up.

Responsibility or no, Rachel's pregnancy was Gideon's fast ticket away from her.

"I'm getting married," Gideon said.

His grandfather beamed, leaning across the table at the elegant restaurant Grove, and clasped Gideon's hand firmly.

"Congratulations, son," he said, tightening his warm grip before his grandson could pull away. "Iva and I have been hoping for such an announcement from you, and we're thrilled that you've finally found the right woman."

As he settled back in his seat, he readjusted the napkin on his lap and turned a pleased smile onto Iva. "You know what that means, my dear," he said. "I'll be able to start my succession plan and half-retire in the next year."

Gideon frowned. "Succession plan? Retire? *You?*" He laughed, although he knew it must sound forced, based on the way Iva was watching him.

"Of course, my dear boy. I promised myself—and Iva —that once you settled down and decided to get married, whenever it was, I would start easing up myself and begin to retire."

His grandfather was *so* pleased. Gideon didn't ever think he'd seen him as happy, other than when he'd first introduced him to Iva.

She was still looking at him, her bright blue eyes steady. But there was worry painted in them.

She hadn't congratulated him.

She hadn't said a word, in fact.

Gideon felt his middle twist and he took a sip of water laced with lemon.

The ring he'd bought for Rachel weighed down his pocket. Its box bore the gold-stamped logo of one of the finest jewelers in Grand Rapids, and he knew Rachel would be pleased to flaunt it.

He was going to bring it to her after dinner tonight. Perhaps he should have invited her to join them at Grove, but somehow he knew it would be best to talk with Grandfather—and Iva of course—first.

The ring itself had been easy to select: a single, square-cut ice-white diamond set in platinum, two carats of colorless brilliance that would look lovely on any woman's hand—but most especially with Rachel's perfectly manicured, white-tipped fingernails.

The pit of his stomach felt deep and heavy as he'd fingered through the diamonds spread out on a purple velvet cloth earlier today.

How different his choice would be if he were selecting a ring for Fiona. She'd want something as unique as she was; something colorful like bold sapphires, or maybe a dark yellow diamond set in warm or rose gold, instead of colorless ice—

And how foolish of him to allow that thought to enter his mind.

The fact was—the cold fact he had to keep reminding himself— Fiona had seized the opportunity to rush him out of her life the moment he gave her a reason. He'd hardly had the words out; he hadn't even been able to tell her what he was thinking, what he thought was the best option...

Obviously, her insecurities and inability to commit to anything had won out in the end—and, Gideon mused, it was just as well.

Whatever *he* did, he was in for the long haul.

Fiona didn't have it in her to tackle anything for the long haul, and she'd made that clear.

A wife like Rachel Backley—an executive, a power-house of a businesswoman and stunning to boot—would serve him and his grandfather's practice much better than an impetuous, airy-fairy *palm-reader* would. Chances were, Fiona would get bored with her antiques shop anyway and move onto greener pastures within months.

With a start, Gideon realized that both Iva and his

grandfather were looking at him expectantly from across the table.

Kindness, perhaps even pity, glinted in her eyes as Iva spoke. "You don't seem very happy about it, Gideon. Is it too soon for you? Are you rushing into this?"

"No. Rachel and I have been together for over three years, so I wouldn't consider it rushing into anything." Gideon said the words with a deep-seated calm that he absolutely did not feel.

Inside, his stomach roiled and his head hurt.

Gideon Senior stared at him, setting down his drink without looking. It would have ended up in his lap if Iva hadn't snatched it up from a free-fall.

"What the hell are you talking about?" bellowed the older man, sitting up abruptly as the diners at the next table turned to look at them. "*Gideon?*"

"Calm down, dear." Iva had already begun to soothe the troubled waters. "Can't you see Gideon is in shock?"

"*In shock?* Of course he's in shock, Iva—for God's sake, he's marrying the wrong woman. He's going to make the same mistake I made—three times!" The elder Nath made no effort to keep his voice or opinions circumspect and more people were looking.

"Gideon, I'm sure that you knew your grandfather and I were expecting you'd be announcing your engagement to Fiona—not Rachel. And although it's none of our business" —these last words were accompanied by a black glare at her companion— "if you'd like to talk a little about what happened, we'd listen." Her round cheeks seemed deflated, and a paler pink than usual, and the glint usually smiling in her eyes had disappeared.

It was definitely pity and concern that he saw there in Iva's expression—neither of which he felt like responding to.

"It wasn't going to work out with Fiona," he told them simply, having rehearsed this speech previously. "We both realized it before it was too late, thank goodness. We're just not from the same worlds. Rachel's more my type, and I just decided it was time to stop messing around with a bit of eye candy. My life's more serious than Fiona's. She just doesn't get it."

As he spoke those last words, he didn't need to see the frozen expression on Iva's face to realize how arrogant they sounded.

The taste of something bitter filled his mouth and he looked down and away from the disappointed expression on her face.

"It's very sudden, Gideon. Just last Friday, I was at the shop with Fiona and you'd—er—been there the night before. And now suddenly you're announcing your engagement to Rachel. Is there something else going on here?" Iva pressed gently.

He might as well tell them. It was going to be obvious soon enough. "Rachel's pregnant. I told her we would get married."

Grandfather opened his mouth to speak, but a warning look from Iva magically silenced him. He closed his mouth, but his cheeks became mottled as he fought to control his reaction.

"The baby is yours?" Iva asked.

"Yes. I'm doing a DNA test to be certain—I'm not *completely* oblivious to feminine wiles—but I've no reason to believe otherwise." He glanced at Iva. "It was my decision to get married, and she agreed."

Gideon drew in a deep breath and spewed it out slowly, then continued. "She gave me the whole argument that it was better for the child, if the parents weren't in love, not to get married. And that she was more than financially capable of raising the baby on her own with a nanny. She said I could be as involved with the child as I wanted to, but that there was no reason for us to get married. I told her that was ridiculous, and I wasn't about to let my child grow up without a father."

The unspoken words "like I did" hung silently in the air.

"It's the right thing to do," Gideon Senior said, nodding sagely. The color in his face had returned to normal. "Your responsibility is your responsibility and you're right to own up to it, Gideon. I'm proud of you, son."

Iva didn't speak. She took a sip of her Riesling and looked at him, then at Gideon Senior, and then back again, pointedly remaining silent.

"I'll be bringing Rachel to the Children of Grand Rapids Fundraiser at Meijer Gardens in a couple of weeks. You'll have a chance to meet her again then."

"Are you going to tell your father?" his grandfather asked.

Gideon set his water glass down, but kept his fingers wrapped around it. "Yes. I'm planning to visit him on Monday."

The last time he'd visited his father was last June, for his birthday and Father's Day (conveniently within the same week), but Gideon refused to feel guilty about that fact.

He signed in and was approved to enter the prison, and then strode down the long, white, empty halls.

In the last two weeks, his life had flipped from one of laughter, freedom, and pure happiness to one of duty and seriousness. He had enough to feel guilty about. Not visiting his father more than a couple times a year wasn't going on the damned list too.

Gideon took his seat at the table spliced by a wall made of clear Plexiglas. He watched as Gid, as his father preferred to be called, preceded a guard and sat down on the other side of the wall. Both men picked up the heavy black telephone receivers that would allow them to speak to each other.

"Long time no see."

Gideon swallowed a sharp retort. "Hello Gid." He'd long since stopped thinking of him as Dad, or even Father.

"To what do I owe this honor?"

"Thought I'd let you know that I'm getting married." Gideon focused on keeping his fingers from tapping nervously on the counter in front of him.

"Well, that's nice of you." His words sounded sincere, and when Gideon looked up, what he saw in his father's face matched the tone of his words. "I'm glad you've found someone."

"Thank you."

Silence yawned.

"You gonna tell me about her? Is she that redhead Dad was talking to me about? He really likes her."

Gideon snapped his eyes up again, shocked. His grandfather had visited Gid *and* told him about Fiona?

"No…no, it's not her. She was too…uh…flighty. Not serious enough. We didn't have a lot in common. I'm going to marry a woman more like me—down to earth, professional, focused, aggressive. She's the principle of a very hot marketing company that just won the Hottest Midwest Company of the Year from *Fortune*. It's a very prestigious award, and there are a lot of press opportunities and—and other benefits related to it," he added lamely.

"Sounds a lot like you…and your grandfather. But tell me about this redhead who's not serious enough for you. Dad made it sound like you two were destined for the altar."

Gideon suppressed annoyance about his grandfather's big mouth.

He didn't want to talk about Fiona.

He wanted to forget about her.

Yet…the conversations he had with his father—meaningful ones, anyway—were so few and far between that he felt compelled to continue.

Perhaps it was a desire for Gid to understand how he'd molded his son's life because of his lack of responsibility—how, because of his unrealistic pipe dreams and desire to live only for the moment, he had been not only a terrible father, but had created a son who was compelled to be so completely opposite of him.

"She's fun and beautiful and very carefree. I enjoyed being with her, but in the end we decided that we didn't have enough in common to be together. Our relationship was too distracting, and she just wasn't serious enough for the long haul.

"Fiona just didn't have enough focus in her life… enough *goals*." He glanced at his father, who was still very handsome even with graying hair and deep wrinkles around the eyes and mouth.

Gid frowned and looked down. "I know you think I'm the biggest prick that ever tried to be a father—and you're somewhat justified in thinking so—but you're still my son, and I still have an interest in your life.

"I'm 58 years old and'll be in here for another ten years—and then maybe, if I'm lucky, I'll get out on parole. I'm here because I allowed myself to get too caught up in instant gratification, short-term pleasure, and my own addictive weaknesses. I know it, and I'm paying for it. But I don't want to see you do the same thing."

Gideon gaped at his father. "That's absurd! I never live for the instant pleasure—I plan and work and focus, I have goals, and I'm *damned* if I'll ever get caught up in fanciful dreams in order to be a fashionable starving artist like you. I'm *nothing* like you."

"That's my point, Gideon. You're so sure you're going to end up like me that you're swinging so damned hard in the opposite direction—and so your life's nothing but structure and work and duty. Just like your grandfather's. I was just as determined as you are to be the exact *opposite* of my father that I did the same thing."

Gid's voice was earnest and he leaned toward the glass, his deep-set eyes serious. "Gideon, I only talk to you once every month or two months…and only see you a couple times a year—but I can see that you need balance in your life. You need a little fun and a little free spirit and a little creativity. A little art. Maybe a lot of art," he said with a short laugh.

"Letting that in—the creative side of yourself—isn't going to end you up in prison like me. *Not* letting yourself loosen up will turn you into my father—or at least the way he was before Iva.

"Do you want to spend sixty years of your life like that before you realize you made a mistake?"

NINETEEN

WHY OH WHY had she agreed to this?

Fiona scowled at herself in the tall oval mirror and adjusted her sparkling, bronze-colored gown. It brushed the floor and hugged each one of her curves from throat to hip in a shimmering display.

Her shoulders and back were bare, but the gown was high-necked with a choker-like collar that made her look even taller than she was. With her hair piled high on the top of her head, she looked like she imagined a Greek goddess would look, especially if she were a statue cast in new copper.

She leaned forward to brush on shiny cinnamon lipstick, then glanced at the clock. Brad would be here at any moment.

Why oh why had she agreed to go with him?

He'd been so insistent, and Fiona had felt so damned *confined* since breaking things off with Gideon. It had been over three weeks ago, and she hadn't felt like going anywhere or doing anything.

This was not only a chance to get out of the house,

but to enjoy one of her favorite places in an unusual and special way: the annual Children of Grand Rapids Fundraiser was being held at the gorgeous Frederik Meijer Gardens.

The event was after hours, and the patrons would have the opportunity to see the new Japanese tea garden display before it opened to the public. Despite it being mid-November, there would be heat lamps throughout the gardens and large fire pits to add to the ambience and warmth. Inside the sleek and welcoming facilities would be a cocktail party and silent auction, and the guests would move between the inside and outside displays for the evening.

Brad, who'd won his election two weeks ago, certainly wouldn't miss such a public relations opportunity in the middle of his district—and when he'd asked Fiona to be his companion, she'd forced herself to accept.

She knew she needed to do something other than work at the shop and sit at home.

When he knocked at her front door—she was back at her apartment in Grand Rapids tonight, in anticipation of the event—she gathered up the black beaded shawl and matching handbag from the table, then snagged a long overcoat for the ride in the car.

"Hi Brad," she said, opening the door wide enough for him to come in. He looked very debonair in his tuxedo, but, like Carl, the man just didn't do a thing for her hormones.

Damn it anyway.

Oh, this was a bad idea. Maybe she could still get out of it…

"You look gorgeous!" Brad said, literally gawking as he stood on the threshold. "Fiona, you will be the belle of the ball. I'll be the envy of every man there."

Hmm. Maybe it wouldn't be so bad to have her ego stroked like this all evening. She could probably suffer through some excellent food and wine on the arm of the new State Senator if he was going to talk to her like that. After all, a woman needed her confidence shored up every once in awhile.

"I drove myself tonight, and the car is waiting below. Are you ready?" He offered his arm, crooking an elbow, and Fiona reluctantly slipped her hand through it.

Now that she was closer to him, she realized how overpowering his cologne was. His campaign manager should let him know to ease off on it, or he'd be making the babies he was probably still kissing sneeze.

That quirky thought made her smile, and lightened her thoughts as she settled into the sleek Jaguar. It purred like its namesake and the ride from the suburb of Wyoming to Meijer Gardens was smooth but filled with Bradley's chatter about his recent victory and his plans for the future.

He left his car with a valet stationed at the entrance and led her inside to the cocktail party, which was already in full-swing.

***

Gideon felt as if he'd taken a punch to the gut when he caught sight of the elegant couple making their entrance. He stared from across the room as his fingers tightened around a rock glass.

Dear God, it *was* Fiona.

And she was with State Senator-Elect Bradley Forth.

Rachel shifted beside him, bumping into his arm, and he barely noticed when she turned to look up at him. "Gideon? Is something the matter?" Without waiting for him to respond, she looked over. "Is that who I think it is?"

"Who's that?" he asked with nonchalance. Lord, he was getting good at faking that.

"It *is* her. Fiona—was that her name?" Rachel asked ingenuously. Gideon resisted the urge to comment; his fiancée networked like a pro. She never forgot a name, a background, a connection. "She's very striking—especially in that unusual gown with those long legs and all that hair."

Those long legs and all that soft, sweet hair had been wrapped around him, plastered to him, heated him, loved him—

Gideon swallowed a large gulp of club soda and wished for something far stronger.

"I can see why you were attracted to her."

He looked down at Rachel, for there was a note in her voice that seemed off. "Yes, she's very beautiful. But it's over between us—you don't have anything to worry about." But as he spoke, he realized he was saying it more for his own benefit than for hers.

"I'm not worried whatsoever, Gideon. This was—"

Whatever she was about to say was interrupted by the arrival of Gideon Senior and Iva, accompanied by some of his grandfather's cronies from law school.

They exchanged pleasantries with Ben Laslow and Norm van Delt and their wives, and Gideon kept his attention on the conversation at hand and away from the exotic and fascinating distraction across the room.

Just keep your distance.

His resolve was shot to hell, however, when Norm van Delt suddenly said, "Don't I know that woman?"

The group's attention turned as one, fixating on the

cinnamon and bronze column of woman standing next to Forth, now only yards away.

Gideon suddenly realized how Norm van Delt knew Fiona.

He should be relieved she wasn't his date after all— these more staid folk would remember her as the odd, airy-fairy woman who told their futures by reading palms.

"Oh, that's right, Norm, she was doing those palm-readings at that fundraiser a few months ago," his wife told him. "You talked about her for weeks after." To Gideon's (and probably Norm's) mortification, Mrs. Van Delt turned and called, "Yoo hoo! Over here!" and waved to get Fiona's attention from across the room.

Yet Gideon's feet were nailed to the floor. He should have bolted from the area. But all he could do, however, was stand there with a fixed half-smile on his face as disparate pieces of his world merged, clashed, then distorted like the insides of a kaleidoscope.

Fiona saw the group and the beckoning woman almost immediately.

"They must recognize you," she said to Brad as they approached…and then her voice trailed off when she saw Gideon with his grandfather, Iva, and the irritatingly still-slender and very elegant Rachel Backley. She was looking at Fiona with a definite arched-brow look.

"Great," Brad murmured. "Now that I'm elected, my constituents are going to expect all sorts of favors."

But as they approached the group, he extended his hand with a hearty greeting and shook all around the little group. "Nath," he said as he reached Gideon. "Pleasure to see you again. Always seem to be running into you at these things, eh?"

"I remember you, dear," said one of the ladies whom

Fiona faintly remembered. "You were reading our palms at that fundraising event at the JW Marriott back in October."

"Oh, yes," Fiona replied, darting a glance at Gideon.

He stood just outside of the little cluster, his mouth anchored to one side in some sort of expression that could have been a smile. Despite the frozen look on his face, he looked so good it made her stomach flutter and her mouth water. He'd recently had his hair cut, and although that stern look still graced his face, she knew there was warmth and emotion beneath the shuttered expression.

Warmth and emotion that was now being given to Rachel.

Fiona couldn't stanch the flood of memories— remembering how carefree he was when he smiled, and how heated his expression could be when he was trying to argue a point.

How hot and liquid his eyes were when he was moving inside her.

How good that felt.

How *right*.

"Good evening," she said, somehow forcing the words from a dry throat as she turned to greet Gideon Senior.

She shook his hand, remembering with a pang how much she'd enjoyed the seemingly blustery man and his date, the latter of whom was looking at Fiona as though trying to see into the depths of her mind.

"Hello, Iva. I haven't seen you since we found those letters of Valente's." Now why had she said that? The last thing Fiona wanted to do was make Iva feel uncomfortable for not visiting her.

"It's been far too long, dear, I know," Iva replied.

There was what seemed to be genuine regret in her voice. "Hollis and I were in California for an extended visit—but now that I'm back, we'll have to have lunch again. *Soon.*"

"I'd like that," Fiona said—even though she wasn't certain she would.

It was one thing to enjoy Iva's company—and that of the other Tuesday Ladies...but now that Gideon was out of the picture, it might be more bittersweet than anything.

She smiled, and then turning—having no choice but to greet the elegant woman standing very close to Gideon. "It's Rachel, isn't it?"

Fiona forced herself to put sincere warmth in her voice and made sure she made good, solid eye contact with the elegant dark blond who was standing hip to shoulder with the man Fiona loved. "Congratulations to both of you."

At the last phrase, Fiona finally looked at Gideon, head-on, and when their eyes met she was stunned at the blankness—bleakness—therein. His gaze contained emptiness, only emptiness—not even the cool professionalism she'd known—and she couldn't suppress her own wave of grief.

Somehow she shook Rachel's hand, but Fiona simply couldn't make herself touch Gideon—especially those gorgeous hands.

Before he even had the chance to offer, she turned to the other couples, whom she barely knew and who would be a wonderful distraction, and reintroduced herself to them.

The ladies babbled about her palm-reading, and even the men—for all the stiff-necked properness of their proper old money and power—seemed fascinated by her talent.

"You've never read *my* palm, Fiona," Brad said with an inflection of intimacy that made her cringe.

She'd never even allowed him to kiss her, let alone given him cause to use that tone.

"I should have asked you to do it before the election —but now that we know I've won, maybe there's something else you can tell."

Fiona laughed brightly, studious in keeping her gaze from checking Gideon's reaction to Brad's comment. "I wouldn't have been able to tell you if you'd win the election anyway...but I should be able to tell you whether you'll find success in your new job."

Relieved to have something to focus on—even if she didn't want to broadcast the lack of their non-existent intimacy, she took Brad's hand and turned it palm-up.

And then she almost dropped it.

Fiona had never had such an immediate reaction to reading someone's palm before. Intense discomfort and unease washed over her in an awful surprise. She felt as if a black cloak had sudden dropped over her, smothering her.

What was wrong with her?

Fiona blinked to clear her mind, and focused on Brad's hand.

She tried to follow the lines of his palm, but anything she might have read into them was engulfed by her strange feelings of aversion. Nevertheless, she concentrated, traced some of the lines on his hand with her index finger, and babbled something—she would never remember what—about him being a success and having a happy life with two children and a wife and several other comments that sounded palm-reader-like. She was relieved to notice that at some point, Gideon and Rachel had stepped away, and that made her slightly more at ease.

Slightly.

Nevertheless, as soon as she could—after the comments about her reading died down—Fiona excused herself from the little group before someone else asked to have their palm read.

Brad wanted to accompany her as she put distance between herself and the others, but with a playful little laugh, she told him, "I'm just going to step into the powder room for a minute. Why don't you stay here and talk to your constituents for a bit? I'm sure they have a few things on their minds."

The chuckles from the group followed her as she stepped away, and it wasn't until she'd made her way across the room that she felt able to breathe again.

Between unexpectedly seeing Gideon and his fiancée, and then having the strange reaction to Brad, Fiona definitely needed a few minutes to herself.

Her knowledge of the layout of the facilities at the Meijer Gardens aided her in her quest for privacy, and Fiona had no trouble finding a small alcove where she could stand and pretend to admire a modern metal sculpture while trying to get her composure under control.

She felt a presence behind her almost immediately, and, half-expecting—*wanting*, and yet *not* wanting—to see Gideon standing there, she turned.

Her heart plummeted.

"Iva. I'm so glad to see you again...and I want to apologize for my comment about you not coming by. I didn't mean to put you on the spot—it was very rude, and I feel terrible about it." She heard herself babbling, but she couldn't stop. She was afraid what would happen when her emotions caught up with her.

"Fiona, *dear*," was all Iva said before pulling her into her sweet-smelling embrace.

The short, plump woman hugged her tightly, and for a minute, Fiona didn't want to let go. She blinked hard, trying to keep surprise tears from spilling from over her eyes and ruining her makeup.

"I wasn't offended at all," Iva said into her ear. "I was afraid you wouldn't want to see me—at least, not for awhile. I should be the one apologizing for not coming by. I wasn't certain what had happened between the two of you. And, well...you know Gideon. He wouldn't say anything about it."

Tears knitted into the corners of her eyes and Fiona felt a huge lump forming in her throat. How could this woman she barely knew evoke such an honest response in her when her own mother never could?

Finally, Fiona pulled from the comforting embrace, only slightly embarrassed by her emotional reaction. It had felt good to let someone hold her—to let herself grieve for a minute.

"You love him," said the older woman, looking up at her with sad blue eyes. "Just like I love Hollis."

Fiona swallowed over the heaviness in her throat, considered lying, but then nodded. "Yes."

"He's making a terrible mistake, Fiona," Iva said, beginning to dig around in her handbag. She pulled a tissue free and offered it to her. "I know you're not used to such a small purse."

Fiona smiled again and blew her nose. "Thank you. I don't know what's wrong with me...well, actually, I sort of do. Something happened tonight."

"What do you mean?" Iva's eyes turned sharp. "Did

Gideon *say* something to you? Or that woman Rachel?"

"No, no," Fiona replied quickly. Not only did she want to change the subject, but she needed to tell someone about Brad. And Iva, of all people, would understand. "When I picked up Brad Forth's hand just now to read his palm, something strange happened."

"You weren't hit with a bolt of lightning and fell madly in love with him, were you?" Iva demanded.

"No…in fact, it was quite the opposite. Exactly the opposite. I felt this surge of dislike rush through me. I almost dropped him—his hand, I mean. That horrible sensation made it difficult to focus on what I was reading, and I just made some stuff up. I just wonder what caused me to react that way."

"Does he frighten you? Perhaps you shouldn't be alone with him, Fiona." The older woman was dead serious, and she gripped Fiona's hand tightly. "Don't forget we still don't know who's been breaking into the shop and trying to find—well, whatever they're trying to find. Has anything new happened in the last few weeks, Fiona?"

Fiona shook her head. "No, nothing. And Helga and Captain Longbow don't really have any news."

"I don't trust that man," Iva said. "That politician. Ever since I first met him, I had a…feeling about him."

Fiona rushed to clarify her experience. The last thing she needed was Iva saying or doing something about Brad…

"It wasn't necessarily that Brad *frightened* me when I touched his hand—after all, I've been alone with him many times, and he's never raised the hair on the back of my neck like tonight. He's never given me cause to feel uncomfortable around him before.

"I think it must have just been the fluke of a

moment…maybe he's just another dishonest politician, and it came out in his palm." She shrugged off the older woman's concern even as her insides remained tight and nauseated. "I've already decided I'm not going to see him anymore anyway. He's just not my type."

"Well, he is Valente's grandnephew," Iva said with a gentle smile, looking at her with a gleam in her blue eyes. "We'll get to the other stuff in a minute—about that foolish boy Gideon—but first, I found out some things about your benefactor that might explain your ghost."

Fiona raised her eyebrows, glad to have something to focus on instead of her riot of emotions. "You did some research at the library?"

Iva nodded. "Along with Maxine and Juanita, of course. They had to be involved once they heard about everything from Orbra. They scrolled through the microfiche, and I looked up some other resources.

"Fiona, do you recall that I mentioned the name Josef Kremer as being familiar to me? I can't believe I didn't remember right away—but he was a Nazi war criminal. The son of one of Hitler's elite, and very much involved with the inner workings of the Third Reich. Kremer—the son—was thought to have escaped Germany and fled to Argentina with some of the others."

"I haven't heard of him myself, but I'm sure you're right. What do you think his connection to Valente was? Do you think he killed Josef Kremer? And maybe the blackmailer knew it. Maybe Kremer killed Gretchen, the love of Valente's life, and Valente avenged himself on Kremer by taking him out."

Iva was nodding. "Perhaps. It's possible. What a romantic story that would be. I thought I would let you know what I learned about Kremer—so maybe if you come across any more hidden drawers with secret letters in them, they might mean something to you."

"Hidden drawers?"

Fiona nearly jumped out of her skin at the sound of Brad's voice behind her.

"I'm so sorry, ladies. I didn't mean to interrupt. I just realized my wallet is missing, Fiona, and wondered if you'd seen it."

"I don't remember seeing it anywhere. When was the last time you had it?"

"I know I had it when I stopped by your shop this morning—I wanted to make sure our date was still on for this evening," he added, winking at Iva. "But I haven't had need of it since, and I'm wondering if I left it there, at the store. I'd taken it out of my pocket while looking for a business card, and I'm thinking I must have left it on the table by that walnut secretary—you know the one, Fiona, don't you? Would you mind if we stopped by on the way home tonight to look?"

"Of course not," she replied, waving away his hang-dog expression. "Although I'm sure Carl would have noticed if you left it there, and he'd have called me."

"Well, I'd feel better if I had the chance to check. Maybe it got knocked to the floor. Anyway, ladies, I didn't mean to interrupt. Fiona, are you hungry or thirsty? Would you like me to get anything for you?"

Iva glanced at Fiona and then turned a sudden dazzling smile on Brad that Fiona recognized as one hiding an ulterior motive. It was the smile Iva utilized when she wanted to bend Gideon Senior to her will without him realizing it.

"Mr. Forth—can I call you Brad?—I'd like to ask you a few questions about your platform—now that I'm one of your new constituents," she added with a tinkle of a laugh. "There are a few things I'm not certain I'm in agreement with."

"Certainly, Mrs.—er

"*Ms.* Bergstrom," she replied.

"Yes, then, Ms. Bergstrom. If I could just—"

"My Ladies Guild at the library in Wicks Hollow might be interested in having you come in to speak with us—and we usually have quite an attendance." She fluttered an old-lady look that made her appear fluffy and disingenuous, and Fiona had to hide a smile. "In particular we want to know about your position on legalizing marijuana."

"Oh," Brad said, drawing himself up into formal, very rigid pose. "Well, I'm definitely against the legalization of marijuana, Ms. Bergstrom."

"Well, that's going to be a big problem then," Iva replied, still in her easy-going-slightly-batty old lady tone. "Because the entire Ladies Guild grew up in the Sixties and Seventies, and half of us had pot plants growing in our dorm rooms at college!"

Fiona smothered a smile at the shocked expression on Brad's face, then realized Iva was giving her the perfect chance to escape...and escape she would.

But as she stepped out of the alcove, she came face to face with Gideon.

She'd known it would happen—both hoped and feared it would, if the truth were to be known—and she was always honest with herself, at least.

But the sight of him—his tall, familiar, handsome form—still made her draw up quickly, and her insides jerk and flutter.

"Fiona." His tone sounded as though he'd expected to see her—so he had the advantage. She never liked that.

"Hello, Gideon." She would remain cool. Not too stand-offish, and certainly not deer-in-the-headlights speechless.

In fact, she would seize control of the conversation since he'd obviously sought her out. "I must say, you look absolutely delicious in that tux."

Fiona couldn't believe her own audacity when she reached out to tug on the collar of his jacket, then slide her fingers on down to smooth it into place.

He was warm and solid even under that brief touch, and she immediately regretted her boldness. "I've always said you fill out a tux better than pretty much anyone I know…with the exception of Robert Downey Jr. as Tony Stark." She grinned cheekily even though her insides churned.

Gideon finally found his tongue, startled by Fiona's sudden appearance, and then by the onslaught of her icy calm. Surely *she* wasn't faking nonchalance too?

"Thank you for the compliment. You look stunning as well…just, *gorgeous*…but I don't want to stand here and mutually admire each other for the next ten minutes, Fiona."

"Whyever not?" She was practically batting her eyelashes at him—a sure sign she was hiding something. "We spent several weeks doing little more than that, didn't we?" Her smile bordered on suggestive, but her eyes were still flat.

Gideon reached for her, wrapping his fingers gently but firmly around her wrist before she could sidestep him.

"Are you dating Forth now?" he asked before he checked the words with his brain and realized they sounded petulant and jealous, and were utterly and completely out of line.

Nevertheless, he didn't give her a chance to respond before directing her around a corner and through a door —and suddenly they were outside in the Japanese tea garden.

The faint trickle of water burbled in the quiet, and a large, shallow, metal bowl contained a roaring fire. A cloudy sky above allowed glimpses of a half-moon and part of a starscape. The air was chill and brisk, and smelled faintly of burning wood.

"Well, it's not the riverfront at the JW Marriott," Fiona commented, bringing to mind the last time they'd both attended an event and ended up in a private setting by the river. She drew her beaded wrap a little closer. "And no I'm not dating Brad. As if it's any of your business. You've always had a craw up your butt about him for some reason, haven't you?"

Gideon had no reason to feel the relief, but it washed through him. Then it was replaced by irritation with himself for his selfishness. Just like his father.

"Did you want to talk to me about something Gideon?" She'd stopped and turned to look up at him. Her gaze searched his, but it was cold and emotionless. He wanted to warm it again, to melt away that reserve and see her easy and giddy.

He reached to touch her hair, piled tall on her head, leaving her long, elegant, sexy neck and shoulders bare. His mouth went dry.

He knew exactly how warm her skin would be, how it would smell like spice and sweet and something exotic...how she'd shiver, and catch her breath if he pressed his lips to that spot just below her ear—

He dragged himself back to reality. "I just wanted to know that you're all right. I think about you...often." Twisting a loose coil around his finger, he rubbed the silky strands between the pads of his fingers until she stepped back and the lock slipped from his fingers.

"I'm doing just fine, Gideon. How about you? Are you happy? Picking out names? Will there be a Hollis Gideon the Fourth, or are you waiting to learn the sex? Decorating the nursery? Planning a wedding—or did you elope?"

He felt like he'd been punched in the stomach, then grief and anger, emptiness and fury rushed over him.

It was his own fault for seeking her out, for getting this close to her again. He should have just stayed away, across the room, with his fiancée.

It would have been much safer.

Yet impossible to do.

"I love you, Fiona." The words shocked him as much as they did her, and he gaped for a moment before trying to backpedal. "Oh, God, I'm sorry. I shouldn't have…"

Her entire face had frozen. Now, it sagged, then drew tight with incredulity. Her eyes snapped wildly as she got in his face, the words tumbling out. "You didn't really just say that, did you, Gideon? I had to have imagined it. How *dare* you do this to me—to *yourself*—and to Rachel. *How dare you.*"

Gideon had never seen her so angry—so cold and detached and deadly furious.

It was frightening and illuminating at the same time. He thought for a moment she was angry enough to strike him, but instead, she whirled and stalked away, her feet clipping hard on the stone pathway as she disappeared into the night.

He stared after her, ill and ashamed.

Empty.

Then the sound of clapping…slow, steady, mocking… reached his ears.

Gideon turned to see Rachel, leaning against one of the tall columns that created a stone archway.

He turned cold.

"Nice job, Gideon."

"Oh, God, Rachel…I am so sorry." He went toward her, his whole body numb, his brain frozen. Misery, shame, desolation warred inside him. There was nothing he could say.

Rachel allowed him to take her hands, but she didn't move away from the column against which she leaned. "What in the hell was that?" she said in a clipped voice.

Her fingers felt warm in his freezing hands. He scrambled to pull his thoughts together…but the only thing he could focus on was the image of Fiona's shocked, loathing expression before she turned away.

Forever. Gone. Forever.

"Rachel…I'm sorry. I'm sorry you heard what you— thought you heard," he said, gathering his best lawyerly defense: admit nothing.

Then, he realized with a deep, heavy thud in his heart that he wasn't going to lie. Or obfuscate.

The truth was, he did love Fiona.

He owed it to her—or at least, to his memory of her— to be honest about that.

"It's over with me and Fiona, Rachel. That was…that was just goodbye. I told you, I'm not going to walk away from my responsibility. And you and I are so well-suited to each other."

"Obviously not as well-suited as you and Fiona. My God, this garden was sizzling with the chemistry between the two of you." She withdrew her hands, her voice bitter and Arctic. "And you've never said you love me. Ever."

"I care about you very much Rachel," he said quickly.

But, again: he wasn't going to lie. "And I'm going to be a wonderful father. I would never let you raise our baby alone, Rachel. I want to be a part of—"

"This is the 21st century, for God's sake. Do you think I want—or need—a *pity* husband? A *man* to take care of me? You *bastard*."

She was the one who cracked him across the face with her hand after all—the cool, controlled business-woman, not the wild redhead.

He didn't bother to lift his hand to the stinging cheek. He'd deserved it. *Oh*, he'd deserved it. "That's not—I'm not going to be a pity husband—"

"Well, whatever you are, it's *not* going to be a husband. Mine, anyway." She was already working the diamond off her finger. "I don't need you, Gideon. I don't need a damned husband."

"But I'm the father—"

"Yes. That's right. But I sure as hell am not going to marry a man who's in love with someone else." She whipped the ring at him, and it glittered as it bounced off his arm and tumbled into the bushes. "What sort of woman do you think I am, to take *leftovers*?"

"Rachel, I—"

"Stop it, Gideon. Just *stop*." She stared at him, heaving, her eyes black with fury. "Don't say another word."

TWENTY

"ARE you sure you don't mind leaving already?" Fiona asked as Brad draped the wrap over her shoulders. All of a sudden, she was cold.

Chilled to the bone.

Oh, Gideon.

It had been all she could do to stop the angry tears before Brad—or someone else—noticed them.

"Not at all. I was ready to go too." He flashed a smile at her as they stepped out to his Jaguar.

Fiona settled into her seat, her heart still hammering with anger and her veins still jumping.

How dare that stiff-assed lawyer tell her he was in love with her when he was planning to marry someone else?

What did he want—a wife, a child, and a palmist on the side for when he was ready for some fun?

True, he didn't look as though he was having fun. In fact, he'd looked down right miserable. But that wasn't her fault, and there was nothing she could or would do about it. He'd made his bed, and so on.

"I still want to stop by the shop to see if my wallet's there—I know it's down in Wicks Hollow, but I'll feel better once I check."

"Oh, right." Fiona had forgotten about that detour. She settled back in her seat and closed her eyes in an effort to relax, already looking forward to slipping into bed and having a good cry. She'd planned to go back to her apartment tonight, but with the detour to Wicks Hollow, she'd probably just stay at Ethan's.

It was after ten o'clock, and Violet Way was deserted of people and vehicles, as the tourist season was well past and the autumn night was chill and dark.

Fiona dug the keys from her handbag, wondering with a spur of apprehension whether The Lamp—Gretchen's Lamp—would be playing any tricks tonight. It had never done so when anyone else was with her in the shop, but tonight had been so full of upheaval and surprises that she rather expected something else crazy to happen.

The little bell jingled when she opened the door, and she stepped over immediately to disarm the security system. After punching her code into the keypad, she turned on the closest lamp and watched as Brad walked toward the middle of the half-lit shop.

"Don't turn on any more lights," he said, turning to face her.

"What? How are you going to find your—" Fiona's mouth stopped when she saw the gun pointing at her.

The gun *in his hand.*

"*Brad?*" Her stomach squeezed and she couldn't catch a breath.

"We don't need any more lights on in here."

His face had shifted into a mask that Fiona barely recognized. Even in the half-light, she read his expression: ugly and determined. "What's going on? Why do you have a gun pointed at me, Brad?"

"I tried to do it the easy way, Fiona. Really I did. But nothing seemed to work out right."

She didn't know whether she should move or just stand there. That pale glint of metal pointing at her didn't help her focus on her choices...all it did was freeze her mind.

"What are you talking about? You don't need the gun for anything. I'll *help* you." Fiona kept her voice calm and soothing as her brain began to function. "This won't be good for your political career, you know," she said reasonably.

"I tried to find it on my own...the stuff that Valente left. But you've hidden it so well that I couldn't." His words rambled and the tone of his voice sounded surprised and confused.

"I don't have any idea what you're talking about. I haven't hidden anything—"

"What is this about *hidden drawers?* You found hidden drawers in here, didn't you? What was in them?" He moved toward her, lurching as though his legs had numbed. The gun stayed steady, focused at her. "I heard you tell that old lady tonight. Where are they?"

Fiona's heart stopped as Brad grabbed her arm, pulling her closer as he aimed the gun at her middle.

"If you would tell me what it is you're looking for, I'll help you to find it." She tried to keep her voice calm and steady as she frantically searched for a way to escape this horror.

But his fingers dug into her upper arm and he gave a rough jerk—unexpected and sharp, so that her head snapped back and forward, leaving her disoriented and dizzy.

"Valente had secrets, you know…you must know what they are, or he would never have left this shop to you. It has to be *here*. Now show me the hidden drawers."

With a vicious shove, he thrust her away from him and she slammed hip-first into the edge of a table, then stumbled and tripped on her gown, tumbling to the floor. A lamp on the table teetered, then fell off the table, landing with a crash next to her. Fiona began to pull herself up as he came to stand over her, his stance threatening as he pointed the gun two inches from her forehead.

"Now. Show me the hidden drawers."

Her throat was too dry to swallow, though she tried. Her fingers were numb with cold and fear, and she could barely make them move to clutch the table for support as she staggered to her feet. Her hip stung from ramming the edge of the top, and she'd ground her knee into a shard of glass as she struggled to stand.

"There's a—a drawer in that big desk over there." Fiona kept her voice steady and cool, despite the reality that had begun to set in.

Brad Forth was a political figure, completely in the public eye. He had a gun, and he wasn't about to let anything ruin his career, now that he'd won.

Fiona was suddenly, sickeningly certain he had no intention of letting her tell the tale of what happened here tonight—once he found what he was looking for. She was going to conveniently disappear.

Just like Gretchen had.

"Valente was a criminal, you know, Fiona." His words became conversational, now that it appeared that she was going to comply. "He was a horrible man. And ugly one. His real name was Kremer…Josef Kremer. Ever heard of him?"

Fiona gasped in spite of herself. "*He* was Josef Kremer? The Nazi war criminal?" She gaped at Bradley, who seemed to relish the moment of her shock. "Valente?"

"My great-uncle…yes, and his father too, who was one of Hitler's elite. They were infamous, notorious anti-Semites." He laughed darkly, then prodded her with the gun. "The drawers please."

She limped toward the back of the store. That explained why Valente had been blackmailed about the whereabouts of Josef Kremer. He hadn't *killed* Kremer—he *was* Kremer. He couldn't let anyone learn his true identity.

"Look, I'm not going to tell about your great-uncle," she told him, pausing to turn and look back. "I don't really care. No one really cares anymo—"

"Get going!" He shoved her again, and she fell forward again, this time flat on her cut knee, her palms slapping onto the floor. They stung and the sharp pain zipped up her arms. "I'm tired of you playing games with me—you pretend you don't know what I'm talking about, playing hard to get, toying with me…Well, tonight I'm going to take care of you and my uncle once and for all….no more waiting, no more games. Tonight, I'm in charge."

Gideon could still hardly believe it.

He was free…free of an obligation that had torn at him, pulled at him, for weeks.

It had been an ugly moment with Rachel.

An ugly, mortifying situation when he'd realized—belatedly, and only after having made a complete ass out of himself—how much of an *ass* he'd actually been all along.

To Rachel *and* to Fiona.

But now, thanks to a woman with too much sense and pride to settle for his half-assed decision to marry her—he was set free.

He would *make* Fiona take him back. He loved her; he knew she loved him.

He *hoped* she loved him.

A dark worry clouded his moment of elation. What if she didn't?

What would he do then?

He'd fight for her—and be damned if he'd spend the rest of his life looking for a more "suitable" woman.

Fiona was the only one for him…despite her quirky ways and off-the-beat habits, he'd found what he needed. She'd brought fun and spontaneity into his life, and she'd even forced him to look beyond hiding his sketches in a drawer.

His dad was right, Gideon reflected, pacing as he waited for the valet to bring his car.

Damn Gid. First time in his entire life, Gideon's father had actually acted like a father and given him something worthwhile to think about.

"Gideon?"

He turned to see Iva standing there. She had a sort of arrested look on her face. "Your grandfather and I are leaving now—just waiting for him to bring up the car. I…thought I just saw Rachel climbing into a car. To leave."

Unspoken were the words: without you.

"Yes," he replied.

"Is everything all right?" Iva said. "With the two of you?"

He sighed, loosening the tie at his throat. "I suppose it depends who you ask. We've broken off our engagement."

Iva did a very poor job of hiding the elation that leapt into her eyes, but her voice was calm and properly sympathetic. "I see." She waited a beat before continuing, "I never had the chance to tell you that I admired you for walking away from something you really wanted in order to do what you thought was your duty—as misguided as I thought you were…"

"What do you mean?"

"I mean, you walked away from Fiona to do what you thought you *should* do. Needed to do. You put—again, misguidedly—someone else's needs before your own, and in many ways that's very admirable. But… what kind of man would you have been without Fiona in your life? Now you have the chance—"

"Fiona dumped me before I even had the opportunity to talk with her about the situation with Rachel." He should have been feeling elated, relieved, and giddy… but it was more of a desolation that crept over him.

"Oh, Gideon. That was self-defense. Pure self-defense. She had to dump you before you walked away from her—that way *she* would be the one left standing. You scared the hell out of her, and when she saw you acting all mopey, she knew the writing was on the wall."

"Maybe."

"She cares about you deeply, Gideon," Iva said as his grandfather's sleek Mercedes pulled up at the curb. "Everything will work out all right. Call her."

Fiona's fingers shook as she fumbled the spring on the hidden drawer to show Bradley, who bent close enough that his fading cologne nauseated her. She'd never be able to smell Blue Water again without wanting to puke.

If she lived to smell *anything* again.

"There's nothing in here," he growled, jabbing her shoulder with the gun. "Where's the journal? The bank book?"

His eyes darted about like fleas, hopping from Fiona to the desk to the gun. "Where are they?"

He yanked her to her feet and she tripped over the hem of her gown, staggering into him. He pushed her away and she fell again, the weight of her piled-up hair sagging to one side.

"I don't know what you're talking about, Bradley. I haven't seen anything like that, I swear it." Panic began to dart through her, muzzing her brain and numbing her face. The man was insane.

"I know he left them for you. There must be another hiding place. Get up…unless you want to take a break?" His sudden leer transformed his eyes from glassy to intent. "You've been teasing me for months…if you want to take a break to make that up to me right now, I certainly wouldn't mind that." His expression was lascivious as he stood over her, gun aimed at her head, one hand on the fastening of his trousers.

Fiona pushed back the surge of nausea. She looked up at him, braced by her hands behind her on the floor, sprawled in a pool of sequined gown. Now her intense reaction to reading his palm made sense. Somehow tonight, his growing desperation had come past the mask he'd worn for months.

Brad stepped closer, one foot planting on the material of her gown, holding it—and her—in place. "We'll have a little bit of fun, then we'll get back to work. I'm sure by that time, you'll be much more accommodating." He laughed, and it was nothing like the polite, gentle chuckles she'd heard from his politician persona. This was a deep, roiling, nasty laugh.

What had happened to change him so quickly from the polite, debonair politician to this half-mad, leering person?

All at once her attention was drawn to The Lamp where it sat on the walnut desk behind Bradley. It glowed a soft color and then went out abruptly. An idea crystallized in Fiona's mind.

"I think you should know—there's a ghost here," she told him, making her eyes wide and fearful. "Gretchen's ghost."

He laughed again. "Don't be frightened, my dear. You've been wanting this for months." He bent toward her, menace in his eyes, and suddenly there was a loud crash.

Fiona, who'd half been expecting something, started, but Bradley jolted as though he'd been pushed. He whirled around to look beyond the desk, into the darkness, where the sound had come from.

Just then, The Lamp came on, glowing whiter and brighter than Fiona had ever seen it.

"What the he—" Bradley's words choked off when a palpable chill filtered through the air—sudden, subtle, but unmistakable. "What kind of game are you playing here?" He whirled back to Fiona, brandishing the gun, swinging it sharply toward her.

She staggered to her feet just as the gun smashed into her temple.

Pain exploded, and everything went black.

TWENTY-ONE

GIDEON PEERED in the front window of Fiona's shop. It looked as though a few lights glowed within, but there certainly wasn't any sign that she and Brad were in there.

Glancing up the street, and then in the other direction, Gideon tried to make sense of the babbling phone call he'd received twenty minutes ago from Iva. He'd just pulled into his condo's parking lot—after trying to call Fiona, as suggested, and getting no answer.

"You have to find Fiona!" Iva had exclaimed as soon as he'd answered his phone. "She's in danger!"

"What are you talking about?" Gideon asked, frowning, even as he turned the ignition in his car back on. "Iva, you don't need to play matchmaker any more. I'm going to—"

"Gideon, after we got home, I did a Tarot reading tonight—my first one ever—and it said that Fiona's in *danger*. You have to find her! She went somewhere with Bradley Forth, and I'm sure he's going to hurt her!"

"You did a Tarot reading and you want me to use that

as an excuse to hunt her down? Iva, you know I love you but—"

"Gideon! This is your grandfather. Now listen to me —forget what Iva said about her Tarot reading—this is serious. Fiona did a palm reading on Bradley tonight and—"

"Not you too!" Gideon exploded. Had his whole world gone mad? "Look, I'm going to go home and—"

"*Gideon!*" His grandfather thundered. "I'm going to hang up and call the Wicks Hollow police. Do you want me to tell you what's going on first or not?"

"What?" Now his heart was starting to pound. "*What?*"

"When Fiona did the palm reading on Forth tonight, she told Iva that she had the most immediate, forceful reaction to him—one of dislike and fear. She sensed something was wrong, but she didn't know why. Forth told her he wanted to go to her shop to look for his wallet, which he thought he'd left there…but I saw him use his wallet to pay for a drink tonight. *He was lying to her to try and get her back to the shop. He's up to no good, Gideon.*"

"All right. I'm on my way to the shop from my condo. Twenty minutes, max. *Wait* to call the police until I check back in with you, okay? Just in case Iva's wrong."

He disconnected the call and immediately called Fiona's cell again, but of course she didn't answer.

And based on the fact that she rarely did, he knew it might mean nothing. But he'd had to try.

For all he knew, the wallet line was a ruse for Bradley to get Fiona into bed at his house.

Or sprawled over that big old desk in her shop.

He banished those thoughts as he sped down the highway, ignoring the fact that he was well over the speed limit, and trying to figure out how he'd explain Iva's Tarot-card reading warning to a cop if he got pulled over.

His car squealed a little as he turned the corner off the exit ramp, then purred down the streets of Wicks Hollow till he got to Violet Way.

The shop was dark. There was a car across the street, but he didn't recognize it. However, it was a sleek Jaguar —just the sort of vehicle a politician like Bradley Forth might drive. Maybe they were somewhere else.

Like Ethan's cabin. Or even Fiona's apartment— which Gideon himself had only been to once.

Just about to turn away from the dark shop and plan his next step, Gideon noticed a faint light in the back of the shop come on, then go off. Then, moments later, a very bright light glowed from the back.

That did it.

He tried the door, and to his shock and amazement, it opened. Unfortunately, bell above jingled as he slipped in, making his presence known.

"Fiona?" he called.

Only three lamps had been lit, and the shadows loomed tall and dark. Everything was silent and eerie. Gideon felt a shiver crawl up his spine as he stepped a few more paces into the shop. "Fiona, are you here?"

"She's a bit indisposed at the moment."

The voice snapped through the air and Gideon turned to face Bradley Forth—who had a gun pointed straight at him.

His insides tightened and he gritted his teeth, ignoring the threat of the weapon. "If you've hurt her, I'll kill you."

Forth laughed. "You sound like a frigging B-movie

actor, Nath. Why don't you step this way before my trigger finger shows you how happy it is to see you."

"Where's Fiona?" Gideon snapped, but turned as the gesturing gun insisted he do. There was no sense in getting himself shot before he found out what was going on.

The metal poked him in the back, but they hadn't taken two steps toward the bowels of the shop when a gust of wind blasted toward them.

Gideon paused, frowning. The gust was cold and sudden, and brought with it the strong scent of roses... and then it was gone. The gun jabbed at him, and Gideon saw Forth look warily around the shop.

"What is that?" Forth said furiously.

Gideon didn't reply, but the hair on the back of his neck had lifted. And all at once, he remembered Fiona's babbling about unplugged lamps and odd things happening in the shop.

He tripped and nearly stumbled over something in his path.

"Fiona," he gasped, heedless of the gun behind him, and fell to his knees beside her crumpled body. Thank God there was no blood, and she was breathing...but she wasn't moving and her skin felt cold and clammy.

He didn't have a chance to do anything more than touch her face before Forth stalked up beside him. "She's all right—for now. You being here is going to make this a lot easier for me, Nath. I was going to have to stage this to look like another break-in, but now I can just make it look like a lovers' tryst gone bad."

He stepped back, the gun still clutched in his hand as he gestured around the shop. "A few candles, a bit of wine, and a little carelessness...you knock the candles over and the whole place goes up in smoke—the two of you along with it."

Gideon pulled slowly to his feet, taking care not to make any sudden move. "All right, Forth. What am I missing?" He leaned casually against a table, noticing a short brass statue of a Buddha that looked like it'd pack a good wallop.

"My uncle was not a nice man. He was one of Hitler's elite, and somehow managed to escape here in Grand Rapids. If it ever came out that Nevio Valente was the notorious Josef Kremer, I'd be ruined. My political career would be over hardly before it started."

He glared down at Fiona's still figure. "The old man wrote everything down. He had a journal and put *everything* in it—even boasted to me once about how he'd bashed his old lady on the head because she'd tracked him down and threatened to expose him. That was Gretchen. Must be the body you found here.

"The old bastard made me sit and listen to him, time and time again, over and over. He promised he'd leave me the money, but there wasn't any mention of it in the will. Nothing. And then he gave this shop to *her*. It was a slap in the face, after all I'd done for him, sitting and listening and keeping it all a secret for years."

"Were you the one blackmailing him?" Gideon asked.

"Me? No, damn it. Wish I'd thought of it, to be honest, but once he told me about his past, I knew I couldn't because he'd know it was me. But I *believed* Uncle Nevio when he told me he'd leave me the bank accounts and the journal so I could destroy them. It was Rudy and Viola who were blackmailing him.

"Uncle Nev knew it was them all along, and he damn well paid them—that I can't understand." Bradley shook his head, and his expression darkened. "The damn journal's around here somewhere—and I can't find it, so the whole damned place is going to be torched. Can't take the chance it'll be found. I'd hoped to track down the numbers of his bank accounts in Switzerland…but your damn girlfriend wouldn't tell me that either." He brought back his foot and, before Gideon could react, rammed his toe viciously into Fiona's still body.

Gideon's vision blazed red, and he caught himself just before making what would have been a fatal move toward Forth—for the gun was still pointed at his abdomen.

"Now, now, Nath…I didn't realize you had a temper like that. Why don't you just—"

Forth didn't finish his sentence, for all of a sudden, another whoosh of *something* blasted by them.

It was stronger than before, palpable and cold, and it ruffled their hair. The strong, sudden scent of roses was accompanied by a faint moaning, whistling sound.

"What the *hell* is going on?" Forth whirled, and Gideon took his chance, surging toward him.

Forth turned in that split second, swinging his gun, just as Gideon slammed into him. As they fell, Gideon banged his head on the edge of a heavy table, and heard the clatter of the gun as it tumbled to the floor.

They rolled, crashing into tables, chests, and other furnishings. Lamps, figurines, and metal vases tumbled to the floor as they fought in the shadowy light.

Pulling to his feet after a particularly vicious blow to his face, Gideon staggered into a table and closed his fingers around the heavy metal Buddha.

As he turned to face his attacker, holding the statuette close to his body, he found himself facing the barrel of the gun once more.

"Say goodbye to your girlfriend, Nath," said Forth,

tightening his finger on the trigger. "I promise to take good care of—"

The lights went out, plunging the shop into total darkness. Gideon didn't hesitate, taking advantage of the surprise darkness to dive behind a large china cabinet.

The sound of the gun's retort filled the space, echoed in the open area above...then, silence.

Gideon silently shifted backward, trying to keep his breathing soft and silent.

It was so dark...dark enough that he couldn't see his hand in front of his face. Then he noticed two tiny lights glowing from the back of the shop, and Gideon felt his body numb as the lights moved, coming closer...and then he recognized them as belonging to the cat, Gretchen. She was stalking them, moving toward them, her glowing yellowish eyes fixed, unblinking, in a manner that made the hair on the back of his neck rise again.

His attention whirled to the front of the shop when a light suddenly blinked on...then off...then another came on...then off...and then another and another.

Gideon gaped at the display, and, in the dim light, saw Forth staring at the blinking lamps. Even in the soft glow, he noticed the other man's jaw sagged in shock, and he could make out the gun hanging uselessly by his side.

One light stayed on, and all of a sudden, the moaning sound returned, along with another blast of wind—this time as though it were coming down the stairs from the second floor. It was as loud as a train, roaring and terribly cold, and beneath it that eerie moaning noise.

"What's going on in here?" Forth shrieked, his eyes wild.

A crash splintered the air, and Forth jumped, whirling

around and fired in the direction of the noise, the sound metallic and sharp compared to the horrible moaning sound. He shot again, and something near the front of the store exploded into pieces.

Gideon stood there, frozen in fascination and horror. His hands had gone clammy and his heart raced as he wondered, too, what was happening—but whatever it was had served to distract Forth. Gideon gripped the Buddha statue, hefting it gently in his hand as he slowly edged his way closer to his assailant.

Suddenly, all of the lights went dark. He heard the other man's gasp, then Gideon jolted when Forth fired his gun into the silence.

Then, nothing. It was dark—black—and silent and cold…very cold.

And the smell of roses was very, very strong.

Gideon thought he heard a whimper from the other man, but he did nothing but tighten his grip on the statue and edge closer: silent and slow and using the furnishings for cover.

The air moved. Something cool brushed past Gideon, then past Forth—who gave a low shriek.

Then all at once, every light in the shop blasted on at full brightness. Gideon saw the frozen, terrified look on Forth's face before everything went black again.

The sound of heavy, short breathing rasped in the air, grating in the silence. A stale smell permeated the room, growing stronger and closer over the essence of roses, filling Gideon's nose with such horror that he wanted to choke. It didn't smell rank or putrid…it just smelled cold and stale and *dead*.

He drew in a deep breath through his mouth, trying not to smell it, and trying to remain calm. A soft groan from somewhere in the depths of the shadows alerted him to Fiona's movements—he could sense her not far from him on the floor, and Gideon carefully stepped closer to her. He felt her shift against his foot just as the roar of wind came through the room again. This time, it was a tornado: violent and vicious, loud and cold.

Bradley fired again, and then once more, unbelievably, all was still. The wind, the light, the smell…all of it was gone.

But this time, when Gideon turned slowly in the blackness, he saw something that made his hair lift all along the back of his neck.

It was an amorphous shape…greenish, yellowish, and it *glowed* in the dark as it wisped like curls of smoke right in front of Bradley Forth.

The man's illuminated face was frozen in an expression of slack-jawed terror, and he gasped for air as though something was dragging the life out of him.

The shape…the *ghost*, for lack of a better word, swirled gently, and, as Gideon watched, the glow metamorphosed into something that resembled a figure.

A woman.

He watched. The hair and nerve endings all along his arms vibrated alarmingly as the figure took shape, the face evolving into a clear, detailed image…one that was so familiar to him that he glanced down to make sure Fiona was still there next to him. She moaned, shifting against his feet, and he reached down to comfort her with his touch. Then he looked back up.

"Gretchen." He whispered her name. The ghost's name.

His fingers were cold, but he realized he wasn't frightened.

Still gripping the smooth statue, slick now from the sweat on his palms, Gideon watched the ghostly figure seep back into nothingness as though her work was complete.

There was darkness, then another loud crash next to him. Then the lights flashed on long enough for Gideon to bring the statue down on the back of Bradley's head.

Then, there was abrupt, dead, silence.

TWENTY-TWO

WHEN FIONA OPENED HER EYES, she saw Gideon's face close to hers, his eyes bright with concern.

She blinked, struggling to make sense of her murky thoughts. Something was wrong…her brows drew together and she swallowed, her dry throat rasping with the effort.

Then she remembered: Brad Forth. She must have tried to cry out a warning, for Gideon covered her lips with a pair of gentle fingers.

"Shh…he's not going to hurt you, baby…He's gone."

"Brad…?" she managed to whisper.

"Yes, Brad. I must say, I'd rather hoped *my* name would have been the first thing you said…" He smiled gently. "Instead of his."

Fiona couldn't hold back her own painful grin. She didn't know what happened, or how Gideon had managed to be there, but he was—*and* he had made a rare joke.

Two miracles in one night.

He pressed a kiss to her forehead, murmured something that sounded like "I love you" and then pulled away to look down at her.

His face was so dear to her, so handsome and familiar and so *wanted*…Fiona felt like she was going to get lost in the warmth and love in his eyes.

Something had changed with him. The shutters had fallen from his face, and it was open, glowing, soft.

Fiona became aware that they weren't alone and she struggled to sit up on a sofa. People were moving around, talking, lights were on…

They were in the shop, she realized, her mind still foggy as she recognized the back room. Yes, that was right—Brad had brought her here, then pulled a gun on her.

She shuddered, and Gideon pulled her close to his warm, solid body that smelled—not of overpowering cologne, but of maleness and strength. Goosebumps lifted on her bare arms, and he smoothed his beautiful hands up over her skin, gently caressing her chilled arms.

"What happened?" she managed to say, just Helga van Hest walked up to them.

"How are you Fiona?" she asked, reaching for her wrist to check her pulse before she could reply.

"I'm fine. I just…want to know what happened."

Helga gave Gideon an ambiguous look, then replied, "Bradley Forth has been taken into custody for assault, battery, and attempted murder. Thanks to Gideon here, he was apprehended before he could escape—or perpetrate his ultimate goal."

It was Helga van Hest's very straight face that told Fiona that was only part of the story. But before she could ask more questions, a medic was there, poking and prodding on her everywhere.

Finally—once pronounced well enough to go home and, thankfully, not to the emergency room—Fiona demanded, "What happened, Gideon?"

He told her that Iva and Hollis had been worried about her, and that was why he'd tracked her down at the shop—only to be accosted by Brad Forth.

"How did you get the gun away from him?" Fiona asked.

Gideon looked uncomfortable, as though he couldn't find the words. "He got—er—uh—distracted, and I smashed him on the head with that Buddha statue."

"Distracted?" But Fiona was already beginning to suspect what had happened.

Gretchen's Lamp—perhaps even Gretchen herself—had helped them out.

She reached to touch Gideon's cheek. It was warm and prickly from the stubble that had already begun to spring up, and she slid her hand around to cup his jaw. How she'd missed touching him!

Then she remembered Rachel, and jolted back from him. *Oh God.*

"Where is she? Rachel?" Her joy drained away.

"She's not here, Fiona. She's not going to be here…it's over between us."

"No, Gideon, you can't—" With every last remnant of strength and integrity, Fiona turned to look at him, fierceness in her eyes. She wouldn't let him do that.

"Shush, baby…shhh…It's over." He pressed a kiss with exquisite tenderness to her forehead. "Rachel and I —err—agreed it would be best if we didn't get married after all. I'll still be involved in the baby's life, of course —my child's life—but not with the mother. Not with Rachel."

"Gideon…" She realized her face was buried in his

broad shoulder. It smelled so *good*. So familiar, so deli-cious…so like *him*. "Are you sure?"

He nodded against her, his face bumping into the top of her head. "Yes. We both agreed, Rachel and I. Fiona, I've been lost without you…I want you in my life. I told you tonight, I *love* you. I…I want to be with you." He stopped suddenly, then plunged on, "I know you were scared, and things were moving too fast before. We can slow things down, but—"

"*No*," she said quickly. "No to slowing things down. I love you, Gideon. I could barely get through the words, telling you to be with her…"

He held her for a long moment there on the floor, in the corner and away from Helga and Captain Longbow, and the sheriff's team, who'd come in to help with gathering evidence.

Suddenly a familiar peremptory bellow reached their ears. "Gideon! Fiona!"

Gideon Senior and Iva burst upon them, both demanding to know if they were all right. Gideon's grandfather's glasses were askew, and Iva was wearing some sort of house slippers…and they both carried worried and concerned expressions on their faces.

"For God's sake, sit down, Iva." Gideon Senior yanked a chair over for them and propelled her into it. "You can see they're all right now, so you can stop your yammering."

Fiona saw that despite his harsh words, his attention raced over Gideon and herself to make sure they were, indeed, all right.

Trying to make light of the situation, she looked at Iva and grinned. "Reading Tarot cards now, are you?"

Iva flushed and looked down at her hands. "Well, I thought I'd give it a try. My first time, and since you were on my mind…and Gideon, and the whole situation with Bradley Forth…well, I just meditated on you and pulled a few cards."

Gideon Senior rolled his eyes, smiling broadly now that all was well. "*Foolishness.* Such foolishness I never heard, eh, Gideon? What are we going to do with these two women and their penchant for the mystic?"

Fiona felt Gideon shift beside her, and she looked to see a very sober expression on his face. "Grandfather, I have to say…I'm never going to poke fun at them again." He hesitated, then glanced at Fiona and closed his mouth.

She took a quick look at Iva, who was watching intently, and then reached to touch Gideon's face. "You saw her, didn't you? Gretchen?"

He nodded and Iva gasped in what could only be described as disappointment. "Do you mean she showed herself to *you*?" She looked around as if to catch sight of the Ghostly Presence herself. "After all the research and work we did, she didn't even show herself to *us*?"

Gideon Senior's mouth was hanging open. "What are you saying, son? You think you saw a ghost?"

Gideon bit his upper lip, raised one eyebrow as though he didn't believe it himself, and nodded. "I saw a ghost." He said the words and looked over at Fiona. "It was definitely Gretchen, and she looked just like you—except for the hair."

"You *really* saw her?" Iva asked, her blue eyes perfectly round and her cheeks flushing in excitement. Her disappointment seemed to have ebbed. "What did she do? What did she look like? *What happened?*"

"She scared the bejesus out of Bradley Forth," Gideon replied with great relish. "She was kind of greenish-yellow, and she had a hell of a gust of wind behind her. It felt like a damned tornado in here. She broke a lot of lamps—a lot of things. I don't know if it was the wind or just her...moving things." He shook his head. "I wouldn't have believed it if I hadn't experienced it for myself...but I did." He looked into Fiona's eyes with an uncertain gaze—as though he were afraid she'd laugh at him.

Before she could respond, Joe Longbow called out from across the room. "Fiona, did you see this mess over here?"

She and Gideon pulled to their feet when they saw where he and Helga were standing—next to the big old desk where Gretchen's Lamp had stood.

The old white lamp was no longer in its spot on the desk—now it lay smashed on the floor.

"Right over here was the last crash I heard," Gideon told Fiona as they stooped to look at what remained of the lamp. "Gretchen must have destroyed it as her last act."

"What's this?" Fiona reached for a wad of papers—a small notebook that had been folded in half and lay among the shards of milk glass. "It must have been inside the lamp."

As soon as she pulled it out, the glass tinkling to the floor under it, she knew what it was. "Valente's journal," she and Iva said at the same time. They both squealed with giddy delight, though with Fiona's head aching so, hers wasn't quite as high-pitched as Iva's.

They all looked at each other, Helga making furious notes on a neat steno pad and Joe Longbow scratching his head. "Journal?"

"That's what Bradley Forth was looking for," she told them. "And some bank books too."

Iva took the journal and flipped through it, then dug

for reading glasses. As she leaned over her shoulder, Fiona squinted, but couldn't make out the brown spidery writing that had faded over time.

"I'm sure it must tell the whole story in here," Iva said, shoving her readers in place. "It'll say that he was Josef Kremer, one of Hitler's elite, and that he came here to start a new life after the war."

"And that his first love—Gretchen—found him, and when she came to visit him, he killed her for fear she'd divulge his identity. He actually killed the woman he loved—or at least had loved once upon a time."

Gideon looked at Fiona, warmth shining in his eyes as he clasped her hand. "I just want you to know, my love, that no matter how long we're married, and how angry you might make me...I'll never bash your head in and leave you in a closet under the stairs." He grinned a crooked, gentle grin.

Fiona felt a wave of love and tenderness as she fell into his gaze. She smiled, reaching to touch his warm, dear face. "Another joke from you, Gideon? Two in one day? Are you really the man I love, or are you an imposter?"

She leaned forward to press a kiss to his mouth, and felt like she'd come home. This was where she'd be, this was where she'd stay. Her home, her life, her commitment...her responsibility.

"I love you Gideon. And if that's a proposal, I'll accept it...but you're really going to have to stop making so many jokes."

were you intrigued by the little spitfire Bruce Banner, Juanita Acerita's papillon? I'd like to introduce you to the inspiration for little Brucie—my own darling papillon named Ranger.

He's just as feisty as Bruce Banner, and ridiculously cute, as you can see. If you follow me on Facebook, Instagram, or Twitter, you'll find that I often post pics or videos of Ranger.

He likes to lay on top of the floor vent in the kitchen when the furnace is running, so he can stay warm. What a life!

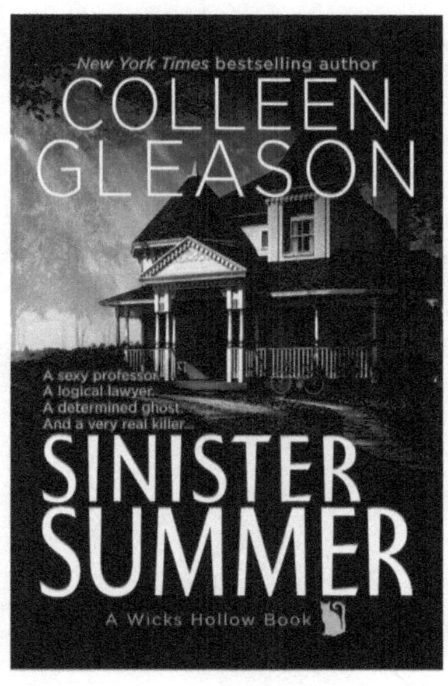

A sexy professor.

A logical lawyer.

A determined ghost.

...And a very mortal killer.

Diana Iverson needs a break--from her stressful job, from her philandering boyfriend, and from the rest of her fast-paced life. When she inherits her eccentric Aunt Jean's Wicks Hollow home, Diana takes a much-needed vacation in the cozy little town.

But when the lake house becomes the scene of multiple break-ins, Diana begins to suspect Aunt Jean's death was not as innocent as it seems.

And then there's Ethan Murphy, the sexy college professor

who lives next door… He appears to know a lot more about Aunt Jean than he should, and Diana doesn't trust him.

But most of all, there's Aunt Jean herself…who seems determined to communicate with Diana from beyond the grave…

NOW AVAILABLE!

LEARN MORE AT AMAZON.COM

A sexy blacksmith.

A CEO turned innkeeper.

A haunted speakeasy.

And a very desperate killer…

Leslie Nakano needs to make a major life change—getting away from the dog-eat-dog corporate world, as well as getting past a personal loss—so she buys a large turn-of-the-century mansion in Wicks Hollow, with plans to renovate it and turn it into an inn.

She doesn't care about the rumors that it's haunted—she just wants a new life.

But she sure wouldn't mind finding the missing gems that belonged to Red Eye Sal, a bootlegger who lived in the house during Prohibition.

Blacksmith Declan Zyler, who has more work than he can handle, working on historical restorations, has suddenly acquired a fifteen-year-old daughter he never knew he had. This turns his life upside-down when he decides to take on the role of single father.

When Leslie hires Declan to restore the iron staircase in her inn, neither of them realize they are disturbing a spirit from days gone by…and until they determine how to put that ghost to rest, neither Leslie nor Declan will be able to move on with their lives.

NOW AVAILABLE!

LEARN MORE AT AMAZON.

Don't let announcements and news get stuck in
your spam folder! Sign up for SMS/Text messages and
help keep your inbox uncluttered.

Not sure how? Here's a cheat sheet diagram:

Colleen Gleason is an award-winning, New York Times and USA Today best-selling author. She's written more than forty novels in a variety of genres—truly, something for everyone!

She loves to hear from readers, so feel free to find her online and say hi!

Get SMS/Text alerts for any
New Releases or **Promotions!**

Text: **COLLEEN** to **38470**

(You will only receive a single message when Colleen has a new release or title on sale. *We promise*.)

If you would like SMS/Text alerts for any **Events** or book signings Colleen is attending,

Text: **MEET** to **38470**

Subscribe to Colleen's non-spam newsletter for other
updates, news, sneak peeks, and special offers!
http://cgbks.com/news

Connect with Colleen online:
www.colleengleason.com
books@colleengleason.com

<u>The Gardella Vampire Hunters</u>

Victoria

The Rest Falls Away

Rises the Night

The Bleeding Dusk

When Twilight Burns

As Shadows Fade

Macey/Max Denton

Roaring Midnight

Raging Dawn

Roaring Shadows

Raging Winter

Roaring Dawn

<u>The Draculia Vampire Trilogy</u>

The Vampire Voss: Dark Rogue

The Vampire Dimitri: Dark Saint

The Vampire Narcise: Dark Vixen

Wicks Hollow Series

Ghost Story Romance & Mystery

Sinister Summer

Sinister Secrets

Sinister Shadows

Sinister Sanctuary (Summer 2018)

Stoker & Holmes Books

(for ages 12-adult)

The Clockwork Scarab

The Spiritglass Charade

The Chess Queen Enigma

The Carnelian Crow

The Lincoln's White House Mystery Series

(writing as C. M. Gleason)

Murder in the Lincoln White House

Murder in the Oval Library (Sept 2018)

The Marina Alexander Adventure Novels

(writing as C. M. Gleason)

Siberian Treasure

Amazon Roulette

Sanskrit Cipher (forthcoming)

Writing as Alex Mandon

The Belle-Époque Mystery series

Murder on the Champs-Élysées